HONG KONG BLACK

ALSO AVAILABLE BY ALEX RYAN:

Beijing Red

HONG KONG BLACK

A NICK FOLEY THRILLER

ALEX RYAN

CROOKED LANE

NEW YORK

Copyright © 2017 by The Quick Brown Fox & Company LLC.

Published in the United States by Crooked Lane Books, an imprint of The Quick Brown Fox & Company LLC.

Crooked Lane Books and its logo are trademarks of The Quick Brown Fox & Company LLC.

Library of Congress Catalog-in-Publication data available upon request.

ISBN (hardcover): 978-1-68331-028-0
ISBN (ePub): 978-1-68331-030-3
ISBN (Kindle): 978-1-68331-031-0
ISBN (ePDF): 978-1-68331-032-7

Cover design by Lori Palmer.
Book design by Jennifer Canzone.

Printed in the United States.

www.crookedlanebooks.com

Crooked Lane Books
34 West 27th St., 10th Floor
New York, NY 10001

First Edition: May 2017

10 9 8 7 6 5 4 3 2 1

PROLOGUE

The Necropolis of Qin Shi Huang
Xianyang (capital of China)
State of Qin
213 BC

Unification.

And punishment.

These were the things that kept Li Si awake at night. As chancellor and principal advisor to Qin Shi Huang, the First Emperor of China, Li's job was to transform vision into reality. Of all the beasts that roamed the earth, only men possessed this great and unique power—the power to manifest the ethereal into the corporeal. But not all men had the will. Only great men. Divine men. Men such as himself. The creation of the world's greatest empire, governed under singular rule and law, was proof of his greatness as chancellor. He and he alone was the architect of this momentous feat, and he had accomplished it through unification.

And punishment.

Li glared at a pile of horse dung on the footpath and sidestepped the offensive mass. This sort of filth was unacceptable inside the Emperor's necropolis. The necropolis complex, although still under construction, was a sacred place and should be maintained as such. He filed the infraction away in his mind. Someone would be disciplined; he would see to that. As he made his way east, to

1

the standing terracotta army, he could not help but marvel at the magnificence around him. The necropolis of Qin Shi Huang was the largest construction project in all of China; hundreds of thousands of laborers and craftsmen had been conscripted for the task. The necropolis was a microcosm of the empire, complete with an imperial palace, map room, and tomb mound at the center. It was designed to embody all aspects of daily imperial life and provide the Emperor with everything he would need to rule in the afterlife. Unlike his forbearers, who, upon death, demanded burial sacrifice of their attending staff, Qin Shi Huang had chosen to construct a legion of life-size terracotta doppelgängers to stand in for his host of advisors, servants, and soldiers. This shift in burial policy was Li's doing; he had no intention of sacrificing his life for a man he intended to outlive. He had already begun making plans and alliances, secretly selecting Qin Shi Huang's successor to ensure he would remain chancellor when the Emperor died.

He had worked too hard the last twenty years to let something as mundane as death rob him of power.

Craftsmen and laborers bowed their heads as Li strode along the outer wall, but he paid them no mind. The necropolis had two walls—an inner and outer—encircling the tomb mound. Inside the inner wall, statues of bureaucrats, courtiers, and advisors were staged, ready to serve the Emperor in the afterlife. Bronze chariots and horses, with drivers and guards, waited ready to transport and protect the Emperor wherever he might choose to go in the great beyond. Between the inner and outer walls, terracotta entertainers, artisans, and strong men engaged in their craft—immortal spectacle for Qin Shi Huang. The imperial stables were located outside the outer wall. The Emperor had decreed that real horses would be buried with terracotta grooms ready to service them in the immortal life. But the most impressive element of the Emperor's mausoleum did not reside inside the necropolis. To the east, Li could just make out the columns of the terracotta army in the distance. Over six thousand life-size warriors were already completed, each soldier painstakingly handcrafted and unique. No two warriors in the Emperor's legion were the same.

He picked up his pace, driven by compulsion.

Every day he searched their faces.

Every day he returned unsatisfied.

Ten minutes later, he was lost among the ranks, scanning their painted clay faces for his own. He had forbade the master craftsmen from using his countenance, but his unsettled heart told him that somewhere in this clay army, there was a soldier wearing his face. He would find it, and when he did, he would have the statue destroyed. The afterlife was a fool's fantasy—Li was certain of this, which is why he had devoted all of his energy and faculties to accumulating as much power and pleasure in life as possible. *Death is not transcendence*, he told himself, and yet still he searched. Service to this Emperor in one lifetime was enough. He would not risk the same fate for eternity, no matter how unlikely the odds.

His gaze flicked from face, to face, to face.

No . . . no . . . no . . .

It's here. Somewhere. I know it is.

As he searched for his doppelgänger, Li felt a thousand eyes on him.

Gooseflesh stood up on his forearms.

A surge of panic washed over him, and suddenly he found it difficult to breathe. Someone touched his shoulder. He whirled around. No one was there . . . except the clay soldiers. They were everywhere. Surrounding him. Enveloping him. Painted clay irises watching him, following his every move . . . mocking him.

He began to run.

"Chancellor Li," a voice called from behind him.

Li froze in his tracks.

"Chancellor Li," the voice beckoned again.

The voice sounded human enough, maybe even familiar. He turned slowly, beginning to question his sanity.

An imperial guard—a *living* imperial guard—greeted him with a deferential bow of the head. "I'm sorry to startle you, Chancellor."

Li straightened his shoulders. "A mind can play tricks in a place like this," he growled. "You would do well to remember that next time you seek my audience."

"My humblest apologies, Chancellor," the guard said, the fear evident in his voice.

Li suppressed a smile. The guard was afraid of retribution, thoughts of the Five Pains undoubtedly swirling in the young man's mind. *Good. He should be afraid, the fool.*

"Why have you disturbed me?" Li asked, regaining his composure.

"The Emperor has summoned you, my Chancellor. He is waiting for you in the map room."

"Very well," the chancellor said. "You may escort me."

The imperial guard bowed his head. "As you command."

Li followed the young guard back to the necropolis, passing through the outer and inner walls, until he reached the map room. The map room was the Emperor's favorite place to loiter, and Li understood why. It was a marvel, depicting the whole of the empire with miniature topographical precision. Mountains and valleys, carved in three-dimensional relief and painted in vivid color, stretched across the room. Rivers made of liquid mercury snaked and shimmered, giving the illusion of flowing water. Miniature buildings dotted the countryside, forming villages and cities linked by winding cobblestone paths. It was a breathtaking experience every time he looked upon it.

"You summoned me, Emperor," Li said, bowing to Qin Shi Huang.

"Chancellor Li," the Emperor said. "I am ready to receive your report."

A knot formed in Li's stomach. "The report . . ." He had no idea which report Qin Shi Huang was referring to and fumbled for words as he tried to remember what he'd possibly forgotten that would warrant a private summons.

"The trial report," the Emperor said with equal parts irritation and exasperation. "For the Elixir of Life presented by the shaman of Shennong Dengto Mountain."

Li clenched his jaw to suppress the irritation hiding just beneath the surface. Unlike the Emperor, he was not enchanted by the never-ending stream of alchemists and shamans that flowed through the palace, peddling potions and teas purported to restore youth and vigor. He was of the mind to have these charlatans—with their unverifiable claims about the Elixir of Life—buried alive and then exhumed a week later to prove to the Emperor that they spouted nothing but lies. But the Emperor demanded proof in the form of scientific trials. Each elixir was evaluated for efficacy using a royal proxy over a period of eight weeks. If the test subject regained his youth, then the alchemist of the elixir would be rewarded with his weight in jade. No rewards had been paid to date.

"Ah yes," Li said at last, nodding vigorously. "I'm sorry, my Emperor, but the formulation from Shennong Dengto is not the Elixir of Life. No immortal benefits were observed."

Qin Shi Huang kicked a miniature mountain, spraying pebbles and dirt across the miniature kingdom. "Punish the shaman," the Emperor seethed.

"But you have always prohibited the punishment of the holy men and alchemists who bring their potions and elixirs to the palace."

"I grow weary of being played the fool," the Emperor said. "The day is getting late, Chancellor Li. The Elixir of Life must be found. Spread the message throughout the kingdom—the reward for the elixir is great, but the consequence for deception will be severe."

"Yes, my Emperor," Chancellor Li said with a bow. "How shall I punish this charlatan?"

Qin Shi Huang eyed him. "You are the architect of punishment—inventor of the Five Pains—are you not?"

"I am."

"Then decide his crime and punish him accordingly."

"Yes, Emperor. I will see it done," Li said, bowing again to take his leave. This time, he could not conceal the pleasure inside and grinned broadly. Too long had these frauds and deceivers prayed on the Emperor's obsession. Now, finally, he could mete out the justice they deserved.

"Oh, and Chancellor," the Emperor called after him. "Make preparations for one final pilgrimage to Zhifu Island. This time I will find Penglai and meet the immortals. This time I will find the Mountain of Immortality."

"But sire, you have been to Zhifu Island twice already and found nothing."

"Yes, but this time will be different," the Emperor said, turning his attention the map of his kingdom. "Because this time you are coming with me."

Li's smile evaporated. "As you command."

He left the map room in a foul temper. *Zhifu Island . . . Zhifu Island!* A pilgrimage would take six months, possibly more depending on the Emperor's whims and health. Li did not have time for this foolishness. Did the Emperor not realize the irony of this decision? A third unsuccessful pilgrimage to Zhifu and back would undoubtedly be the death of him. Gritting his teeth, Li passed judgment on the shaman from Shennong Dengto before he'd even reached the imperial palace. For the crime of deceiving the Emperor of China, the shaman would be subjected to four of the Five Pains: permanent tattooing of the crime across the forehead, amputation of the nose, amputation of one hand, and amputation of the genitals. He would be spared the fifth and final pain, public execution by quartering. For the crime of deceiving the Emperor, Li intended to make the shaman of Shennong Dengto a walking ambassador. Everywhere the man traveled henceforth in the empire, everyone would know his crime.

Everyone would soon understand the fate of a man who claimed to be able to cheat death and lied.

PART I

CHAPTER 1

Beijing, China
1835 hours local—Day 1

Nick Foley gritted his teeth.

A voice inside his head was whispering for him to give up. This was one mission he simply wasn't qualified for. A second voice chimed in. *Ring the bell, Foley. You don't have what it takes,* taunted the ghost of Senior Chief Gunn, Foley's infamous ball-busting instructor at BUD/S.

Nick wiped the sweat from his brow with his sleeve and picked up the plastic carton of chicken stock—well, he hoped it was chicken stock. He'd purchased it based on the little caricature of a chicken in the upper-left corner because he couldn't read a word of the Chinese hanzi decorating the carton. He poured a little more of the tawny liquid into the grainy mess that was supposed to be risotto. It was beginning to look like, in choosing risotto for his first ever "home-cooked" dinner date, he had bitten off more than he could chew.

So to speak.

He stirred the fresh liquid in as he poured. The rice grains were still rock hard. He cursed under his breath and tried to face the problem head on. This was not how risotto was supposed to look. The question now was whether to add more chicken stock, more white wine, or just keep stirring. If he were cooking for anyone other than Dash—the beautiful and brilliant Dr. Chen Dazhong of the Chinese CDC—then he wouldn't be freaking out. But this was the woman who danced in and out of his thoughts countless times a day. He'd curated this first *real* date in his mind a hundred times, and he wanted it to be perfect.

Now here he was, torpedoed by risotto.

There was a knock on the door. He looked up at the wall clock in a panic; there was still a good half hour before Dash was supposed to arrive. *Of all the times to be early . . .*

He covered the risotto pan with a lid and wiped his hands on the dish towel draped over his shoulder. The raw lamb chops sat unseasoned on the cutting board, and he had forgotten to preheat the oven.

Damn it.

He took a deep breath, mustered a smile, and headed for the door.

His smile evaporated when he pulled it open.

"What the hell are *you* doing here?" Chet Lankford, the CIA's ranking man in Beijing, was the last thing he needed tonight—doubly so because he didn't want Dash to know he was still in contact with the man.

"Good evening to you too," Lankford said, slipping past him into the living room.

Nick left the door open. He had no intention of letting Lankford stay.

"Nice apartment, Foley," Lankford said, looking around.

"Thanks," Nick said, his hand still clutching the doorknob. "But you need to go."

"Is this how you treat all your guests?"

"Seriously, Lankford, get the fuck outta here," Nick said, beckoning him back to the entry. "Please."

Lankford flashed him an Oscar-winning passive-aggressive smile and sat on the sofa.

Nick sighed and shut the door. "Your timing is terrible."

"I can see that," Lankford said, glancing toward the kitchen. Nick expected a snide follow-up remark, but instead the CIA man sighed. Lankford looked tired. And stressed. "Don't worry, I'll only take a minute."

Nick nodded. "All right, now that you've made yourself at home, what's on your mind?"

Instead of answering the question, Lankford's attention shifted to an ornately painted cube topped with a bow that was sitting on the coffee table. He picked it up for closer examination. "What is this thing? Some kinda Chinese Rubik's Cube?"

"It's called a puzzle box, and it's none of your business," Nick said, walking over.

"What does it do?" Lankford asked, turning it over in his hands.

"Like I said, it's a puzzle box—figure out the puzzle, and there's a hidden chamber inside. I just finished rebuilding it, so please be careful."

"You fix puzzle boxes?"

"Puzzle boxes, old cars, shot-up Navy SEALs . . . Fixing stuff is fixing stuff. It's what I do."

Lankford nodded, impressed. "The artwork is exquisite. Five elements: metal, water, wood, earth, fire . . . and the balancing forces, yin and yang. Do you mind if I try to solve it?"

"Yes, I do mind, actually," Nick said, gently commandeering Dash's prized childhood gift from his clutches and returning it to the coffee table. He was about to sit down beside Lankford, but a sudden fear of ruined risotto drove him running back to the kitchen. Lankford pulled himself off of the couch with a grunt and followed Nick to the stove.

Nick removed the lid from the pan and swore.

"Risotto?" Lankford asked.

"Supposed to be."

"You need more chicken stock," Lankford said, then leaned in and sniffed. "And more white wine. And probably salt."

"Thanks," Nick said, pouring a little of both into the pan and reaching for the salt as he stirred.

"Dr. Chen will love it," Lankford said coyly.

Nick ignored the probe and raised an eyebrow. "So why exactly are you here?"

Lankford put a finger to his lips in the universal hush sign, then pointed to the ceiling. Nick nodded. Yes, the Chinese were almost certainly listening. The Chinese government made no secret about watching and listening to foreigners living and working in their cities. Nick was American—and former military—so it was guaranteed that he was under surveillance, even if he was not now associated with Lankford. When Nick, Dash, and Lankford had teamed up with China's elite Snow Leopard Counterterrorism Unit to stop a bioterrorism threat, they may have earned the formal gratitude of the government, but no matter how grateful the Snow Leopard Commander might be, he now knew who Lankford was and why he was in China. For Nick it was, at a minimum, guilt by association.

"I was in the neighborhood—thought I'd stop by and say hello."

Nick rolled his eyes.

"Also, I could use a favor."

"I've told you before, I'm not interested in working for your tech company."

Lankford smiled. "Yes, you've been quite clear about that, but that's not why I'm here."

Nick was about to make a sarcastic reply when his phone chirped. He picked it up and read the text, then slammed the phone onto the counter. "What the hell did you do, Lankford?"

The CIA man looked genuinely confused and picked up Nick's phone to read the SMS, which turned out to be from Dash:

Nick . . . so sorry but had to fly out for work.
Reschedule? My treat? My apartment? Call you in a
few days or when I can.

"I didn't do this," Lankford said, setting the phone down.

"Bullshit," Nick said as he threw his dish towel in the sink.

"Nick," Lankford said, grabbing his arm. Nick turned to face the CIA man. No Team guy would screw a buddy like this. "Seriously, man. All of our thrust and parry aside, I had nothing to do with this. I like the girl, really. I'd love to see the two of you together."

Nick sighed, leaned forward, and rested his hands on the kitchen counter. He knew he shouldn't feel this dejected over a canceled date, but the buzzkill hit him hard. He exhaled and tried to shut down the mental vitriol his subconscious was slinging around.

"She's giving you a rain check at *her* place," Lankford said. "Compared to the ambience you've got going on here in your Spartan studio—I'm just saying, it can only be a step up."

Nick shot him a look.

"No offense," Lankford added.

"Hmm, I suppose you make a good point," Nick said, cracking a smile.

"It's what I do."

"Are you this annoying with all your friends?"

"Pretty much."

Nick grabbed two beers from the fridge, popped the caps, and handed one to Lankford. Lankford extended the neck of the bottle in a toast. "To Dash and rain checks."

They clanked bottles.

After his first swig, Nick said, "So tell me about this favor you need, Chet." Suddenly, he found himself very curious about what was going on in the CIA man's world, something he didn't want to admit to himself and sure as hell wouldn't admit to Lankford.

Lankford made the hush sign again and pointed his index finger toward the ceiling. Then he lifted the lid to check the "risotto." Nick saw that the little grains were now sticking to the bottom of the pan, a small funnel cloud of dark smoke rising from the center of his culinary disaster.

"This looks basically inedible, dude," Lankford said. "Turn it off, put your lamb chops in the fridge, and let me buy you dinner. Think of it as recompense for tonight."

13

"Fine," Nick said. He dropped the pan into the sink, where it hissed when it hit the wet surface. Then he packed up his lamb chops, tossed them into the fridge, and turned to Lankford. "Your treat."

"Of course."

"Where?"

"I know a place."

The countersurveillance dance from Nick's apartment to the restaurant took over half an hour, and Nick figured every minute over thirty upped the stakes of whatever it was Lankford wanted to tell him. When they were finally settled into a booth, sipping on bottles of Tsingtao beer, Lankford ended the suspense.

"I'm missing a man," he said, suddenly looking five years older.

Nick was a SEAL—or used to be—so the weight of "a man left behind" was not lost on him. He looked around the room. No one seemed to be paying them any mind, so he leaned in. "Tell me?"

"His name is Peter Yu. He was conducting routine surveillance in Xi'an and missed a check-in. I didn't think anything of it, at first—lots of check-ins get missed, and we have a protocol for that. But then he missed another and then a third. I have managed assets in Xi'an—you know, guys we pay for information. They checked his apartment and his office—he's gone."

"Gone where?"

Lankford clenched his jaw and balled his hand into a fist on the table.

"Well, I don't fucking know, Nick. If I did, he wouldn't be missing, would he?"

Nick pursed his lips.

"Sorry," Lankford said after a beat. "I'm tired."

"It's fine," Nick said—and meant it. Two months ago, Lankford had lost an agent on his watch—a talented rising star in the Beijing office named Jamie Lin. Lankford had bonded with the girl, had thought of her as a surrogate daughter. Her murder had hit him hard. *Best to tread lightly on this one*, Nick thought.

"What was Yu working on?"

Lankford placed a silver tablet computer on the table between them.

"I loaded his reports on this. Feel free to take a look, but I suspect you won't find anything interesting. I didn't. Yu was fairly new to the post and was spending the majority of his time sniffing around for anything that didn't smell right. Routine monitoring and surveillance mode, you know the gig. His official cover was as a branch manager for ViaTech, mostly business development and IT staffing for some of the big Chinese tech companies in Xi'an."

"Placing talent?"

"Exactly, to keep an eye on government contracts, tech transfer, pipeline R&D, cyber, and so on."

"So what do you want from me?" Nick asked, feigning apathy. He didn't want to care, but he did. His mind drifted to Afghanistan and the brothers he'd lost. When he left the SEALs to join a charitable NGO, he'd intended to leave the clandestine life behind. But here he was, dining with the CIA's ranking official in China, talking spook shit. He didn't regret the decision to leave the SEALs, and he didn't regret working for an NGO. But Lankford's tale of a missing American operative stirred old, powerful feelings.

No man is left behind.

It was the mantra of Special Operations and an ethos of the SEALs. Since their birth under Kennedy in the early 1960s, not one SEAL had been left behind on the field of battle, alive or dead. His desire to help find Yu was not something he could ignore or resist—it had been spliced into his very DNA.

Lankford pushed the still untouched tablet computer closer to Nick. "I was hoping maybe you could poke around Xi'an for me."

"Poke around Xi'an?" Nick echoed, cocking an eyebrow at Lankford. "What the hell does that mean?"

"I can't trust my assets in Xi'an with this. They're all managed assets. In my experience, the minute a managed asset thinks he's in any real danger, he turns. They'll do the scout work for me, but that's about it. I need someone I can trust to go to Xi'an and try to pick up Yu's trail."

"I thought you had *people* for shit like this!"

"Of course," Lankford said. "But thanks to you, your girl-friend, and your buddy Commander Zhang, my entire operation in Beijing is outed. My *people*, as you say, are blown. Peter Yu is proof of that. Anyone I send could be in real danger if the Chinese government is behind Yu's disappearance."

"Yeah," Nick agreed, leaning in with a tight smile. "But then wouldn't I also be in danger? You know for damn sure that they're watching me. No mystery there. Zhang was explicit—get caught working with you and the CIA again, and he'd person-ally kick my ass out of China on the next available flight."

"He was just trying to rattle your cage."

"Oh, I see how it is. Since I'm not on your payroll, I'm expend-able. Is that it?"

Lankford looked irritated. "It's not like that, Nick. You have a real NOC. You don't work for me, as you love pointing out. You conduct legitimate business in Xi'an. Hell, you were there just a few weeks ago, if I'm not mistaken. No one would find it curious if you traveled back to Xi'an for Water For People, or Habitat for Humanity, or whatever the hell tree-hugging shit it is you do for a living." The tension in his voice was rising now.

"Relax, Chet. I was just kidding," Nick said. Then, under his breath he added, "Well, sort of."

Lankford said nothing. He just held Nick's gaze with tired, desperate eyes.

Nick flashed him a half-baked smile. "Isn't this the part of the conversation where you're supposed to pull out the red pill and the blue pill and tell me I have to choose between taking the trip down the rabbit hole or going back to living my normal, boring life?"

Lankford tapped the tablet computer with the tip of his index finger and said, "Red pill." Then he tapped Nick's beer bottle. "Blue pill . . . Look, Nick, it really is that simple. Either you go to

Xi'an and look for my missing man, or you stay in Beijing, hang out, drink beer, and learn how to cook risotto."

Nick grimaced.

"Look, you said you're a fixer—and I need your help to fix this mess. You're either up to the challenge or you're not."

Nick stared at the tablet. No matter how much Lankford loved to mock him, the work he did with Water 4 Humanity was important. Access to sanitary drinking water was the most fundamental of human needs. In the few short months he had worked for W4H, he had helped provide life-giving water for thousands of poor and indigent Chinese, most of them children. He believed in the mission, and yet here he was, bantering with Lankford about spy games. The truth was obvious. He wouldn't be having this discussion if the NGO career fulfilled all his needs. The chase and gunfight in the tunnels of the Beijing Underground City, solving the mystery of Jamie Lin's murder, stopping a bioterrorist minutes before he killed thousands of innocents—all of that had made Nick feel alive, but they weren't the things that would make him say yes.

Peter Yu was an American operator in a foreign land, a kindred spirit . . . a brother by proxy.

"Okay, here's the deal," Nick said. "We have a satellite office in Xi'an, where we manage projects in the north and west—mostly around the low mountain villages outside of Yaojiagouzhen. I'm sure I can invent some reason to go there and check in with my regional managers on those projects. While I'm in Xi'an, I'll stop by Yu's apartment and report what I find. Will that help?"

"Yes. Thank you, Nick," Lankford said with more sincerity than Nick had ever heard from the sarcastic spook. "All of Peter's reports are on the tablet—zipped in file number one. All of his assets' reports are zipped as file two. Fair warning—there's not much to work with. The third and final file contains the details of his official cover in Xi'an and his redacted personnel file."

Lankford pulled a small gift-wrapped box from his coat pocket and slid it over. The card on top read, "Thanks for everything."

Nick looked up and arched his eyebrows.

"Don't get too mushy or excited on me," Lankford said. "It's an encrypted burner. Call me if you need help or if you find anything. Anything at all. That being said, save your minutes, because once you start using it, our friends will get to work cracking the encryption. The number for my encrypted burner is in the speed dial."

Nick slipped the tablet and the gift box into the pocket of his barn jacket.

"Thanks for this, Nick. I mean it."

"I know you do, Chet. I hope I can help."

Lankford stood up from the table.

"I thought you were buying me dinner?" Nick said.

"Should've eaten before you let me screw you," Lankford said with a chuckle. "You're a SEAL—even you know that."

The waitress arrived and set a plate of steaming beef noodles in front of him. Nick looked from his food back to Lankford, but the spook was already gone.

Shit, Nick thought as he dug into the spicy fare. *Here we go again.*

But this time, he realized he was smiling.

CHAPTER 2

Somewhere over China
Citation X, cruising at 24,000 feet

The first time she flew on a private jet, Chen Dazhong felt like a celebrity. No waiting in line, no security screening, no baggage hassles, free concierge-level service, and comfortable leather captain's chairs—these were the VIP luxuries of chartered air travel that the everyman dreamed about. For Dash, that first magical flight had been four years and many jaunts ago. Tonight, the magic was gone. Tonight, she did not feel like a celebrity. Instead, she was very much aware of the flip side of being *that* someone who is whisked away on a private jet at a moment's notice. Being that someone carried obligation and risk. It carried high expectations and even higher stakes. Tonight's free ticket from Beijing to Hong Kong was a thinly veiled ride on the devil's chariot. They were flying her to the gates of hell . . . in Hollywood style.

The call from Commander Zhang had come unexpectedly, while she was dressing for her dinner date with Nick Foley.

"It's happening again," Commander Zhang had said when she'd answered her mobile.

"What's happening again?" she'd asked, a lump already in her throat.

"Dead civilians. Except this time, it's different . . ."

"Different how?"

19

"Words don't do it justice. You'll just have to come see for yourself."

A black sedan had picked her up in front of her apartment ten minutes later.

Now here she was, with her "go bag" propped on the empty seat beside her, en route to tackle China's second bioterrorism event in as many months. As the CDC's senior representative on China's Quick Reaction Bioterrorism Task Force, she was both a first responder and a primary investigator. She had been hand-picked for this role by the Director of the CDC—namely, because of her success in starting up China's first Ebola relief hospital in Liberia. Her decisive leadership in the field and her exemplary safety record during the relief effort had reflected positively on the Chinese CDC—and China as a nation—in the eyes of the international community. Her heroism in the days following a bioterrorism attack in the western desert city of Kizilsu had cemented her position as a permanent task force member.

Now rumors were circulating at the CDC that she was next in line to become the department head of the Office of Disease Control and Emergency Response (DCER). It was a promotion she did not relish because it would mean forfeiting her current position as a lead researcher of emerging diseases. Any department head position, especially as head of DCER, would take her out of the laboratory . . . probably for the rest of her career.

She had joined the CDC as a scientist. Research was her passion. The promise of discovery was the thing that got her out of bed in the morning, not ladder climbing. She was no bureaucrat, but that didn't matter. Her future was not her own. She was being groomed to someday become the first woman Director of the Chinese CDC, an honor and a burden she wholeheartedly did not want. Which left her in the unfortunate and awkward position of knowing that the only way to change her fate was to sabotage her own career, something she simply could not bring herself to do.

The cabin steward approached her with a hesitant smile. "May I get you something to drink, Dr. Chen? Tea, water, a soft drink beverage?"

"Coffee, please," she said.

"Any milk or sugar?"

"Yes, sugar, please. Be generous with the sugar."

"My pleasure. Anything else?"

"Yes, how much longer until we land?"

The young man checked his watch. "Thirty minutes, approximately."

She nodded, and he departed to fulfill her request.

From the moment the plane landed in Hong Kong, a tidal wave of bioterrorism operations activity would sweep her off her feet and carry her wherever it would. For the next twenty-four to thirty-six hours, she would work nonstop, without sleep or a proper meal, until the biological threat was identified and contained. On the Quick Reaction Bioterrorism Task Force, she shared tactical and operational command with Commander Zhang of the Snow Leopard Commando Counterterrorism Unit's Ninth Squadron, as well as Major Li Shengkun of the PLA's Nuclear Biological Chemical Regiment 54423 out of Shenzhen. Together, they formed the holy trinity of China's bioterrorism defense strategy. Together, they had the power to marshal every resource that the CDC, the Army, and China's National Police Force had available.

Tonight, she prayed they wouldn't have to.

Her mind drifted to Nick. She wondered if he was upset with her. *Probably.* She had, after all, canceled their date thirty minutes before she was supposed to arrive. His response had seemed cordial and forgiving enough. She retrieved her mobile phone and reread his text message reply:

Completely understand. No worries.
Talk soon and be careful.

If she took Nick's message at face value, then he was not upset with her. They were both working professionals who traveled regularly. Work interrupts life. Plans change. Nick understood this. But on the other hand, his reply was very succinct. Almost terse. Clearly, he was irritated with her, which was why he'd said so little. And there was the fact that he didn't even *acknowledge* the offer she'd made in her text message to make up the dinner date at her apartment. Maybe he'd been planning a romantic dinner. Maybe he'd been hoping she'd spend the night. If he'd miscon-strued her acceptance of his dinner offer as a romantic invitation, then that would be a problem. She wasn't sure if she was ready for a romantic relationship with Nick yet. It was too soon. Just two months ago, she had been married . . .

Besides, she told herself, *how can I have a romantic relationship with a former American SEAL, given my position in government? It would not be tolerated.*

And yet, the thought of his touch made her flush.

She sighed and shook her head.

What's wrong with me? I'm thinking like a schoolgirl.

The cabin steward returned with her coffee and set the cup down on the tray next to her. "Can I get you anything else, Dr. Chen?"

"No, thank you," she said.

He nodded and returned to his seat at the back of the aircraft.

She raised the cup to her lips and sipped. Hot and sweet—just the way she liked it. She sipped greedily, until the little white por-celain cup was empty. She stared out the window at the twinkling lights dotting the landscape below.

Her left upper eyelid began to twitch.

Great, not this again.

She was nervous, caffeinated, and chronically sleep-deprived, so it was no wonder that "the twitch" had reemerged from its eight-week hibernation with a vengeance. Sometimes the spasm lasted only a few seconds; sometimes it tormented her for hours.

Twitch.

She felt the nose of the jet dip as the pilot began the descent into Hong Kong. Her stomach suddenly felt queasy. She'd done everything mentally possible to avoid thinking about "the event" in Hong Kong during the flight. But with touchdown only min-utes away, she couldn't help but wonder what twisted, hellish nightmare she was walking into this time.

Twitch, twitch . . .

She didn't know if she could handle another Kizilsu.

Twitch.

Whatever it was, one thing was certain: there would be pain and misery.

And dead bodies.

Clenching her jaw, she pressed the pad of her left thumb against her eyelid and prayed that this time, the machinations of her imagination were more dreadful than reality.

CHAPTER 3

Hong Kong International Airport
Lantau Island

Dash peered out the porthole window and saw a figure dressed entirely in black, waiting for her on the tarmac. The plane taxied to a stop and the cabin steward unlocked and cracked opened the Citation's access hatch. The wind howled through the gap, and the young man struggled to maintain control of the staircase as he lowered it. The landing had been white-knuckle choppy, and now she understood why. Lightning flashed on the horizon; a violent gust of wind buffeted her back from the opening. A storm was brewing. She pulled her shoulder-length onyx hair into a quick ponytail, zipped her jacket up to her neck, and stepped off the plane.

As she strode to meet the Snow Leopard Commander, the go bag slung over her shoulder bounced rhythmically against her right hip. Their eyes met, and the left corner of Zhang's mouth curled into a coy half smile. Tonight, he was dressed in the SLCU's signature all-black tactical gear and looked particularly imposing.

And handsome.

"Dr. Chen," he said, extending a hand to greet her.

"Commander." His grip was so firm, it was like shaking hands with a granite statue. "Good to see you again."

24

"You as well. Although I wish it were under better circumstances." He gestured to a black Mercedes GL idling ten meters away with its headlights on. "That's our ride."

"Where are we going?"

"To the helo," he said.

She climbed into the back seat of the Mercedes SUV, and Zhang slid in beside her.

"Go," he barked at the driver, and the GL's V-8 engine roared to life, throwing her back into her seat.

"Has anyone briefed you?" Zhang asked, turning to face her. Worry lines creased his forehead.

"No," she said.

"It'll be noisy on the helo, so I'll bring you up to speed now," he said. "At approximately 1700 local, dead bodies began washing up on Tung Wan Beach."

"Tung Wan Beach," she echoed. "Is that on Cheung Chau Island?"

"Yes. It's one of the most popular and crowded beaches in Hong Kong. So you can imagine the pandemonium that erupted when corpses started floating in. Supposedly, a seven-year-old girl and her father were playing in the waves when the first body drifted by. Its arms tangled around the girl's legs."

Dash shook her head, mortified at the mental imagery. "That poor girl is going to be emotionally scarred for life."

"Not just her," Zhang said. "At least a dozen swimmers and windsurfers had similar encounters."

"Wait a minute, just how many bodies are we talking about?"

"Last I heard, the count was up to eighteen."

"And the beach? Please tell me it has been quarantined . . ."

"Yes. The local police weren't sure what they were dealing with. Because of the condition of the bodies, they called us, and I made the decision to mobilize the task force and implement your quarantine procedures."

The Mercedes skidded to a stop twenty meters away from a blacked-out Changhe Z-11 tactical helicopter that was already spinning up its rotors.

"I have to ride in that?" she said, gawking out the window.

"What, you don't like helicopters?"

"I've never ridden in one," she said, opening the passenger door. "And to be honest, I don't particularly like the idea of flying around in something that doesn't have wings. It's not natural."

"You'll love it," he said, stepping out of the SUV behind her. "I promise to fly nice."

"Whoa, whoa, whoa," she said, clutching his arm. "Don't tell me you're the pilot?"

"Of course. That guy in the pilot's seat is just warming her up for me," he shouted over the rising roar of the rotor wash. "Relax, Dr. Chen, it'll be fun . . . Now duck your head and stay with me."

She did as instructed, jogging in a crouch toward the helicopter. The rotor wash buffeted her this way and that—almost knocking her over—but Zhang kept her on her feet with a steadying hand on her back. When they reached the fuselage, he helped her into the copilot's seat and then swapped places with the pilot. He put on a green headset embossed with a David Clark logo on the side. He motioned for her to do the same. She fit the padded cups over her ears, and immediately, the roar of the rotors and engines dropped at least ten decibels.

"Electronic noise-canceling," Zhang said, his voice crisp and clear over the shared comms channel. He reached over adjusted her boom mike so that it was two centimeters from her lips. "There, now you're ready to go."

"Thanks," she said.

She watched him complete a sequence of preflight checks while he called the tower for what she assumed was permission to take off.

"We've got some weather coming in, so it might be a little bumpy," he said. "You ready?"

"Do I have a choice?" she asked, but the helicopter was already airborne.

She felt her stomach drop as the tarmac fell away at a startling speed. She had never accelerated vertically in an aircraft before, and the sensation was unnerving. Wind shear pounded the fuselage, suddenly rolling and tipping the helo simultaneously. She clutched at her armrests and cursed. She looked at Zhang, expecting to see him clench-jawed and serious, but instead, he was grinning ear to ear.

He's actually enjoying this, she thought.

"Relax, Dr. Chen," he said, laughing. "You're with me, remember?"

She watched him work the pedals, cyclic stick, and collective control with expert efficiency, dynamically compensating as the wind tossed them around. After a few minutes, she relaxed her death grip on the armrests. She mustered the courage to look out the window and admired the Hong Kong skyline shimmering off to her left. They flew along the east coast of Lantau Island and then banked left over the ocean. Before she knew it, they were hovering over a small, crescent-shaped island.

"There it is, Cheung Chau Island," he said over the comms circuit.

"That didn't take long."

"Only fifteen kilometers by helo."

"Where are we going to land?"

"There's a helo pad at the south end of the beach, next to St. John Hospital. We set up our command post there."

As he descended toward a circular landing pad, the wind picked up again, shaking them terribly. Clinging to the armrests for dear life, she said, "When we were in the SUV, you said you made the decision to mobilize the task force because of the condition of the bodies."

"That's right," he said, his gaze focused on the landing pad.

"So what is the condition of the bodies?"

"Bloated and disfigured," he said without affect. "But the eyes are what concerned me and made me think of the nanobot bio-weapon we encountered before."

"What about the eyes?" she asked.

"Do you remember the dead Russian we found in the stairwell of your apartment building?"

"Yes," she said. "He didn't have any eyes."

"Exactly," Zhang said as the helo touched down. "And neither do these corpses."

A shiver ran down her spine. "Qing is dead. I ensured that the technology was destroyed. I don't understand how this could be happening again."

"Neither do I. That's why I needed you here."

A lightning flash arced across the sky. The deep, rolling bellow of thunder followed a second later.

"It looks like it could get ugly out there," she said as Zhang began flipping switches to shut down the helo.

He turned to face her. "You have no idea."

CHAPTER 4

Tung Wan Beach
Cheung Chau Island

The rain pelted Dash's blue exposure suit in fits and spurts—chaotic punishment from a storm both angry and indecisive. The hood, goggles, and M5 antimicrobial mask she wore already made it hard to hear, see, and talk, but the gusting winds and pounding waves amplified the problem. Tonight, Dash felt more like a scuba diver battling the surf than a bioterrorism first responder.

On the positive side, at least she had light.

Zhang had ordered twelve massive halogen floodlights set up along the sidewalk that formed the perimeter of the crescent-shaped beach. The lights were spaced at ten-meter intervals and positioned approximately fifteen meters back from where the storm surge was pummeling the beach. Portable gasoline generators churned, while black electrical cabling snaked everywhere in between. How Zhang had found the equipment to make this happen on such short notice was beyond her. Logistics was one step away from magic as far as she was concerned.

The sand shifted beneath her booties as she walked toward the two rows of corpses. The bodies—naked, gray, and bloated—were staged three meters back from the breakers. In her peripheral vision, she saw another corpse bobbing in the surf: a new arrival.

She nudged Zhang, who was walking at her side. He looked at her, his eyes obscured behind fogged goggles. She pointed to the body at the water's edge, and he nodded. They continued trudging through the sand and the wind until they reached the nine corpses. Dash took a knee beside the body on the end—a male in his midtwenties, she guessed, based on the level of fitness.

She wiped rain splatter from her goggles with the back of her gloved hand, but this only had the effect of smearing the water droplets. She cursed under her breath. If she had to imagine the worst possible conditions for investigating a bioterrorism event, tonight came damn close.

"Am I crazy, or is that an incision?" Zhang shouted, pointing to the corpse's torso.

She cocked her head to try to see out of a clear patch of goggle lens. To her horror, the corpse had a single longitudinal incision that ran from the base of his neck down to his pubis. The incision was closed with heavy, black suture—whipstitched with little regard for anything other than speed and utility. Dr. Frankenstein's stitchwork could be called elegant compared to this effort.

"This body was cut open. Possibly autopsied," she shouted back, over the howling wind.

She scanned the rest of the body, inventorying the damage. Where there should have been eyes, instead she saw two gaping, purple holes. A jagged triangular crater filled the space normally occupied by a nose. She reached out and pulled back the lips, expecting to find all the teeth missing. Yes, suspicion confirmed. She shifted her focus south and was aghast to find the man's genitals had been excised, along with both of his hands.

"Barbaric," she muttered.

"What'd you say?" Zhang said.

"This is barbaric," she hollered.

Zhang nodded.

"I'm going to work my way down the line."

"Roger that."

The second corpse was a female, also midtwenties. Like the first, this body was eyeless and marred with a longitudinal frontal incision, but unlike the male, she was not missing her nose, hands, and feet. The third corpse, male, had no incision on the torso but was missing his nose, hands, feet, and genitals.

"What's that on his forehead?" Zhang asked.

She leaned in to inspect the third victim's forehead. "Looks like a tattoo," she said, trying to make out the hanzi characters.

"Does that say *Hanjian*?" Zhang shouted.

"I think so," she said, crabbing her way down the line, checking the other corpses. Two more corpses had the same forehead tattoo and were also missing noses, hands, and genitals. The others were missing only their eyes and had longitudinal incisions. Except for the first body, only those without tattoos had longitudinal torso incisions.

"What the hell is going on here?" Zhang shouted.

"I have no idea, but I can tell you this," she hollered. "This is not the work of a biological weapon."

"So what now? Do you want to lift the quarantine?"

"No. Not yet. Better to err on the side of caution."

"So what do we do?"

"We need to move all the bodies to a secure location, where I can begin testing and autopsy work. Somewhere with controlled access, where the media can't bother us."

"Already taken care of," he hollered over a thunderclap. "Our favorite Major from Shenzhen should be arriving within the hour. He's arranged for the bodies to be transferred to the Gun Club Hill Military Hospital in Hong Kong."

Dash smirked behind her mask. "Knowing how Li operates, he'll have taken complete control by midnight. We'll be able to catch an early-morning flight back to Beijing and wash our hands of this."

"Don't count on it. Li's a team player now, remember?"

"After what I did in Beijing with the nanobot vaccine, I wouldn't be so sure. The man hates me. He tried to have me kicked off the task force."

"True," Zhang said. "But he failed. I'm on your side, remember? No matter what."

31

She met his goggly gaze. "Thanks, Zhang. That means a lot."

"Don't thank me yet. We still have another helicopter ride to take."

"No way, hotshot," she said, shaking her head. "I'm taking the ferry over. Even if it means I have to ride with the bodies."

CHAPTER 5

Xi'an Hilton Hotel
199 Xinjie Street, Xincheng, Xi'an, China
Day 2

Post-ischemia-reperfusion-injury mitigation.

Nick shook his head.

Not cyber, not aerospace, not defense . . . Before his disappearance, Peter Yu had inexplicably been focused on a biotech company engaged in research on ischemia-reperfusion. Lankford hadn't mentioned anything about that in Beijing when they had last spoken. Probably because Lankford didn't have a fucking clue what it was. If it weren't for Nick's SEAL Eighteen Delta medic training, he wouldn't either.

Ischemia: a lack of blood flow and oxygen to tissue.

Reperfusion injury: damage caused to tissue when blood flow is restored after a period of ischemia.

Why would a CIA operative tasked with collecting intelligence on defense and aerospace contractor activities be interested in obscure biomedical research?

"Sir?" the hotel valet said, shaking Nick from his fugue. "You want me hail you taxi?"

"No, thanks," Nick said. "I have a rental car."

"You park in garage? You want me get it?" the young valet said, eager to move Nick along.

"No, thank you," he said, nodding at a compact Geely parked down the curb. "That's me."

"Next time, you no park here, okay? Valet only, okay?"

"Sure, sorry," Nick said and made his way over to his rental.

It had taken him only ten minutes to check in and drop his bag off in the room; now he was ready to head out for the day. He'd chosen the Xi'an Hilton because it was about equidistant from the Water 4 Humanity offices at Jianguo 4th Alley, just south of Dongguan Commerce Block, and Peter Yu's apartment overlooking Huancheng Park. A stop by the NGO office had been mandatory to keep his cover intact in case he had been followed from Beijing. For all he knew, there could be eyes on him right now. He had made the stop short and sweet before coming to the hotel, and now he could focus on the mission.

Damn you, Chet Lankford. You've got me thinking like a spook already.

It had taken all his energy to appear focused when his team of young and eager NGO volunteers briefed him on the various projects they were running out of the Xi'an office of W4H. They had been confused by his visit—probably assuming they'd done something wrong—but he had been quick to reassure them his visit was routine. He'd used the time during their PowerPoint presentations to mentally pore over the information that Lankford had provided.

The reports from Lankford's local assets—Chinese civilians on the CIA payroll, whom Yu was managing—had been useless: *Yu was still missing. His car was still parked in his reserved spot. He had not been observed at his apartment or his office for days. He had not communicated with any of the assets about plans to travel or changes to their tasking. He was last seen at dinner with a local Chinese woman, no name or description provided.*

The heavily redacted file on Yu himself was also frustratingly lacking in substance: *Peter Yu, age thirty-two, only child born to first-generation Chinese immigrants. Fluent Mandarin. Bachelor's degree in political science from UVA. Recruited as a senior by the CIA. After graduation, went straight to the Farm, where he finished* *top half in his class. Then three years spent working at <<redacted >> in the civilian sector under an OC, before being accepted to the Elliot School at George Washington University, where he earned a dual master's in international affairs and Asian studies. After leaving GW, the Company sent him back to the civilian world, where he worked at <<redacted >> as a <<redacted >>. Six months ago, he joined Lankford's team, standing up a tech staffing company in Xi'an.*

Yu's staffing company had no ties to ViaTech, a fact not lost on Nick. The events in Beijing two months ago had blown Lankford's cover and had revealed ViaTech to be a CIA front company. But Yu had never worked for ViaTech, so there was no reason to assume that Yu's cover was compromised. Nonetheless, any possible paper trail connecting Yu to Lankford was something Nick would have to investigate.

After three hours at the office, he turned down a lunch invitation and headed west in his Geely along the South Ring Road West. His Chinese driver's license gave him considerable freedom but had been hell to acquire. The Chinese didn't recognize his international driver's permit, and the only way to get a Chinese license was to endure considerable testing in a system far more bureaucratic than in the States. In the end, it had been easier to get a license in Hong Kong, one of only two licenses valid to convert to a Chinese license, the other, strangely, being a license from Belgium. He was in Hong Kong frequently with W4H, so it had been the path of least resistance.

He imagined his NGO team had been glad he'd cut his impromptu visit short. He'd offered to meet them in the morning to drive up to the Yaojiagouzhen project, and they had all eagerly volunteered to join him. They had not traveled tens of thousands of miles to China to sit in an office, so going into the field—even with the boss—would be a treat. Nick would see what he could find out about Peter Yu today, inspect the water project at Yaojiagouzhen tomorrow, and be back in Beijing by tomorrow night.

He crossed over the ring canal around central Xi'an on Tianshuijing Street and merged left onto the Huoyaoju Alley after circumnavigating the circle. A moment later, he pulled into the lot at Huoyaoju number thirty-two. The dull, nondescript building stood in stark contrast to the colorful buildings on the far side of the park, but Peter Yu's apartment on the fifth floor would have a great view of both. Nick locked the car and made a great effort not to look around as he crossed the street and buzzed himself into the building with the key card Lankford had provided. He needed to look like he belonged here, in case someone was watching.

He rode the elevator up to five, an operation that again required the key card, and then walked confidently to unit 512 on the west side of the building. With the traditional metal key clipped to the key card, Nick let himself into Yu's apartment and shut the door behind him.

The apartment screamed "American expat technophile." The furniture was sleek and modern. To the left, two Eames lounge chairs with matching ottomans—probably Chinese knock-offs—sat facing an enormous LED television. The TV hung over a black modular entertainment center decked out with a Bang & Olufsen stereo, an Xbox gaming system, and a satellite box. To the right, a glass dining table was positioned under a window and flanked by two polished aluminum chairs. Beyond the dining area was a pass-through bar to a contemporary kitchen. He padded into the kitchen and found it to be fastidious, save for some unwashed dishes in the sink. He opened the refrigerator to find what he deemed ordinary fare for a bachelor: leftovers, condiments, beer, and butter. He opened the freezer door: ice cubes, ice cream, a bottle of vodka, and frozen vegetables. He shut the fridge and freezer doors, made his way out of the kitchen, and walked down a short hallway leading to what he presumed was Yu's bedroom.

The bedroom door was cracked open four inches. He assured himself that the room was unoccupied, but his adrenaline jumped as he approached the threshold. He paused to listen, wishing for a Sig Sauer to clutch in his right hand. Hearing nothing, he eased the door open with his left foot.

The hollow wood door swung easily on new, silent hinges.

He glanced left and right, clearing the corners out of habit, then exhaled with relief.

Directly ahead, an unmade queen-sized bed dominated the bedroom. A cell phone charger cord was draped across the top of a bedside table, with no cell phone in sight. A pile of dirty laundry lay strewn on the floor of the open closet on the left. He peeked inside: trousers, dress shirts, and two suit coats hung from hangers in the otherwise Spartan closet. Finding no wall safe or file cabinet, he turned back to the bedroom. On the facing wall, he spied a stainless-steel Tag Heuer sports chrono resting on top of an IKEA-style dresser. He left the watch untouched and opened each of the drawers in turn, finding nothing but neatly folded clothes. On the right-hand wall, Yu had set up a tiny modern desk and task chair. Nick inspected the desk and opened the lone underhanging drawer: no computer, no USB drives, no notebook, no journal, and no tablet PC.

Shit. There's nothing of interest here at all.

He exhaled with annoyance.

Only one thing was certain—if Yu had met a violent end, it hadn't happened here. There was no sign of forced entry and no indication the apartment had been searched. The state of the apartment gave off a life-as-usual vibe. However, that wasn't necessarily a positive sign either. This was exactly how agents were trained to evacuate their personal spaces when things got nasty. The only detail of interest, in Nick's opinion, was the conspicuous absence of a computer. Lankford confirmed that Yu had been issued a Company notebook computer, and the prospect of finding the machine had been the primary impetus for Nick entering the apartment. If Yu had known he was compromised or in immediate danger, his first action would have been to scuttle his laptop. The laptop had not been found in Yu's office, according to Lankford, and Nick found no evidence of one here either. Again—interesting, but alone it meant nothing.

Nick wandered back into the living room and looked around one last time—checking in and behind the entertainment center. He felt himself getting antsy. Time was ticking. If he was being followed by Chinese G-men, then he preferred to be outside if they confronted him. Satisfied there was nothing else here to find, he decided to leave. At the apartment door, he paused and looked over his shoulder one last time to see if anything new caught his eye. It didn't.

He reached for the doorknob and found it already turning.

A surge of panic washed over him.

Go into character, he told himself. *You're an American expat catching up with a friend from back home. No laws against that.*

Instead of retreating, he grabbed the knob and swung the door open.

A young, diminutive Asian woman looked up at him. She gasped and backpedaled, dropping a silver key on the tile floor of the hall.

"Who the hell are you?" Nick demanded in English, hoping to keep the woman off balance. "And where is Peter?"

The girl tried to speak, but all she managed was a soft clucking noise. She swallowed hard and then tried again. "I am Lihau," she said, this time in perfect English with a slight Irish lilt. "Peter's girlfriend. Who the hell are you?"

CHAPTER 6

Suantang Dumplings Beef Noodles Restaurant
Two blocks from Peter Yu's apartment
Xi'an, China
1715 hours local

The girl who called herself Lihau was trying not to look worried as she sipped her tea.

Nick fought the urge to pity her. Nothing was ever what it seemed in the world of espionage—Lihau's concern for Peter Yu seemed genuine enough, but Nick didn't trust his instincts today. When he was deployed in Afghanistan, he'd gotten pretty good at reading the Pashtun. He'd learned how to detect when they were bullshitting him and when they weren't. But parsing the tells and decoding fictions employed by tribal Afghanis in no way qualified him to suss the truth from a woman who could be a Chinese agent trained by the Ministry of State Security. He reminded himself of the facts: Lihau had found him inside Yu's apartment; she'd had a key; she spoke fluent English; and her arrival had coincided almost perfectly with his. Taken together, the odds were better than average that Lihau was a spy. Unfortunately, ascertaining that for certain was something he simply did not consider himself qualified to do.

Of course, that wouldn't stop him from trying.

"So when did you last see Peter?" Nick asked, deciding it best if he controlled the conversation.

"It's been four days since I've heard from him," she said.

"Is that unusual? I mean, do the two of you talk regularly?"

"Peter travels often for business. Sometimes we go a couple days without talking, but we always text. He hasn't responded to any of my text messages."

"Are you worried?"

"Yes," she said and sipped her tea. She glanced at him over the rim of her cup. "Why do you have a key to Peter's apartment?"

If he hadn't had time to prepare for the question, she might have caught him off guard.

"Usually, I don't," he answered. "But when I told him I was coming to town, he offered to let me stay at his place. He left a key with the building manager for me."

"Funny, he didn't mention you were coming," she said, eying him.

"And he didn't mention to me that you two lived together."

"We don't," she said with a defensive edge and glanced away.

Hmmm . . . if she's an agent, she's either been working Yu and has lost him, or she's already gotten her man, and now she's tying up loose ends.

"Your English is excellent, if you don't mind me saying," he said, probing. "Where did you learn?"

"I studied English in primary school, of course, but I became fluent during my graduate studies abroad in Dublin."

Nick nodded, confirming his earlier suspicion about the hint of an Irish accent. "What did you study in Ireland?"

"Molecular biology."

"Oh, so you must work with viruses and bacteria?" he asked, silently praying he wasn't stumbling into another bioweapon case.

"Yes and no. My particular area of expertise is CRISPR," she said absently, looking out the window.

"What's a crisper?"

She chuckled. "CRISPR is an acronym. It stands for Clustered Regular Interspaced Short Palindromic Repeats, which are segments of prokaryotic DNA that convey adaptive immunity in bacteria and archaea. But when someone says they work with CRISPR, what they really mean is that they are using CRISPR Cas9 proteins for genome engineering. Even though CRISPR Cas9 was discovered in bacteria, it can be utilized to edit genes in eukaryotes."

Nick had absolutely no freaking idea what she was talking about, but he committed her last sentence to memory for later. "Sounds interesting," he said.

"It is," she said.

He waited for her to elaborate, and when she didn't, he shifted gears. "So how did you meet Peter?" he added with a grin, trying to sound more familiar.

"We met at my work," she said, her face lighting up. "Well, sort of. We met at a coffee shop just outside my company's offices here in Xi'an. He had just tried—unsuccessfully—to get a meeting with the human resources people. His company does IT staffing." She looked at Nick again as if to see if he knew that.

"Yeah, so I heard," he said. "Peter has done quite well for himself since he left George Washington University."

"Yes." She looked at her teacup and then smiled at some fond memory. "Anyway, that was a couple of months ago." She blushed. "Things went very quickly with us."

Nick smiled at her. "Did Peter ever get a staffing contract with your company—what was the name?"

"Nèiyè Biologic. And no, he did not. He used to complain all the time about it, but now he says it doesn't matter because fate had other reasons for bringing us together. He said if his meeting with HR had gone better, we might never have met."

"I'm sure he meant it, Lihau. He was never slick enough to make something like that up."

"Thank you," she said, smiling warmly at him. Then, with a pent-up urgency that surprised him, she reached out and grabbed his wrist. "Do you think something terrible has happened to him? It is not like Peter to ignore my text messages and voicemails."

Either this girl is in love with Peter Yu, or she's the best damn liar I've ever met.

"I think he's fine," Nick said, again resisting the urge to emotionally invest in her. He had to assume she was working him—just as he was working her. "I'm sure he got called away on business and hasn't been able to reach you because he's been traveling."

"Perhaps," she said and pulled her hand away. "But since he knew you were coming to visit, you'd think he'd have at least tried to call you."

A very good point.

"Maybe he tried and couldn't get me? I'm not sure, Lihau. I'll tell you what—I know you're worried—how about I get in touch with Peter's boss? If Peter's traveling on business, then I'm sure his boss would probably know something."

"You know Peter's boss?" she said, confused.

"Yeah, of course," Nick said with a laugh. "How do you think Peter got this job in the first place?"

She nodded and chuckled politely. "Okay."

"Okay, what?"

"Can you call him now? Peter's boss . . ."

"Uh, sure."

Shit. Now what?

Nick thumbed the volume control down on his phone as he dialed Lankford's number. After a few rings, the CIA man picked up.

"So what the hell is going on in Xi'an, Nick?" Lankford demanded. "And why are you calling me on your personal phone? Did you find him?"

Nick looked at Lihau and smiled.

"I got his voicemail," he said, loudly so that Lankford would hear, get the idea, and shut up. "I'll leave a message." He waited a moment, pretending to wait for the beep, and then spoke into the phone again: "Hi, Mr. Lankford, it's Nick, Peter Yu's friend. I'm in Xi'an, and Peter is not in his apartment and won't answer his phone. I'm here with his girlfriend, Lihau, and she is worried about him because she can't reach him either. Can you call me back when you get this and let me know if, perhaps, he is traveling on business? We're both worried. I'll wait for your call. Again, it's Nick Foley, Peter's friend. Thanks. Bye."

Nick clicked his phone off.

"I'm sure he'll call me when he gets the message."

"I hope so," Lihau said.

A wave of paranoia suddenly washed over him. He'd fucked up and used Lankford's name. Lihau hadn't flinched, but that didn't matter. He'd voluntarily linked both himself and Yu to Lankford. But Lankford's cover was blown, so now he was blown. If Lihau was a spy, he had just become a loose end she would need to tidy up.

He did not want to be a loose end.

He pulled out enough renminbi to cover the tab and tossed the loose bills onto the table.

"I'm sorry, I have to go," he said, standing. "If you give me your mobile number, I'll call or text you the moment I hear anything from Peter."

She looked taken aback at his abrupt exit, but she quickly collected herself. "Thank you," she said, and then she jotted a phone number down on a scrap of napkin and slid it over to him.

"No problem." He slipped the number into his left pants pocket. "Nice to have met you, Lihau."

"You too, Nick."

He turned and walked out of the café, very much feeling her eyes on his back as he headed out the door. He crossed the street and turned right, striding hard and straight toward the lot where he'd parked his rental car a couple of blocks away.

"I'm an idiot," he muttered under his breath. "Dropping Lankford's name like some goddamn rookie."

The interaction with Lihau had been necessary, and he'd handled himself like a pro until the very end. His gut told him that Lihau really was Yu's girlfriend, but he didn't dare take any chances. The longer he stayed in town, the more risk he assumed. Realistically, he'd probably discovered everything worth discovering in Xi'an pertaining to Peter Yu's disappearance. He quickly cataloged his findings: one, Peter Yu wasn't dead in his apartment;

two, he supposedly had a Chinese national girlfriend named Lihau who worked for a biotech company called Nèiyè Biologic—the same company that Yu's files indicated the agent had an interest in, not coincidentally, he was sure; and three, his computer was missing. He'd have Lankford look into Nèiyè Biologic and Lihau. Yu wasn't deep undercover in some NOC—nonofficial cover—so in his "routine monitoring and surveillance" role, as Lankford had put it, dating a cute girl like Lihau was probably okay. Hell, it probably helped solidify Yu's cover with . . .

Something felt wrong.

Nick glanced to his left.

He spied a sleek, black Mercedes two-door coupe with dark windows parked first in a row of cars directly across the street from the lot where his Geely was waiting. Something about this particular car set his "spidey sense" tingling. Was he being paranoid? Hell, there were Mercedes everywhere in the financial district of Beijing, and from what he could tell, Xi'an was no different. German luxury imports were a prominent status symbol among China's nouveau riche. Nick squinted, trying to see if the car was occupied, but he couldn't make out anything inside the dark cabin.

From his current position, he'd have to turn his back on the Mercedes to cross the vacant lot to his car. *Get a grip, dude, that's just some hotshot banker's ride parked in the pole position.*

He slowed and retrieved the key fob from his pocket, using the opportunity to glance behind him while pretending to look at the fob, and then began walking toward his car. As he closed the distance, he repeatedly pressed the unlock button on the fob. Ten meters away, his rental car chirped, and he thought he heard the doors unlock. The urge to look back over his shoulder was all consuming, but he resisted, listening instead for the sound of tires on pavement and a Mercedes engine growling.

Five meters.

Three meters.

Two.

One . . .

A scream of tires and a throaty roar sent an electric surge of adrenaline through him. He whirled around to find the black Mercedes hurtling toward him on a collision course that would cut him in half. Somehow, the car had closed half the distance almost silently before the driver had punched the gas.

Reflex took over.

He crouched and, at the very last second, leapt vertically into the air like a cat. In his mind's eye, he would land in a squat on the hood of the Mercedes after it crashed to a stop against his Geely. But physics ripped this plan to shit. There was a horrifying scream of metal obliterating metal as the hood of the Mercedes passed beneath him. On impact, both vehicles traveled farther than he expected, and so instead of landing as he had envisioned, the Mercedes's windshield clipped his lower legs, cartwheeling him in the air. He came down hard, his left hip and rib cage hitting the roof. The impact knocked the breath from his lungs, and he tumbled off the roof, onto the pavement beside the passenger door.

He gasped for oxygen like a fish out of water—puffing and suffocating despite being surrounded by an infinite supply of air. As a SEAL, he'd had the wind knocked out of him enough times that he knew not to panic. His breath would return, but his opportunity to take control of the situation would not. Hyperventilating, he kept low and crabbed across the pavement until he was squatting behind the rear bumper of his Geely. He heard angry shouting in Chinese from inside the other car.

A second later, there was a sharp click to his right.

Catching his first real breath, Nick peeked his head around the bumper and watched the right passenger door open. An expensive Italian dress shoe appeared below the sill, followed by a gray-suited pant leg.

With all the fury he could muster, he exploded like a defensive lineman on the snap of the football—driving his shoulder into the door with all the power his heavily muscled, two-hundred-pound frame could offer.

A faceless howl echoed behind the tinted glass window as the door-to-frame compression crushed the finely appointed tibia of his assailant with a horrifying crunch. Nick stepped back from the door and juked left. When he saw a hand reach for the torn pant leg, where blood was gushing from a compound fracture, he grabbed the wrist and heaved backward, using his weight to yank the man out of the car.

He heard another crack as the man's skull smacked the B-pillar, and then the killer tumbled facedown onto the pavement at his feet. Still controlling the wrist, Nick took a knee and fluidly rotated the arm until he felt it snap. The Chinese man howled again in agony and dropped something he had been clutching in his other hand. Nick's gaze followed the clatter to the iconic, blocky muzzle of a Glock 43 nine-millimeter pistol lying on the pavement just in front of the left rear tire. Nick released the fallen hit man's wrist and snatched the pistol. Crouching, he peeked inside the Mercedes through the still-open passenger door. The driver's seat was empty, and the door was open. He caught a fleeting glimpse of gray suit tails moving left. Instead of charging to beat the driver to a face-to-face shootout at the rear of the Mercedes, Nick crouched low and bolted over the first thug. He moved toward the front of the car, which was buried a good twelve inches into his rental, and took cover behind the open passenger door. He raised the Glock, sighting between the open passenger door and the C-pillar.

The driver rounded the rear of the Mercedes, crouched and leading with a pistol . . . just not crouched enough. The instant the driver's head came into view, Nick squeezed the trigger. Twice. The first round pulled sparks in its wake as it skimmed the C-pillar and then laid open a deep gash in the man's left cheek before evaporating his left ear in a pink puff. The second bullet hit the assailant in the forehead and then exploded the back of his head in a red geyser. The driver slumped out of view.

Still sighting over his pistol, Nick scanned the interior of the car through the passenger door one final time, bobbing up and down in case another thug lurked in the back seat. Finding the car empty, he scanned quickly in both directions for a second hit squad closing on his position. To his left, nothing. To his right, he saw cars backing up at the corner. He watched someone step out of a car, point, and then raise a mobile phone to his cheek.

Damn you, Lankford.

Nick took a knee beside the groaning hitman at his feet and tore back the man's suit jacket. He pulled an extra magazine from the thug's belt and then a long black leather wallet from the inside pocket of his coat. He slipped the extra mag into his left front pant pocket and the stolen wallet into his shirt's breast pocket. Then he turned to assess his rental car. The driver's side was completely caved in by the nose of the Mercedes.

This piece of shit ain't going anywhere.

Using the butt of the Glock, he knocked out the remaining shattered glass of the driver's side window, reached in, and grabbed his backpack from the front passenger seat. After slinging the bag over his shoulder, he tucked the Glock into his waistband at the small of his back, hiding it under his untucked shirt. He dodged right around the two mangled cars, moving quickly and with purpose, while fighting the mounting sensation that he needed to run. He cleared the parking lot and headed toward a cluster of buildings across the street. He ducked down a one-way street and then circled back around behind the complex, moving north and crossing a block and a half behind the stalled line of traffic at the intersection adjacent to the parking lot where the gun battle had just gone down. He could hear a cacophony of horns blaring as traffic piled up behind the gawkers. Head down and eyes up, Nick kept moving, putting as much distance as possible between him and the chaos behind. His ankle ached, and his left hip throbbed, but he forced himself not to limp.

Another block down.

Cold sweat streamed from his armpits.

The sirens will start any minute now . . .

He spied Xi'an Park ahead and hoped it would be crowded with tourists. As he walked, he unzipped his backpack and pulled out the spare collared sport shirt he always carried. Rare was the day he made it to five o'clock without having to change shirts. Today, he was thankful to be a sweaty bastard. He slipped the new black shirt over the teal one he was wearing. Then he calmly exchanged his personal mobile phone for the encrypted phone buried at the bottom of his backpack. He pushed and held the number one and then waited for the call to connect. After three rings, the line clicked, and his call went to voicemail.

"Leave a message," a woman's voice said.

"You need to come get me," he panted. "Call me back immediately. I need EXFIL right fucking now. The shit hit the fan. Get me an extract point. Now." The last word was louder than he'd meant it to be. He ended the call but kept the phone in his hand as he weaved deeper into the park. A moment later, the phone vibrated.

"Status?" said Lankford's cool but strained voice.

"Intact and on the move. Someone put a contract on me. I evaded the first attempt, but I am not sticking around so they can try again. I killed a man, Lankford."

"When?"

"Five minutes ago."

"Chinese national?"

"Yes."

"Jesus, Foley. You were supposed to poke around, ask some questions, not go fucking Rambo in Xi'an."

"Tell that to the motherfuckers who just tried to run me over with a Mercedes. I need a rendezvous address and EXFIL ASAP."

"All right, I'm texting you the address to a safe house in Xi'an. It is about a mile and a half from your target location. Are you near there?"

"Yes."

"Okay, I'll text you the four-digit code for the lock. Once you're inside, text me, and I'll give you follow-up instructions."

"What about the EXFIL?" Nick huffed.

"I'll have you out of Xi'an by morning."

"And then what?"

There was a long, uncomfortable pause, and then Lankford sighed.

"I'm sorry you got pulled in, pal, but I see no choice here. You gotta go black until we get this sorted out."

Nick's mind raged between the urgency of his situation and how pissed off he was that today was the end of his life and career in China. He thought about Dash, who had become an important part of the new life he was trying to build. *Damn you, Lankford.* Zhang had made it crystal clear after the chaos in Beijing a few months ago—any *activity* outside his NGO job and his ass would be on the first plane out of China. But he'd just killed a man, and that crime warranted punishment far more severe than eviction. Thanks to Lankford, he was probably going to spend the rest of his life rotting in a Chinese prison.

He forced the nightmare from his head and focused on his current objective—survival.

"How the hell can I go black in Beijing? People know me. Where will I hide?"

"Not Beijing," Lankford said. "You're going Hong Kong black."

The line went dead.

Nick walked deeper into the park. The encrypted phone vibrated with the arrival of a new text message.

He read the message, deleted it, and slipped the phone into his pocket. Forcing himself to walk even slower, more casually, he corrected his heading to the east. As he walked, he passed an elderly couple strolling hand in hand. He smiled and nodded; the old woman smiled back, showing off a mouth in desperate need of reconstructive dentistry. Nick glanced at his watch. He would be secure in the safe house in half an hour or so.

Provided that no one else tried to kill him.

And that the Chinese authorities didn't arrest him.

Thank you very much, Chet fucking Lankford.

If only Dash had come to dinner . . .

CHAPTER 7

Gun Club Hill Barracks and Military Hospital
Kowloon, Hong Kong
0900 hours local—Day 3

*T*hirty-eight.

Thirty-eight was the final tally of mutilated corpses that had washed up on Tung Wan Beach and had been transferred to the Gun Club Hill Barracks Military Hospital for examination. Yesterday, Dash had presided over the autopsies of the first eighteen victims in the hospital's immaculate autopsy suite, and today she would have to do it again. She was neither a coroner nor a forensic pathologist, but lately she was beginning to feel like one. Nightmarish memories of the investigative autopsy she'd conducted on her best friend—former CIA agent Jamie Lin—tormented her still. She hated autopsies, and now she could add this fresh batch of grotesqueries to haunt her dreams.

When she had entered medical school, she had done so despite a deep-seated aversion to blood and gore. From the beginning, her interest in medicine had been academic, not clinical. She'd had no interest in being a practitioner. Her dream was to immerse herself in the universe of the microscopic—a place where cells rallied to defeat pathogenic invaders in an ever-waging war invisible to the human eye. But to become a specialist in infectious disease, she first had had to complete all the requisite training of her profession, and that had meant gaining proficiency in evaluation, diagnosis, dissection, surgery, and patient care. It was not until she had completed her residency that she finally was able to spend her time doing what interested her—looking through a microscope. That was why she had joined the CDC, to conduct epidemiological research on emerging infectious disease, but within eighteen months of being hired, she found herself pulled out of the lab yet again, this time treating Ebola patients in Liberia.

"Where did you go to medical school?" Major Li asked from across the autopsy table, breaking her train of thought.

"Fudan University," she said.

Li grunted an acknowledgment. She couldn't tell if it was grudging respect or disdain for her alma mater.

"What specialty did you pursue in residency?"

"Internal Medicine," she said, probing a kidney. "This kidney shows early signs of necrosis. The other is missing." She glanced at the young Army nurse, who was acting as her scribe. "Make a note of this."

The young woman nodded and dutifully typed an entry into the log.

"And after that, you studied in America?" Li continued.

"Yes. I was accepted to Johns Hopkins, where I completed a fellowship in Infectious Disease and also earned my masters in epidemiology and biostatistics."

Qualified enough for you now, Major?

Li said nothing.

She glanced up at him.

She couldn't see the smug smile on his face because of the antimicrobial surgical mask he wore, but she knew it was there—baiting her to defend her qualifications to be on the Quick Reaction Task Force. The irony was that Li knew her credentials inside and out. He knew everything about her, and he had used every possible weakness he could exploit as grounds for her removal from the Task Force. After the events in Beijing two months ago, his vendetta against her didn't surprise her. In the final hours of the crisis, she'd asked for his help in exchange for a promise and had then deceived him. But what other option had fate offered her? If given the choice between helping Li advance his career and impeding development of the world's most lethal and covert biological weapon, she'd pick the latter every time. Li, however, didn't see it that way. He was bent on quid pro quo, and he would not stop until he succeeded in derailing her career and sullying her reputation. Thank God for Commander Zhang and for her boss, CDC Director Wong. Together, they'd thwarted Li's efforts in Beijing—an embarrassing loss for the Major that only stoked the fire of contempt burning inside the man.

And so here she was, stuck in an autopsy room, dissecting mutilated corpses with the man who hated her most in the world . . . while the man who adored her most was back in Beijing, wondering why she'd stood him up on a romantic dinner date. She sighed. A part of her wished that she had been fired from the Task Force, because that would have meant more time in the lab conducting research, more time with her beloved microscopes, which never engaged in petty politics, and more time with Nick.

"Why the sudden interest in my education?" she said at last, breaking the silence.

"Just curious," he said. "Your proficiency at autopsy surprises me, given your specialty."

"Thank you," she said, shifting her focus from Li to the cadaver's pancreas.

"It was not meant to be a compliment," he said. "Just an observation."

"Instead of making observations about my CV, Major, maybe you should focus your attention on the mutilated woman on the exam table and make observations that might be helpful to this investigation."

Before Li could respond, the steel door to the autopsy suite swung open, and Commander Zhang strode into the room.

"Mask, Commander," Li barked, glaring at Zhang.

With a wry smile, Zhang pulled a crumpled surgical mask from his pants pocket. He slipped it over his nose and mouth without breaking stride. "It smells terrible in here," he said.

"What did you expect?" Li came back. "Roses?"

"I don't know how you can stand it," Zhang said, eyeing them both.

Zhang was right; the room reeked. Although she'd acclimated to the smell, she knew the stench of the decay in the room was nauseating. The amount of decomposition had been exacerbated by the time the bodies had spent in the sea.

"What have you got, Dr. Chen?" Zhang asked, taking a place by her side at the table.

Dash felt an upsurge in both confidence and energy with Zhang's arrival. She'd been stuck most of yesterday with Li, and his ceaseless scrutiny and unmitigated derisiveness leeched her qi.

"First, the good news," she said. "None of these people appear to have been infected with a biological agent, nor do I find any evidence of the nanobot bioweapon we encountered in Kizilsu. We're still waiting on final confirmation from tissue samples sent to the lab yesterday, but in my professional opinion, these deaths were not caused by a bioterrorism event. Pending receipt of the laboratory results, I recommend lifting the quarantine at Tung Wan Beach."

Zhang exhaled his relief audibly. "That's very good news."

"And grounds for us to stand down the task force," Major Li interjected.

"Let's not rush handing this off to the Hong Kong Police just yet. Especially while we're still waiting on laboratory confirmation," Zhang said, shutting Li down. He turned back to Dash. "Please, go on, Dr. Chen."

"All the victims are mutilated, but I propose we divide them into two categories: Category A are individuals who are missing organs, and Category B are individuals who have been tattooed and mutilated. It is difficult to ascertain times of death because the bodies have been in the ocean, but I can say with ninety percent confidence that all these people died within the past two weeks."

"How long were the bodies in the water?" Zhang asked.

"Based on the amount of degradation, I'd guess less than forty-eight hours," she said.

Zhang nodded. "That matches well with my theory."

"What theory is that?" asked Li.

"That these bodies were either dumped or lost at sea during the recent storms. Two days ago, the harbor control suspended ferry transit due to high sea state and typhoon-strength winds, but merchant traffic continued. Yesterday, I tasked the Coast Guard with conducting a sonar sweep of the waters around Cheung Chau Island."

"A sonar sweep? Looking for what?" said Li, dubious.

"Floating bodies, an unreported shipwreck, or anything else unusual. It's not uncommon for merchant vessels to lose unsecured cargo overboard in violent weather."

"Have they found anything so far?" Dash asked.

"Not yet," Zhang said and leaned over to stare into the open, empty chest cavity of the corpse on the table. "Completely gutted, huh?"

Dash nodded. "Heart, lungs, pancreas, liver, and one kidney missing."

"What about the other kidney?"

"Not removed. It shows early signs of necrosis."

"Is that significant?"

She nodded. "It helps confirm my working theory."

"Which is?"

"Organ harvesting. The organs excised correspond to the organs most in demand for transplant: heart, lungs, liver, kidneys, pancreas, and corneas. As you might expect, the cadavers with missing organs—the bodies I'm putting in Category A—all appear to have been relatively young and healthy. In the case of this woman on the table, they left the degraded kidney because it was unsuitable for transplant."

"I assume these organs are sold on the black market after they're harvested," Zhang said.

"I've heard rumors of this sort of thing before, but I never imagined an operation was being conducted at this scale."

"How quickly after an organ is removed does it need to be transplanted?"

"Ideally, as soon as possible. Tissue degradation from ischemia commences once blood flow is stopped, but under optimal conditions, hearts and lungs can remain viable three to four hours, kidneys and livers, six to eight."

"That's what I thought."

"Also, you should know that we found traces of anesthesia in blood samples taken from the aorta."

Zhang screwed up his face. "Meaning?"

"Meaning that these people were not willing organ donors. We're not talking about living-will scenarios here. Somebody put these people to sleep and took everything. They never woke back up."

"That's psychotic," Zhang said.

"What's more," she said, her eyes downcast, "the internal surgical precision I'm seeing is exemplary. The quick and dirty post-op stitch-up is misleading. This is not some back-alley hack job. These people were anesthetized and operated on in a surgery suite by a team of skilled surgeons. To think of something like this being performed in a Chinese hospital makes me ill. We're talking about murder, Zhang—the premediated, cold-blooded murder of people to steal their organs."

"And what about the other cadavers—the Category B bodies with tattooed faces that had their noses, hands, and genitals hacked off. Any working theory on those people?"

"Maybe," she said, crinkling her nose at a fleeting memory of some disturbing text she'd read in a history book once. "But I need to spend some time researching on the computer before I'm ready to discuss it."

"Okay, fair enough," Zhang said. "Have we made any progress identifying any of the victims so far?"

"We've fingerprinted all the corpses with hands and submitted the paperwork to your man, Sergeant Tan, to run a search in the database," she said. "For the victims missing hands, eyes, and teeth, we'll need to rely on DNA samples. Major Li and I are collecting tissue samples as we go."

"Don't get your hopes up," Zhang sighed heavily under his mask. "The national DNA registry is extremely limited and has records for only a small percentage of the civilian population. If the victim isn't a soldier or a criminal, odds are we won't find anything."

"I know," she said. "I figured as much."

"Anything else?" Zhang asked.

She glanced at Li, who nodded, apparently reading her mind. "We did have one outlier among the dead—a male, early twenties, who was tattooed, mutilated, *and* missing his internal organs. This body was the only one we collected that seemingly fit into both categories."

"Hmm, interesting," Zhang said. "I assume he was missing his hands?"

She nodded. "Along with his eyes, teeth, nose, genitals, and feet."

"And the tattoo?"

"Same as most of the others—TRAITOR—inked across the forehead."

"Did you get a tissue sample?"

"Yes, and I was hoping you could—"

"Expedite?" Zhang said, cutting her off.

"Exactly."

"I'll see what I can do."

Zhang's phone buzzed in his pocket. He retrieved it and took the call. "Zhang . . . yes . . . yes . . . where? Excellent work. Ready the helo pad and instruct the dive master to make preparations to dive." He ended the call and slipped his mobile phone back into his pocket. "It appears our friends in the Coast Guard have found something submerged and drifting ten nautical miles off the coast of Cheung Chau Island."

"You're flying out to meet them?" Dash asked.

"Of course," he said, turning to leave, his voice brimming with excitement. "I'll call you as soon as I'm out of the water."

"Commando, helicopter pilot, *and* scuba diver?" Dash called after him.

Zhang looked back at her over his shoulder. "Oh yes, Dr. Chen . . . all that and so very much more."

She rolled her eyes but couldn't help but grin at his bravado.

He winked at her and then headed for the exit.

"Wait," Major Li shouted abruptly. "I'm coming with you."

Dash watched Zhang's shoulders stiffen, but he did not break stride as Li trotted to catch up. As the autopsy suite door was swinging shut behind them, she heard the Snow Leopard Commander's parting words: "The Coast Guard is reporting sea state six today. I really hope you don't get seasick, Major."

CHAPTER 8

D3
CCG-1115 **Hai Twen,** *South China Sea*
6.5 nautical miles southeast of Cheung Chau Island
1140 hours local

Zhang watched Major Li clinging to the aft deck rail with white knuckles—vomit dribbling down the man's chin and spackled across the front of his uniform. While the eighty-eight-meter-long patrol boat CCG-1115 was able to plow through the two-meter swells with ease, the incessant pitching and rolling was doing a number on the Army officer. For a man unaccustomed to the sea, the rhythmic rise and fall of the fantail would be more nauseating than any roller coaster at Hong Kong Disneyland. Zhang touched the tan-colored scopolamine antinausea patch affixed behind his left ear and grinned at his compeer.

He felt no sympathy for Li.

A soldier should always be prepared.

He'd warned Li of the rough conditions, but the Major had insisted on tagging along, rattling off something about protocol and compartmentalization. Zhang knew Li's real motivation—control. Li wanted control of the information; he wanted control of the operation. The question nagging Zhang was why. Was it about satiating Li's ego, or was something else going on? Li had already demonstrated a propensity for jumping the chain of command.

When the Major had secretly lobbied to have Dr. Chen kicked off the task force, it had opened Zhang's eyes to how the man operated. Now he couldn't help but wonder if Li was back to his old tricks, routing information outside the task force. Did the Major have a secret agenda? Was he reporting to a secondary chain of command?

"How can you dive in these conditions?" Li groaned, wiping a fresh spattering of vomit from his left cheek, where the wind had spread the mess all the way up to his ear.

"Carefully," Zhang admitted. "It'll be dangerous near the surface, but once we're at depth, things should settle down."

Li opened his mouth to say something but then changed his mind and leaned over the rail to dry-heave, his stomach apparently empty at last. Zhang watched the Major retch in agony until he couldn't stand it anymore and turned to monitor the Coast Guard team as they set up the dive command station on the helo deck. Thankfully, the sea state had calmed from a strong six to a manageable five over the past hour. Rough seas were bad for scuba diving and nasty for landing helicopters. He was certainly competent at both activities, but a rescue diver and naval aviator he was not. Landing his Z-11 on the patrol boat had been precarious, and he had forced Li to suffer through two aborted attempts before finally sticking the landing. Hard to say which, the harrowing landing or the seasickness, would ultimately leave the Army officer with the worst memory. After landing, Zhang's helicopter was moved into the hangar deck beside the ship's own Harbin Z-9 helicopter.

Zhang turned his attention forward, looking up and along the superstructure of the impressive ship. Formerly the *Haijian* 15, a surveillance vessel of the first Marine Surveillance Flotilla, the *Hai Twen* CCG-1115 was one of the Chinese Coast Guard's most capable ships. With the formation of a unified Chinese Coast Guard in 2013, dozens and dozens of naval assets had been reassigned, and the CCG-1115 was one of them. Although he had not had frequent occasion to work with the Coast Guard, their professionalism and competency so far today had impressed him. The

CCG-1115 was presently on loan from the North China Sea Fleet for training exercises with the South China Sea Fleet, which was stationed 120 kilometers northwest of Hong Kong, up the Pearl River in the port city of Guangzhou. He was fortunate the asset was available to help with the search.

From the corner of his eye, Zhang saw Lieutenant Chung approaching. Chung's 3mm wet suit hung open at the chest, and he wore sunglasses, the combination making Zhang chuckle. The young Snow Leopard looked at Major Li dry-heaving over the rail and flashed Zhang a conspiratorial grin.

"How's the station keeping going?" Zhang asked before Chung had time to get a wisecrack in.

"The bridge team is doing an exemplary job tracking the object and matching its set and drift," Chung said. "It's moving south-southeast at two and half knots with the current. The dive should be manageable without DPVs."

Zhang nodded. "Good, I hate those damn things. The name of the game on this dive is going to be buoyancy control, and those vehicles make static hovers a living hell."

"Fin down, take a look, and fin back up. Easy day, Commander."

"Don't be overly confident, Lieutenant," Zhang warned. "The ocean is unforgiving. Just because the current is stable now doesn't mean it will stay that way. This is going to be an untethered dive, due to the rough surface conditions. After a big storm, there's no telling what we'll encounter."

"Yes, sir," Chung said, tempering his bravado.

"What's the depth of the object?"

"Twenty-six meters," the young counterterrorism officer said. "I recommend we base our decompression table on a maximum depth of just under thirty-five meters; that gives us fifteen minutes for a no-decompression limit. It's conservative, but I suggest that we follow this protocol, as decompression stops with these surface conditions would be a challenge."

"Agreed," Zhang said. "If we stay under thirty meters, we can squeeze out a few more minutes."

"Twenty minutes if we stay above the thirty-meter mark. More than enough time to dive, examine the object, and return to the surface. If the object looks retrievable, we can call for topside to drop a winch cable and try to retrieve it."

"Agreed," Zhang said. "But diving on a nonstationary object is dangerous, Mr. Chung. You are not to enter the object without my express permission. Disturb the air bubble keeping the object at neutral buoyancy, and it could plummet very deep, very fast, taking anyone stupid enough to be inside down with it."

"Understood, sir. The investigation of the object will be performed and controlled by us and us alone. The ship's rescue divers will serve as safety divers for the duration of the dive in case we run into any problems."

Zhang ran through his mental checklist, ticking items off on his fingers as he did until he came to something they had not discussed. "What's our comms plan?"

"The comms package is run from the surface using the built-in EM-OTS2 comms in our dive masks, but I secured OTS D2 transmitters as well, so you and I can communicate over a secure channel."

"Excellent. Thank you, Mr. Chung. Feet wet in ten."

The young officer saluted, an unnecessary courtesy in these conditions, but no doubt a show for the PLA Major anguishing on the rail. Then Chung turned and headed back to the makeshift dive command post.

Zhang approached Li, who was still clutching the deck rail, his forehead pressed against the back of his hands. Zhang put a hand on the Major's shoulder. "Go belowdecks, Major," he said. "Find yourself a nice piece of a real estate somewhere amidships and get horizontal. The fantail is the worst possible place to loiter."

Li looked at first as if he might object, but instead he gave Zhang a weary, defeated nod. "Will you brief me on what you find when you get back?" Li said, his voice hoarse, ragged, and almost pleading—a nice change from his usual arrogant affect.

"Of course," Zhang said.

"What do you think you'll find down there?"

A great question and one he had no answer for.

"Hopefully, a clue to whatever the hell is going on," Zhang said. "Now go get some rest. I'll see you in an hour."

Li nodded, suppressed a belch, and then headed forward, his hand dragging across the rail as he swayed and stumbled his way belowdecks. Zhang shook his head at the Army man and then made his way to the dive station to gear up.

Fifteen minutes later, Zhang, Chung, and the two Coast Guard rescue divers were standing shoulder to shoulder on the ship's stainless-steel dive platform. The platform resembled a window-washer's station, except instead of being raised and lowered manually along the side of a building, this platform was designed to be hoisted into and out of the sea by the CCG-1115's stern service crane. They waited until the grate decking of the platform was positioned just above the tops of the highest swells. On Zhang's mark, the four divers took a giant stride off, stepping in unison into a receding wave. The ship's engines were at idle as a safety precaution to prevent the divers from being shredded by the twin propellers should the unpredictable currents and waves drive them forward.

Zhang kicked hard, leading the team deep as fast as possible to get away from the rough surface chop. He equalized pressure in his ears continuously during the rapid descent. At six meters, the wave action began to wane. By fifteen meters, it disappeared almost completely.

"We have you on sonar. Stay tight, so we keep a nice return," came the voice of the surface dive coordinator in Zhang's headphones.

The dive mask Zhang wore covered his entire face but bore no resemblance to the steel diving helmets of old. Inside the mask, a fighter-pilot-style respirator cone covered his mouth and nose, which permitted easy voice comms and minimized fogging, but it still relied on a rubber to skin contact seal for watertightness. His earphones were held in place by a neoprene band fitted inside his wet suit hood. As he scanned the area, an annoying smear appeared on his facemask, making it hard to see at the ten o'clock position. He wiped his gloved hand across the Plexiglas until it cleared up, then he glanced at his depth gage.

Twenty meters.

It was getting dark. The anemic daylight from the rainy, overcast sky above was now almost completely filtered out at depth. Zhang clicked on the lights attached to either side of his mask by each temple. The LED illumination was unsatisfactory, lighting less than a one-meter sphere around his head. Particulates and slimy floaters filled his field of vision.

Is that oil? Maybe we're dealing with a sunken vessel after all, he thought.

Zhang's earphones crackled, and he strained to hear a garbled report from the dive coordinator over the roar of the howling winds topside.

"Say again, louder," Zhang replied.

"Descent on target. Sonar holds you directly over the object— five meters and closing," the dive coordinator repeated, this time shouting to be heard over the background noise.

"Roger," Zhang said into his microphone.

"How is your visibility? Do you see the object?" the coordinator yelled.

"Visibility poor," he replied. "No visual contact yet."

"All I see is this slime," one of the safety divers said. "What the hell is this stuff anyway?" The young man's voice sounded tense and unsure.

"Looks like oil," Chung answered.

"It's not oil," came the second Coast Guard diver's voice, more relaxed than his partner. "It feels oily, but it is light in color, and the droplets are loose and small—not the consistency of machine oil."

When Dr. Chen had performed autopsies on the bodies in Kizilsu during the bioterrorism attack a few months ago, Zhang had witnessed a foul-smelling, light-colored grease pooling in metal dissection pans. Could this be the same thing? He shuddered and forced the terrible thought away.

"Dark shadow bearing two-seven-zero and just below us," came Chung's voice over the comms channel.

Zhang looked in the direction the junior officer was pointing but saw nothing except flickers of light reflecting back from whatever was dispersed in the water. He realized he had a greasy feeling on the back of his hands as well. Then he saw something—an orange-yellow blob in the distance.

"I see it too," Zhang said.

He glanced at the depth gauge on his wrist: twenty-five meters. He glanced at the dive counter: eleven minutes burned. That left them only fourteen minutes to investigate whatever it was.

"Where did it go?" one of the safety divers asked.

"Sonar now holds the object at a depth of twenty-seven meters. I repeat, twenty-seven meters," the dive coordinator reported.

Zhang squinted, but he too had lost sight of the object.

Shit, it's sinking.

"I see it," Chung said. "Follow me."

Zhang saw his lieutenant kick deeper and followed him, the orange blob now taking on a geometric shape through his oil-coated faceplate. The object looked triangular. It appeared to be made of metal, and the bulk of it disappeared into the darkness after only a half meter.

"What the hell is that?" Chung asked.

At first, Zhang didn't answer, but as he finned around to the left for a different perspective, the mystery revealed itself as the triangle morphed into an elongated container.

"It's a Conex box," he said. "This is the top corner of a shipping container."

This could be it, he told himself.

If this container had broken loose from the deck of a cargo ship leaving Hong Kong in the storm, it could have drifted here in the current. Of course, cargo vessels lost containers overboard all the time, many incidents going unreported. This Conex box could have been at sea for months, or years, and could have come from almost anywhere on the planet. He glanced at his watch again—ten minutes to sort it out.

"Spread out a bit," he said.

The four divers spread out over the large box, and now their combined lights showed much more clearly the rectangular shape of an orange cargo container, floating at about a forty-five-degree angle and listing another fifteen degrees to the left. A small trail of bubbles dribbled out from the topmost corner and danced upward until they disappeared. Zhang finned along the top of the box, moving deeper and checking his depth gauge as he did. There were no corporate markings on the top of the box nor on the right side that he could see with the light from his mask.

"Safety divers, maintain depth here. Watch our backs as we examine the container more closely."

"Roger," one of the divers responded.

Chung finned along behind him as he explored the length of the container. So far, he had not seen any holes or penetrations in the walls of the container. When they reached the deep end, he looked at Chung. Chung nodded, and they pulled themselves down and around the edge to inspect the loading end of the container. As expected, the cargo box had hinged double doors. The doors were shut but not locked, which was fortunate, since they did not have any cutting equipment. A ten-digit serial number was painted on the upper corner of the left-hand door. Zhang nudged Chung and pointed at it.

"Commit that number to memory," he said.

"Yes, sir."

Zhang grouped the numbers—31 29 937 224—and created a singsong mental pneumonic and rehearsed it three times in his head. Then, he checked the time: five minutes left on the no-decompression timetable. He looked at the door handles and then at Chung, who raised his eyebrows behind his Plexiglas dive mask.

"You said we weren't going to open the doors," Chung said.

"No, I said nobody goes inside," Zhang said. "We're here. It's unlocked. I think we're obligated to take a peek inside."

"Shouldn't we just get a cable on it? What about the air bubble?" Chung said.

Zhang nodded. "By the time we rig for a cable we will be out of time on our no decompression limits. If we wait to make a second dive, we might lose it. We need to have a look while we can. We'll open the lower door. All the air will be trapped in the top half."

"Copy that."

Chung swam beside him, and together they grabbed a metal handle that operated as a lever. When rotated, the handle lever shifted a linkage connected to upper and lower locking bolts, which, in theory, would allow the lower door to drift open.

"Easy," Zhang said as they pulled down on the handle. An air bubble the size of a soccer ball burped out as the locking bars began to shift.

Zhang froze. "Careful. Be ready to clear quickly in case the container loses buoyancy."

"Check," Chung grunted.

Zhang reapplied pressure to the handle. It moved ten degrees and then stopped. They both pushed, but it wouldn't budge.

"It's stuck," Chung said.

Zhang looked up and then down, his headlights illuminating the top and bottom junctions of the two-point locking mechanism. "The upper locking bolt is out, but the bottom one is still engaged. Just a little more."

Chung nodded. Zhang pushed hard and heard Chung grunt over the comms circuit. The handle barely moved. They tried again, finning and pushing harder. With a metallic *tang*, the handle suddenly shifted as the bottom locking-bar popped free. Aided by gravity, the massive steel door swung open much quicker and with more force than Zhang expected. The edge of the door clipped the top of his mask, knocking it crooked on his face. Greasy salt water instantly flooded his mask. With both hands, he straightened and repositioned it. With the seal reestablished, he looked toward the surface and pushed hard on his regulator purge valve to clear the water from the mask cavity. As air evacuated the water, the stench hit his nostrils, triggering a reflexive gag. Acutely aware that vomiting in his mask at thirty meters below the surface would be a serious problem, he fought back the urge.

A panicked, static-filled scream echoed over the comms circuit.

Zhang blinked, trying to clear his blurry vision, but then realized it wasn't his eyes that were the problem. A thick, greasy film now coated the inside of his mask, robbing him of clarity. He couldn't tell what the hell he was looking at. He was seeing double, now triple . . .

"Chung?"

But as a fourth body came into view, he understood.

A dozen corpses had now drifted out of the Conex box, and Lieutenant Chung was thrashing about in the middle of a throng of bloated bodies—eyeless sockets wide, mouths gaped open in silent screams. As Zhang strained to identify which body was Chung, he noticed that something else was wrong. The momentum of the swinging door falling open had caused the container to rotate on its axis. Zhang watched in horror as an enormous bubble of air and buoyant oil burped out from the top corner of the now open doorway.

"Swim clear," he shouted at Chung, but it was too late. The cargo container began to sink, falling toward them at a steeper angle as it began a death slide to the bottom of the South China Sea. Zhang saw Chung's legs disappear into the container. A heartbeat later, an edge smashed painfully into Zhang's shoulder as he too was engulfed in the coffin's maw. Zhang knew that the container was falling toward him, but the sensation that the box of corpses was breathing him in overpowered all logic. He heard the desperate, futile cries of the safety divers over his headset, but he couldn't speak. A swarm of rotting corpses converged on him, their loose, wrinkled skin reflecting a ghostly gray in his headlights. Flaccid arms and legs were everywhere, ensnaring his own. An eyeless face pressed against his mask. He pushed it away, his fingers tearing off a hunk of hair and rotten scalp. He kicked hard, trying to propel himself backward, away from his undead assailants, but he was surrounded.

"Chung!" he screamed. "Where are you?"

His fingers sunk into the gooey face of a female corpse, and he watched in horror as it disintegrated under his touch. Panic was taking over now as he desperately tried to clear corpses out of his way to find Chung. Then he felt something firm, something rubbery; he grasped it and realized it was Chung's dive fin. He tugged at it.

"Chung, is that you?"

"Commander?"

"I got you Chung. Hang on."

The pressure in his ears was building rapidly with their descent, but he didn't dare free a hand to use his mask's equalizing assembly to plug his nose and equalize. He pushed another dead body clear and kicked with all his strength against the momentum of the sinking container. Dragging Chung behind him, he worked his way through the mass of corpses—their bellies flayed open wide, their eyeless sockets mocking him in the devil's dim light—toward the open door.

Zhang reached out his left hand, and his fingertips found purchase on the edge of the container. His ears were burning with pain now, and he wondered how much longer until his eardrums would rupture. With a primal howl, he hauled Chung out of the container by the fin, all the while praying it would not slip off. He heard a *thunk* as Chung's tank smacked against the container door while the young officer sailed past him. Grinning triumphantly, he hoisted himself out of the opening, flipping himself upside down, over the edge, and out. He watched a blur of orange sail past him as the cargo container plummeted toward the bottom of the sea.

Zhang felt a hand grasp his calf just above the ankle.

He looked down and met Chung's wide-eyed gaze. "You all right?" he asked.

The young officer stared back at him, catatonic.

Zhang reached down and grabbed Chung by the straps on his BC vest and pulled him up until they were staring at each other mask-to-mask.

"It's over," Zhang said. "You're okay. We're safe."

Chung nodded, his mind in another place.

Zhang checked his depth gauge—they had plunged an additional ten meters, to a depth of nearly forty meters. He imagined the additional nitrogen in his body, saturating his blood, waiting to bubble out on the ascent and cause embolisms in his brain, joints, and lungs. "Listen to me, Chung. It's time to go up."

Chung nodded.

Only now did he register all the chatter on the comms circuit, with the dive coordinator and safety divers frantically calling for status reports.

"We are okay," he said, giving a thumbs-up to the safety divers hovering ten meters above. "I repeat, we're okay, but we exceeded the no-decompression limit, so we'll need a slow ascent and decompression stop to avoid the bends."

"Roger," the dive coordinator said. "It's still pretty rough up here. I'll lower the dive platform to fifteen meters. You can decompress there and not have to worry about station-keeping."

"Copy that, and much obliged."

Dragging Chung behind him, Zhang began the ascent.

"If you don't mind me asking," the dive coordinator said, "what the hell happened down there, Commander?"

Nightmarish imagery from their battle for survival inside the sinking, corpse-filled container flashed across his mind's eye. "I'll spare you the gory specifics . . . Let's just say we got our asses kicked by a box of dead people."

CHAPTER 9

Commander Zhang shuddered despite the steaming-hot water raining down on his ocean-chilled skin.

If Dazhong could see me now, shaking like a child, what would she think?

The time in the cargo container had felt like an eternity, but in actuality, he'd been trapped with the corpses for less than a minute. Dazhong, on the other hand, had probably logged over twenty hours of autopsies with the dead in the chilly basement of the Gun Club Hill Barracks. Would seeing him like this shatter her image of him as the fearless, unflappable Commander of China's elite Snow Leopard Counterterrorism Unit? Or would she empathize? Would she wrap her arms around him and comfort him as a kindred spirit also ensnared in this most morbid of investigations? Or would she gaze at him with his father's eyes—disappointed eyes for a son who never measured up—no matter how high the bar was raised?

He silently chastised himself for being so weak.

He'd seen plenty of blood. Plenty of death. *This is no different,* he told himself.

But it *was* different.

70

There was a twisted malice at work here—mutilation, exploitation, and punishment. The mind behind this operation was sick and callous. *A sociopath*, he surmised. Someone even more deranged than the butcher of Kizilsu, Chen Qing, and that was saying something. Whoever was behind these murders had to be stopped, and Zhang was going to be the one to do it.

He wasn't sure how long he lingered in the shower, but it was long enough to stop his shaking. Long enough to exceed the hot-water ration for a dozen sailors. Long enough to scrub the skin of his face and neck until it was red and tender, trying to rid himself of the oily residue of the decomposing corpses. Still, the smell—or at least his paranoia of the smell—persisted. He leaned his head against the wall, took one last shuddering breath, and then turned off the water. Reaching for his towel, he pulled the shower curtain open and came face-to-face with Major Li.

"What the hell are you doing?" he snapped, wrapping the towel around his waist and wondering how long the Army officer had been standing outside his shower.

"I need a briefing on what you found during the dive," the Major said, his hands clasped behind his back. "You promised me you would brief me as soon as you surfaced."

"You want to be briefed right now?" Zhang said, gesturing sarcastically to his towel. "Would it please the Major if I made the report naked?"

"Your state of dress or undress is irrelevant. You promised me a report, and I'm still waiting."

"You're unbelievable," Zhang muttered, shoving his way past Li into the officers' locker room. He let the door slam closed on Li behind him, but not surprisingly, the Army officer pursued him, unfazed. Zhang sighed, tossed his towel into a bin by the door, and opened his locker.

"What did you find?" Li persisted.

"We found a cargo container," he said, stepping into a pair of boxer briefs.

"And?"

"And what?" Zhang said smugly, turning to look at his agitator.

Li flushed with irritation. "Tell me about the bodies inside. What was their condition? Were they like the others? What identifying marks were on the container? Why was it hovering submerged like that? Where did it come from? Must I spoon-feed you the obvious questions that need to be addressed in a proper report?"

Zhang's pulse quickened; he'd had enough.

"Be careful, Major," he said and stepped toward the Army man until their faces were inches apart. He towered over Li, but the Major did not flinch. "I am the ranking member of this task force now. This is not an Army operation. I do not report to you. I will share the details of my investigation of the container when I please, as I please. If that arrangement is unsatisfactory to you, then I am happy to request your replacement on the grounds of insubordination."

Li hesitated a beat, and when he spoke again, his tone had lost its edge. "Very well, Commander. As a task force team member, my only wish is to assist in the investigation. I can't do that in the dark, but I should have waited for you to share the information when you were ready. I heard your experience down there was . . . difficult. I apologize for disturbing you. I should have waited."

Zhang nodded and returned to dressing in silence. Maybe he had overreacted. Maybe Li was really trying to help. The man had connections in circles that Zhang did not, and he could marshal the vast resources of the Army if necessary. A man like Li was far better to have as an ally than as an adversary. The only trouble was, Li was smarter than him. The man was cunning and insidious, and he was playing a game that Zhang didn't quite understand. One misstep on this operation, and Li would be back in front of the Central National Security Commission, whispering slander and hyperbole in Deputy Chairman Hu Zedong's ear, this time about Zhang as well as Dazhong. As much as it chafed, he had no choice but to play the game he hated most—the game of politics.

"The Conex box contained at least fifty bodies, probably more," Zhang said, his voice measured and professional. "The warm ocean-water environment was hard on the corpses, so they already looked much worse than the corpses we retrieved from Tung Wan Beach two days ago. That being said, I suspect they are from the same source as the others, based on similar traits."

Zhang sat on the room's only bench to put on his boots.

Li took a seat beside him—annoyingly close. "Similar traits?"

"Yes, like missing hands, empty eye sockets, missing noses. I think some had the forehead tattoos as well, but it was dark, and I had other concerns to deal with."

"Why was the container floating in the first place? With all that weight, why didn't it sink to the bottom?"

Zhang remembered something a pathologist had told him years ago when he had recovered a body floating in the Yangtze River. The doctor had explained that after death, the bacteria in a body continued to flourish. If unchecked, the bacteria produced gas, which resulted in the bloated appearance and the eventual "floating" of a corpse that had once been submerged. He imagined the gases from all those bodies filling the container with air. As the buoyancy of the container increased, it began a slow ascent up from the bottom. He had neither the energy nor the inclination to explain any of this to Major Li, so he simply said, "A large air bubble was trapped inside."

Li nodded. "In that case, do you think there are more containers out there stuffed with corpses and drifting around?"

"Your guess is as good as mine."

"Do you think the container was carried out here by a ship and sunk on purpose to dispose of the bodies?"

"That's one possible theory, especially if the people wanting to dispose of the corpses didn't know the decay process would produce enough gas to float the box," Zhang said, rubbing his chin. "Then again, there's also the possibility that this and other containers were washed overboard from the deck of a cargo vessel during the storms."

"Is there any way to identify the container and where it came from?"

Zhang repeated the serial number he had committed to memory, reassuring himself that he still remembered it. Then he said, "I didn't see any serial numbers or markings. It doesn't mean the container didn't have any. They may have been painted over, or maybe I just didn't see them. Everything happened so quickly."

"That's unfortunate," Major Li said, holding Zhang's gaze and probing for more behind the words.

"No matter," Zhang said and checked his unmarked uniform in the mirror. "We know the container sank at this location. We can mount a second expedition using pressure suits or even a submersible to recover it. But hopefully, that won't be necessary."

"Why so?"

"Because the DNA samples that Dr. Chen collected from the corpses at Tung Wan Beach should yield the information we need to get this investigation moving."

Li sniffed but said nothing.

Zhang made a decision in that moment and put it into play. He needed time to track the serial number from the container, and he wanted to do it away from Major Li.

"I'm glad you insisted on coming, Major," he said and clasped the Army officer's shoulder. "At least a half dozen bodies, maybe more, escaped the container and are slowly floating their way to the surface. I need someone to remain behind onboard to head up the collection and evaluation efforts."

"Where will you be?" Li asked, the suspicion unmistakable in his voice.

"I must fly back to the mainland and check in on Dr. Chen and her progress," Zhang said. He exited the small locker room with the Army Major in tow.

"I'm certainly better suited to working with Dr. Chen than supervising dredging operations out here with the Coast Guard," Li countered.

Zhang stopped as they reached a ladder well. He turned and narrowed his eyes at Li. "Dredging operations? Really, Major. Must you be so insensitive?"

"You know what I meant, Zhang."

"How is evaluating corpses here any different from doing it at the Gun Club Hill Hospital? With the exception of the waves, it's not. You're more qualified to evaluate the bodies than the crew of the *Hai Twen*. And you're looking so much better than the last time I saw you on the fantail, Major. Just don't eat anything, and you'll be fine."

"But—"

"I've made my decision," Zhang said, silencing the man.

"Very well," Major Li said in his most pejorative tone.

"Excellent," Zhang answered. "I will inform the ship's captain that you will be remaining aboard. Keep me informed of any progress, Major."

He turned and climbed up the ladder before Li could renew his protest. The decision of whether they attempted another excursion to retrieve the container at the bottom, he would leave to the ship's Commanding Officer and Li. Even if they did manage to get the serial number off the sunken container, in the worst-case scenario, he would have a six-hour head start on Li trying to track the Conex box. Until he understood Li's end game, he would do everything in his power to stay one step ahead of the Major.

CHAPTER 10

CIA safe house
Amalfi complex, Discovery Bay
Lantau Island, Hong Kong
1400 hours local

Nick imagined that going black in Hong Kong would be reminiscent of CIA lore of old—a blown agent forced to hide out in the bowels of a dangerous, alien city, with no support, no money, and no creature comforts. He expected Lankford's CIA safe house in Hong Kong to be some small, dirty, rat-infested basement apartment in the slums, where the violence of the neighborhood drug dealers was as much a threat as the invisible enemy in chase.

He was wrong.

Going black in Discovery Bay had nothing in common with his imagination.

He stared out the sliding-glass door at a swimming pool and, for a fleeting instant, actually considered swimming laps.

"Just keep your head down and lie low," Lankford had said after his EXFIL from Xi'an. *"Everything you need will be provided. Your only responsibility until we get this figured out is to avoid being seen."*

Simple enough instructions . . . in theory.

The Discovery Bay safe house was, in actuality, a duplex condominium located in the heart of one of Hong Kong's most affluent and thriving expat communities. Nick's condo shared a BBQ deck and oversized in-ground pool with an attached sister unit. Both units were owned by the same front company—a Hong Kong–based property-management outfit called Blue Star Properties—which maintained several degrees of separation from ViaTech and Peter Yu's staffing company. What made it work, Nick suspected, was that the property-management company was a legitimate real estate investment firm that had been purchased ten years ago by the CIA through a series of blinds.

According to Lankford, the unit Nick was staying in was reserved exclusively for US assets, while the sister unit was rented out year-round to unaffiliated local and international businesses—including well-heeled British and American families on vacation. In other words, Lankford's high-value CIA agents and assets were separated by a wall and a shared pool deck from legitimate renters next door—adding another layer of normalcy that kept prying eyes from raising their eyebrows. At present, Nick's neighbors were supposedly four Chinese telecom middle managers in Hong Kong for business meetings with China Mobile. For the duration of his stay, Nick was *Justin Reynolds, Senior VP of International Sales for Holden Cosmetics,* out of Ireland.

The arrangement was genius, he had to admit.

"Anything you need, sir?"

Nick looked up at the young woman who stuck her head in from the kitchen.

"No thanks, Jing-Wei," he said and smiled at the tiny woman who matched the sound of her name perfectly.

She smiled back and headed into the kitchen.

He'd had a ham-and-cheese panini for lunch and a large coffee at the coffee shop a short walk north in DB North Plaza. He was doing his best to keep his head down and lie low, but damn it, he was starting to go stir-crazy. His midday walk along the promenade had let him stretch his legs and had given him the fresh air he desperately needed. Unlike in mainland China, here in Discovery Bay, he actually blended into the crowd. Keeping a low profile was easy in a sea of Western expats. Besides, he'd been attacked in Xi'an—why would anyone go looking for him three thousand kilometers away in Discovery Bay?

Nick glanced at his watch. Lankford would be arriving from Beijing within the hour. He was eager to see the CIA man; they had plenty to sort out. While he appreciated Lankford's people extricating him from Xi'an and stashing him in the safe house, he was still bitter that his reluctant agreement to do the man a "favor" had wrecked his life—perhaps irreparably so. Everything he had worked to build in China over the past six months, both professionally and personally, was at risk. Lankford had allowed him a quick call to Hon Bai, his boss at Water 4 Humanity, to let him know that a death in the family required him to fly back to Texas for a few weeks. Bai had been very understanding, giving his condolences along with an offer to "take as much time as he needed." Nick had also insisted that he be allowed to call Dash, but he had yet to make that call. He wasn't sure what to say; he'd know when the moment was right.

Lankford's minions had tried to take Nick's personal cell phone, but he'd refused, telling them they'd have to be content with his promise not to use it. Without his phone, he would not be able to see if Dash called or texted him. As long as he was stuck in the safe house, his mobile was her only lifeline to him. Funny, he doubted *she* thought of it that way, but he certainly did. He wondered if she was thinking of him at all. Was she feeling guilty about the dinner date? Was she eager to reschedule? The last thing he needed was for her to think that perhaps he was angry with her for canceling on him. He understood the rigors of her job, probably better than anyone she'd ever dated. Were they actually *dating*?

Nick sighed, reached for the remote control, and switched on the seventy-inch flat-screen TV with satellite reception. He thumbed through news channels broadcasting from all corners of the world and then tossed the remote back on the table. No mention of a homicide and shootout in a parking lot in Xi'an on any of the Chinese news stations, CNN, or the BBC. He rose from the couch, walked to the glass doors, and stared at the swimming pool. Again.

A double chime announced the front door opening, and Nick instinctively moved left, toward the corner. A Chinese man entered, saw Nick, and smiled.

"You must be Nick," the man said, his thick Texas drawl taking Nick by surprise.

"And you are?" Nick asked, his hand on the butt of the sub-compact nine-millimeter he wore in a holster on the small of his back. Like the other weapons he now had at his disposal, the pistol "came with the apartment" and had been given to him en route by the field agent who had escorted him to Discovery Bay.

"Jeremy Reimer," the man said and plopped down on the couch. "I know I look more like a 'Ping or a 'Huang,' but my momma called me Jeremy, and my dad was a Reimer, so there ya go."

"You're from Texas?" Nick asked, taken aback.

"No. I'm just fucking with you," the spook said, his Texas drawl disappearing. "Boss said you were a Texas boy, so I thought I would give you my best Dallas twang. I'm actually from Seattle."

"No shit? You had me fooled. You nailed it."

"Accents are sorta my thing," the man who called himself Reimer said with a cocky grin.

"You speak Chinese?" Nick asked.

Reimer rattled off something in Mandarin. Nick wasn't even close to fluency in Chinese, but he'd heard enough Mandarin spoken over the past six months to know that Reimer commanded an expert level of proficiency in the language.

"Say again?" Nick said with a chuckle. "In English this time."

"I said, 'Mind if I change the channel? I'd like to check the football scores.'"

"Be my guest."

Reimer snatched the remote and changed the channel to ESPN. After seeing that no discussions concerning football were being aired, he looked back at Nick. "First time in Disney South?"

Nick nodded.

"You the guy the boss is coming to see?"

"I guess," Nick said and sat in the low, black leather-and-chrome chair beside the couch. "If the boss is Chet Lankford."

The man looked at him strangely. "Yeah, well, he's my boss. He's not yours?"

"No," Nick said, "Lankford is . . ."

A friend? A colleague? Just what the hell is he to me anyway?

". . . an associate, I guess."

"An associate, huh?" Reimer said with a laugh. "I guess that makes you a task force boy, then, huh?"

Nick said nothing, and the man laughed again and waved a hand.

"Yeah, yeah, I know—you could tell me, but then you'd have to kill me. Relax, I don't give a shit. I'm just stopping over tonight on my way elsewhere, so we don't have to get to know each other."

Nick laughed to himself and shook his head. "Sorry, I'm a bit edgy after Xi'an."

"I don't blame you."

"You heard what happened?"

"Yeah," the agent said and plopped his feet up onto the coffee table. "I got the download this morning."

"Lankford has you working the case?"

"Nah, just needed a place to stay en route to my next assignment."

"Oh," Nick said.

"Don't worry, he's bringing two guys with him to help out. They should be here any minute."

"Two guys?"

"Yeah, shooter types." Reimer looked at Nick and sized him up with a twinkle in his eye. "You know, muscle—guys like you."

Nick laughed—a real laugh this time. "Rrrright."

The door opened again with a double chime, and Lankford walked in, a scowl on his face, flanked by two guys who—like Reimer said—looked very much like former operators. Both of the plainclothes soldiers scanned the room and then moved past Lankford to check out the rest of the condo.

"Can we have the room, Jeremy?" Lankford said.

"Sure, boss," Reimer said, standing. "I'll get settled in. Any room you want me to take?"

"Any room not occupied by our guest is fine."

The young Asian CIA man looked like he might say something funny, thought better of it, and then disappeared up the stairs. Lankford collapsed onto the couch beside Nick. An awkward pause lingered between them while the CIA station chief from Beijing rubbed his temples.

"So?" Nick began.

Lankford raised a finger, his eyes still closed and his other hand still rubbing a temple. Anger swelled in Nick's chest, but he swallowed it down. This wasn't really Lankford's fault—he knew that.

Lankford was a good man. Two months ago, he had risked his life to help Nick and Dash stop a madman, saving thousands of innocent lives and taking a bullet in the process. Nick owed Lankford, which was one of the reasons he'd agreed to help look for Peter Yu. That debt, in Nick's mind, had still not been repaid. Everything that happened in Xi'an was just bad luck—the shitty things that happen in war and, he supposed, in covert operations. Lankford could have walked away and left him in Xi'an, but he didn't. He got him out. He got him safe.

Lankford opened his eyes and gave Nick a tired smile. "How are you holding up?"

Nick gritted his teeth. "Fine."

"You always this melodramatic? Tell me how you really feel," Lankford laughed.

Nick couldn't help but laugh at himself along with Lankford. "I suppose hanging out at your million-dollar condo while things get sorted out is better than rotting in a Chinese prison."

"Yeah," he said and gestured at the well-appointed space. "Just 'cause you go black doesn't mean you have to live like an animal."

"You OGA guys are soft," Nick prodded. "Going dark downrange with the Teams meant living inside a hollowed-out tree for a week."

"Right," Lankford said with a grin. "We don't like to rough it here." He looked far off for a moment and then mumbled, "Way better than the 'Stan.'"

Nick looked down. He'd forgotten that Lankford had been in Afghanistan as well. He wondered if things had gone better for the CIA man than they had for him. It had been difficult for Nick to trust Lankford initially because of his sordid history with spooks downrange. One of Lankford's CIA brothers had been responsible for bad intel that had resulted in the worst night of Nick's life. He forced away the haunting memory of the charred remains of an Afghani girl.

No room for the past today, he told himself.

"Bring me up to speed on all your supersecret spy shit. Who's trying to kill me, Chet?" he asked and leaned forward, his elbows on his knees.

Lankford shook his head.

"I don't know, Nick." He hesitated and looked at his hands. Then he looked back up and held Nick's gaze. "I need to tell you something. About the girl."

"She was a spy? I fucked us, didn't I?"

"Nope, just a civilian molecular biologist working for Nèiyè Biologic, like she claimed."

A wave of relief washed over Nick, but it was short-lived. A new worry bubbled to the surface. "Tell me you found her before they did. Tell me you got her out," he said, more statement than question.

Lankford shook his head solemnly.

"Damn it!" Nick popped to his feet and began to pace. "It's my fault."

"No, it's not, Nick."

"If I hadn't sat down with her—"

"Enough," Lankford snapped. "You didn't do anything wrong, so stop beating yourself up. The only person responsible for the girl's death is the asshole who ordered the hit."

"How . . . how did they do it?"

Lankford looked genuinely pained. "Does it matter?"

"Yes, it fucking matters."

The CIA man sighed. "Staged to look like an accident, but we both know how these things work. The hit went down the night before last."

"Who's responsible?"

"I don't know," Lankford said, anger in his eyes. "I have to guess it was the Chinese government, on to our CIA operation in Xi'an. I'm not blaming anyone, but by helping you, I outed myself to your Snow Leopard friend, Commander Zhang. After that, our entire operation in China was blown."

Nick thought a moment about Zhang. He felt a weird kindred connection with the counterterrorism operator, despite their different national loyalties. He didn't see Zhang killing an innocent girl—an innocent Chinese civilian especially. He didn't see Zhang's people killing Yu either. Despite the doom and gloom Nick was feeling, Lankford still didn't have confirmation of Yu's death. Maybe Peter Yu was in some deep, dark hole being interrogated. Nick guessed there could be other entities in the Chinese military and intelligence apparatus that would have no qualms about kidnapping or killing an American spy, but these entities operated deep, deep, deep in the shadows. It was doubtful even someone as connected as Zhang knew about such operations.

Nick stopped pacing and looked at Lankford. "If you're blown, then why did Langley leave you in play? If staying is so dangerous, why not call everyone back and start over from scratch?"

Lankford gave him a pitying smile. "It's not that simple, Nick. If the Company pulled me out, then the next cover set would be made immediately, because the Chinese would be watching for them. Better to leave me in place as an impotent operator, run some low-level shit so I look like I'm still in play, and build a new operation under their noses while they watch me dick around."

Nick nodded. As insane and dangerous as it sounded, the plan made sense.

"So you had Peter Yu running a 'low-level shit' kind of operation so you could look like you were still in play. Is that what you're telling me?"

Lankford shrugged. "I guess you could say that. I'm not saying we had him dangling. We kept several degrees of separation between his NOC and my blown cover. Still, you have to plan for a breach under such circumstances, so we kept his work low-threat to the Chinese—nothing that would warrant getting him arrested, deported, or God forbid, assassinated. He was just using the IT staffing company to poke around and make it look like the Yankees were still business as usual. He wasn't going after high-value targets or Chinese state secrets. It's not like I had him out there by himself with orders to poke the bear. His task was to look at Chinese suppliers with ties to the defense complex and the West. Apparently, he also thought his task included banging his Chinese girlfriend."

"You didn't know about Lihau?"

"No," Lankford said simply and leaned back on the sofa.

"So having a girlfriend in your line of work is not okay?"

"No, Nick, fucking the enemy is not okay. Mirror or not, he was still a field agent, and everything he did was supposed to be part of his cover and reported to me in detail. Lovers are not the same thing as marks. He got the girl killed because he was selfish, careless, and lazy."

"Her name was Lihau," Nick said. In his professional opinion, the girl was in the wrong place at the wrong time because she fell in love with the wrong guy. She was not the enemy, but he didn't say that. "You keep calling her the girl, but she had a name: Lihau."

Lankford screwed up his face.

Nick let it drop. "What's a mirror?" he asked.

"Just an expression," Lankford said. "Yu's assignment was a mirror image of an operation—not real, but not exactly fake either. In this case, his staffing company activity in Xi'an was meant as a ruse."

Nick nodded. "You said he was careless and lazy. Was that really your opinion of him?"

Lankford groaned a sigh and suddenly looked exhausted. "I'm venting, Nick."

"I know that, but I'm being serious. Was Peter Yu a careless field agent?"

"We only worked together a short time, and I didn't know him before."

"Was that his rep?"

"Not from what I hear."

Nick pursed his lips. "Maybe he wasn't."

"Wasn't what?" a now irritated Lankford asked.

"Careless. Maybe Yu was working Lihau as an asset. You said he was looking at Chinese companies with ties to defense and the West. What about the company she worked for?"

"I know, Nèiyè Biologic," he said. "Billion-dollar Chinese firm. The CEO has been on a buying spree, vacuuming up bio-tech start-ups and research facilities in Europe, the US, and Canada. But there was no military or defense connection. We looked hard at them and didn't find shit. It's hard to imagine that poking around Nèiyè Biologic would get a CIA agent killed."

"It's equally hard to imagine that the Chinese government would disappear a CIA agent, put a hit on me, and kill a Chinese civilian scientist. You said it yourself, Yu was working on low-level shit. This isn't Cold War Berlin, where being a spy gets you garroted in an alley. If they knew you were CIA after our adventure in the Underground City, they could have tossed you out or arrested you or whatever. They let you stay—probably to watch you—so why kill one of your low levels and then go after me?"

"I don't fucking know, Nick."

Nick sat back down on the sofa next to Lankford. "There has to be something else here, something we're not seeing. Who stands to gain from taking out Yu? What is their next move?"

"Yeah, well, that's the problem with not seeing . . . you're fuck-ing blind to next moves."

"Then let me help," Nick said, surprised to hear the words coming out of his mouth.

"We tried that already, and look where that got us," Lankford said, gesturing to them on the sofa. "My cover as station chief is blown, and you're a marked man, which, if I'm not mistaken, makes us the two most useless assets in China."

"I'm still handy with a gun," Nick said and smiled, trying to lighten the mood.

"Yeah," Lankford said. "But you're a terrible spy. The log says you went to the plaza today, wandered around with a coffee, and ate lunch on the dock. What the hell, man? Which part of 'lie low' don't you get?"

"How is that not lying low? We're in Discovery Bay. The only people here are expats. You didn't say I was confined to quarters. Who the hell is going to rat me out—that family with three kids I passed, waiting for the Disneyland shuttle? Oh, wait, I know—the rich, fat Russian and his skinny, young blonde who asked me for directions?"

"Be a fucking professional," Lankford growled, getting to his feet. "This is serious."

"I'm not a fucking professional," Nick snapped back, springing to his feet, now toe-to-toe with the shorter CIA man. "I left the Teams for a different path. I traded in my M4 for a shovel, and I was happy to. But you dragged me into your world, and now I'm back in the suck all over again—always looking over my shoulder, waiting to kill or be killed."

"Screw you, Foley," Lankford said. "You dragged me into your world and ruined my operation in China first, remember? Your Boy Scout sob story about wanting to save the poor is getting tired. Don't you dare pretend you've checked out. You're aching to be in the game. I saw it in your eyes in Beijing, and I see it in your eyes now."

"Bullshit."

"It's not bullshit; it's the truth you refuse to recognize. Just like you refuse to admit that the only reason you're still in China is because you've deluded yourself into thinking that someday Chen is going to let you into her panties, and the two of you are going to ride off into the damn sunset. She's on China's Quick Reaction Bioterrorism Task Force. She's being groomed for the CDC director position. Wake up, Nick—you and Dash are never going to happen."

Nick balled up his fist to strike the CIA man, but discipline trumped rage. He took a deep breath and stepped back. Looking at Lankford, he did two rounds of four-count tactical breathing. Lankford was spun up too—his cheeks bright red and his jaw set.

When his pulse rate had slowed below a hundred, Nick said, "We're both stressed and exhausted. Let's take a break." He picked up *Strong Vengeance*, the Jon Land novel he'd been reading, and tucked it under his arm.

"Where are you going?" Lankford asked.

"To get some coffee," Nick said, his tone daring the CIA agent to tell him not to.

"Nick," Lankford called after him.

Nick paused, his hand on the doorknob.

"Get me a vanilla latte, will ya?"

That was as close to an apology as he'd get from Chet Lankford. "Sure," he said, looking back at the CIA man.

"And feel free to put it all on my tab."

Nick chuckled. "Don't worry, I always do."

CHAPTER 11

CIA safe house
Amalfi complex, Discovery Bay
Lantau Island, Hong Kong
0315 hours local—Day 4

*I*nsomnia blows.

Nick rolled over on his back and sighed.

He watched as the palm trees outside cast dancing shadows on the ceiling in the soft, blue glow from the pool lights. The bed was comfortable, the air was cool, the pillow was soft, and he was exhausted—all together, he should be passed out and five hours deep into the monster sleep he'd hoped to get tonight. But here he was, staring at the ceiling and mulling over his argument with Lankford:

"Don't you dare pretend you've checked out. You're aching to be in the game. I saw it in your eyes in Beijing, and I see it in your eyes now."

"Bullshit."

"It's not bullshit; it's the truth you refuse to recognize. Just like you refuse to admit that the only reason you're still in China is because you've deluded yourself into thinking that someday Chen is going to let you into her panties, and the two of you are going to ride off into the damn sunset. She's on China's Quick Reaction Bioterrorism Task Force. She's being groomed for the CDC director position. Wake up, Nick—you and Dash are never going to happen."

He had almost decked Lankford for saying it . . . but why? Why did Lankford's words make him so angry? Was Lankford right? Was Nick living in a fantasy world, trying to be a man he wasn't while trying to seduce a woman he could never have? He ripped the cotton sheet off his torso and tossed it aside in aggravation.

They say the truth hurts . . . Well, fuck the truth. I can be who I want to be. I can date who I want to date—regardless of her nationality or profession.

He was trying not to obsess about Dash but was clearly failing. He couldn't help it; he was worried about her. *Where is she? What is the biological threat she's investigating? Is she in danger? Has she forgotten about me because she's spending all her time with Commander Zhang?*

He rolled onto his side, facing the wall opposite the window.

The shadows changed.

Nick frowned and felt his muscles tense. For a moment, the shadow on the wall looked less like a palm tree branch and more like a . . .

A second shadow joined the first—hunched in a combat crouch. The figures swiveled, and Nick immediately recognized what could only be the barrels of their long guns. As the shadows crept across the wall, Nick rolled out of bed and onto the floor. He moved toward the dresser where his Sig Sauer lay, ducking at the waist to keep below the sight line of the window. From a squat beside the dresser, he reached up and snatched the nine-millimeter pistol, chambered a round, and crabbed silently over to the window.

He took a deep breath and popped his head above the windowsill. He scanned left to right for only a millisecond and then ducked back down. The imagery from his sweep populated his mind's eye—nothing unexpected. Nick frowned and raised his eyes above the windowsill again, this time for a longer look: the pool deck was empty and well-lit in a green-blue hue from the submerged lights; the perimeter fence was intact, and the gate was closed; there were no moving shadows, no dark figures crouched in corners, no one stirring at the condo next door.

Was it all a trick of the light? Was this a delusion of a paranoid mind racked with insomnia? Or were the CIA branch guys making a sweep of the property? He had to imagine this facility had a state-of-the-art alarm system and cameras strategically located throughout and around the property. Yet no alarm was sounding . . .

He heard a chirp that was immediately choked off—like a smoke detector warning of a low battery. Then silence. Nick pulled on a pair of jeans and a T-shirt and slipped his feet into his camp shoes. He slid quietly to a position next to his bedroom door, watching the shadows on the wall for anything else alarming. Clutching his gun in his right hand, he waited and listened.

His pulse thumped loudly in his ears.

A floorboard creaked somewhere outside his room.

Then a toilet flushed, spiking his adrenaline. He smirked and lowered his gun—

An explosion shook the entire house, cracking the glass in his bedroom window.

Breacher charge . . . They're coming for me.

Two deafening booms followed—flash bangs, he assumed. A heartbeat later, pistol fire crackled before being drowned out by automatic rifle fire.

He shifted to the left of the door, keeping the muzzle of his Sig trained on it. He crouched low and pressed his shoulder against the wall. The door burst open, and a rifle barrel moved through the doorway, the muzzle spitting fire. The bed exploded in a cloud of wood chunks, fabric shreds, and down feathers. He angled the muzzle of his Sig around the doorframe and fired three times at torso level. The machine gun barrel jerked up toward the ceiling, still firing. Paint and stucco rained down on him from above until the rifle went still and clattered to the ground.

He reached out and grabbed the receiver of what looked like an Israeli-made assault rifle—*IMI Galil*, a voice whispered in his head. He tugged it toward him, but the rifle was attached to a black-clad assassin by a woven nylon sling. Heaving with all his might, he dragged the rifle and its dead owner into the bedroom.

He scanned the limp body and then pulled a bloody ski mask off of the killer's head, revealing half of a Chinese face. The other half was a mass of bloody bone and gray matter. This fucker wasn't coming back. Nick slipped his pistol into his waistband, snapped out his folding knife, and cut the rifle sling. Pistol shots echoed in the hallway outside, coming from the bedrooms to his right. He snatched two extra magazines from the dead man's vest and shoved them into the waistband of his jeans at the small of his back. Then he went to a combat kneel and aimed down the dark hallway over the iron sight.

"Foley—you intact?" a voice called from the room to his left.

It was Lankford.

"I'm good—you?"

"Intact," the CIA man hollered back. "How many do you . . ."

His question was cut off by more rifle fire. Nick thought he heard a grunt and then a moan.

"Lankford?"

No reply.

Nick fired blindly into the hall and down the staircase. A barrage of heavy return fire tore chunks out of the wall and door-frame beside him. He backpedaled into the room.

"Lankford!" he shouted.

Still no reply.

In seconds, the assaulters would overwhelm him.

Time to go.

He fired another prolonged burst into the hallway, and as the barrage of return fire came, he dashed to the window. He scanned outside. Still clear, but he had no idea who or what might be lurking beyond the fence. It didn't matter, because he sure as shit couldn't stay here. He scooped up his backpack with his left hand, slung it over his shoulder, and fired the rifle at the cracked window, spraying back and forth until the window shattered. Another barrage of gunfire echoed in the hall, and then he heard boots pounding on the stairs.

He heard a familiar *tink* and in his peripheral vision saw a grenade roll into the room.

91

Without a second thought, Nick launched himself out the second-story bedroom window.

He felt the white heat of the explosion on his back before he heard it. The concussive energy of the blast funneled through the window, propelling him farther than his leap alone could have. Without the grenade—it occurred to him as he was flying through the air—he would have fallen short of the pool and splattered on the pool deck instead. A half second later, he hit the water, landing at an awkward angle. His left arm got wrenched backward, and his left cheek smacked the surface so hard that he saw stars . . . but the cold water quenched the burn on his neck and accepted him without breaking his bones. As he sank to the bottom of the pool, dragged down by the weight of his clothes and gear, an eerie, blue quiet enveloped him. He expected tracers to zip through the water at any second, but the bullets never came.

If only I could just stay here . . .

He kicked off from the bottom and swam to the far side of the pool. With a grunt, he hauled himself out of the water and rolled onto the deck, his rifle back up, trained on the window he had just leapt from. Muzzle flashes lit up the window from the inside. Flames danced in the window and licked up the walls from the fire now raging inside his bedroom. He heard voices barking instructions in a foreign language but in a cadence familiar to operators. Another explosion shook the building as a second grenade exploded a hole in the back wall of Lankford's bedroom.

Nick stifled the urge to shout the spook's name as debris rained down in the yard and splashed into the pool. He scanned the yard for Lankford—maybe he'd gotten out before . . . Then he saw something smoking a few yards from him that made his heart sink. A boot. *Lankford's boot.* The condo shuddered, creaked, and then collapsed in on itself, the back half of the structure giving way. Nick looked away. Lankford was gone.

He was alone—again.

He ducked into a tactical crouch and moved to the fence line, easing right into the bushes. From the shadows, he scanned the rear of the complex over his rifle but saw no movement. Thick black smoke was now pouring out of the shattered glass doors that led from the living room to the pool deck. He heard shouting from his right and looked over to see three black-clad figures standing over five Chinese businessmen from the other half of the duplex. The executives knelt beside the pool, arms raised. One captive was naked, three wore silk pajamas, and the last was in boxers. A much younger woman—a professional, Nick guessed—was sobbing. Before Nick could decide what to do, one of the black-clad men barked an order, and the other assaulters delivered five rapid gunshots, exploding the businessmen's heads in geysers of blood and brains. The young girl shrieked hysterically and then was silenced with a bullet of her own. He had just watched the cold-blooded murder of six completely innocent people. Either the killers assumed that they too were CIA, or they were just keeping things neat and clean.

With the executions complete, the three killers moved as a pack back toward the CIA half of the "safe" house. Nick raised his rifle and took aim at one of the black-hooded heads . . .

Lankford's dead, along with everyone else inside the house. Going out in a blaze of glory won't help anyone.

He lowered his rifle and crept along the wall to the back corner. After a quick glance behind him, he rolled over the fence and disappeared into the dense tree line behind the row of duplexes. As he moved deeper into the woods, he performed a rapid self-assessment. He was bruised and sore but had sustained no injuries. The wail of approaching sirens convinced him it was time to ditch the assault rifle. He still had the compact Sig Sauer pistol tucked in his waistband. He transferred the Sig and extra mags to his backpack and hid the machine gun under a patch of ground cover and fallen palm fronds. Then he turned west and began the trek away from Discovery Bay. He had to get off Lantau Island, and his best hope was to catch the first ferry of the morning at Mui Wo.

Time was his enemy.

His body was not among the dead in the safe house.

When the men who were hunting him realized that . . . the hunt would begin anew.

CHAPTER 12

Silvermine Bay Ferry Pier
Mui Wo, Lantau Island, Hong Kong
0605 hours local

Nick sat alone on a wooden bench.

The green-painted slats were dappled with dew. A somber fog hung over the bay, and the heaviness of it matched his mood. His jeans were still damp from his plunge in the pool, making it impossible to warm up despite the hot cup of coffee he clutched in both hands. An overwhelming fatigue was making it hard to stay sharp. It had been like this in the Teams. He would go hours, sometimes days, running a hundred miles an hour with his hair on fire, but the moment he was confronted with a few minutes of inactivity—waiting for a helicopter or, in this case, a ferry to Hong Kong Island—the exhaustion would cave in on him like an avalanche.

His head bobbed with microsleep.

Unacceptable.

He had to stay sharp; his life depended on it.

He stood and checked the time. The next ferry was scheduled to dock in five minutes. Five minutes left on Lantau. Five minutes for the men hunting him to take their shot. Whether you're waiting for salvation or waiting to die, five minutes is an eternity. He scanned the other passengers milling about the pier, looking for malevolent cues. No furtive glances. No nervous body language. No hands buried deep in long coat pockets . . .

His heart rate ticked down a notch.

He glanced out at the water. The ferry was on approach and slowing. According to the posted schedule, this was the high-speed ferry, crossing the bay to Pier Five in only thirty-five minutes. Getting off Lantau alive was his first and only priority at the moment, but the minute he stepped foot on Hong Kong Island, he'd need to find a place to hole up. He was short on resources, which meant he'd need to stay somewhere cheap, and that meant somewhere in the unsavory part of town. Fate, apparently, was not without an ironic sense of humor. His vision of hiding out Cold War–style in a slum was soon to be a reality.

During his trek from Discovery Bay to the pier at Mui Wo, he had crept through the backyards of a row of luxury homes, looking for a target of opportunity. Crime was virtually nonexistent in the wealthy enclave on Lantau, a fact he'd hoped to exploit. Along the way, he'd gotten lucky and found a house with the rear sliding-glass door open. The screen door had been shut, but a flick of the blade, a slit in the screen, and he was in. The homeowner had been fast asleep on the sofa in front of the TV with the volume plenty loud enough to mask Nick's entry. He'd taken the man's mobile phone from where it sat charging on the kitchen bar, had snagged one of two sweat shirts draped on a barstool, and, on his way out the door, had snatched the man's reading glasses from the end table next to the sofa. Then he'd slipped silently back into the night.

An incomprehensible announcement in Chinese, followed by a garbled translation in broken English, told him that the six twenty ferry to Hong Kong Island was now boarding. Nick fell in behind a small group and moved through the turnstiles. He crossed the short boarding ramp to the ferry, which could easily carry ten times as many people on a busy weekday. His internal alarm was quiet; he didn't see or feel anyone's eyes on him. He drained the last of his coffee, handed his ticket to the man in a blue suit at the top of the gangway, and then stepped down onto the ferry deck. Most of the passengers stayed indoors on the first deck, so he moved up the double row of stairs to the second deck and then forward to the bow, where he took a position on the outdoor deck beside the wheelhouse. He looked out at the water and inhaled deeply through his nose.

The ferry sounded one prolonged, ear-piercing blast from the steam whistle atop the wheelhouse beside him—signaling to the world it was getting under way—and then pulled slowly and quietly away from the pier. Nick scanned the pier, parking lot, and coffee shop one last time: no one staring, no one phoning his departure to another team. Whoever had attacked the condo either assumed that he was dead, his body burned to ashes with the other Americans in the fire, or they had been unable to track his movements. He prayed for the former.

Leaning on the balcony railing, looking at the Hong Kong morning skyline, his mind drifted to Lankford. With considerable pain, he wondered if maybe Lankford had been right. He had been cavalier in Discovery Bay. He was no spy, that was true, but he knew better than that. Had his carelessness in wandering around Discovery Bay and NB North Plaza's coffee shop and restaurants resulted in the safe house getting made? Was it possible that he was inadvertently responsible for Lankford's death—not to mention the deaths of the other American operators and the innocent businessmen in the duplex next door?

The man asks for my help, and in exchange I get him killed . . . Fuck!
Now I have another teammate to mourn for a lifetime.

He was tired of death, tired of killing . . . tired of loss and guilt. He'd left the SEALs for this very reason. He'd come to China to find ways to make people's lives better instead of finding ways to end them. He'd joined an NGO to replace violence and destruction in his life with charity and construction, but now here he was, immersed in violence and regret.

Again.

Is violence my fucking destiny?

He practiced his four-count tactical breathing until he had his emotions under control. Then he boxed the thoughts away. He needed to focus on the mission. Like it or not, he was on a mission, and that mission was to stay alive. Someone had disappeared Peter Yu; killed Yu's girlfriend, Lihau; assassinated four CIA agents; and murdered a handful of innocent Chinese businessmen whose only sin was unwittingly renting half a duplex from the CIA. That same someone was also hell-bent on killing him, though he had thwarted that plan twice. If he couldn't figure out who was the puppet master, then eventually his enemy would finish the job.

Nick rubbed his temples.

Think, damn it. Who could be responsible for this?

The hit on the safe house had government black ops written all over it, but last night's assault in the heart of Discovery Bay was overkill, even for a very pissed-off Chinese government. As a former operator himself, he saw a glaring tactical-strategic disconnect. Too risky. Too messy. He tried to imagine Commander Zhang—cool, calculating, and cautious—briefing the Snow Leopards on last night's op . . .

No way. Impossible.

He thought back to his last conversation with Lankford in the safe house. With his cover blown, Lankford admitted he was treading carefully—biding his time until his replacement could stand up a new operation with new agents and new NOCs. Lankford wasn't out there poking the bear—quite the opposite, in fact.

But who else has the balls and the resources to go after the CIA with impunity if not the Chinese government?

When unmasked, the operator he'd shot last night had looked Chinese. That wasn't proof of anything concrete, but it did tell Nick the assaulters were probably domestic. He hadn't seen any markings or insignia on the dead man's kit, collar, or shirtsleeves. Could they be mercenaries? Chinese mafia?

Maybe . . . but one thing is for certain: this all started with Peter Yu.

Nick looked at the stolen mobile phone in his hand. Right now, he felt more alone in the world than he ever had before. No SEAL teammates to watch his six. No Lankford waiting in the wings, a reluctant yet reliable ally just a phone call away. The gravity of his situation hit him. He was about to embark on a quest to unravel and end whatever the hell *this* was, and he would have to do it alone. Maybe the best thing to do was travel directly to the American embassy and get the hell out of China. He was long overdue to head home to Texas and see his family. But then who would stop the killing spree that Peter Yu's snooping had set in motion? Something terrible was going on, but it was hidden just beneath the surface. He could feel it in his bones. His subconscious knew why he had nicked the phone, even if his conscious self didn't want to admit it. He needed help.

He needed Dash.

He powered on the phone and dialed from memory.

Dash's recorded voice came alive on the line in sweet, singsong Chinese. He didn't understand a word, but he loved hearing her greeting because she sounded happy. After Beijing and what her psycho of a husband had done to her, she deserved to be happy.

He wondered, red-faced, if he was now about to fuck it all up.

The voice suddenly switched to English: "If this is Nick, leave a message and don't stop calling until you get me." Her voice had a smile in it, and he closed his eyes a moment, squeezing them tight after the beep.

He almost hung up, but the words came out like a stampede.

"Dash, it's me, Nick," he said. He opened his eyes and looked out at the silhouetted, fire-painted sky that was Hong Kong at sunrise. "We need to talk. I'm in trouble, and I could use your help. But don't call this number. I'll call you back in a few hours from another phone. I hope everything is going okay on your trip, and I . . ."

I what? Just say what were you going to say, you sentimental jerk.

"I missed not seeing you the other night. Anyway, please keep your phone on, and please don't tell Commander Zhang that I called. Gotta go, bye."

He ended the call and shifted his gaze from the sunrise to the dark eddies swirling in the water alongside the ferry. Then, with a sudden fury, he hurled the phone out into the bay. He watched it splash into the water and disappear into the black.

Disappear into the black . . . just like he was about to do.

CHAPTER 13

0625 hours local

Despite scrubbing herself raw in the hotel shower last night before going to bed, the fetor of death still clung to Dash. After bathing, she had liberally applied scented lotion to her hands, arms, and face, but it made no difference. The stink of rotten flesh and chemicals seemed to have seeped into her. Even now, hours later, she could still smell it.

God, what if it never goes away?

She inhaled deeply through her nose. Did she actually reek of corpse, or was she imagining it? *Maybe it's all in my head.* She dragged herself out of bed and padded to the bathroom, suddenly compelled to brush her teeth.

She had worked late last night, pushing herself to finish the last of the autopsies so she wouldn't have to go back. Working without Major Li had been both a blessing and a curse: a blessing because she wasn't subjected to his persistent and abrasive scrutiny, a curse because completing the casework without him opened the door to the very post facto criticism and critique he loved to levy. In her opinion, Li lived and operated in the world of hindsight. With hindsight on his side, he was never wrong, and everyone else was.

By the time she'd made it back to her hotel room, it had been nearly midnight. After showering, she'd fallen asleep immediately, only to be awoken an hour later by a nightmare. In the dream, she was back on Tung Wan Beach, where the bodies had first been discovered. As she inspected the corpses with hacked-off noses and gaping holes for eyes, they reanimated en masse and dragged her, kicking and screaming, out into the surf, where they drowned her. When she woke, she was disoriented and gasping for air in the dark. It had taken her several seconds to realize where she was and that she was not drowning. After that, she'd tossed and turned in bed, haunted by a revolving carousel of gruesome imagery from her dream and what she'd witnessed in the autopsy suite over the last two days. She'd finally managed to fall back asleep around four AM. Two hours later, her alarm had gone off.

She rinsed her mouth and put her toothbrush away. Then she met her reflection in the bathroom mirror. She looked ghastly— thin and pale, with dark circles under her eyes. In the field, she almost never wore makeup, but today she needed it. She opened her travel makeup kit, used concealer under her eyes, and brushed some color onto her cheeks. Then she applied some lip balm. She sighed. What she really needed was twelve hours of sleep.

She hadn't eaten anything yesterday. Autopsies and appetite were mutually exclusive. To make it through today, she'd have to break her compulsory fast. She was already feeling a little light-headed, and the day had just begun. She needed sugar.

And caffeine.

God, I could go for a bing and a cup of coffee right now.

She wandered out of the bathroom to dress for the day. As she shrugged off her nightshirt, her mobile phone chimed on the nightstand. Glancing at it, she saw that she'd missed a call while she'd been brushing her teeth. She didn't recognize the number. It chirped again, and a pop-up indicated that she had voicemail. She played the message:

"Dash, it's me, Nick. We need to talk. I'm in trouble, and I could use your help. But don't call this number. I'll call you back in a few hours from another phone. I hope everything is going okay on your trip. I . . . I missed not seeing you the other night. Anyway, please keep your phone on, and please don't tell Commander Zhang that I called. Gotta go, bye."

She sat on the edge of the mattress. The smile from hearing Nick's voice—from hearing that he missed her—suddenly evaporated as the other more ominous elements of the message began to register: Nick was in trouble. Nick needed her help. Don't call him back; he would call her. Don't tell Commander Zhang that he'd called.

What the hell is going on?

Despite his instructions, she immediately redialed the number he'd called her from. The phone rang seven times, and the call went to voicemail. An unfamiliar male voice rattled off a recorded greeting in Chinese.

Definitely not Nick.

She ended the call and began pacing the room in her underwear. What kind of trouble was he in? Trouble with his job? Or something worse . . . trouble with the government? Had he lied to her about his identity? About his job? It wouldn't be the first time a man she cared about had lied to her. It wouldn't be the first time an American "friend" had lied to her. Maybe Nick had agreed to work for Chet Lankford. Maybe his assignment was to befriend her and deceive her, just like Jamie Lin had done.

She shook her head.

No, no, no. These are crazy thoughts, she chastised herself. *Nick is not a spy. Since the day we met, he's always been truthful.*

Her phone chimed in her hand. She checked the screen and was surprised to read a text message from Commander Zhang:

Let me know when you're up. Breakfast is my treat. Much to discuss.

She texted him back:

I'm up. Whenever you're ready.

She hadn't heard from Zhang or Major Li since they'd abruptly left to go out on the Coast Guard ship, and she was curious to learn what they had discovered. She wandered over to the hotel dresser and pulled open the middle drawer to retrieve a clean outfit.

A loud, staccato knock on the hotel room door gave her a start.

Clutching her clothes to her chest, she walked to the door and looked through the security peephole. She saw Commander Zhang's handsome face, huge and distorted through the fisheye lens. He was grinning.

"Hang on a second," she shouted through the door. "I'm not dressed yet."

"I thought you said you were ready," he called back.

"I didn't realize you were standing outside my door," she laughed, dressing quickly.

"I hope you're hungry," he said.

"Famished. What did you bring me?"

"Bings and coffee . . ."

Smiling, she unlocked the security bolt and opened the door.

He handed her a paper sack and an insulated cup.

She made a show of inhaling the coffee aroma. "My hero," she said, taking a tentative sip through the tiny hole of the plastic lid. Not too hot, not too cold . . . perfect.

Zhang smiled but made no move to enter her room.

"Come in," she said, gesturing toward the room. "I don't bite."

"Are you sure? They have a café in the lobby."

"It's a big room. I have a sofa and a table," she said, leading the way.

He shut and locked the door behind him and followed her to the sofa. She watched him make a quick-second survey of the room before he fixed his mocha-colored eyes on her.

"This is nice. Much better than the rooms on base," he said. "Good decision to book here."

She shrugged and retrieved one of three bings from the paper sack. "Just a place to sleep," she said and took a giant bite of pastry. She angled the bag toward him, offering him to partake. "They're delicious."

He grabbed a pastry, took a bite, and set the sweet bun down on a napkin on the coffee table.

"You must have some news," she said, chewing, "or you wouldn't have tracked me down at six thirty in the morning. Did you find something out there with the Coast Guard?"

"A shipping container drifting below the surface, full of bodies."

"What?" she gasped, nearly choking. "Were they like the others?"

He nodded solemnly.

Her stomach roiled at the thought of a shipping container filled with dozens of mutilated corpses. "How many bodies can you fit in one of those shipping boxes?"

"I don't know . . . a lot."

The obligation of having to conduct more autopsies hit her like a brick. "Did you recover the bodies?"

"Unfortunately, no. Things got complicated," he said, shaking his head. "I almost lost a man."

She could tell from the look on his face that he was holding back. Over the years, she'd become skilled at reading between the lines when talking to men. *I almost lost a man* was both a statement and an omission.

"Are you okay?" she asked, following her intuition.

"Yes, but it was close. We disturbed an air bubble in the container, and when it vented, the container sank, dragging us down with it. We barely made it out in time."

She reached over and squeezed his hand. "I'm glad you're okay."

He flashed her a cocky grin. "Just another day in the office."

She shook her head at him and then looked down at her half-gobbled bing on the table. With the renewed talk of corpses, her appetite was waning again. On top of that, she felt emotionally conflicted. On the one hand, she was selfishly relieved not to be receiving a new load of bodies for autopsy, and on the other, she was mortified at the scale of the organ-harvesting operation. Whoever was behind this was a sick, twisted, malevolent soul.

"But it wasn't a complete loss," he continued. "I managed to record the serial number on the side of the Conex box. The container is registered to Ya Lin Transport out of Macau, so I had one of my men run over to their office and start asking questions. The

Logistics Officer at Ya Lin claims the serial number belonged to a container that disappeared from the loading docks at Haikou New Port on Hainan Island six weeks ago."

"Do you believe him?"

"We made calls to the port authority at Haikou New, and the dock manager confirmed that a loss report was filed by Ya Lin thirty-one days ago for two containers. They searched the dock-yard but never found them."

"So it's a dead lead?"

"I'm not sure. We're going to stay on it. My men are having the terminal managers pull the cargo manifests for all vessels that embarked out of the Port of Hong Kong for three days before the bodies appeared on the beach. We're going to cross-reference those lists with all customs bill-of-lading submittals and look for matches and mismatches."

"You're thinking that somebody stole that container, loaded it up with bodies, and tried to sneak it out in a shipment of legiti-mate cargo? That way, even if the container was discovered, the only documentation would point to Ya Lin."

"You think like a criminal, Chen," he said, his lips curling at the corners.

"Not my fault. I was married to one for many years, remember?"

"I remember," he said, sipping at his coffee.

She thought for a second and then asked, "Even if a manifest shows that the container was loaded onto a particular ship, how does that help us now? The container fell overboard during the storm. It's at the bottom of the ocean."

"It gives us another clue—the name of the ship. We can look at the carrier's freight contracts. See who their customers are. Maybe that container was loaded with a batch of legitimate cargo we can trace. I don't exactly know what breadcrumb we might find; I'm just hoping to find one."

Her stomach growled loudly, interrupting them. Zhang raised his eyebrows, and they both laughed.

"Damn, sounds like someone's hungry." Then, gesturing to her half-eaten sweet bun, he said, "Eat your bing."

She picked up the pastry and renewed her nibbling. "Anything back on the DNA samples yet?"

"Sergeant Tan expedited the check on the fingerprints and DNA samples you collected."

"Already?"

"You did ask me to expedite."

"I'm impressed," she said. "Go on."

"No hits."

"Not a single ID?"

"No, not one. So I had Tan run them through the Interpol database."

"And you found something?"

"No."

She met his gaze and could tell he was toying with her. He was holding something back. "You're not telling me something," she said, her curiosity piqued.

"What I'm about to tell you doesn't leave this room, understood?"

She nodded. "Of course."

He narrowed his eyes at her.

"What?" she said, exasperated. "Who am I going to tell?"

"When we didn't get a match on the Interpol global DNA database, I queried the US Defense Medical Epidemiology Database."

"That's a classified database."

He nodded.

"But how did you . . ."

"I have a friend in Pudong who works with Unit 61398."

"I don't even want to know," she said, shaking her head.

"Which is why this conversation stays between us."

She nodded. "I already promised. What did you find?"

"We got a DNA match on the sample from the male body that fit into both categories—mutilated and missing organs. An American named Peter Yu. Supposedly, Yu works for an IT staffing company in Xi'an, but something doesn't smell right to me. I'm certain Yu was working for the CIA."

Dash felt her cheeks flush. "The CIA?" she echoed. "That means he was working for Chet Lankford."

"Undoubtedly."

"Doing what?"

"I don't know. I have people looking into that now."

"Are you going to confront Lankford?" she asked, her nerves on fire at this bizarre twist.

"No."

"Why not? You know he's CIA."

"It doesn't work that way."

"Then let me ask Nick."

"Nick Foley?" Zhang fixed her with a perturbing stare. "Foley has given testimony that he does not work for the CIA. Are you telling me otherwise?"

"No, no," she said, shaking her head emphatically. "Nick does not work for the CIA, but I do know Chet Lankford has tried to recruit him on multiple occasions. We can use this knowledge to our advantage. Nick helped us before; maybe he would agree to help us now."

"What are you proposing?"

"He could meet Lankford for drinks and subtly inquire about Peter Yu."

Despite the scowl on his face, she could see he was toying with the idea. If Zhang agreed, it would give her the perfect excuse to fly back to Beijing, meet Nick in person, and find out what sort of trouble he was in.

"No," Zhang said at last. "It's not a good idea. Foley is an American expatriate, and his loyalty lies with the US and Lankford. We can't afford to reveal anything about this case to him, no matter how tempting it might be."

"Nick risked his life for China before and saved thousands of lives," she said with a scowl. "I don't know why you refuse to give him the benefit of the doubt."

"Don't be naïve. Nick Foley risked his life for *you*, not for China," he fired back. "And just so we're clear, I've already given him the benefit of the doubt. Which is why I allowed him to stay, to live and work in China, instead of canceling his visa or turning him over to the Guoanbu as procedure dictated. If I were to contact the Ministry of State Security right now and lay out all the facts, do you think they would be as understanding as I have been?"

She met his gaze and recognized the cold, hard truth. The *only* reason Nick was still in China was because of Zhang—the same man who had just delivered coffee and her favorite pastries at sunrise. She swallowed, but the lump in her throat persisted. "No, I don't suppose they would."

Zhang sighed and walked to the window.

She stared at him, backlit against the Hong Kong skyline, and experienced an upwelling of conflicting emotions: admiration and anxiety. Attraction and irritation. Even though he hadn't verbalized his feelings for her, Zhang clearly had romantic intentions. Until now, she'd tried to ignore the chemistry between them, but she felt it. There was a spark. Which made Zhang's handling of Nick's visa all the more surprising. With the click of a mouse, he could have had Nick deported, clearing the way for him to pursue her unencumbered. Zhang knew she had feelings for Nick. Why make it complicated? Why make it into a competition?

Because he's a soldier. Because he's a man . . .

Winning her heart by deporting the competition was the coward's strategy. It wasn't valiant. It wasn't honorable. *It wasn't enough.* Men like Zhang and Nick would never be satisfied with love by default. She was a mission to be completed, a battle to be won. For Zhang, triumphing over Nick to gain her love and affection was the ultimate aphrodisiac.

Of the conflicting emotions battling for control of her mood, irritation ultimately triumphed. She wasn't a prize to be won. She wasn't the victor's spoil. Who she chose to love was her decision. No way in hell would she let her love life transform into some alpha-male courtship cage match.

She glanced at her phone.

It would ring any second, with Nick on the line.

Why? Because Zhang was in her hotel room at an inappropriate hour, and that was how the universe worked when it came to these things.

"I think you should go," she heard herself say.

Zhang turned. "Did I say something wrong?"

"No," she said too quickly. "I just need to finish getting ready. I have a lot of work to do today, and, uh, as much as I'd love to drink coffee and chat, I really need to get back to the autopsy suite."

"Of course," he said, stiffening. "I'll see you on base, Dr. Chen."

And with that, she watched Zhang let himself out, his coffee and half-eaten bing left behind to go cold and stale.

CHAPTER 14

Nèiyè Biologic Corporate Headquarters
Lintong District, Xi'an, China
0730 hours local

Xue Shi Feng sat at his desk, reading the latest batch of manufacturing KPI reports. It took concentration to read the information because he was hungry.

He was always hungry.

There was a knock on his office door. He pressed a hidden button on his desk to release the magnetic door lock, and his secretary stepped into the room. Chow Mei was his twelfth secretary in as many years, but she had lasted longer than all the others—almost four years now. He'd hired her because she was exquisite to look at, but she'd proven to be much more than just vapid eye candy in a pantsuit. She was ambitious. She was observant. Most importantly, she possessed a skill none of his previous assistants had. Mei was a connector. A hub. The left ventricle of Nèiyè Biologic, keeping time and pumping the lifeblood of the company—employee gossip—to sustain the organism. KPI reports were informative management tools, but they paled in comparison to the insights Mei possessed. It had taken him a long time to recognize this. It had taken him even longer to figure out how to tap the vein.

With most people, compulsory persuasion was always the most direct and efficient means of extracting secrets. But with

Mei, compulsion was akin to using a hammer to extricate a model ship from a glass bottle—a self-defeating exercise. Gifts and flattery were equally ineffective enticements. Only in a moment of furious epiphany did he realize that the ante for a seat at the gossip table was the same currency as the payout—information. The more salacious, the more consequential, or the more personal the details he was willing to share, the greater her reciprocation. At first he'd resented her for this, but over time, he'd come to appreciate it as nuance rather than nuisance. Just as he'd come to appreciate her as an oracle rather than an adversary.

"I'm sorry to disturb you, sir," Mei said with downcast eyes. "The hospital called."

"Go on," he said.

"Your mother is asking for you . . . The doctor said she doesn't have much time left."

"Clear my calendar after lunch," he said. "And have a car ready for me at one o'clock."

"Of course." She looked up to meet his gaze.

"Is there something else?"

She took an empathetic step toward him. "Just that I wanted to say I'm sorry. I know this is a difficult time for you."

"Thank you, Mei. She is truly a remarkable woman, my mother."

Mei nodded. "I wish I could have met her."

He took a deep breath. "Did you know that I was born here, in Xi'an?"

She shook her head but took a curious step forward.

"It's true. And when I was born, I didn't cry."

"You must have been a very brave baby."

"No," he laughed. "When a baby doesn't cry at birth, it usually indicates a health problem. My muscle tone was so poor that the doctor told my mother I was not strong enough to survive infancy. He told her to make funeral arrangements, but my mother was defiant. She took me home and vowed to save her only son. But my suckle reflex was so weak, I could not feed at her breast. Three times an hour, she roused me and expressed milk into my mouth. And when I was too weary to swallow, she would cradle me and massage my neck. This ritual went on for months, but despite the physical and emotional toll, she never gave up. And when my father began to verbalize his desire that she let me die so that they could try for a healthy son, she told him to go to hell. You see, my mother loved me unconditionally, despite my curse. She did not forsake me in my time of greatest need, and so I will not forsake her in hers."

He saw that Mei's eyes were rimmed with tears. "Why are you telling me this?"

"I don't know," he sighed. "Maybe so you can understand how I came to be the man I am today."

She tucked a loose strand of hair behind her left ear. "My father desperately wanted a boy. Even now, twenty-eight years later, he has not forgiven me."

"Forgiven you for what?"

"Being born," she said, setting her jaw.

"It appears our fathers have something in common," he said with a wan smile.

"Yes," she mumbled. "They're both bastards."

At this, they both laughed, while she tried to discreetly wipe away the tears that had begun to trickle down her cheeks.

"Thank you, Mei," he said after a beat. "That will be all."

She nodded and turned to leave, but at the threshold, she stopped and looked back at him. "Sir?"

"Yes?"

"Um, I thought you might want to know, I heard talk that Dr. Chow is being courted by Sinovac."

"Oh, really? Do you have any thoughts on why Dr. Chow might be unhappy here?"

"If his department head would approve his most recent R&D request, I think Dr. Chow would find the happiness he seeks."

"Very well," he said. "I'll keep that in mind."

And with that, she disappeared out the door, leaving him alone with his KPI reports and his hunger pangs.

He typed a quick and succinct e-mail to Dr. Chow's depart-ment head, instructing him to fund Chow's R&D request and to unburden fifty percent of the man's workload so he could begin work on the new project immediately. Had Chow been in sales, the retention carrot would have been a generous bump in incentive comp. Had he worked in operations, Feng would have countered Sinovac's offer with a promotion giving the man greater authority. But Chow was a research scientist, and neither of these things were the proper motivation. To retain Dr. Chow, all he needed to do was remove the obstacles preventing him from pursuing his passion—CRISPR research. Chow was one of Nèiyè's rising stars. Feng needed Chow and had no intention of letting the man get poached by Sinovac.

As Chief Operations Officer and the functional number two at Nèiyè Biologic, Feng's job was to manage issues—like the pos-sible defection of Dr. Chow—before they became problems. But as the company grew, the number of issues had multiplied expo-nentially. Of late, all he had time to do was put out fires—trying to wrangle chaos into order, turn incompetence into productivity, and fill the growing leadership void left by the company's increas-ingly absent founder and CEO, Yao Xian Jian. Feng was already working eighty hours a week, not including his off-the-books project work. The stress was starting to take a toll. He was fray-ing at the edges. His gaze fell on the top-left drawer of his desk, the one filled with "emergency" rations. He was so damn hungry. He closed his eyes and took a deep, centering breath.

Discipline. Self-control. These were his weapons.

Pain was his reward. If he could resist now, he would reward himself later.

He took another deep, cleansing breath, then opened his eyes. The craving crushed, he turned his attention back to his com-puter. A new e-mail in his in-box appeared from Yao Xian Jian's assistant. The CEO was in Hong Kong but would be returning this evening and was requesting a private dinner. Feng screwed up his face at the monitor. He knew what this was about, and he wasn't looking forward to having the conversation yet again . . .

Feng had been with Yao from the beginning, entrusted since day one with managing the day-to-day operations of the business while Yao did what he did best—defy expectations. Despite the man's eccentricities, he was brilliant. He also had a knack for wooing investors and turning investment capital into enormous returns. Over the past twelve years, he and Yao had developed a portfolio of biotechnologies, prescription drugs, and genomic insights that had yielded hundreds of millions in profits for the shareholders. Now Nèiyè was the fastest-growing biotechnology company in China and was gaining attention on the world stage. And despite all their success, the crown jewel in the Nèiyè portfolio of biotechnology breakthroughs was one they intended to keep hidden from the world.

The phone on his desk beeped. He noted the *blocked* message on the caller ID. He'd been waiting for this call; he picked up the receiver.

"Yes?"

"I'm calling with a status report on our operation on Lantau."

"Go ahead," Feng said.

"Are we secure?" the voice asked.

Feng screwed up his face in annoyance. He was a busy man, and busy men don't have time for validating the obvious. This line was always secure.

"Of course," he said.

"The operation failed."

"How?" Feng asked, squeezing his eyes shut. The morning news had been buzzing with stories about the explosions in the wealthy Discovery Bay neighborhood. How could the operation possibly have failed, given the body count?

"The target was not among the casualties."

Feng hissed air through his teeth. "Are you one hundred percent certain?"

"Yes," the voice said calmly. "I have contacts inside the local police force. The American's body was not among the dead."

"How is that even possible? From what I'm seeing on television, you blew up half the neighborhood."

Silence hung on the line, his operator apparently understanding that the question was rhetorical. After a beat, the man said, "I do have one piece of good news. We confirmed the American's identity. His name is Nick Foley. He presently works for Water 4 Humanity, an international NGO, but he has a military history. He was a US Navy SEAL. Knowing this, and seeing how he has evaded us twice, I think it is safe to conclude that he is working as an intelligence operator."

"Can we confirm this?"

"I have a relationship with an informant in the Ministry of State Security. It will be expensive, but I can make the inquiry. But before you decide, I have other information that I believe provides all the confirmation we need. Cross-referencing the casualty list suggests that the home we hit was an American CIA safe house."

Feng took a long, cleansing breath. The hunt for Nick Foley was getting more complicated by the minute, and the timing couldn't be worse. The irony of the situation was not lost on him. The harder he tried to protect their secret, the more attention he drew to it.

"And you did not know the property was occupied by CIA before you made the hit?"

"No, sir."

"Find Nick Foley," Feng growled, on the verge of losing control. He took a deep breath and centered himself. "Spare no expense. Kill him if you must, but I would prefer that he be brought to me for questioning."

"Understood," the man said. "The search is already under way. My police contact located him on security footage from the Mui Wo Ferry Pier. He departed on a ferry a few hours after the failed operation. We also have him disembarking a half hour ago."

"Where?" Feng interrupted.

"Pier Five in downtown Hong Kong."

"Then what are you waiting for? Go get him!"

"Yes, sir," his operator said. "I have numerous assets already—"

Feng hung up.

His stomach was on fire. He glanced at the upper-left drawer of his desk, and his mouth began to water. He reached for the knob but then abruptly stood. He walked away from his desk, putting physical separation between himself and the food. He looked out the window at the massive, low-set building in the distance. Beneath its sixteen-thousand-square-meter dome roof stood First Emperor Qin Shi Huang's perfect army—seven thousand stone disciples—hardened, unwavering, and eternal. He admired them. Revered them, actually. If only his operators were that perfect, things wouldn't be spiraling out of control.

But his men knew the price of failure.

They would either find Foley or die trying, because the alternative was worse than death.

PART II

CHAPTER 15

Yue Ko Street at Shek Pai Wan Road
Aberdeen District, Hong Kong
1745 hours local

By willpower alone, Nick rose above the fatigue.

Like all covert operations, maintaining mental acuity was the number-one precursor to success. *Stay alert to stay alive*, he told himself. If the bullets started flying, his adrenaline would take over, and everything would get real simple real quick—shoot the asshole trying to shoot him, and run away. *Fight and flight*, Darwin's governing principles. But he couldn't let it get to that. He'd cheated death twice in as many days, and the last thing he wanted to do was press his luck. Right now he needed to be a countersurveillance machine—a CIA of one—and find a safe place to hole up and bed down.

God help me, he mumbled, looking south toward the Aberdeen Ferry Pier.

He pretended to be annoyed, checking his watch repeatedly to signal to any would-be observer that someone was keeping him waiting. He'd scouted this area extensively. He knew all the buildings by heart now. Behind him was the rundown hotel that catered to the workers from the nearby shipyards and the Wai Shing Plastic Tyre & Battery company down the road. The sign on the hotel's neon marquee was written in Chinese only, so he couldn't pronounce the name. This was the type of lodging he was looking for—a place where no sane American expat would dream of booking a room. A place the men hunting him might overlook.

After five minutes, it was time to move. He hadn't spotted anyone surveilling him. As he wandered, he looped back endlessly on his route to clear his six. The city was wet from days of rain. Gutters ran murky brown, and the stench of food waste and wet cardboard filled the back alleys. He'd found his way to the bowels of Hong Kong, where tourists and businessmen alike rarely ventured. From the time he'd left Pier Five, he estimated he'd walked twelve miles in endless loops and back tracks, stopping at shops and vendors to check behind him, searching for faces and vehicles that might appear more than once, and then repeating the loops to shake any tails he might not see. During that time, he had slowly changed his appearance—buying a black ball cap from a street vendor; slipping into a public restroom, where he ditched his too-small sweat shirt; buying two new nondescript sweat shirts from another shop and then looping back; finding another restroom; and ditching the second sweat shirt and putting on the third. He found a backpack by a bus stop, empty with a broken strap, and flung it over his shoulder. In an alley, he transferred the contents from his original backpack into the dirty, broken one. He carried both for an hour or so. Then he walked through an alley, ditched the first backpack and the sweat shirt, mussed his hair, and tossed his cap. He emerged from the same alley and returned the way he came. Later—as a misting rain picked up—he bought a white plastic rain poncho from a street vendor and sat on a bus-stop bench, drinking a coffee and pretending to read a magazine for a half hour, resting his legs and his aching back. He covertly lifted a cell phone—with a twinge of guilt—from an old woman's purse when she sat down beside him. When a bus stopped and burped out a throng of passengers, the elderly woman boarded. He followed her, acting as if he was going to board too, but at the last second, he changed directions and darted into a souvenir shop just as the bus pulled away. Pretending to search through the worthless plastic junk, he watched the street for any evidence of a tail chasing after the bus, but he saw nothing suspicious. He left his poncho beside a rack of plastic junk, bought a candy bar, and walked out, turning left and heading back the way he had come.

Tired of the drudgery and wet and weary from the rain, he decided he'd reached the point of diminishing marginal returns. He knew his limits, and it was time to stop before he became numb and sloppy. SERE school in the Teams had not prepared him for this environment—miles from any desert or jungle. He'd spent too long trying to be creative while worrying that the countersurveillance routine he was using might not be adequate against professional covert operatives. He needed to lie down before he fell down.

Nick completed one last loop around the block and made his way to the neon marquee of the local hotel, where he hoped to find a room that didn't deplete his limited funds. He pulled the door handle, but it shuddered against a lock instead. He peered inside and made eye contact with an old man who eyed him suspiciously. Nick raised his eyebrows expectantly. With a scowl, the old man pushed a button, and Nick heard a metallic click. He pulled the handle, and the door swung open easily. The lobby was shabby and stank of human excrement. Nick tried to resist wrinkling his nose and hoped the offending odor was only indicative of a plumbing problem and not something more horrifying. Along the wall, two men sat on a bench and played dominoes on a square of cardboard they balanced between their two laps. The one closest to him shouted something, making Nick jump, but then laughed, his toothless partner joining in with a delighted howl. Neither man turned to look at him. Nick walked over to the old man behind a flip-up bar-style counter.

"Do you speak English?" he asked.

The man barked something over his shoulder loudly, and Nick fought the urge to bolt for the door, imagining a giant man with a baseball bat being summoned from the back room. Instead, a small boy appeared in the doorway, clad in a too-small T-shirt with Mickey Mouse smiling beneath a row of Chinese characters.

The boy was barefoot, wearing threadbare acid-washed blue jeans and a Los Angeles Lakers hat off center on his head.

"Who you look for?" the boy demanded. "What you want?"

"I need a room," Nick said. "Do you have any?"

"Maybe," the boy answered and then said something to his grandfather in Chinese. Then he turned back to Nick. "You pay money in up front. One hundred dollars US for the night."

Nick suppressed a grin at the prospect of haggling with a child over a hotel room. "How old are you?" Nick asked.

"I'm nine," the boy said and squinted at him. "How the hell old is you?"

Nick chuckled. "Older than that. How did you learn such good English?"

"Mickey Mouse," the boy said and pointed to his shirt, but he didn't smile. "You are wanting the room? You not have money, then you getting the hell out."

"I have money," Nick said with confidence while silently fretting over how long his money would actually last. "But a hundred dollars is too much. I'll give you two hundred dollars for the week."

The boy looked at the old man but didn't pass on the offer yet.

"Three hundred dollars for you being here a week."

"Tell you what," Nick said, narrowing his eyes at the boy. "Two hundred for Grandfather, and fifty for you."

The boy smiled and looked at him more carefully.

"You are American?"

"No, South African," he said, figuring a nine-year-old native Chinese speaker would not recognize the difference in accents.

The boy spoke in quick, clipped Chinese to his grandfather and then nodded at Nick.

"Pay first."

Nick reached into his right pocket, where he had put some of his American currency, and made a show of uncrumpling a bunch of small bills and counting them out. The last thing he needed in this neighborhood was word getting out that a foreigner with loads of cash had taken up residence in this dump. He handed the bills to the boy, who double-checked his count before handing the cash over to his grandfather.

"No funny business, or I'm throwing you on the street," the boy said, eyeing him from under the bill of his ball cap.

Nick decided he liked the kid and suddenly wondered if the soul of some forty-year-old New York wheeler-dealer had gotten reborn in this kid's body. "No funny business, I promise," he said.

He followed the boy through an iron gate and then up two flights of stairs. The boy led him down a short hall, where Nick stepped over no fewer than five large, wet stains on the carpet runner. Nick counted the doors and also the number of paces to each door. There was a black door with a push bar at the end of the hall that he noted must be a stairway exit. He made a mental note to check whether it led to a door that was accessible to the outside or padlocked, making even an emergency exit impossible.

The boy unlocked a door on the right and held it open for him. The room was disgusting but adequate. What was not adequate was the lack of a window.

"No good," Nick said, shaking his head. "I need a window—a window near the fire escape I saw on the front of the building."

"This is room for two hundred dollars."

Nick shook his head again, emphatically this time. "For the fifty dollars I promised you, I need a room on the front, with a window, near the fire escape."

The boy glared a moment but then suddenly smiled and laughed.

"Okay, you is dirty dog. Coming with me." He gestured for Nick to follow him, and they trudged up two more flights of stairs.

The new room was nearly identical to the first, except for a single window on the opposite wall. A dirty mattress lay on the floor up against the left-hand wall. In the far right corner was a sink, the porcelain stained orange from iron in the hard water dripping audibly from the faucet. A cracked, rectangular wall mirror hung above it on a single nail. The "toilet" was nothing more than a wooden crate with a hole cut in the center over what he presumed was a hole in the floor leading to God only knew where;

he refused to let his imagination wander. He sighed. *This* was exactly how he'd imagined Lankford's off-the-grid CIA safe house would look.

"This will do," Nick said. "Sheets for the bed?"

"Fifty dollars is for week."

"I don't have another fifty dollars."

The boy shrugged. "You don't be having sheets."

Nick decided any sheets the boy provided would likely be as disgusting and infested as the mattress. He made a mental note to buy a couple bath towels and some soap when he went on his next countersurveillance run.

"Fine," he said and handed five ten-dollar bills to the boy. "That's for you. Thank you."

The boy grinned at him with gray teeth. "Here the key. No funny business, got it?"

"Got it."

The boy handed the key to Nick and then left, closing the door behind him. Nick dropped his go bag, and a cockroach scurried across the floor and disappeared under the wooden "toilet" crate.

"Jesus," he mumbled. "I'd rather sleep in a dugout on the side of a mountain in Afghanistan than in this shithole."

He collapsed cross-legged onto the floor beside the filthy mattress. He had absolutely no idea what to do next. Admitting that was both liberating and humiliating. He was a frigging Navy SEAL, one of the world's most elite warriors, and yet here he was, crippled by uncertainty and self-doubt. He was completely alone. In the SEALs, he'd always been part of at least a three-man team. Even if he got separated, he was never really alone. But there were no teammates looking for him now. No QRF was on standby, ready to pop up over the horizon and hose the bad guys with fifty mike-mike and whisk him away. With Lankford gone, his umbilical cord to the CIA had been cut. He'd made Lankford promise to keep the CIA chain of command in the dark about his involvement. Assuming Lankford kept his part of the bargain, that meant there was no one at Langley who even knew that former Navy

SEAL Nick Foley had gone black in Hong Kong and needed help. His shitty hotel room might as well be a prison.

This was how he'd felt in quarantine in the Artux People's Hospital in Kizilsu two months ago. No . . . this was worse. At least during that operation, he'd always had the option to walk away. It had never been about him. This was all about him. Somewhere out there, someone wanted him dead, and the only people who had any insight into the matter were already dead.

He pulled his mind away from his worthless pining and self-doubt. He made a quick security survey of the room for defense, countersurveillance, and emergency egress. The fire escape was accessible from the window, which made a reasonable emergency exit but also made for an increased risk—the exit might well serve as an entrance for someone else. Nick rose and walked to the window, scanning the street from a safe distance back before approaching. He saw nothing on the street nor in the windows of the low building across the street. He twisted the lock at the top of the window, and it spun off in his hand and clattered to the floor. Nick closed his eyes and laughed, shaking his head. He would need some sort of stick—or better yet, a metal bar—to properly secure the window. He banged along the joint with the top window, frozen from paint and swollen wood, and then muscled the window up. It made it halfway and stuck beyond even his strength. No matter—in a real emergency, the window would shatter with little effort. He stuck his head out and measured the distance to the fire escape as less than two feet—an easy distance for him in a hurry but equally as simple for someone else coming in.

He slid the mattress to the corner to the right of the window—out of any sight line of the fire escape. Then he pulled the light bulb out of the rusty socket over the sink—it didn't light up anyway, he found—and leaned far enough out the window to toss it onto the fire escape without breaking it. It settled in the rails at the top of the last black metal step. In the dark, it would be invisible, and a boot would crush it easily—and make a noise he would easily hear. Hardly foolproof, but this was all about belt and suspenders—even if he felt he was wearing no fucking pants.

The door was about as hard to breach as a sheet hung in a door-way, but again, he would have to deal with it. He placed puffed rice cereal on his mental list for the store on his next outing. He would sprinkle it all over the dirty carpet in both directions from his door, giving him some warning before the door was breached.

Nick sat back down and sighed, bone weary and suddenly barely able to keep his eyes open. He needed rest. Right now, the weapons he most lacked were rest and a clear head. He lay back, his head against his bag instead of the filthy mattress. He would let his mind run the checklists that it would run without or without his permission—the years in the Teams were something you could never scrub from your DNA. Unfamiliar emotions—from both fatigue and the realization that he was far out of his element—surged to the front of his mind.

I'm such an idiot. All I had to do was say no. When Lankford asked me to go to Xi'an, I should have just fucking said no.

A wave of anger suddenly washed over him. He was angry with himself for jeopardizing what he had built in Beijing—professionally with the NGO and personally with Dash. Why had he caved in to Lankford? To fulfill some juvenile desire to get back in the game? To live up to the ethos—no man left behind—of the Team he had decisively left for a new life? Or was it something else, something deeper, a flaw inherent to his character? For as long as he could remember, he'd always had trouble saying no—doubly so to someone asking for help. He was a fixer—a mender of broken bodies, a rebuilder of broken things, and a solver of people's prob-lems. Those who knew him casually would say it was his greatest strength; those who knew him intimately might argue it was his greatest liability. Lankford had recognized it and had played him like a fiddle.

Spook bastard.

"Last laugh's on you, buddy," he shouted. "Because you're dead, and I'm . . . I'm still fucking here."

He choked down an upswelling of emotion—guilt, regret, and sadness all swirling together. Over the past two months, Lank-ford had become a friend. Hell, the man had taken a bullet in the Underground City for him and Dash when they barely knew each other, but the stakes had demanded it. Memories of Lankford barging into his apartment uninvited and making wisecracks played like a movie in his mind. He felt his eyes rim with tears, and yet he couldn't help but smile at the spook's larger-than-life personality. He wanted to be angry at the CIA man and blame him for all of this, but in his heart, he couldn't. Lankford was looking out for one of his agents; Lankford had been doing the right thing by asking Nick to help investigate Peter Yu's disappearance.

He took a deep breath and exhaled, trying to center himself.

All roads lead back to Peter Yu . . .

Leave it alone, he told himself. *Digging deeper will only make things worse.*

But he couldn't leave it alone. His thoughts gravitated to Dash. Who better than a brilliant CDC investigator, whom he trusted implicitly, to look into the shady activities of Nèiyè Biologic? Together, they could piece it all together, just like they'd done with Chen and his secret biological weapons program. Together, they could ferret out who was trying to kill him. He got to his feet and started pacing and arguing with himself:

You're doing it again. By involving Dash, you're no different than Lankford. She'll say yes, and then you'll be putting her life at risk.

She works for the Chinese government. She has resources, and she has access to Zhang.

Zhang won't help you. He doesn't even like you.

But there's camaraderie between us. He's a Snow Leopard; I'm a Navy SEAL—we're cut from the same mold, brothers-in-arms in the War on Terror.

He shook his head. How far would that camaraderie get him with the Snow Leopard Commander after Zhang found out he'd broken his promise and had started working with Lankford? Zhang's warning had been clear: get caught working with the CIA, and his visa would be revoked.

Shit.

Who else could he trust?

Maybe he could make his way to the American consulate unnoticed, but what in the hell was he supposed to say to the ambassador's staff? It would be his word against whoever was trying to kill him. With Lankford dead, Nick didn't even have proof that he had been working with the CIA. His role had been off the books. If his adversary was the Chinese government, then it would be his word against Beijing's. What if he became implicated in a conspiracy against the Chinese? He would have no standing with the consulate. It was conceivable that he could be handed over to the very people trying to murder him.

He glanced at his watch. He'd wasted too much time worrying and debating with himself. His gut told him that before making his next move, he needed help, and his heart told him the only person he could trust was Dash. It was settled; he would keep trying Dash until he reached her. He knelt by the window and scanned the street in both directions. He saw nothing that sparked suspicion: no mysterious van parked across the street, no smoking man in a trench coat at the corner watching over a newspaper, no Kevlar-clad assaulters firing automatic weapons and tossing grenades . . .

If they came for him here, the outcome would not be in his favor.

He sat back down on the dirty floor and leaned his head back against the wall. He needed to do more countersurveillance in case the little boy or his innkeeper grandfather started talking about the "South African man" with US dollars staying at their hotel. He also needed to secure several burner phones with prepaid minutes so he could call Dash.

But right now, he needed to rest his eyes.

Just for a few minutes.

After a quick catnap, it would be dark.

Then he would sweep the neighborhood . . . find a shop to buy some food, bottled water, some soap and towels . . .

And then he would text Dash . . .

And . . .

CHAPTER 16

A loud crash woke him.

The adrenaline rush hit Nick like a lightning strike. He was on his feet, weapon in hand, scanning the dark room for human-shaped silhouettes and movement. Operating entirely on reflex, it took his mind a second to catch up with his body:

Hong Kong, shitty hotel, fifth floor, single window with fire escape access to the alley . . .

Ambient city light leaking through the shoddy curtain was just enough for him to validate that he was alone in the room. He pressed himself against the right-hand wall and trained the muzzle of his weapon on the door. He heard a thud in the hallway outside and then muffled voices.

They've come for me.

He slipped his finger from the trigger guard onto the trigger. He inched closer to the door, listening, ready for the door to fly open in a shower of splinters at any moment.

Then someone started shouting in Chinese.

Male, possibly drunk.

A reply came, also in Chinese.

Female, angry but scared.

One didn't have to speak fluent Chinese to recognize what was going on—a domestic dispute had apparently migrated from a nearby room into the hallway. He exhaled, shifted his finger back to the trigger guard, and waited. More arguing ensued, followed by crying and then more shouting.

Definitely domestic.

Nick checked his watch: 01:11.

Instead of taking a catnap, apparently he'd gone comatose and had slept for over six hours.

"Entirely unsat, Foley," he whispered, silently chastising himself in the dark.

The plan he'd devised to go out after sundown and buy supplies was shot. At this hour, the streets would be deserted, and the stores would be closed. He walked back to the dirty mattress on the floor and sat down cross-legged on it. He picked up the stolen phone from the floor and debated whether he should try Dash. She was undoubtedly sleeping, but the longer he waited, the more things spiraled out of control. He would only be able to use the old lady's phone once before trashing it. He desperately needed a cache of burner phones, which meant another trip to the streets for shopping.

"Fuck it."

He dialed her number, and to his surprise, she picked up before the second ring.

"Chen Dazhong," she answered, cool and professional.

"Dash, it's me, Nick," he said.

"Oh, Nick, I was hoping that was you," she said, her voice transforming instantly. "Are you okay?"

"I'm okay," he said. "At least, for the moment."

"Where are you?"

"In Hong Kong, but that's all I should say for now. Can we meet?"

"Yes, yes, of course. Name the time and place, and I'll be there."

The odds were low that his "acquired" phone was being traced and monitored, but given the number of near misses he'd had recently, he decided to take precautions. He'd leave her stepwise instructions somewhere en route to the meeting—a Cold War dead-drop technique—that way he could monitor her approach and see if she was being followed. He'd already decided he wanted to meet in Victoria Park. It worked well for all the typical counter-surveillance reasons: good visibility, public place, limited car access, and lots of tourists.

"At eight AM, go to reception at the Excelsior Hotel. I'll leave instructions for you there."

"Okay, I can do that."

"Good," he said. "And Dash?"

"Yes?"

"Be careful."

She was quiet for a beat, and he could feel her smiling on the other end of the line. "Nick?"

"Yes?"

"You too."

He ended the call before the need for intimacy trumped opsec. He sighed and looked down at his hands in his lap: gun in the right, mobile in the left. Was this his life now? Was this how he would be forced to spend the rest of his days in China—in the dark, ready to shoot, his only connection to the world via anony-mous burner phone?

Some fixer I am . . . I can't even keep my own life from falling apart.

Despite his best efforts, he could not fall back asleep. Instead, he spent the rest of the night scenario planning. He left the hotel before sunrise, hours before his meeting with Dash, to conduct countersurveillance runs. No way was he going to put her in dan-ger. If a single hair prickled on the back of his neck, he'd abort the meeting. He walked the dark streets of southern Hong Kong Island in endless loops before catching the number thirty-eight bus, not far from where he'd started in Aberdeen. He got off at North Point Ferry Pier, made another series of loops, changed his sweat shirt, swapped ball caps, and dropped his backpack into a large canvas rucksack he'd bought. On his return to the bus stop, he let the first number-ten bus depart without him, waiting and watching for anyone who loitered with him and didn't move along with the crowd. No one did. When the next bus arrived ten minutes later, he boarded and took a seat in the back. He rode to a stop near the Hong Kong Central Library, where he disembarked and walked an indirect route to the Excelsior Hotel. At the hotel, he chatted up the concierge for ten minutes, asking questions, giving compliments, and telling jokes until he'd built a comfortable rapport. Then he scribbled instructions for Dash on a piece of hotel stationery, sealed it in a hotel envelope—both obtained from the concierge—and left the envelope at reception. He poured himself a cup of coffee from the hotel's complimentary coffee bar station and departed the lobby at zero seven thirty. He expected Dash to arrive promptly at eight, if not early, to the Excelsior. That gave him time to make a pass through the park before looping back to the hotel to scrub her for ticks before meeting at the Hill Knoll Pavilion in the park.

Nick entered Victoria Park west of the jogging trail. He stopped at the circular fountain, scanning for anything or anyone suspicious before making his way north to the Hill Knoll Pavilion. Halfway through his sweep, his heart seemed to freeze midbeat, leaving a heavy void in the center of his chest. He forced himself to scan casually past the man standing twenty meters away, talking on his phone by a park bench. Nick was certain the small Chinese man in jeans and a short black coat had been looking at him, but more telling was the way the man turned his head away when Nick looked in his direction. The man looked familiar—or was it just his coat?

Nick mentally scanned the catalog of figures and faces he'd logged since he'd left his hotel hours ago. In his mind's eye, he tried to make a match. He had seen him on the number thirty-eight bus. He felt certain he'd seen that same nondescript short black jacket . . . but the man on the bus had been older. Or had he? Nick tried to recall the passenger's face and clothing. The rider had also been wearing jeans, just like this guy.

Nick shifted his rucksack onto his shoulder and brushed his forearm across the subcompact Sig Sauer in his waistband, validating that it was still there. He had nine rounds in the weapon and four additional magazines—two in his jeans pockets and then two more in his backpack—which were stuffed inside the ruck-sack and therefore virtually inaccessible in a firefight. He pulled out his phone as if checking a text message and began walking a slow circle around the fountain. He pretended to type a text, periodically glancing at the man by the bench as he did.

Suddenly, the man laughed loudly and then sat down on the bench. He leaned forward, putting his elbows on his knees. Now the man was paying no attention at all to Nick, but Nick was sure the guy had been watching him a moment ago. Nick walked to the far side of the fountain, keeping his head turned just enough to keep the man in his peripheral vision. The real test would come if Nick headed west toward Great George Street to leave the park. If the dude stood and followed, then Nick had problems.

He turned west and walked ten paces before stopping and taking a knee as if to tie his shoe. In the process, he glanced back toward the bench on the opposite side of the fountain. The man was now off the phone, had pulled a tablet from his case, and was looking at something on his device, apparently paying no attention to the fact that his prey was escaping. Could there be others waiting for him? Perhaps the man was texting them right now to ambush Nick as he crossed under Gloucester Road.

Instead of leaving the park, Nick turned south. He decided to loop around the fountain on the footpath north of the playing fields and observe his would-be observer from behind. After several meters, he turned east, taking the tree-lined sidewalk. He opened up the range, then turned north, merging onto the jogging path. He walked north until the fountain came into view through the trees. The man still sat on the bench, head bowed, his back to Nick. From the right, a woman approached the bench. She tapped the black-coated man on the shoulder, careful not to spill the two coffees she held, and then smiled at him. He stood up, and they embraced. The woman handed him a coffee, and they sat together on the bench. Nick let the breath hiss slowly out between his clenched teeth and then forced his shoulders to unwind.

He glanced at his watch. Just enough time to loop around the pavilion and work his way back to the Excelsior Hotel for Dash's arrival.

Fifteen minutes later, from his observation hideout in Tung Lo Wan Garden, he spied her walking east on Gloucester toward the park. He was wholly unprepared for the effect seeing her had on him. She was dressed simply—in khaki pants, a light jacket, and sensible shoes. Her onyx hair flowed behind her as she dodged pedestrians on the sidewalk. She walked with confidence, but like a woman who had no idea how beautiful she was. The sight of her took his breath away. She was a vision of femininity, and a wave of longing washed over him.

He shook his head and tsked with his tongue.

No time for that now.

He shifted his gaze, scanning behind her. He looked for ticks, assuming that if she was being observed, it was by a team, with watchers passing her off to one another as she passed their positions. He let her pass, clearing her six as best he could, before stepping out of the little playground park and onto Gloucester behind her. She doglegged around the median, pausing for traffic before jogging over to the other side of the street and entering the park. He trailed her up the hill to the pavilion, keeping his distance. A mother and her two small children were playing on the two ancient iron cannon barrels. Dash stopped to watch them, taking a seat on the concrete wall next to two cartoonish statues depicting laughing heads. He watched her cross her legs and look around, and when she didn't see him, she sighed. While she waited, she began chewing her pinky nail on her left hand. When she noticed she was doing it, she shook her head in irritation and crossed her arms.

Nick watched the area for several minutes, but nothing set off his antennae. He circled west for a last change of vantage points before approaching her. When she saw him, all the darkness in her face evaporated, and she jumped to her feet and ran to him. He resisted the urge to throw his arms around her, but to his surprise, she had less control and wrapped her arms around his chest. She pressed her tight body against his, and then she tipped on her toes to look at him. For an instant, he thought she might kiss him, but she stopped and smiled instead.

"Oh my God, Nick," she said, gazing at him. "I was so worried about you. You made me wait so long between the voicemail and when you called me back."

"I'm sorry," he said, "but there was no other way."

"It's okay, just promise you won't do that again."

He pulled away slightly and scanned around them. His internal metronome was keeping time, and they'd loitered long enough. Time to move. Yes, he was being paranoid, but he could almost feel invisible forces climbing up all sides of the hill around the pavilion, moving into position for a strike. The high ground would be useless with him being the only shooter and possessing only one pistol. He smiled at her and then said, "We should walk."

Dash reached for his hand, and he shifted to her other side—leaving his shooting hand free and taking her right hand in his left. Her skin was warm and soft, and her hand felt so natural in his. He cleared the area as they walked and led her off the west side of the hill onto a walking path that led south into the trees. Once the pavilion disappeared behind them, she spoke, squeezing his hand as she did.

"What on earth happened to you? Where have you been? Your message—the call—you sounded like you were in such trouble."

"I am," he said tightly. "I hate that I need to involve you, but I need your help. I'm sorry, Dash . . ."

"It's okay," she said. "I'm always here for you."

She looked at him expectantly, and he suddenly wasn't sure where to begin. More important, how could he tell her about helping Lankford and the CIA without losing her trust?

"I was in Xi'an," he began, but she interrupted immediately, turning to look at him, her face surprised and her eyebrows suddenly knitted tightly.

"Xi'an? Why were you in Xi'an?"

He sighed. Trying to compartmentalize the information as he told the story was pointless. If he truly wanted her help, he'd have to come clean. The sooner he did that in the conversation, the better things would go. "I was doing a favor for Lankford," he said, keeping his tone light.

"Lankford?" Dash stopped and looked up at him. "Don't tell me you're working for Lankford."

"I'm not working for him, I swear."

"But Lankford asked you to go to Xi'an."

"Yes, but it's not what you think," he said.

"But he works for the CIA, Nick. If he wanted you to go to Xi'an, then it was on behalf of the CIA."

He ran his fingers through his hair. *This is not going as smoothly as I'd hoped it would.*

"Nick? Answer me, please."

"Lankford wanted me to go to Xi'an because an American expat there had gone missing. He asked me to stop by the guy's apartment, ask a few questions, that's all."

"And what happened?"

"The guy wasn't there, and when I started asking questions, it ruffled someone's feathers, and that someone put a hit on me. Two goons tried to kill me in downtown Xi'an in broad daylight."

"And that's why you came to Hong Kong?"

"Yeah, Lankford got me the hell out of there and put me up in a CIA safe house on Lantau Island."

"But Lantau . . ."

"I know," he said. "That was for us. I escaped, but . . ."

"But what?" she said, her voice nervous now.

"Lankford didn't make it, Dash."

Her face lost all its color, and she let go of his hand, her hand going to her mouth.

"Dead?" she breathed.

"Yeah."

"Who did this?" she said softly. "Who killed Lankford?"

"I don't know," he said. "All I do know is that the people who killed him are the same people who didn't like me asking questions about Peter Yu's disappearance."

Dash froze. "Wait a minute. Did you say Peter Yu?"

"Yes," Nick asked. He grabbed her by the shoulders and turned her to look at him. "Do you know him?"

"We have his body," she said. "It was recovered in the investigation I'm working on here in Hong Kong."

Nick's jaw dropped open. How was that possible? Was fate determined to pull them together once again into a new and terrible horror? Was that their destiny? The coincidence bordered on insane, and Nick wondered, for a moment, if he was losing his mind. He felt Dash's worried eyes on him. He swallowed hard and said, "Then that means Lankford's murder and the two attempts on my life are also somehow connected to your case."

"Yes," she said absently, her mind somewhere else, evidently unfazed that the universe was once again conspiring against them. "We have to tell Zhang."

"No, you can't," he said, squeezing her shoulders until her eyes came back to him. "I don't think Zhang will be understanding once he learns I was helping Lankford. Besides, we don't know who's hunting me. It could be an element inside the Chinese government."

"*I* work for the Chinese government," Dash said, a sharp sting now in her voice. "This is not an American action movie. My government is not in the business of assassinations, nor is it in the business of butchering civilians and dumping mutilated bodies in the South China Sea."

"Mutilated bodies?" Nick asked, now completely confused. "What the hell are you talking about?"

Dash shook her head. "I'm getting ahead of myself. Finish your story first," she said, "then I will tell you everything I know."

CHAPTER 17

Dash walked beside Nick in a dreamlike state, her fingers clasped inside his strong, calloused hand. She had been fully unprepared for the raw emotion she was experiencing. Knowing that two attempts had been made on Nick's life in forty-eight hours in two different cities had her stomach in knots. And to learn that Lankford had been murdered in a secret CIA safe house did not bode well. Despite arguing to the contrary, she couldn't help but be concerned that a black ops division of the Chinese government was involved. Who else would have the audacity and the means to hunt down and kill American CIA operatives in China?

With worried eyes, she looked at Nick.

He smiled tightly at her. "Are you okay?"

"Yes, but I'm still trying to process everything you told me."

"I know," he said. "It's a lot to take in . . . Your turn now. Tell me more about the mutilated bodies you mentioned before." His eyes were far away, seemingly searching for new angles in the case. She had seen that face before, when Nick had helped her and Commander Zhang work their last case. She was glad to have him on their side again.

"Maybe we should wait until we get back to my hotel," she suggested, giving his hand a double squeeze. She was suddenly feeling very nervous and questioned whether it was wise to be having this conversation as they walked through Hong Kong.

"Understood," he said, and she felt the muscles in his hand tighten ever so slightly. "Did you take public transportation here?"

"No, I have a car. It's parked at the Excelsior."

He grunted at this.

"What?"

"I don't like parking garages."

"I used valet."

"Okay," he said, hesitating. "That should be okay."

He led her south for another few minutes before turning west toward Gloucester Road. At the sidewalk, he stopped.

"There's no crossing at Kingston," she said, eyeing the metal barriers along the median dividing the northbound and south-bound lanes.

"Yeah, I know," he said, looking south down the sidewalk, "but I don't like the look of that guy hanging out by the Great George Street underpass."

She gazed down the street, wondering who Nick was talk-ing about and how his vision could possibly be so much sharper than her own. When she turned back to him, she didn't like the expression on his face. Something about the way his eyes swept across the area around them made her nervous. She'd seen this look before—over the barrel of an assault rifle, right before all hell broke loose.

Nick shifted his gaze across the street to a delivery van stopped with its flashers blinking, idling in front of a store called D-Mop. She watched him study the unusual traffic pattern formed by the Gloucester flyover and the bidirectional loop roads where they intersected Kingston. He suddenly pulled her to his side and started walking south at a quick pace. She looked at him in sur-prise. "I thought you didn't want to go this way."

He flashed her a fake smile. "I changed my mind."

Something was wrong; she could feel it.

They walked half a block before he stopped, pivoted, and pulled her close. At first, she thought he was going to kiss her, and she at once felt both excited and terrified, but instead, he pulled her into a hug and whispered in her ear.

"Relax," he breathed in her ear, his breath warm on her neck. "Need to check something."

"It's okay," she stammered and felt a stirring she had not felt in years.

"C'mon," he said, abruptly releasing her and resuming the brisk trek south. They were now just a half block from the pedestrian underpass at Great George Street. A car horn blared behind them, making her jump. She turned, and in her peripheral vision, she saw a Volvo delivery van executing an insane U-turn at Kingston and Gloucester, knocking over a section of the median divider and heading straight for them. The next series of events happened in a blur.

The van skidded to a halt at the curb in front of them.

Nick grabbed her roughly by the meat of her bicep and jerked her behind him as the side door slid open and two men leapt out. The first thug was tall with a tattooed neck, dressed in a hooded sweat shirt. The second was short and stocky, clad in dark jeans and a black jacket. A woman sat in the driver's seat, watching with expressionless eyes through the slider door. The attackers rushed Nick in unison, but Nick managed to land the first blow—the heel of his right boot arcing through the air and connecting with the thick man's face. A nauseating crunch followed, and blood exploded from the short thug's mouth. The doctor in her diagnosed a jaw fracture, nasal fracture, and likely zygoma fracture as the man collapsed in a heap in front of them. A cervical spine injury was also likely from the violent whiplash the man's neck suffered from the kick.

The second attacker hesitated a beat, eyeing his fallen partner before lunging. Something silver flashed through the air, and Nick barked a curse. He twisted at the waist, his arms windmilling in a series of blocks and strikes. He grunted as he took a kick to the thigh from the knife-wielding thug. As Nick backpedaled, so did she, but her heel caught, and she stumbled and fell. When she looked up, Nick was dodging another knife thrust from the stocky man. She watched in awe as Nick transitioned from defense to offense, spinning again, this time driving his left elbow into the other man's temple. The thug growled and slashed wildly at Nick's throat, but Nick dropped into a crouch, and the blade sailed harmlessly by overhead. Nick pulled a gun from his waistband and angled the barrel up. The stocky man's eyes went wide, and he tried to slash downward, but it was too late. Two rapid pops echoed, and fire arced from the muzzle of Nick's gun. The man's head jerked back, and blood and brains spattered over the side of the van.

Nick jumped to his feet and stepped on the back of the other writhing thug's neck while taking aim at the woman in the van. "Hands where I can see them," he commanded.

Getting to her feet, Dash repeated the command in Chinese to the driver. Instead of raising her hands, the woman raised a pistol. Nick's gun barked twice more, and the van began drifting slowly down the street. As it passed in front of Dash, she cataloged the details: a woman slumped over the steering wheel, half of her head missing, and blood splatter everywhere on the interior of the windshield. There was a star-shaped fracture in the glass, and in the center of the star was a chunk of bone from the dead woman's skull. Dash's mouth filled with bile, and for an instant, she thought she might vomit but swallowed it down, steeling herself.

"How far can you run flat out before you need to rest?" Nick asked, looking at her shoes.

"I don't know. A kilometer or two?"

He grimaced. "C'mon, let's go," he said and jerked her by the wrist back into the park.

"What about my car?" she said, running beside him.

"Too many witnesses back there," he said, his eyes scanning. "The park is our only chance. We need to put some distance between us and the scene, then figure out transportation."

They had only run a few minutes before she began to get winded. She had never been one for exercise, especially running.

"Keep up," he said, pulling her by the wrist.

"I'm trying," she huffed.

"At least you wore smart shoes," he said, guiding her through patches of trees.

Three minutes passed, and her lungs were already burning. She looked at Nick and saw that he was breathing through his nose, running effortlessly, scanning with his eyes as they ran. In that instant, she was both furious and humiliated: furious because she was literally being forced to "run for her life" and humiliated because she was so badly out of shape compared to Nick. She could not remember the last time she'd actually run anywhere. Fitness was something she simply hadn't been able to cram into her busy, work-driven schedule. And yet despite the voice in her head telling her she must slow down and rest, she forced her legs to stride longer and faster. After a few paces at speed, Nick glanced at her.

"You're doing good. Keep it up."

She glanced sideways at him and noticed that the entire left side of his chest was a mass of blood, which soaked through his sweat shirt. The fabric was torn to his shoulder, and beneath gaped a jagged knife wound across his chest.

"You're hurt," she gasped.

"I'm okay," he said, but blood was dripping at an alarmingly fast rate from his left fingertips.

"We have to stop," she huffed. "You're going to bleed out if you keep running like this."

He looked over his shoulder, then scanned right and left before slowing to a walk. He looked down at his chest and frowned. Then he bunched up his shirt in his fist and pressed it into the gaping wound. "You're right. I should probably keep pressure on this."

She stared at him, panting. The wound looked horrible.

"We have to get you to a hospital."

"No," he snapped. "No hospitals."

"But Nick, that wound needs to be closed."

"Then you're going to have to do it," he said, eyeing a passing jogger.

"All right," she said grudgingly. "But if you pass out before I get to it, I'm calling an ambulance."

"Fine," he grumbled. "But I'm not going to pass out."

She looked around and realized they'd crossed the park and were standing just north of the swimming pool and tennis courts. In the distance, on the opposite side of the park, she heard sirens now.

"Time to go," she said, shrugging off her jacket and handing it to him. "Here, drape this over your shoulder and chest and follow me."

She led him out of the park and across Hing Fat Street to Lau Li Street, where a line of red taxis waited, idling along the curb. They climbed into the first one, and she ordered the driver to take them to her hotel, promising to pay triple his fare in tips if he hurried. As the taxi lurched away from the curb, she turned to look at Nick. His color was good, and his eyes looked sharp.

"You doing okay?" she asked him.

"Yep," he said. "You have supplies in your hotel room?"

"No, but I know where to get them. It's close." She reached out and put a hand on his thigh. "Don't worry, I'll take care of you."

"I know," he said, scooping up her hand in his. "You're the only person in the world I trust right now. I want you to know that."

She tried to think of something to say but couldn't find the right words. So instead, she raised his hand to her lips and kissed it.

CHAPTER 18

Zhang pushed open the glass lobby door, balancing two coffees and a bag of pastries to share with Dazhong. Her face had lit up yesterday when he'd arrived unannounced, bearing treats. Was it overkill to play the same card again? He paused midlobby, doubting himself. His gaze went to a nearby trash receptacle, and he contemplated tossing the coffee and pastries in it.

He was terrible at this sort of thing.

He was terrible with women.

Well, not all women—just the ones he had feelings for. Which was ironic, because in the eyes of women he didn't care about, he could do no wrong. Women like the two receptionists behind the counter—one young, one old, both undressing him with their eyes—would tolerate his worst behavior and come begging for more. Traveling in uniform, like he was today, only seemed to amplify the phenomenon. For years, he reveled in this power, channeling his inner Casanova at will, but after getting to know Dazhong, he'd lost interest in shallow. He'd lost interest in easy.

Dazhong had never looked at him like the two receptionists did. She looked at him like a sister looks at a brother: with admiration and sometimes with affection, but never with longing. No matter what it took, that was something he intended to change. What he needed now was a "do-over" with Dazhong for yesterday. Things had been awkward between them after they'd argued about Nick. He'd only visited her once in the autopsy suite, and that was to invite her to lunch—which she declined. Later, she'd left the base without saying good-bye. Hopefully, that awkwardness could be erased with a gesture of goodwill. He flipped a mental coin and decided to stay the course. Nodding at the girls at the front desk, he headed straight for the elevators, coffee and pastries in hand.

He'd called Dazhong early this morning on her mobile. When she didn't answer his call, he drove to the base hospital. Signal coverage was terrible in the hospital basement, so he figured she'd simply missed his call. But when he found the autopsy suite vacant and the attendant said she hadn't been in since late last night, he decided she must have driven herself to exhaustion and was still deep asleep in her hotel room. He would have let her sleep—Dazhong had a habit of pushing herself to her limits—but the information he had was too important. He needed her insight on what this new connection to a biotech company might mean for their investigation.

He tapped on the door with his foot, not wanting to spill the coffee, and called her name softly through the door.

"Dr. Chen?" he said, feeling guilty about waking her. "Sorry to bother you, but duty calls."

The light behind the peephole dimmed, and then he heard hushed voices. Was it the TV, or did she have company? Unwelcome company? He shifted the coffee carrier to his left hand and found the grip of his sidearm with his right.

"One minute, Commander," Dazhong called through the door. There was a tension in her voice, but she did not sound under duress. A beat later, the lock clicked, and the door opened. She stood in the opening, smiling at him, but her face seemed tense.

"Is everything all right?" he asked, trying to see past her.

"Yes," she said. "But I need to tell you something before you come in." She bit her lower lip. Then he noticed the stain on her blouse.

"Is that blood?"

She looked down at her chest and then back up at him.

"Yes, but I'm fine," she said. "Before I let you in, I need you to promise me something."

He narrowed his eyes at her. "Promise you what?"

"Promise me you'll listen to what my guest has to say and that you won't overreact."

He tilted his head right to look around her, but she mirrored his movement, blocking his view.

"I can't promise that."

"Then I'm afraid you can't come in," she said and started to close the door in his face.

He stopped it with the toe of his boot. "Fine, I promise," he growled.

"Good," she said with a hint of victory, reopening the door. "Nick is here."

"What?" he shouted.

"You promised," she scolded and began to shut the door again.

This time he caught the door in his hand. Then, taking a deep breath, he forced himself to say in a calm voice, "What I meant to say was, why is Nick Foley in your hotel room?"

"Because someone is trying to kill him," she said, her voice cracking.

"I thought I told you explicitly not to contact him."

"And I told you that he could help us."

"Oh, for Christ sake, just let him in," a familiar American voice called from inside the room. "Otherwise everyone on the floor will hear the conversation."

Dash opened the door and stepped aside. Foley sat shirtless, reclined in an armchair under a floor lamp. One of the bedside tables was being used as a surgery caddy and was covered with wads of bloody gauze, surgical instruments, and suture packs atop a blue drape. A deep gash, beginning in the middle of Foley's left pectoralis just above his nipple, stretched like a crooked red finger up and over his chest. The wound ended on the front of his shoulder, where it had split apart the edges of the tattoo that covered his shoulder and extended to his mid-upper arm. Little streams of blood, dried but still shiny, snaked down his chest and the inside of his arm. Zhang felt suddenly foolish, standing there with coffee and pastries.

"Commander Zhang," Nick said. "I can't tell you how happy I am to see you."

Zhang set down the coffee and pastries on a console table and marched over to Nick. "What happened here?"

"Thanks for your concern, and no, it's not as bad as it looks," Nick said, his voice ripe with sarcasm.

"You think this is a joke, Nick Foley?"

"No," Nick said, shaking his head and wincing in pain for it. "Believe me, there is nothing funny about what's happened to me over the past forty-eight hours."

Dash slipped on a fresh pair of latex gloves and took a seat on a footstool beside Nick. Picking up a needle driver and a new pack of sutures, she said, "I went to meet Nick at a park, and they came for him. They attacked us in broad daylight."

"Capture/kill operation," Nick interjected. "With a bias toward the *kill* end of the spectrum."

"Nick fought them off, and we escaped, but he got stabbed in the process. The knife went deep, but Nick's chest muscles are big, so thankfully it didn't penetrate the chest cavity. The wound gets shallow as it goes to his shoulder. I closed two deep layers already, but I'm not a surgeon. Hopefully, it will be all right."

"Did you give him antibiotics?" Zhang asked, leaning in to look more closely at the nasty wound.

"Of course," Dash said as she began running a new layer of sutures just beneath the edges of the skin. "I gave him some cefazolin intravenously."

Zhang stood up and crossed his arms on his chest. Eyeing the American, he said, "Why are you in Hong Kong, Nick? Who is trying to kill you? And most importantly, what have you been doing to cause this mess?"

Nick looked at Dash. "Start at the beginning?"

She nodded without looking away from her stitchwork.

Nick blew air through his teeth and looked up at Zhang. "I know that interrogation is kind of your thing, Commander, but I respectfully ask that you let me tell my whole story without interruption. When I'm done talking, then you can erupt like a volcano. Fair?"

Zhang clenched his jaw at the American who—despite Zhang's generous treatment after embroiling himself in the task force's last incident—still had the audacity to patronize him. "Very well. Tell your story." He resigned himself to listening as the former SEAL began to recount the saga of the past few days. But no sooner had Nick uttered the name Peter Yu than Zhang raised a hand to stop him. "How do you know Peter Yu?"

"I don't, but that's the reason I went to Xi'an—to look for Peter Yu."

Zhang's face flushed with anger. This was it. Nick Foley was a spy. Time to spring the trap. "The same Peter Yu who works for the CIA?"

"Yes," Nick said.

"So you admit it, you work for the CIA?"

"No," Nick said, screwing up his face. "Of course not."

"But you went to Xi'an to find Peter Yu because Chet Lankford asked you to?"

"Yes."

"Because you work for Lankford?"

"No, I told you, I don't work for Lankford."

"But you do work for the CIA?"

"No," Nick said, his voice becoming agitated. "I don't work for the CIA."

Zhang swallowed, trying hard to keep his promise to Dazhong. "If you don't work for Lankford, and you don't work for the CIA, then which agency do you work for, Nick Foley?"

"For the thousandth time, I work for an NGO called Water 4 Humanity."

"Nick, I'm going to arrest you now," Zhang said. "I don't have time for games; I don't have time for lies."

"I'm not lying," Nick insisted. "I went to Xi'an because an American had gone missing, and Lankford was powerless to do anything about it. He asked me, as a favor, to stop by Yu's apartment and snoop around. That's all I agreed to do. I swear."

Zhang shook his head. "I like you, Nick. And I'm grateful for what you did in Beijing, but I simply cannot tolerate being deceived. This is the end of the road for us."

Dazhong stopped her stitchwork and looked up at him. "Before anyone is arrested, will you please keep your promise and let Nick tell you the rest of his story?"

Zhang sniffed. Foley certainly wasn't going anywhere in his current condition. And despite the lies, he did not perceive the American as an immediate threat to either his or Dazhong's safety. For the sake of his relationship with her, he would indulge the request, then he would arrest Nick. "Very well, finish your story, Nick. When you're done, then I'll arrest you."

This time, he let Nick talk without interruption to the end. By the time the former SEAL had finished, the initial anger Zhang had felt had morphed into something more complex—an amalgam of emotions leaving him both conflicted and confused. The events surrounding Lankford's death bothered him. Yes, Lankford worked for the American CIA, but this was already well known and being handled. Their countries had been playing spy games with each other for decades, and there were unspoken rules. The Chinese government did not send murder squads after men like Lankford. Men like Lankford and Foley were valuable political bargaining chips—too valuable to be squandered. And despite the obvious nationalistic conflict of interest between his and Nick's chosen occupations, Zhang had to admit that this did not feel like an East-versus-West shakedown. The operation that seemed to matter here was Peter Yu's attempt to infiltrate Nèiyè Biologic, not the broader implication of the CIA trying to place moles in Chinese biotechnology companies.

"Apparently, I left him speechless," Nick said, breaking the silence.

Dash looked up from her suture work again to meet Zhang's gaze. "What do you think? Do we turn our investigation to Nèiyè Biologic?"

"I've never heard of this company," Zhang said. "I can't say—"

A sharp knock at the hotel room door caught him midsentence.

"Please don't tell me you brought friends with guns," Nick said. "I assure you, that won't be necessary."

"I summoned no one," Zhang said and turned to Dazhong. "Are you expecting company?"

"No," she said.

"May I help you?" Zhang called out to the door, switching to Mandarin.

"It's Major Li," a voice said from the other side of the door.

Zhang turned and looked at Dazhong.

The expression on her face left no room for interpretation.

"Now is not a good time, Major," Zhang said loudly. He glanced at his watch. "Dr. Chen and I will meet you on base at fifteen hundred for a briefing."

"Unacceptable," the Army man said. "I'm not leaving, so you might as well open the door, and we can conduct the briefing now."

Nick shook his head.

"You don't get a vote," Zhang said to him.

"When Li sees Nick, there's no telling what he'll do," Dazhong whispered. "I don't trust him."

Before Zhang could answer, the lock clicked, the doorknob turned, and Major Li let himself into the room. Behind him stood a man in a black suit wearing a nametag and holding a key card in his shaky right hand. His expression was both sheepish and apologetic. Major Li walked into the room and let the door slam behind him without a word or glance at the hotel manager. He scanned the room, and his gaze settled on Foley.

"Who is this man, what happened to him, and why is he here?" the Major asked, his eyes surveying the American from head to toe.

Dazhong started to answer, but Zhang cut her off.

"This is Nick Foley," he said. "Mr. Foley is an acquaintance of Dr. Chen, he was injured in an assault on Dr. Chen's life this morning, and he is here receiving medical treatment for his wound."

A vulpine smile spread across Li's face. "I know exactly who Mr. Foley is. I know about his involvement with the last case. I know about his service record with the United States Special Warfare community. I also know that he received an official warning from you, Commander Zhang, not to involve himself in matters of Chinese national security again and that to do so would result in either his prosecution or immediate expulsion from China, but nevertheless, here he sits."

Zhang glanced at Foley, who was warily eyeing Major Li.

Foley claimed he did not speak Mandarin, but whether that was actually true, Zhang did not know. Zhang himself often feigned ignorance of English when it was strategically useful for him to do so. The anxious expression on Foley's face was not sufficient evidence to settle the matter. He glanced back at Li and saw raw animosity for the American in the Army officer's eyes. What happened next took him by surprise. The words seemed to pour from his lips before he had a chance to police himself: "I invited Mr. Foley on board as a special consultant for this case. His strategic insights and counterterrorism experience proved invaluable on the last case, so I enlisted his services."

"This is unprecedented. Some might call this treasonous," Major Li said.

Dazhong leaned in and whispered something in Foley's ear, translating, no doubt.

"I don't see how Mr. Foley's cooperation could be construed as treason, Major."

"Oh, I'm not talking about Foley's actions—I'm talking about yours, Commander."

Zhang felt the blood rush, hot and angry, to his cheeks. He opened his mouth to speak, but Dazhong beat him to the punch.

"Gentlemen," she said in English. "For Nick's benefit, I ask that the remainder of the conversation be conducted in English. Otherwise I will be forced to translate, which will be a terrible distraction while I try to close this wound. And second, instead of arguing about how and why we got to this place, our time would be better spent discussing how we best move forward."

Li shot her a sour look, but he didn't argue.

Zhang resisted the urge to shake his head at the circus playing out before his eyes. *What a fucking mess*, he thought. *Wherever Foley goes, mayhem seems to follow, and I'm the one who has to manage it.*

"I'll take your collective silence as agreement," Dazhong said. "Now, Major Li, since our last discussion, new information has been brought to light. Prior to the attacks, Nick was investigating Peter Yu's disappearance. Peter Yu, it seems, was working for the American CIA, and before his death, he was investigating a biotechnology company in Xi'an called Nèiyè Biologic. Are you familiar with this company?"

"I know of it," Li said. "If I'm not mistaken, they specialize in biotechnology and bioinformatics. Are you suggesting that Nèiyè Biologic is somehow complicit in the murders and the attack on Mr. Foley?"

"I am suggesting that the connection is more than coincidental and is not one that we can ignore," she said and then turned back to Nick's wound.

Li stepped forward and looked down at Dazhong's handiwork. He watched as she resumed pulling the running suture along, slowing as she approached the edge of the tattoo on Foley's shoulder. She chewed her lip as she worked, apparently trying to line the edges up perfectly. Li smirked. "Pointless, Dr. Chen," he said. "The scarring will undo your tedious effort to align the edges."

Zhang saw her jaw tighten, but she made no comment.

"It's fine," Nick said. "She's doing great."

Li shifted his gaze to Foley's face. "Whatever you think your role on this task force is, Mr. Foley, I can assure you it ends now. Consider whatever promises or assurances Commander Zhang might have given you to be null and void. He has overstepped his authority."

"I'll leave that to you two gentlemen to sort out," Nick said with an easy smile. "Consider me here to help."

Li took a step back and turned to Zhang. "The Coast Guard was able to raise the cargo container. I retrieved the serial number and sent instructions to your man Chung this morning to run a search. I copied you on the e-mail."

"I saw that," Zhang said, suppressing a grin. "Good work, Major."

"What cargo container?" Nick asked.

"I never got a chance to tell him about that," Dash said, cutting the suture at her knot and picking up a new—this time blue—suture to begin her final layer of wound closure.

Zhang filled Foley in on their gruesome discovery, then turned to Li. "Lieutenant Chung has already made some headway on tracing the container. That particular Conex box, and one other, went missing from the loading docks at Haikou New Port on Hainan Island six weeks ago. A loss report was filed by the owner, Ya Lin Transport, thirty-one days ago for both containers. Now we know that at least one of the containers was on a ship either coming from or going to the Port of Hong Kong during the last month. Chung is going to cross-reference the traffic lists with all customs bill-of-lading submittals to look for matches and mismatches in case someone was trying to sneak it out in a shipment of legitimate cargo. If we get a match, we'll learn the name of the ship, and we can look for a tie to Nèiyè Biologic. In the meantime, we need to start investigating Nèiyè Biologic and its employees."

"Hold on," Nick interrupted. "None of this makes sense. Why would a biotechnology company be illegally transporting mutilated corpses? We know Peter Yu was murdered, but who are the other victims? If they were murdered too, then why?"

Dazhong jumped in now, and Zhang saw a look in her eye that meant she was processing something important. "I've been thinking about the autopsy results. A minority of the victims were obviously tortured—this is not up for debate. I think it is safe to conclude these people were murdered, and the bodies were dumped for disposal." She turned to Nick. "This whole thing reminds me of your American mafia movies, only on a much bigger scale. The forehead tattoos are also significant. Most of the tattoos say 'Traitor.' One victim was tattooed as a 'Liar,' and the single mutilated female was tattooed 'Whore.' When I first saw the tattoos, they struck me as significant, but I couldn't remember why. Last night, I spent time researching on the computer and rediscovered the Five Pains."

"The Five Pains?" Zhang said, cocking an eyebrow at her.

"Yes, the Five Pains was a system of corporal punishment implemented by the First Emperor of China, Qin Shi Huang. But the Emperor was not the architect of the Five Pains; the mind behind the madness was his chancellor, Li Si. While there is nothing original about the use of corporal punishment in ancient China, Chancellor Li was the first to codify the Five Pains into edict. Li Si's objective in doing so was to make living examples out of criminals and slaves—tattooing the crimes across an offender's forehead and then amputating a nose or limbs so that the price for breaking the law was advertised for all to see. Whoever is doing this is a modern-day disciple of Chancellor Li. He is punishing his victims for perceived offenses and sending a message to the world: 'This is what happens to you when you cross me.'"

"That is all very fascinating," Nick said, "but you said those victims were only a fraction of the bodies you recovered. What about the ones without forehead tattoos and missing appendages?"

She nodded patiently, and Zhang realized she had not read Nick fully into the case. That made him feel better. She turned to him with an approval-seeking look.

"The unmolested corpses fall into a different category, and although they are not missing appendages, they are missing critical organs. Over the past two days of autopsying, I made several new observations. First, all of these victims were young—under the age of forty—and empirically healthy. I believe most, if not all, hail from the working class—as seen from the condition of their skin and muscles, calloused hands, and sun-worn faces. The paucity of DNA records in our national citizenry database supports this claim. Such individuals, if taken from the rural regions, would be difficult to trace and even more difficult to ID by anyone other than immediate family members. These corpses all had detectable levels of general anesthesia in their tissues. Their kidneys, livers, eyes, hearts, pancreases, and lungs were consistently, uniformly, and expertly removed—work that could have only been performed by a skilled surgeon." She looked from Nick to Zhang and then added: "And when I say a skilled surgeon, I mean a transplant surgeon. It's unthinkable to imagine such sinister work being secretly performed in hospitals all across Mainland China."

"Wait a minute," Nick said, shifting uncomfortably under the blue towel, where he had been sitting perfectly still since Zhang's arrival. "Are you saying that these people were murdered for their organs? Illegal organ harvesting is the stuff of urban legend. I never imagined it actually happened."

"Neither did I," Dazhong said. "But whenever large sums of money are involved, you'll find someone willing to break the law to obtain it."

Nick shook his head. "I don't know," he said. "This company—Nèiyè Biologic—is an international biotechnology firm worth hundreds of millions, if not billions, of dollars. Are you suggesting they're paying doctors to murder innocent Chinese citizens so they can pawn the organs on the black market?"

"I agree it's a strange hypothesis," Dazhong said, "but Peter Yu's mutilated body, and this gaping wound across your chest, says that Nèiyè Biologic *is* involved. The question is not if, but rather how and why."

Zhang turned to Li. "You've been unusually quiet, Major. What is your opinion on the matter?"

Li sighed. "Why are you assuming that Nèiyè Biologic is selling the organs on the black market?"

"What else would they be doing with them?" Zhang said.

"I don't know, but if this operation is truly of the scale you're hypothesizing, then why haven't we heard rumors of it before? And how have they managed to consolidate all the mutilated corpses from multiple hospitals around the country without notice? More important, why go to all the trouble in the first place? Why not dispose of the bodies locally and individually?"

Zhang looked at Dazhong and Nick. Their expressions seemed to mirror his own gut response to Major Li's insight. "I don't know. Those are good questions."

"I think this operation is localized, if not in Hong Kong, then somewhere within a hundred kilometers. That is why the bodies are consolidated, and it is the reason I was so keen on recovering the shipping container. I'm also of the opinion that Nèiyè Biologic is not operating alone. I think a third party may be involved," Li said.

"By 'third party,' you mean a hospital?" Dash asked.

Li shrugged. "Not necessarily a conventional hospital, but a facility outfitted for organ harvesting, transplant surgeries, and waste disposal without government oversight."

"Such a facility would be very difficult to conceal," Zhang said.

"Unless it's hiding in plain sight," Nick mumbled.

"What was that, Nick?" Dash asked, touching his arm.

"I said unless it's hiding in plain sight. You know, the same strategy governments often use for their secret installations. Maybe the facility also operates as an outpatient clinic, or a manufacturing plant, or even a morgue."

"Exactly," Li said. "This theory satisfies Occam's razor, whereas our other theory of distributed organ harvesting does not."

"Okay," Zhang said, "here's what we're going to do. Major Li will continue working with Lieutenant Chung at the Port of Hong Kong to find a paper trail linking the shipping container to Nèiyè Biologic or a third-party partner. Dr. Chen and I will investigate this new theory and make a list of potential facilities that could be a match for organ harvesting, transplants, and disposal. We'll meet back here at nineteen hundred hours to regroup."

"What about me?" Foley said, looking back and forth between Zhang and Dazhong.

"You stay here," they both said in unison.

"Great," Foley sighed. "Sounds a lot like house arrest."

Zhang shrugged. "Would you prefer the alternative? Perhaps an arrest that leads to a much less *comfortable* accommodation?"

CHAPTER 19

Nèiyè Biologic Corporate Headquarters
Lintong District, Xi'an, China
1330 hours local

Xue Shi Feng returned from his lunch appointment hungry, despite stuffing himself with two extra portions of Singapore street noodles with fried beef. He was disappointed with himself. Hunger had won the midday battle, and consequently fasting through dinner would be hell. He was in such bad temper, he didn't even look at Mei as he walked past her desk en route to his office.

She hailed him anyway.

"Sir?" she said. "A moment, please?"

He stopped and forced a smile before turning to face her. "Of course, Mei. What do you have for me?"

She rattled off five messages, informed him of one cancelation and two additions to his calendar, and finished by asking him about his visit to the hospital yesterday, all without pause.

In reply, he simply said, "Thank you, Mei, and the hospital visit was fine."

"How is your mother doing? Did the doctors have anything new to report?"

"She was in good spirits," he said. "But the dialysis is beginning to take a toll. I've never seen her this weak. If we don't find a suitable donor soon, I'm afraid she won't survive the summer."

"I've taken the liberty of ordering a nice bouquet of flowers for her room to brighten things up," Mei said. "I hope that's okay."

He smiled at her. "Of course. What would I do without you, Mei?" He turned to walk to his office, but she wasn't finished.

"Sir, there is a gentleman holding on line one," she said to his back. "He's been on hold for twenty minutes, and he refused to give me his name. Do you want me to insist on taking a message?"

"No, that won't be necessary," he said. "Transfer the call to my private line. Thank you."

He entered his office and shut the door behind him. On cue, the private line on his desk began to ring. He wondered if his private line wasn't as secure as he had believed, in light of all that had happened and the involvement of the American CIA. He needed to be cautious. He picked up the handset and said, "Yes?"

"You have a delivery in the basement," a male voice said.

"Understood. Anything else to report?"

The caller hesitated a beat before answering. "Not at this time."

The statement was a lie, but Feng deciphered the subtext. The team in Hong Kong had still not recovered Foley, and the team leader was delaying in hopes that his next report could be good news. A foolish game, but that was human nature.

"Very well," Feng said and hung up the phone. Without bothering to look at his computer, he headed for the private elevator located at the back of his office. He realized he was rubbing his hands together and stopped himself, again frustrated with his lack of discipline. He entered the stainless-steel elevator, turned a key, and pushed the lowest of the three unmarked buttons at the bottom of the stack. The elevator descended rapidly, and moments later, he felt a heaviness in his gut and legs. The cab stopped twenty meters beneath the ground level of the Nèiyè Biologic headquarters building, a stately glass-and-steel edifice designed to Yao's tastes. The door swished open, and he exited. A black-clad security guard—holding a short-barrel rifle across his chest—straightened immediately.

Feng ignored the guard and strode past a half dozen brushed-metal doors before stopping at the last door on the left labeled

"Mechanical Room." He removed the key card hanging from a lanyard around his neck and swiped it across the reader. The door opened with a metallic click and then a hiss from the positive-pressure ventilation system. All the rooms on level zero had precision-engineered ventilation systems. Level zero was not depicted on any of the building's official engineering or architectural plans. Its construction and existence were the company's *second* most closely guarded secret, and it was only accessible via two of the building's twelve elevators. Level zero was, in the truest sense, a shadow company that existed within Nèiyè Biologic. He walked past the rows of air-handling units, circuit-breaker boxes, compressors, water pumps, and stainless-steel pressure vessels until he reached another door. This access point required dual authentication. He swiped his security badge, and then a red image of a handprint appeared on the black glass screen beside the reader. Feng placed his palm on the red outline, watched it turn green, and then heard another *click-hiss* as the metal door opened.

The clean room looked like any operating room in any hospital in the Western world, save for the cement floor and the absence of bright light. A row of locked cabinets hung bolted to the far wall over a countertop and wash station with a pedal-operated faucet. A long metal operating table was pushed up against the wall to his left; atop the table lay a tray of polished stainless-steel surgical instruments. Only three people in the company had access to this room, and only three people understood its purpose. But Yao never came down here. He didn't appreciate the beauty of pain, nor did he understand the tenets of leadership. From the very beginning, he had happily delegated the responsibility of discipline and punishment to Feng.

Over the years, Feng had come to think of this room as his own private sanctuary. A place where he could speak candidly and be himself. A place where he could liberate his demons and hone his surgical skills. Having access to a place like this changes a man . . . changes him for the better.

In the center of the room sat the condemned, a black hood over his head and his arms strapped to a metal chair with leather restraints. The chair was similar to a phlebotomist's workstation, with wide, flat armrests. The legs of the chair were positioned directly over a round, metal floor drain. The man strained against the restraints, bobbing and cocking his head in an effort to try to see the new arrival through the hood. Feng noted the raspy breathing and saw his hands begin to shake in terror and anticipation. Feng walked to the table and picked up a single instrument. This one looked like an ordinary letter opener, only its 304 stainless-steel edge was honed extrathin and razor sharp.

"Who's there?" the man asked, his voice muffled through his black shroud. "Is someone there?"

Feng didn't respond but instead walked over to the prisoner, stepping so his footfalls could easily be heard by the condemned. As both a practitioner and disciple of the Five Pains methodology, Feng understood torture. Were Chancellor Li Si alive today, Feng would happily debate the great man on the merits of adding a sixth pain.

Anticipation.

Feng reached out a hand and stroked the back of the prisoner's left hand. The man gasped and tried to recoil, but the restraints held fast at the wrist. Feng began to circle the chair as he spoke. "Have you ever heard of Prader-Willi syndrome?"

"What? No . . . I don't know what you're talking about."

"Prader-Willi syndrome," Feng repeated. "It's a rare and devastating genetic disorder in which certain genes are deleted or unexpressed on chromosome fifteen. I can even tell you where: location Q eleven to thirteen. In my case, just four little genes are missing," he said, shaking his head. "It turns out that only four microscopic snippets of DNA are all it takes to turn a man's life into a living hell."

"I'm sorry about your disorder," the man in the chair said. "If you could please remove the hood, we could discuss why I'm here. If it's money you want, I can pay."

Feng ignored him. "The physical manifestations of Prader-Willi include poor muscle tone, behavioral problems, cognitive disabilities, impaired sexual development, short stature, and my personal favorite—chronic and omnipresent hunger. I'm not sure what hunger feels like to you, but for me it is torture without respite."

"I'm sorry. I can only imagine how horrible that must be for you."

"Can you? Can you really imagine what that feels like?"

"Yes, yes. I can empathize. It must be terrible."

Feng smirked and shook his head. "No, I don't think so. I don't think you can possibly imagine what hunger feels like to me. As a child, I used to think that a wolf lived inside my belly, always howling and licking, scratching and biting. No matter what I ate, how much I ate, or how often I ate, the wolf was never satisfied. What choice did I have but to appease him? When you're seven years old, and you're so hungry you can't suppress the discomfort long enough to read a book, or play a sport, or even sleep through the night, what choice do you have but to eat? And so I ate. I ate with the same ferocity as the beast in my belly. And by age nine, I was morbidly obese. I was obese and hungry and angry. You see, most people with Prader-Willi are dim-witted—which, in my opinion, is actually a kindness—but not me. No, not me. Fate had other plans for me. I understood the repercussions of my actions. I chose to overeat, despite the knowledge of its futility, despite the knowledge that it was slowly killing me, one pound at a time . . . and despite the fact that my condition made me a target for ridicule."

Feng paused and stared at the man in the chair. As he talked, he felt his burden begin to lighten. The routine was always the same. The hooded stranger took on the role of a priest behind the curtain; this torture chamber became his confessional.

"But then one day, a boy in my class showed me a great kindness—he saw me struggling to control myself at lunch, and he offered to give up his lunch if I would do the same. 'Instead of talking and dining together,' the boy said, 'we will talk and fast together.' It was the first time I had ever skipped a meal. It was the first time I had ever deprived the wolf. That boy taught me the meaning of self-control, of discipline, of willpower. That boy changed my life, and his name was Yao Xian Jian."

The hooded man had stopped struggling against his bindings now. His breathing had normalized . . . He had been drawn into the story. This pleased Feng.

"With Yao's help, I learned how to meditate. I learned how to focus my qi and resist the call of the wolf. Yao introduced me to kung fu, and we learned from the same teacher. Over the next five years, I gained control of my weight, improved my muscle tone, and honed my mind and body into what they are today."

"Are you still hungry?" the hooded man asked, taking Feng by surprise.

"Always," he growled.

"Then how do you do it?"

"Discipline, willpower, and self-control—that is how I cage the beast." Feng suddenly grabbed the hooded man under the jaw and tilted his head back. "Do you know why you are here?"

"No. I've operated the ship exactly per the contract."

Feng let go of the man's jaw and resumed circling the chair. As he walked, he drew his finger lightly across the flat surface of the long, narrow blade. "Rule number one, never lie to me. For each lie you tell, you will be punished."

"I'm sorry, I'm sorry," the man stammered.

"Your reckless departure from Hong Kong harbor during a storm resulted in the loss of sensitive cargo. Because of your negligence and stupidity, you have exposed our operation to the authorities."

"The weather is beyond my control," the man cried. "We had patients. They told me if I didn't keep the schedule, people would die."

"The ship had electrical shore power, did it not? Despite what *they* said, the choice to embark into such a storm was within your control as ship's captain. Properly fixing the shipping container to the deck was also under your control. But you were easily intimidated, impatient, and lazy, which tells me that you lack discipline and self-control. I do not tolerate such weakness in myself, and

I do not tolerate it in my employees. If I permit undisciplined behavior, it will spread quickly within the empire like a cancer. Cancer must be excised. You will serve as both an example and a warning to others."

"No!" the boat captain screamed. "Please, I can make this right, I promise."

"I know you can," Feng said softly into the man's left ear through the hood. "You are hereby sentenced to the Five Pains."

Feng smelled the stench of urine as the man's bladder let go.

With his left hand, he pulled the back of the hood, forcing the boatman's head back and his face up while pulling the fabric taut across the face—the outline of eye sockets becoming clearly visible. Without hesitation, Feng sunk the blade into the man's left eye, careful to plunge the blade only a centimeter or two, lest it travel too deeply and enter the brain, making the rest of the ceremony moot. He spun the blade around in a short circle, pulled it out, and then plunged it into the right eye as the man howled in agony. The deed complete, Feng pulled the blade out and then removed the hood from the man's head. The boat captain was blind now, his eyeballs having been burst and his optic nerves severed, the visual machinery necessary to register even the light in the room completely destroyed. Blood and clear liquid streamed down the man's cheeks and dripped from his chin after mixing with the bubbles of saliva from both corners of the man's mouth. With an expert flick of the wrist, Feng removed what was left of the mutilated eyeballs and heard them splat onto the concrete floor.

"Stop! Please, stop. I'm sorry. I am so sorry. I have a wife and children!" the man shrieked.

Feng placed the blade onto the instrument table. He picked up a flat bar of ink-stained needles preloaded in the pattern for the symbol of failure. It would take far too long to tattoo the condemned creature's forehead longhand, but he did yearn to try that someday. He needed to slow down, force himself to take the time to savor each stage of the Five Pains.

After completing the forehead tattoo, he debated with himself what to cut off next: nose, hands, or genitalia? His eyes fixated on the bone saw, and a wave of anticipation washed over him, sealing the decision. He clasped down on the man's right hand, pinning the arm to the armrest. Then he drew the saw blade across the wrist as the boat captain screamed. He felt blood spray onto the back of his hand and then glanced absently at the clock on the wall. He had hours until his afternoon meeting with Yao. Plenty of time. He smiled and began to saw slowly back and forth, this time putting his weight into it.

"The second pain," he said softly, and while the condemned man screamed in agony in the soundproof room, the wolf in Feng's belly went silent.

CHAPTER 20

Nick's chest burned liked hellfire along the knife wound. The lidocaine injections Dash had given him earlier for his stitches had long since worn off, and now even the lightest touch of the cotton T-shirt he wore was irritating. The combination of pain, lack of sleep, and being cooped up in Dash's hotel room all afternoon alone had put him in a foul temper.

He glanced at the bedside alarm clock for the tenth time in ten minutes.

Where the hell are they?

To his growing dismay, he hadn't heard from anyone since the team had separated six hours earlier. He'd resisted the urge to call Dash for the past hour, but now the desire to check in with her was becoming overwhelming. Clutching the burner phone in his right hand, he began to pace the room. Using his burner was probably safe, but there was no way to know with certainty. Any electronic communication he initiated put her at risk and should be reserved for only true emergencies.

Jesus, dude, relax. They still have fifteen minutes, he told himself.

But he couldn't relax.

Whoever was gunning for him had come after him three times, twice in broad daylight in the center of a major metropolitan area. Which begged the question: was his adversary insane or untouchable?

Possibly both.

The door lock clicked.

Nick tensed and turned to face the door. The door opened, and Dash walked in with a paper sack in her right hand and Commander Zhang in tow. She smiled broadly at Nick, and he smiled back. Zhang shut the door behind them and engaged the dead bolt.

"Welcome back," Nick said.

"How is your chest?" Dash asked, walking straight to him. She handed him the paper bag with her left hand and immediately pressed the back of her right hand to his forehead.

"It aches, but other than that, I feel fine," he said.

"Your forehead is cool to the touch," she said. "That's a good sign."

"You pumped me full of antibiotics. I should hope so."

"Any bleeding under the incision?"

"I don't think so."

"Let me see it," she said.

He obliged and lifted his shirt. Like a good doctor, she studied the wound and gently probed with her fingers. "It looks okay."

"What did you bring me?" he said, letting his shirt fall and lifting up the bag.

"Dinner," she said with a smile. "I figured you were probably hungry."

"Starving." He opened the bag, and the unmistakable aroma of cheeseburger and French fries filled his nostrils. His stomach immediately growled with approval, and he reached in and pulled out a McDonald's quarter pounder with cheese wrapped in paper. "You got me Mickey D's?" he said with a boyish grin.

She grinned back. "What's the American expression . . . calming food?"

"Comfort food," he said and took his first giant bite. "Thank you, Dash."

"You're welcome." She sat down on the edge of the bed and gestured for him to do the same.

He complied while inhaling another giant bite of burger.

"So," he said with his mouth full of food, "what did you accomplish?"

"We made a list of all the possible facilities that could satisfy the criteria for organ harvesting, transplant surgery, and the storage and disposal of dozens of corpses," Dash said. "As you suggested, morgues were high on our list."

"Any luck?"

"We visited three facilities this morning and sent teams to nine others," Zhang said, taking over Nick's job as dedicated room pacer. "And we found no evidence of foul play. This afternoon, we will make surprise visits to another dozen."

Nick took another bite of burger and couldn't help but smile. Normally, he was not a fast-food type of guy, but the quarter pounder was doing wonders for his mood. He hadn't realized how much he needed nourishment. Amazing how something as simple as a burger and fries could rejuvenate a soul. If only Dash had thought to buy him a milkshake, then the holy trinity of American gluttony would've been complete. He swallowed and forced the inappropriate smile from his face, "Okay, so now what?"

"Now we wait to hear what Major Li has to report," Zhang said. "Hopefully, he and Lieutenant Chung discovered something at the Port of Hong Kong."

Nick nodded. "And after that?"

"After that, I'm going to arrest you," Zhang said with his first smile of the afternoon.

Dash shot the Snow Leopard Commander a disapproving look.

Nick couldn't tell if the man was serious or not. Technically, he had broken his promise to Zhang by "working" for Lankford, but the truth was more complicated than that, and Zhang knew it. Nick put the odds at fifty-fifty that Zhang would make good on the threat. This was China after all, and the political fallout from Nick being associated with Peter Yu and Lankford, and their deaths, could elevate the decision out of Zhang's hands. Yes, Zhang was a kindred spirit, but he was also a soldier, and soldiers follow orders. Nick flashed the Snow Leopard his cockiest grin. "Just promise you'll let me finish my cheeseburger first."

"Yes, of course, Nick," Zhang said. "Enjoy it, because last I heard, they don't serve McDonald's in Chinese prison."

Both men laughed, but Dash didn't. She looked back and forth between them with an incredulous "this isn't a joking matter" look on her face.

Downrange humor, Nick thought. *Guess it's a guy thing.*

"Where the hell are Li and Chung?" Zhang said, looking at his watch, a scowl replacing his smile. "They should be here by now."

The air conditioner unit kicked on, the fan blowing on high and the compressor making a hell of a racket. The cool air felt good to Nick, but Dash immediately hugged herself. Nick had the urge to put his arm around her, but it didn't feel right with Zhang in the room. So instead, he just kept eating until he'd polished off every last crumb of his McDonald's. At ten minutes after seven, Zhang dialed Li's mobile.

After twenty seconds or so, he hung up and with a huff said, "Straight to voicemail."

A beat later, there was a knock at the door.

With a look of relief, Zhang walked to the door, checked the peephole, and then opened it. Too Nick's surprise, there was only one man standing in the hallway, and it was not Major Li but a junior Snow Leopard whom Nick surmised was Lieutenant Chung. The Snow Leopard hurried into the room and shut the door behind him.

The new arrival spoke in rapid-fire Chinese, reporting directly to his Commander without even glancing at Nick or Dash.

Nick watched Dash's face as the young man spoke, and he could tell from her expression that the news was not good. Then she gasped.

"What?" he whispered.

"Major Li is dead," she said.

Nick's mind immediately started to race. If Li was murdered, that meant the entire task force was now in danger. The hotel room was no longer safe. They needed to move, and they needed a plan. Despite the overwhelming impulse to interrupt, he held his tongue until Zhang and the new arrival had finished talking.

Zhang turned and looked at Nick. "For your benefit, I'll paraphrase. As you might recall, Lieutenant Chung and Major Li were working together on tracking the shipping container and trying to identify the ship that lost it at sea. This morning, Major Li was killed in an industrial accident at the Port of Hong Kong."

"What kind of industrial accident?" Nick asked.

"The kind where a shipping container fell on him while he was interviewing a loading superintendent with twenty-seven years' experience at the docks."

"Oh my God," Dash said, her hand clasped to her mouth.

"It was no accident," Lieutenant Chung said in heavily accented but passable English. "At breakfast, Major Li told me he had a new lead he was pursuing, and he was going to meet with a man who he thought could prove it."

"So you found a paper trail?" Nick asked.

Zhang shook his head. "Chung and Li completed their record review last night. They didn't find a single entry documenting the shipping container we found being loaded on or offloaded from any vessel in the Port of Hong Kong over the past three weeks," Zhang said, stepping in.

"I'm not surprised," Nick said. "They probably paid to keep it off the books."

"That's exactly what Major Li said," Chung replied. "So he decided to offer a cash reward and promise of immunity from prosecution to any loading superintendent who would talk to him about the black-market container business."

"Apparently, his instincts were right," Zhang added.

"Now no one at the docks will talk to us," Chung said.

Nick looked at the ceiling and shook his head. "If the people behind this are willing to murder Major Li . . ."

"Then none of us are safe," Dash said, finishing the sentence.

"Yep," Nick said. "This is not about Nèiyè Biologic versus the CIA anymore. This is about Nèiyè Biologic versus anyone who threatens them, including the Chinese government."

"This is bigger than Nèiyè Biologic, Nick. Major Li was right. They must have a partner," Zhang said. "But tactically speaking, I agree with you. We must assume each of us is on the kill list. The enemy has the upper hand right now because they know where to look for us, but we don't know where to find them. It is no longer safe for us in Hong Kong. Let me make some calls," Zhang said, retrieving his mobile phone.

"Wait," Nick said. "Use my burner phone—it's possible your phone is being monitored."

"I'm the Snow Leopard Commander. My phone is both secure and encrypted."

"Try telling that to Major Li," Nick fired back. "Look, until we can get our footing, we all need to go black, not just me."

Grudgingly, Zhang swiped the phone from Nick's outstretched hand and made two calls. Nick couldn't follow either of the rapid-fire conversations, but neither lasted long.

"Mind if I keep this?" Zhang said, holding up Nick's phone.

"Do I have a choice?" Nick said.

"No."

Zhang and Chung dialogued for a minute, then Chung disappeared out the door.

"What's the plan?" Nick asked.

"Chung is going to pick us up at the hotel's loading dock in a nongovernmental vehicle and drive us to a private marina, where I have a contact who owes me a favor. From there, we'll arrange transit by boat to the airport in Zhuhai, where I have another friend who owes me an even bigger favor."

"You actually have *two* friends?" Nick said. "Miracles do happen."

"That's one more than you have, Foley—try to remember that," Zhang fired back. "Anyway, as I was saying, from Zhuhai, we can fly wherever we need to go."

Nick looked at Dash, and they read each other's minds. In unison they said, "Beijing."

"Beijing is our home turf, so in that sense we have an advantage, but it's also the first place our enemy will look for us once we leave Hong Kong," Zhang replied. "I'm not sure if that is wise."

"Yes," Nick said, "but where we're going to go in Beijing, nobody will find us."

"Oh no," Zhang said, shaking his head. "Absolutely not."

"Oh yes," Dash replied with a grin. "We have two questions we need to answer: how big is the black market for organ harvesting, and who is trying to kill us? There's only one man in all of China who might know the answer to both questions, and that man is Gang Jin."

CHAPTER 21

Grandma's Kitchen
Beijing, China

Dash's journey from the hotel in Hong Kong back to Beijing was nerve-racking, uncomfortable, and smelly. It began with a covert EXFIL from the hotel in the back of a delivery van loaded with mushrooms and overripe fruit, commandeered by Lieutenant Chung. After that, they took a five-hour ride on a dilapidated fishing boat that smelled so foul belowdecks that she had actually vomited and needed to spend the rest of the transit to Zhuhai topside. Finally, they took to the skies in what Nick declared "the biggest piece-of-shit airplane he'd ever seen," a Harbin Y12 whose cabin reeked of cigarette smoke and human excrement from the malfunctioning lavatory system. The flight required not one but two refueling stops en route, each time making her wonder if *this* takeoff would be her last. By the time they landed at a private airfield outside Beijing, she was dirty, hungry, and exhausted.

Nick had capped off the journey by informing Zhang, "With friends like yours helping us, who needs enemies?" To which Zhang had replied that he thought it would be safest if Nick rode in the trunk of the loaner sedan for the hour-long drive from the airport into the city. Their juvenile alpha-male banter continued, unabated, all the way to Grandma's Kitchen. The moment Zhang pulled their ubiquitous four-door Geely into a parking spot behind the restaurant, she heard Nick's stomach begin to growl. The aroma of bacon frying and waffles cooking was overpowering, and she wondered who in the group would be the first to suggest a breakfast stop before heading underground.

As Zhang put the transmission in park, she looked over at Nick. The expression he wore told her that he was experiencing the same powerful and disturbing feeling of déjà vu that she was. She had not been back to the Underground City since her husband's death. She had intended never to return, but here they were, getting ready to head below for another excursion into the dark and dangerous underbelly of the capital. Access points to the Underground City were scattered throughout Beijing; all of them were locked, but most were hidden in plain sight. This particular entrance was located in the oddest of places, inside the pantry of Grandma's Kitchen. The entrance had existed long before the restaurant had occupied the location; she had no idea what purpose the structure had originally served.

"Everyone ready?" Zhang said.

"Yep," Nick said, his stomach growling audibly again. "Unless, of course, I can talk you into stopping for breakfast first."

"Sorry, Nick. We're not on vacation."

"Can't blame a guy for trying."

Three minutes and one heated confrontation with the restaurant manager later, the four of them were standing in the pantry of Grandma's Kitchen. The ancient steel door that led to the Underground was concealed behind a shelf of foodstuffs. Nick grabbed the frame and slid the entire rack away from the wall on silent castors.

"This is how you access the Underground City?" Zhang said with surprise.

Nick nodded. "You didn't know about this access point?"

Zhang shook his head. "No. We have a map of dozens of entrances, but this one, I am not familiar with. Unfettered access to the Underground City is a counterterrorism catastrophe waiting to happen. After this incursion, I will give the order to weld this door shut."

An uneasy silence lingered in the air until Nick said what Dash was thinking: "What happens the next time we need to use it? If you weld this door shut, we all lose access."

"You're the last person who should be making such requests," Zhang said, glaring at Nick. "You're under arrest, remember?"

"I understand your concern, but Nick makes a good point," Dash said, playing peacemaker. "After what happened with Qing, I swore never to come back to this place again, yet here we are, only two months later, once again in need of Gang Jin's help. Maybe you should defer any decision on the door until after this is over."

The way Zhang screwed up his face at her comment, he looked like he'd just sucked on a sour lemon, but after a beat, he said, "All right, I'll defer the decision until after I meet this Gang Jin criminal you both seem to think so highly of."

Nick flashed her a conspiratorial smile and pulled the heavy steel door open to reveal a steep, sloping concrete staircase descending into the blackness. Dash reached into the void and swept her palm along the wall until she felt a metal box. She flicked the switch, and a series of battery-powered red LED lights illuminated the stairwell. Her dead husband, Qing, had installed these lights, making frequent excursions into the Underground City that he'd kept hidden from her during their marriage.

Gooseflesh stood up on her neck.

She wondered if it was the ghost of Qing or the breath of cool air exhaled from the mouth of the Underground rushing over her skin.

"Maybe I should go first?" Nick said, jockeying to step in front of her.

"I'll take point," Zhang said, cutting Nick off.

"But you don't know where you're going," Dash said.

"That's never stopped me before," Zhang said with a wry grin, beginning the descent.

It was cool underground, eighteen degrees Celsius year-round, but it felt stagnant. The air had a faint but pervasive odor that she decided must be an amalgam of damp concrete, rodent feces, and mold. It was not an agreeable smell, and it made her stomach uneasy. A drip of water from the ceiling landed on her scalp, sending an involuntary shiver down her spine.

When he reached the bottom of the staircase, Zhang paused and waited for the rest of them.

"Which way?" he said.

"Right," she and Nick said in unison, gesturing to the long, gaping tunnel that faded into the blackness.

Zhang clicked on an LED flashlight and set off toward the heart of the Underground City.

She could not help but marvel at this place—a sprawling subterranean complex spanning eighty-five square kilometers built under the heart of Beijing. The excavation project was launched in 1969 under Chairman Mao's direction and was originally designed to accommodate half of Beijing's then population of six million in the event of a nuclear attack. More than three hundred thousand laborers had toiled for a decade, excavating and building a complex web of tunnels, staircases, ventilation shafts, drinking-water wells, sewage lines, food production and storage nodes, and mixed-use chambers. But the massive undertaking had been terminated during the Cold War, incomplete, unutilized, and unknown to the rest of the world. Plans had been entertained by the government in the years leading up to the 2008 Summer Olympics to convert the Underground City into a tourist attraction with shops, restaurants, and bars, but the plans had fizzled after the money had run out, leaving the Underground City once again forgotten.

Forgotten by most but not all. Eighty-five square kilometers of climate-controlled real estate infrastructure in a city as crowded and expensive as Beijing does not go unnoticed. A vibrant black-market economy of illicit commerce and real estate brokering flourished beneath the streets. Down below, anything could be had for a price—drugs, sex, weapons, black-market tech, and shelter. It was an *Underground City* in the truest sense, with its own law and leadership. Patrolling gangs who worked for Gang Jin—the Underground City's "mayor"—kept order, enforced the rules, and collected "taxes." The money that flowed through the Underground City now was millions more than city planners had dreamed of for legitimate enterprise. This black-market economy was exactly what Dash hoped to exploit. If anyone in Beijing knew how to plug them into Nèiyè Biologic's illegal organ-trade business, that person would be Gang Jin.

They continued down the dark tunnel, toward a dim yellow glow in the distance. As they walked, the light gradually intensified along with her anxiety. The heated banter they'd shared at Grandma's Kitchen was now replaced by brooding introspection. No one was talking. The tang of testosterone in the air among these three alpha males was almost palpable to her. Zhang had asserted himself as the leader, as he should, but it was also evident to her that should the situation take a turn for the worse, Nick was perfectly willing, and perfectly capable, of taking that mantle. Aboveground, such a scenario would never present itself, but down here . . . different rules applied. Although she dared not say it, in the Underground, Zhang was more of a liability than an asset. Were she traveling with only Nick, she was confident that Gang Jin would receive them and give her request due consideration. But bringing two Snow Leopards into Gang Jin's domain without advance warning could be disastrous. He could see such an act as a betrayal of trust—a traitorous and threatening misjudgment that could destroy the fragile alliance they had built during her last visit.

She reached out and touched Zhang's arm.

"Yes?" he said, keeping his gaze forward down the tunnel.

"I'm not sure how to say this, so I'm just going to say it . . . Down here, you can't be Commander Zhang of the Snow Leopards."

"What are you talking about, Dazhong?"

She felt her cheeks flush and hoped he didn't notice. "When we meet Gang Jin, I think it would be better for you to use a cover identity—strategically speaking, that is."

"I'm not afraid of this Gang Jin. He's a petty criminal."

"He's more than that. He runs the entire Underground, and he has connections in a world that we have no access to. If he feels threatened, he'll become defensive and uncooperative. He might even consider me bringing you here a betrayal."

Zhang stopped walking and turned to face her. "You speak of him like he's an equal—like he's one of us. He's not. He should count himself lucky that I'm not sending my entire unit down here to clean the place out."

"She's right," Nick said, stepping up beside her. "Last time I checked, we didn't have an entire unit of Snow Leopards with us for backup. We walk another hundred meters down this tunnel, and the rules change. Down here, Gang Jin makes the rules. Down here, he's in charge. You trusted us once before, and everything worked out. All we're asking is that you trust us again."

Zhang looked back and forth between them and then grudgingly said, "All right, we do it your way. What's my cover?"

"I haven't decided yet," Dash said. "Let me take the lead. Who you are depends on how things are going."

She glanced at Nick.

He nodded.

"Now I suggest everyone put their guns away, so nobody *accidentally* gets shot."

Zhang hesitated a beat but then holstered his weapon. Lieutenant Chung followed suit.

"Much better." Then, striding off toward the dim light down the tunnel, she added, "Now, if you boys would follow me, please."

After a hundred meters, they reached a section of tunnel brightly lit overhead by regularly spaced yellow halogen lights. Fifty more meters and the tunnel joined a hub where other tunnels and hallways connected. This was the spot, she remembered, where Gang Jin's enforcers met them the last time they forayed into the Underground. She stopped, halting the group in the middle of the domed junction. Two dark side passages intersected their tunnel: one on the left, one on the right. In her peripheral vision, she saw movement. Two men, dressed in black fatigues and bearing submachine guns, stepped out of the shadows and greeted them at gunpoint.

"Hello," she said. "I'm Dr. Dazhong Chen, and these are my colleagues. We would like to speak with Gang Jin."

The sentry on the right eyed her with suspicion, then glanced at Nick, Chung, and Zhang in turn. She saw a flash of recognition in his eyes, then the corners of his mouth curled up into something resembling a smirk.

"I remember you," he said in Mandarin. His eyes flicked to Nick. "And him."

He said something to the other sentry, and both men laughed.

"What'd he say?" Nick whispered.

"I'd rather not translate," she said.

The sentry keyed the radio microphone clipped to his shoulder and requested an audience with the Mayor. The reply came back after a short delay, with Gang Jin's voice on the channel: "Bring them to me."

The lead sentry faced the group and said in stilted English, "No weapons."

Zhang sniffed and narrowed his eyes at the hired gun. "I don't think so."

"Okay, then you stay," the sentry said.

Zhang sighed, and he and Chung handed their weapons over to the guard.

A moment later, two more men dressed in matching black fatigues emerged from the far tunnel. These men were also armed, but their rifles were slung casually across their torsos. They approached the first two sentries and chatted in clipped, rapid Chinese. The collected pistols changed hands, and then one of the newly arrived sentries motioned for Dash and the others to follow him.

The sentries led them to what Dash remembered to be Gang Jin's "city center." Upon reaching the reinforced steel door, one of the sentries entered a code into a wall-mounted security keypad. An LED light blinked green, and the magnetic door lock clicked open. The guard turned to her and nodded with his head for them to enter. She looked at Zhang for one final wordless reminder: *Remember, this is my show. You promised to be good.*

He met her gaze: *I'll behave, I promise.*

Taking the lead, she stepped into Gang Jin's operations center and was relieved to be greeted by a genuine, albeit cautious, smile from Beijing's underworld boss. He looked the same as the last time she'd seen him: clean-shaven, neatly trimmed hair, and dressed in a dapper, expensive Italian suit.

"Two unexpected visitors in one day," Gang Jin said, his hand on the back of a chair facing away from them. "What are the chances?"

On that cue, the chair swiveled, and her heart skipped a beat at the sight of the man sitting in it.

"Lankford?" Nick mumbled, eyes wide with disbelief.

The CIA man flashed them both a wry grin. "Surprise."

CHAPTER 22

The Underground City

"How is this possible?" Nick said, staring, mouth agape, at Lankford. "You were in the safe house when it blew up."

"Actually," Lankford said, getting to his feet, "I made it out before you. I saw you egress, but I couldn't call to you. I tried to catch you in the woods, but I'm old and fat, and all you SEALs are fucking ironmen . . ."

Nick stepped up and pulled the CIA man in for a brotherly hug. "I'm glad you made it out, bro."

"Me too, Nick," Lankford said, clasping an arm around Nick's back. "Me too."

"How is it that you're here? And why didn't you reach out to me sooner?"

"I wanted to contact you, believe me, but I wasn't about to make the same mistake three times," he said with a sardonic smile. "What happened in Discovery Bay convinced me that our entire operation was blown. I couldn't trust my network, and I certainly couldn't trust cyberspace. I assumed you'd come to the same conclusion, and when you did, I knew you would find your way here. If you made it out of Hong Kong alive, then it could only mean that some of my spooky ass had rubbed off on you."

Nick laughed and stepped back to get a read on everyone else's reaction to Lankford's miraculous resurrection. Zhang looked dubious, Dash appeared relieved, and the Mayor of Beijing's Underground City was grinning large—hiding whatever his true feelings were on the subject like the chameleon that he was.

"This is quite the unexpected reunion of old friends today," Gang Jin said to the group before his eyes settled on Zhang and Chung. "Except, I don't believe we've met before—"

"I am Commander Zhang, and this is Lieutenant Chung, of the Snow Leopard Commando Counterterrorism Unit headquartered here in Beijing," Zhang said. Nick watched Zhang's eyes survey Gang Jin's operations room, which was not unlike a military tactical operations center. Half a dozen workstations—each with its own computer, flat-screen monitor, and phone—formed a half oval. The half oval faced a large flat-screen TV monitor mounted on the far wall, the screen divided into eight squares—four to a row—displaying different CCTV feeds of underground passages and cavernous rooms. He could tell from his expression that Zhang was not pleased with what he saw.

The Mayor's gaze flicked to Dash, and for a fleeting instant, Nick saw wounded betrayal in the underworld kingpin's eyes. Dash smiled at the Mayor, her eyes reassuring and kind.

"Don't worry, Commander Zhang and Lieutenant Chung are not here in an *official* capacity."

"Which means you do not have squads of Snow Leopards standing by at entry points around Beijing to storm the Underground City?" Jin said.

"Not today," Zhang said, his face stoic.

Nick winced. Of all the responses the Snow Leopard Commander could have given, that was probably the most inflammatory and dangerous.

"Ah, I see," the Mayor said, smiling wryly. "This is a scouting mission in preparation for your assault to take down the empire I've built."

"If I'd wanted to arrest you, Jin, I would have already seen it done. We've known about your—"

Glaring at Zhang, Dash cleared her throat loudly. "Sorry to interrupt, but as I was saying, the *reason* we're here is because we have a serious problem, and we could use your help."

"And what problem is that?"

"As I'm sure Mr. Lankford already alluded to, someone is trying to kill us."

"Hmm," Gang Jin said, rubbing his chin theatrically. "Now, that is a problem."

"We were hoping that given your particular network of contacts, you might have heard something," Nick said.

"Mr. Lankford already explained to me what happened to Peter Yu and how the retaliation began immediately after Nick arrived in Xi'an to investigate his death."

"That's correct," Dash said. "But there's more to the story. Commander Zhang and I were also investigating Peter Yu's death, but Yu is not the only victim. There are dozens and dozens of victims, including one of our team members—Major Li of the People's Liberation Army, who was murdered at the Port of Hong Kong. We believe all these murders are linked to the biotechnology company Nèiyè Biologic, located in Xi'an."

"I'm sorry to disappoint you," the Mayor said. "But I know nothing of this company. Nor have I heard of any contracts being issued on any of you."

Nick pursed his lips. It had been a reach, but he had hoped that the Mayor would have information on both Nèiyè Biologic and the men trying to kill them. If they were involved in illegal organ harvesting and sales, then it wasn't crazy that the underground mayor's enterprise would have had dealings with Nèiyè. He searched the man's face for any signs of insincerity but found none of the typical tells of deception. He turned his gaze to Dash; he'd seen this look before—she was already working on an alternate plan.

"In that case," she said plainly, "what if I told you I wanted to buy a human liver on the black market for transplant?"

"Then, Dr. Chen," the Mayor said, the corners of his mouth turning up, "I would tell you that this is a problem I can help you with."

"What if I told you I wanted the liver immediately and that I didn't have the time or inclination to languish on some waiting list?" Dash asked.

The Mayor smiled at Dash, ignoring the others as if he was having an intimate conversation with the beautiful scientist. "If you're in a hurry, you will have to pay more."

"Money is no object."

"Do you have a moral objection to a compulsory donor?" he said, narrowing his eyes.

"Of course not," she said, still playing the game. "Oh, and did I mention that I want the organ to be a perfect match?"

"In that case," he said, shrugging, "now we're talking business."

She looked at Nick, and he knew where she was going with this.

"In the last several months, have any new players emerged in the market?" Nick asked.

The Mayor nodded. "Yes, and this player has been very, very busy."

"Why?"

"Because, Nick, they are offering designer organs."

"By designer organs, do you mean organs that are genetically modified in a manner so they are not rejected by the recipient?" Dash asked.

"Such a clever girl," Jin said. "Always one step ahead."

Dash ran her fingers through her hair. "Now this is finally all beginning to make sense," she mumbled. "I think I know what they're doing."

"Know what who is doing?" Zhang asked her.

"I'll explain in a minute," she said and looked back at Jin. "Do you happen to be in contact with this *new player*?"

The Mayor laughed. "Oh, Dazhong, when it comes to the black market, I'm in contact with *all* the players."

"Can you set up a meeting for us?" Zhang interjected.

"For you, Commander Zhang, no," Jin said, wagging a finger. "For the lovely Dazhong, maybe. The people who sell these organs are very sophisticated and very, very cautious. This is not something that happens in five minutes. There is a vetting process. And these organs do not come cheap." He turned back to Dash. "What do you intend to do with this liver?"

"The truth is, we don't actually intend to buy a liver. I believe the people responsible for the genetically modified organ trade are the same people responsible for the murders we're investigating and the same people who are trying to kill us. If we follow the money, I'm certain it will lead to Nèiyè Biologic."

"And when it does," Nick interjected, "we're going to take them down."

Jin laughed loudly at this. "I appreciate your honesty, so let me give you some in return. The black-market organ business, while only a small piece of my operation, is a very profitable one. By helping you, I'm destroying a lucrative revenue stream. What incentive do I have to do this?"

"Three days ago, dozens of corpses washed up on Tung Wan Beach," Dash said. "It was all over the news."

"I saw the reports," Jin said. "Tragic."

"What you didn't hear in the news reports is that all these people were victims of illegal organ harvesting. I know this because I performed the autopsies." She pulled out her mobile phone, and Nick watched as she scrolled through her camera roll. She found the digital photographs she was looking for and handed her phone to Jin. The gangster's eyebrows arched, and his jaw tightened at the graphic images. "They were all young and healthy," Dash continued, "robbed of their eyes, hearts, lungs, kidneys, and livers. They were not willing donors, Jin. Let me be clear: these young men and women were kidnapped and then murdered for their organs."

"But this doesn't make any sense. I was told by my contact that these organs are custom grown in a laboratory to match the DNA of the buyer," Jin said, shaking his head at the grotesquery on display.

"Now the puzzle pieces are finally starting to fit together," Dash said, growing excited. "During Nick's investigation in Xi'an, he met with Peter Yu's girlfriend. She claimed to work as a researcher at Nèiyè Biologic and told Nick her area of expertise was using CRISPR for genetic engineering. If what she said is true, then maybe Nèiyè Biologic is modifying the stolen organs after excision, using CRISPR to match the recipient's alleles to ensure major histocompatibility complex matching."

"You're losing us, Dash," Nick said.

"Sorry, I'm getting ahead of myself," she said, turning to the group like a professor teaching class. "To appreciate why any of this matters, you have to understand the postoperative challenges associated with organ transplant. When someone needs an organ transplant, donor organs are screened based on blood type and other physical criteria until the best match is found for the recipient. But no matter how good a match an organ might be, postoperative rejection is a constant threat, because the DNA in the donor organ tissues can never perfectly match the DNA of the recipient. They are, after all, tissues from two different people. Consequently, organ recipients typically must remain on a cocktail of immunosuppressant drugs for the rest of their lives so their immune systems don't attack and destroy the transplanted organ."

"I can't imagine that taking immunosuppressant drugs for the rest of your life is a good thing," Nick said.

"It's not. The antirejection protocol is very hard on a body. The side effects can include low white blood cell count, anemia, liver inflammation, pancreatitis, kidney toxicity, diabetes, hypertension, gout, and the inability to fight infections. In other words, organ transplant is not a Holy Grail solution. The net result is typically life extension, but not without cost. In many cases, the patient is simply trading one set of problems for another."

"Why not just grow an organ in a laboratory like Jin said?" Zhang asked. "Why go through the trouble of stealing organs and modifying them in the laboratory?"

"If they could do this, they would. Some progress has been made in what's called the 'seed and scaffold' approach to growing simple tissue structures like cartilage and skin," Dash said, "but for organs like the pancreas, liver, and kidneys, the technology does not exist. These organs are complex systems that have metabolic needs and must be tied into the body to function and flourish. They do not survive long outside of the body."

"So how is Nèiyè Biologic changing them to match the host if not in a lab?" Nick asked.

"CRISPR is like a cut-and-paste editing tool on a word processor, except instead of modifying lines of text, it is modifying sections of DNA code." She took a deep breath. "This is only a working theory, but I think they are transplanting the organs into the new host and then using a CRISPR protocol to cut and paste the host's histocompatibility alleles in place of the donor alleles to achieve compatibility over a short period of time, thereby rendering the need for immunosuppressant drugs moot."

"Wait a minute," Nick said, scratching his beard. "So you're saying that if Lankford gave me his liver, when they put it in, it's one hundred percent Lankford's cells, but when they use this CRISPR stuff on it, magically they transform into Nick Foley's cells?"

"They are not changing everything over, just the proteins necessary to prevent an autoimmune response, but basically your analogy is correct."

"Jesus," Lankford said. "This is one hell of an operation they've got going on. What do you estimate the market for this sort of thing could be?"

Nick looked to Dash for an answer, and she shook her head. "I have no idea, but what I can tell you is that if this approach is working, the number of candidates for organ transplant would skyrocket, thereby creating a strong demand for organ donors."

"Why is that?"

"Because right now, the best candidates for organ transplant are people who are young and healthy. As I said, the postoperative immunosuppressant drug protocol is hard on a body, especially so for the elderly. To remove that requirement would provide a dramatic opportunity for life extension for the aged population."

"You said that this 'new player' in the black-market organ trade is charging a higher premium for their organs," Nick said, looking at the Mayor. "How much higher, say, for a kidney?"

"A regular kidney sells for around one hundred thousand US dollars. The genetically modified one is going for three hundred thousand," Jin said, still thumbing through the autopsy images on Dash's phone.

"I think that tells us something about the clientele. The only people who can afford these organs are the affluent. What can you tell us about clients you've made connections for?" Lankford asked Jin.

But Jin ignored him, his attention fully devoted to an image on Dash's phone. "How is this possible?" he muttered under his breath.

Nick leaned in to see what Jin was looking at.

"How is what possible?" Dash asked.

"I think that girl was one of mine."

"What do you mean, 'one of yours'?"

"That tattoo—a curled dragon devouring its own tail—is very distinctive. A girl who worked in Club Pink had a tattoo just like that on the inside of her forearm. She was a runaway and ended up here. She told me she wanted to be a doctor someday. I told her I would help her get into university if she could stay drug-free for three months."

"What happened to her?" Nick asked.

"I don't know. She disappeared. She's been gone about a month. The Underground City has a transient population. Runaways move around more than others," he said.

Nick leaned over closer to see the screen more clearly as Jin scrolled through the pictures. He kept swiping until he found the girl's haunting, eyeless visage.

The Mayor grunted his disgust and displeasure at the sight. "It's her."

"I'm sorry, Jin," Dash said.

Nick saw the muscles in Gang Jin's jaw tighten before he spoke. "I didn't realize . . ."

"Nobody did," Dash said, trying—Nick thought—to ease the guilt they could all see he was piling on his conscience.

The Mayor of the Underground City handed the phone back to Dash and said, "I will help you put an end to this. What do you need?"

They listened without interrupting while Dash laid out her plan to go undercover as an intermediary representing a wealthy organ buyer. If Jin could facilitate a meeting, then Zhang and Nick could orchestrate an "intervention"—her word for what Nick knew would likely involve gunfire and death to capture the principals, whoever they were. Once they cracked the facade, they could bring the entire corrupt operation tumbling down and, in doing so, find out how high the conspiracy went. When she'd finished talking, the Mayor looked at Nick and said, "Are you seriously going to let her do this?"

"Absolutely not," Nick said, staring at Dash with a look that would make his feelings—about both her and her plan—quite obvious.

"These are very dangerous people, Dazhong," Jin said, turning back to her. "The client meetings never take place in the Underground City. As a facilitator, I can make the introduction and vouch for your cover story, but if they feel threatened, if something goes wrong, I will not be able to help you."

"I understand, but I won't be alone. I'll wear a wire, and I have the best backup in the world in case anything happens—two Snow Leopards, a Navy SEAL, and the CIA," she said, turning to her friends. "Right?"

A stone-faced Zhang didn't say anything. Then, after a long beat, he slowly nodded. "That's right."

"You can't seriously intend to go along with this plan of using Dash as shark bait," Nick protested.

"Given her medical knowledge, she is the most qualified person for the operation. We are being hunted, and time is of the essence," Zhang said. "I don't see a better path forward."

"Then at least let me come with you," Nick protested. "You can pretend I'm your client—a wealthy American who can't get an organ in the US."

"Be realistic, Nick," Dash said with a patronizing smile. "Look in the mirror. You're the picture of perfect health. No one would believe that you are suffering from renal failure, or liver failure, or any other organ failure for that matter."

"Then I . . . I can be your bodyguard."

"You don't speak Chinese, Nick," Zhang said, placing a hand on his shoulder.

Nick looked desperately at Lankford.

"They have a point," the CIA man said with a shrug.

"She won't be alone," Zhang said. "Lieutenant Chung can be her escort. We'll set up a mobile command center, and the three of us will monitor everything. As soon as she makes contact, we will intervene and grab the organ broker, and then it's our turn to ask the questions."

Nick didn't like the plan, but their options were severely limited. They were targets for assassination, and the only way to turn the tables was to penetrate the enemy's network. He swallowed hard but didn't say anything.

"Good," Dash said, a little too optimistically. "It's settled."

Jin eyed her dubiously like a concerned big brother. After a long pause, he said, "For the record, I agree with Nick, but I'll do as you ask."

"Thank you," she said. "I knew I could count on you."

Jin sighed. "First things first, I need the details of your cover identity. It must be perfect. Like I said, these people don't fuck around."

"Don't worry. It will be solid," Zhang said. "I'll build it myself, and Lieutenant Chung can help me populate the government databases."

"And you'll need to make an earnest deposit. One hundred thousand dollars, nonrefundable."

Zhang screwed up his face. "One hundred thousand US dollars?"

Jin nodded.

"I'll need signatory approval to move that much money. Given our current situation, that's impossible," Zhang said.

"Without the money, you have no chance of securing a meeting," the Mayor said.

After a long, sobering pause, Lankford grumbled. "Give me the routing information, and I'll make it happen."

"You will?" Zhang and Nick said with simultaneous disbelief.

"Those bastards murdered Peter, blew up my safe house along with four of my staff, and tried to kill me and Foley," Lankford said. "Consider this my down payment on revenge."

CHAPTER 23

Qin Shi Huang Terracotta Warrior Museum
Xi'an, China

"Let me do all the talking," Dash said to Lieutenant Chung as they approached the entrance to the museum.

"Understood," the young Snow Leopard Officer replied.

"Even if they ask you a question directly, please defer to me. For the purposes of this meeting, you are my hired security. I do not require your participation in the negotiation, even if things appear to be going badly."

"Yes, Dr. Chen."

"And try to look a little bit more intimidating."

Chung's jaw hardened, and his caramel-colored eyes bore into her with a cold hatred that made her take an involuntary step backward.

"Not *that* intimidating."

His scowl evaporated, and he winked at her.

They walked across the courtyard to the entrance of the museum. She purchased two tickets and moved into one of two security checkpoint lines where tourists were opening their backpacks for inspection. Lieutenant Chung was dressed innocuously in street clothes instead of his usual all-black tactical uniform, but when it was their turn in queue, he provided his Snow Leopard ID to the checkpoint security guard and discreetly informed the young man that he was carrying a concealed weapon. Dash's pulse jumped when the guard's right hand immediately shifted to the grip of his sidearm. Cool and collected, Chung asked that the guard call in the request over the radio to his supervisor, assuring him that arrangements had already been made with the museum director and chief of security. Eyeing Chung with suspicion, the guard made the call. The answer came back after a brief delay, and two minutes later, they were inside the main exhibit hall, incident-free.

Despite being Chinese born and raised, this was Dash's first visit to the Terracotta Warrior Museum. It was something she'd always wanted to see, but the trip to Xi'an was one she'd never taken the time to make. The main exhibit hall, or vault one, was the largest and most famous of the exhibits. The sheer enormity of the space was breathtaking. At 230 meters long east to west, by 62 meters wide north to south, the domed exhibit reminded her of an aircraft hangar. An elevated perimeter-observation track surrounded an open excavation pit, giving visitors a 360-degree view of the two thousand fully excavated warriors standing in parallel columns. An estimated six thousand fire-clay warriors and horses remained to be unearthed.

"This is unbelievable," she said to Chung, staring across row after row of tightly packed life-size figures. "I've never seen anything like this before."

"I don't know," Chung replied. "Looks like every sidewalk in Beijing at rush hour."

"You're just like Zhang. Nothing impresses you guys."

"Oh, that's not true," he said with a sardonic smile. "The new Shenyang J-31 stealth fighter is pretty impressive."

"Boys and their guns," she said, shaking her head for dramatic effect.

She saw Chung's expression suddenly darken. She turned and followed his gaze to a middle-aged Chinese man in a suit approaching, flanked by four security guards. The guards were dressed in uniforms matching the ones worn by the guards at the museum entrance checkpoint. The entourage stopped in front of them.

"You must be Ming Su Lin," the businessman said to her and flashed her a vulpine grin, showing a mouthful of perfectly straight, perfectly white polished teeth. She disliked him immediately.

She forced a smile. "Yes, and this is my associate, Xi Hicheng," she said, gesturing to Lieutenant Chung.

The businessman extended his hand. "You may call me Mr. Lu."

She took his hand and decided he was probably using a cover identity just as she and Lieutenant Chung were. Mr. Lu's grip was cold and hard as stone. She squeezed his hand politely, which he returned with just enough pressure to make her wince. A shiver snaked down her spine. Something was awry with this man. She sensed a keen agitation lurking just below the surface. He reminded her of a wounded animal—unpredictable, dangerous, and in pain.

He released her hand.

Without even acknowledging Chung's presence, Lu turned to face the exhibit, placing both his hands on the railing. "It's a pity," he said, gazing at the exhibit below.

"What's a pity?" she said, playing along.

"This," he said, gesturing to the terracotta army.

"I don't understand."

He didn't elaborate. After a beat, he said, "I'm a descendant of his."

"A descendant of who?"

"The First Emperor of China, Qin Shi Huang."

"Is that so?" she said, trying to navigate her way through the disjointed conversation. "He was a great leader, they say—the first leader to unite China under singular rule and law."

"He was a fool—superstitious and single-minded. The true genius behind all the Emperor's accomplishments was his second in command, Chancellor Li Si."

For a split second, she swore she saw malice in his eyes, but then he smiled warmly at her. "I have a surprise for you," he said, stepping away from the rail. "Come, follow me."

"Where are we going?" she asked, not moving.

"Down into the vault," he said. "I've arranged a private tour, so you can approach the warriors. They are more impressive up close. Every face is unique, did you know that?"

She nodded. "Yes, I think I remember reading that."

"Come," he said, beckoning her.

She glanced at Chung. He gave a single shake of his head.

"I'd rather conduct our business here," she said.

Mr. Lu's smile evaporated. "Impossible," he said, gesturing at the throngs of tourists mulling about. "Either we move to a more private location, or we part company. Make your decision now, because we will not meet again."

"All right," she said after a beat, feeling Chung's disapproving gaze on her. "Let's go."

Mr. Lu's smile returned. "Excellent."

He played tour guide, talking and gesturing as he led her and Chung down into the vault: "Every warrior, horse, and chariot was hand fashioned and intricately painted. Unfortunately, the paint has long since eroded, which is why all the statues are now the color of gray earth. But even without the paint, the diversity in facial structure and expression is remarkable—you can almost feel the soul of each warrior. I believe this authenticity can only be attributed to the fact that artisans did not use molds. Some estimates indicate that hundreds of thousands of laborers were conscripted to build the necropolis and the terracotta army, most of them toiling a lifetime on the project, with death serving as their only release."

She smiled and nodded, feigning polite interest as the man—with his four armed guards in tow—guided her and Chung on an intimate tour of the main exhibit. She knew this type of access was ordinarily reserved only for heads of state. It was a once-in-a-lifetime opportunity, but she was not able to enjoy the moment because her nerves were on fire and her heart was pounding like a bass drum. What game was this guy playing? There had to be some reason for this private tour besides satisfying his ego by showing off his knowledge of ancient Chinese history. She glanced at Chung for reassurance, but the Snow Leopard didn't notice because his eyes were scanning the area.

"Fascinating," she mumbled, turning back to look at Lu during a pause in his monologue.

"But not as fascinating as what I'm about to tell you next. Do you know why the Emperor commissioned the terracotta warriors to be made?"

"Because he was delusional," she said, feeling the chill of a thousand blank stares from the warrior statues. "They say the Emperor believed he could take them with him into the afterlife, where they would serve as his eternal army," she said.

"You know your history," he said with an awkward smile. "But the Emperor was not delusional, just obsessed. He was obsessed with immortality. He was obsessed with finding the Elixir of Life. He spent decades searching for it, organizing pilgrimages all across China. And do you want to know the greatest irony of all this?"

She nodded.

"He died during his third pilgrimage to Zhifu Island. The search for immortality was his ultimate and final undoing. If only the First Emperor were alive today, I would tell him the *truth* about the Elixir of Life and watch his reaction."

She raised an eyebrow at him. "What truth?"

He leaned in and whispered to her, "The Elixir of Life is not a pill or a potion. You could search the world over and never find it—the secret is locked inside each and every one of us."

"Locked inside of us?" she repeated.

"Yes," he said, but when he pulled away, all the excitement and enthusiasm was gone from him. In a flat voice, he said, "I assume you are a proxy, sent here to negotiate on your client's behalf."

"Yes," she said, folding her arms across her chest. "Did you receive our wire transfer?"

"We did."

"Good, so we are ready to proceed with the next steps?"

"Almost, but first, tell me about yourself and your client. Personal history and motivations are a very important part of this process."

She swallowed and regurgitated the cover story they had concocted as a group in the Underground City with Gang Jin's help. He listened thoughtfully, nodding as he did, while he led them out of the vault and into an underground hallway. He paused at a doorway labeled "Restricted, No Access" and waved one of his security guards up to unlock the door.

Chung placed a hand on her shoulder, stopping her. "Where are we going?" Chung asked, eyeing Lu with cold suspicion.

"Vault three," Lu said, "to continue our tour."

"Vault three is that way," Chung said, pointing off to their right.

"He's right," she said, her stomach suddenly going sour.

Lu sighed. "I told you, this is a private tour. We have access to restricted areas, off-limits to tourists. I promise, Dr. Chen, you won't be disappointed."

Dash sensed movement behind her and felt a bee sting on the side of her neck. No, not a bee sting—the prick of a hypodermic needle and the subsequent burn as one of the guards injected her with a sedative. As the fog began to take her, she watched Lieutenant Chung pull his semiautomatic pistol from inside the flap of his jacket.

Muzzle flashes and the roar of gunfire erupted in the tiny corridor.

"No," she heard herself say and felt her knees buckle as the world went black.

CHAPTER 24

Parking lot outside the Terracotta Warrior Museum
Lintong District, Xi'an, Shaanxi, China
1430 hours local

When Nick was with the Teams downrange, the worst thing in the world was to not be out on the mission. It wasn't boredom or wishing you were in the action—though those things were present for any SEAL not operating on the tip of the spear. It was sitting in the TOC—the tactical operations center—listening to the radio comms, watching IR imagery from overhead drones as your teammates converged on a target, seeing the firefight unfold, and knowing you could do nothing to help your brothers. It was the helplessness that men trained to engage had to learn to overcome. As a SEAL, he had not handled "inaction" well.

This was worse.

Nick sat on a narrow, round stool inside the Nissan NV cargo van in front of the dark computer screen. Zhang and Lankford sat crowded in beside him, both on their own stools. Zhang had brought two other trusted Snow Leopards with them from Beijing, explaining that "four Snow Leopards were an exponentially more effective assault force than two," a fact Nick understood well from his time with the SEALs. One of Zhang's men sat behind the wheel in the driver's seat, the other cross-legged on the floor at the back of the van, cradling an assault rifle. A crick in his neck was starting to antagonize Nick, and he desperately wanted to stand and stretch his spine out. Yet despite the extrahigh ceiling in the cargo area, the headroom wasn't sufficient to stand in the van that Lankford insisted on calling the Snow Leopard Mystery Machine—a Scooby-Doo homage that none of their Chinese comrades understood, regardless of how many times he repeated it. After the fifth reference, Nick tried explaining as much to the man, but Lankford was undeterred.

Presently, the CIA man was alternately humming and singing the Scooby-Doo theme song, sprinkling in only those lyrics he could remember.

"Jesus, Lankford," Nick growled when he finally couldn't take it anymore. "Are you always this annoying on a mission?"

"Only when I'm bored."

"Well, try to get unbored, because they just entered the building."

"All right, all right," Lankford sighed. "But you do know the organ broker is not going to show. There's no way *this* meeting goes down inside *that* place. Too crowded. Too much security."

"What are you saying?"

"They're scouting us. They'll stay hidden, get some pictures, validate Chen and Chung's fake identities, and then request a second meeting . . . undoubtedly at night, somewhere where they'll have the upper hand. Trust me, this is not my first rodeo."

Zhang shushed Lankford while wearing a harsh scowl. "I can't hear when you talk so much."

Nick nodded in agreement, but Lankford made a good point, and it calmed his nerves. Through the headset he wore over his right ear—the left earpiece pushed back so he could hear the conversation inside the van—he could hear Dash and Chung talking in clipped Chinese. He waited for Zhang or Lankford to translate for him, but neither man seemed inclined to do so at the moment, which meant either the dialogue was not important or it was very important. Given the intonation of Dash's voice, he assumed the former.

"What's going on?" he whispered to Lankford.

"They're through security," Lankford said.

More talking, then a prolonged pause, followed by a new voice—male, Chinese.

"Well, I'll be damned," Lankford whispered. "I was wrong. The meet is a go."

"Her contact says his name is Mr. Lu," Zhang said, pulling up an employee directory for Nèiyè Biologic. "I'm sure it's a legend, but it's worth checking."

"He's asking them to follow him," Lankford added.

"Where?" Nick asked.

Zhang raised a hand, listening, and then said, "Down into the vault for a VIP tour of the statues."

"I don't like it," Nick said, and his leg began to bounce up and down like a piston. He could tell from the sound of Dash's voice that she didn't like it either. "Did she refuse?"

"Yeah, but . . ." Lankford said, "Lu just gave her an ultimatum."

Her voice sounded very tense now. "We need to pull her, or go in."

"Relax, Foley," Lankford said, but his face was more sympathetic than his tone. "This isn't the SEAL Teams. We can't just kick in doors with a capture/kill agenda and hose down the joint. This is spycraft—it's how the game is played."

"Hang strong, Nick Foley," Zhang said. "They are in one of the most crowded museums in the world, and she is with Lieutenant Chung. He will keep her safe."

"Hang tough," Nick mumbled, and Zhang's left eyebrow rose, expressing his confusion. "The expression is 'hang tough,' not 'hang strong,'" Nick explained. "What are they saying now?"

"He's talking about the First Emperor and the history of the terracotta warriors . . . Everything is fine. Give it time . . ." Zhang suddenly lifted a closed fist.

"What happened?" Nick demanded, trying to make sense of the gibberish in his headphones.

"What did Lu just call her?" Lankford said, his voice sharp.

Zhang jerked his headset off and flung it at the console. "We have a problem," he said, abruptly standing.

"Shit, they're blown," Lankford said. "Lu called her Dr. Chen. We gotta move."

A heartbeat later, Nick heard the unmistakable staccato crack of gunfire over the comms channel. He jumped to his feet and banged his head on the ceiling in the process. Zhang passed a rifle to the driver and tossed the Snow Leopard in the back an extra magazine, while Nick snatched a QBZ-95 fully automatic assault rifle from the rack for himself. He looked over at Zhang, expecting him to order him and Lankford to wait in the van, but to his astonishment, the Snow Leopard Commander simply nodded and passed each of them a tactical vest emblazoned with Chinese symbols above the English words "SPECIAL POLICE GRP."

"We must hurry," Zhang said, and Nick slipped the two additional magazines of thirty rounds each into the magazine pouch on the front of his vest.

He followed Zhang out of the van and shifted automatically into combat mode. The instant his feet hit the ground, he dropped into a low tactical crouch, weapon at the ready. He fell in next to Zhang, but they hadn't made it two steps when the screech of tires caused him to freeze. He spun right and watched a black SUV swerve and lock its brakes, coming to a halt in front of their van. A second vehicle executed the same maneuver behind them, boxing them in. Nick raised his rifle into firing position and pressed himself against the side of the van. He was well positioned to engage the front SUV and had to trust that Zhang's Snow Leopards would take the rear, splitting the threat with him.

The front SUV's doors flew open, and four men stepped out with Chinese assault rifles up and at the ready. Instead of tactical gear, these operators were dressed in dark suits, reminding Nick of the men who had tried to kill him on his first trip to Xi'an. He clenched his jaw and tensed his finger on the trigger guard of his rifle. He took aim through the iron sights of the rifle and placed a mental dot on the forehead of the armed agent closest to him.

Behind him someone, not Zhang, barked something in Chinese.

"Hold your fire," Zhang ordered in English.

Nick kept his finger outside of the trigger guard but kept his weapon up.

"What the hell is going on, Zhang?" Lankford yelled from somewhere behind Nick.

"A misunderstanding," Zhang yelled in English. Then he barked something else in Chinese.

More urgent and angry conversation in Chinese transpired around him while Nick and the Chinese suits played 5.8 × 42 mm brinkmanship.

"Commander Zhang is mistaken. There is no misunderstanding," a female voice said in English as a pair of shapely legs stepped out of the lead SUV. "In fact, I think everything is now crystal clear."

Nick shifted his gaze to the female agent and knew immediately that things had taken a turn for the worse. This woman was angry . . . very, very angry. At first glance, she was a doppelgänger for Dash, but upon closer scrutiny, their resemblance diverged. Where Dash's eyes were kind and empathetic, the female agent's gaze was angry and hard. Where Dash's beauty was soft and feminine, this woman's angular features might as well have been chiseled from stone.

She fixed her eyes directly on him, and as she spoke, it felt as if she was driving an iron spike straight into his heart.

"My name is Agent Ling Ju, of the Ministry of State Security," she announced. "Nick Foley and Chet Lankford, you are both under arrest for espionage against the People's Republic of China."

CHAPTER 25

For a split second, Zhang actually considered shooting the bitch. Yes, it would be impetuous, completely irrational, and even immoral, but in the heat of the moment, none of that mattered. Agent Ling Ju and her men in black had become an obstacle between him and Dazhong, and he didn't *do* obstacles.

"Lower your weapons and step aside," he shouted at her. "This is a counterterrorism operation. You and your men are interfering. Every second wasted puts lives in danger."

Ling flashed him a smug scowl and started to argue, but he cut her off.

The words came with such fury that he drew stares from the gunmen on both sides. "Enough. I said step aside!"

Zhang saw trigger fingers shift from guards to triggers.

"We don't have time for this shit, Zhang," Nick called out. "Go."

"What?" he said, turning to the American SEAL.

"Just go," Nick said. "We're all right."

"How the fuck are we all right?" Lankford demanded from behind him.

"Please, go," Nick said, ignoring his CIA counterpart's protest. "Save her."

Zhang nodded at the American and then turned to Ling. "This isn't over," he growled, then gave the hand signal to his men to move out. Without a backward glance, he took off in a sprint toward the museum, daring Ling and her men to shoot him in the back.

No bullets were fired.

He reached the museum in less than a minute and breached the main doors. The expansive vestibule was on lockdown, with visitors and staff crouched and cowering behind pillars, information kiosks, and in some instances, each other.

"Down in the vault," a woman shouted at him from his left. "I heard many gunshots."

"Which way?"

"That way," she answered, pointing to his ten o'clock.

Zhang signaled to his two teammates to advance. Taking point, he moved in a combat crouch toward a stairwell leading down to the vault. His feet flew down the stairs with blind precision as he sighted over his rifle for threats. At the bottom landing, he took a knee, and he felt his teammates shift into the ready position behind him. At the tap on his left shoulder, he stood, scanned forward, and then swung left to clear his left rear corner. As he scanned for shooters waiting in ambush, his mind was already processing the visual details he'd taken in from the rapid sweep—rows of warrior statues to his right, a deserted corridor leading away into shadow.

No, not deserted . . . There were bodies on the floor.

"Clear," he barked and advanced on the corridor.

Three bodies, none of them Dr. Chen, lay sprawled in the geometries of death. They were dressed as security personnel—in gray trousers and dark-blue blazers—but had short Type 79 submachine guns connected with slings under their coats. The two closest men had bullet holes in their foreheads. The other lay facedown.

Nice work, Lieutenant Chung.

He stepped over the bodies, still scanning over his rifle, and advanced on the closed doorway ahead. At the door, he paused to glance at his fellow operators. Both men nodded. He counted down in a whisper: "Three, two, one . . ."

He breached the door with a sharp, hard kick. He entered the space, his rifle up, finger on the trigger. The room appeared to be a restoration and storage space, containing several statues in various states of repair and numerous wooden crates. In his peripheral vision, he saw black-booted feet sticking out from behind a wooden crate littered with bullet holes. Clearing left and right, he fast-stepped—still in a combat crouch—toward the boots, the pit in his stomach confirming what he would find.

He signaled for his teammates to clear the room while he rolled Lieutenant Chung gently over onto his back. There was no reason to check a pulse—the left side of Chung's head was gone, evaporated by a burst of 7.62 rounds from the enemy submachine guns capable of emptying a magazine in less than two seconds. The crate beside him dripped with Chung's blood and something else unpleasant.

Zhang stood, raising his weapon to the ready. "Status," he barked into his mike. One voice answered in the earpiece in his left ear.

"All clear," his Snow Leopard told him.

Moments later, they were beside him and moving together to a heavy metal door marked "Exit" at the far end of the room. Zhang breached first, clearing the concrete landing that served as a loading dock. He moved swiftly along the concrete apron out into the bright sunlight, his men falling in beside him.

The loading and parking area behind the building was vast—and empty.

Zhang dropped his weapon to his side and lowered his head.

She's gone . . . I've failed.

"Now what?" his teammate asked.

"First, clear the museum and question the witnesses. Also, I want to know if the three dead guards are museum employees or hired help playing dress-up. I presume the latter. Review the security camera footage. I want face shots of these bastards; send the images to my phone. When the local police arrive, let them know it is a counterterrorism operation and we are in charge, but get their help in gathering information. If anyone gives you resistance, call me." He turned his attention to the shorter but solidly built man to his left. "You come with me."

The first operator moved back through the door, which clicked shut behind them. Zhang then sprinted around the building, his rifle in a low-slung position, and across the parking lot to their black NV van, the rear door still open on its hinges. His subordinate kept pace, his own rifle still up. Zhang jumped through the open door into the rear compartment.

"Any trace of our friends from Guoanbu?" he asked.

"None," his subordinate answered, scanning the parking lot. "Nor the Americans."

Zhang sat at the control panel and picked up one of the headsets, pressing one earpiece to his left ear. There was soft static. Zhang switched to the other two channels and heard nothing. Dazhong's transmitter was dead. He tapped the mouse for the center computer in the row, and it flickered to life, but the left window, which should have been bouncing with yellow lines, was flat and still. Zhang slammed his fist down on the counter in frustration, and the other two screens flickered to life, both showing only screen savers with the Snow Leopard emblem in the center of a blue field.

To find the bastard who took her, he needed help.

He needed the Americans back.

Peter Yu had been a CIA asset. Zhang's gut told him that Lankford and Foley knew more than they were letting on about Nèiyè Biologic. By the time the Guoanbu was done with them, Dazhong would be dead.

Zhang grimaced, realizing that what he was about to do was career-ending. In China, it might be life-ending.

Fuck it.

"Get in," he said to the other operator.

Zhang unsnapped his rifle from its sling and moved through the passage to the front. He set his QBZ-95 on the floor and slid into the driver's seat. The other Snow Leopard slipped into the front passenger seat and buckled in.

"Where are we going?" the man asked.

Zhang started the ignition. "Whatever happens," he said, putting the heavy, overpowered van into gear, "remember you were following orders. The agents we are prosecuting are potentially involved in a conspiracy to cover up the murder of dozens of innocents and the assassination of Major Li."

"You really think the MSS is involved?"

"I don't know," he said, answering honestly. "But their intervention enabled the people who killed Lieutenant Chung and kidnapped Dr. Chen to escape. And we know something else . . ."

"What's that, sir?"

"That Nick Foley and Chet Lankford aren't responsible."

"We know that," the young Snow Leopard replied, "but I don't think Agent Ling cares."

Zhang pressed the accelerator to the floor and headed toward the MSS field office in Xi'an. He weaved in and out of the traffic along the four-lane highway, heading into downtown.

"I see them," his comrade said after several minutes, pointing at the two black SUVs caravanning ahead. "What's the plan, sir?"

"The plan is to bluff an assault and take the Americans back."

"Seriously?"

"Seriously. No lethal force, do you understand? We come at them hard, but if they call the bluff, we surrender. Is that clear?"

"Yes, sir." The young man said, looking more and more unsettled as the implications of his Commander's words sunk in.

In the left lane, Zhang closed the gap to the rear vehicle. The SUV's windows were tinted dark, and he couldn't make out the occupants inside. Standard procedure for the Snow Leopards would be for the rear vehicle to clear tails while the lead vehicle transported the detainees. Time to put his tactical driving prowess to the test. With his front bumper even with the SUV's rear tires, Zhang cut the wheel right, hitting the SUV's left rear corner panel. The SUV veered violently to the left, and Zhang felt the van losing control. He jerked the wheel hard into a correction, skidding onto the right shoulder and barely managing to keep the vehicle on the road. With traction regained, he piloted the van behind the SUV and then accelerated clear as the rear SUV spun out of control. In his side mirror, he watched the black vehicle spin off the road, dropping nose first into the ditch on the left highway shoulder.

The lead SUV began to accelerate, but it was too late. Zhang cut left, hitting the SUV in the right rear quarter panel and again accelerating through the impact. The black SUV spun in the opposite direction this time, and Zhang cut his wheel, spinning to a stop beside the SUV, his passenger side coming to rest against the passenger side of the SUV. Zhang and then his teammate were out of the van in seconds, rifles up and trained on the driver and Agent Ling.

"Step out of the vehicle with your hands in the air," Zhang commanded.

"Are you mad?" the female MSS agent asked as she crawled over from the passenger's seat and exited on the driver's side of the SUV. Unlike her driver, who had complied and raised his hands over his head, she placed her hands defiantly on her hips, her right hand near the butt of the pistol on her belt. "You're going to burn for this, Zhang. This is treason."

"It's not treason, Special Agent Ling," Zhang said. He needed to hurry, before the men in the SUV several hundred yards behind regained their composure and came to her aid. "You simply don't have all the information. There are deadly forces at work against us. Our bioterrorism counterterrorism task force has been targeted. Major Li of the PLA has been assassinated, and my CDC team member, Dr. Chen, has been kidnapped. The two Americans in your custody are critical to my investigation. I am afraid you'll just have to trust me on this."

"Trust you?" Ling demanded and took a step toward him, despite the assault rifle pointed at her chest. "You demand my trust as you point your weapon at me? You will go to prison for this."

"I don't have time to debate this with you. You have trusted me once before, though I can see you do not remember."

Ling's face contorted as recognition flickered in her eyes.

Zhang smiled at her and called out, "Nick Foley and Chet Lankford, exit the vehicle and come with me."

The driver-side rear door opened, there was some fumbling, and then Foley and Lankford emerged. Zhang turned back to Ling.

"We met in Juba two years ago, although I was working under an alias. The situation was similar: you were working with incomplete information and nearly made a career-ending mistake then as well. But I moved some chess pieces to help you."

Ling looked at him more closely, her brow knitted up. "That was you?"

Zhang nodded.

Nick and Lankford were behind him now.

"Get in the van," he said over his shoulder. Then he smiled at Ling. "Give me forty-eight hours. That's all I ask; then you can do what you must."

Sudden movement from his left made Zhang swing his weapon that way, his eyes still on Agent Ling. He spied a weapon over the roof of the SUV. His teammate saw it too and swiveled his rifle . . .

"Stop!" Ling yelled, turning to face her men. "Weapons down." Then she looked back at Zhang. "You have forty-eight hours. If you're not back in Xi'an turning the Americans over to my custody, then I'm coming for you."

Zhang lowered his rifle and gestured with his hand for his Snow Leopard teammate to join the Americans in the van.

"I understand," he said.

Ling walked over to him and placed a business card in the breast pocket of his uniform.

"My contact information, should you need assistance finding your way to my office," she said. Then, without a trace of warmth or humor, she whispered, "Consider my debt repaid. Oh, and Commander Zhang, the next time you point a weapon at me or my men will be the last mistake you make."

Zhang nodded, then stepped left, raised his rifle, and fired two three-round bursts into the engine compartment of the SUV. There was a loud squeal and then a hiss of steam. He shrugged.

"In case you change your mind."

His eyes on Ling, he backed away and slipped into the driver's seat of the van. He gunned the engine, spun the wheel, and headed back east on the highway. As they roared past the other SUV stuck in the ditch, two agents dressed in dark suits looked up and shouted inaudible curses. With a smirk on his face, Zhang looked in the rearview mirror at Nick in the back seat.

"That was fucking insane," Nick said, shaking his head.

"You've got balls, Zhang," Lankford laughed, joining in. "Giant, forged-from-steel, Snow Leopard balls. What you just did for us . . . Jesus Christ, I've never seen anything like that."

"No offense, but I didn't do it for you. This case is spiraling out of control, and I need your help."

"Give us the sitrep," Nick said. "What happened at the museum?"

Zhang grimaced. "They took Dr. Chen, and Lieutenant Chung is dead."

"Shit," Lankford said.

"We've gotta find her," Nick said, clutching the QBZ-95 rifle cradled in his lap. "Every second we waste, the chances of finding her alive get worse."

"I know," Zhang said, meeting Nick's gaze, "but I promise, we're not going to let that happen."

CHAPTER 26

Nèiyè Biologic Citation II corporate jet
24,000 feet, cruising altitude, en route from Xi'an to Hong
Kong
1645 hours local

Her mouth was a desert . . . so parched and dry that Dash couldn't gather enough saliva to wet her tongue or swallow. And her eyelids were iron curtains—so heavy that she couldn't muster the energy to open them. Sleep beckoned. She was aware of the rhythmic rise and fall of her chest; the very sensation of breathing was a sweet lullaby.

She let herself drift off . . .

Her bed shook.

Not her bed—she was slumped in a chair.

Where am I?

"Nick?" she mumbled.

She tried to open her eyes, but it was too bright. She tried again, this time squinting until a blurry world grudgingly came into focus. She was on a plane—the private jet en route to Hong Kong. She'd missed her dinner with Nick because they had summoned her to investigate something that happened on Tung Wan Beach.

It was just a dream . . . a strange, terrible dream.

"You talk in your sleep," a voice said.

Adrenaline surged through her body like chemical lightning, scorching the brain fog away and jolting her completely awake.

Sitting across the aisle from her was a man, a man she recognized. The name came to her a heartbeat later: *Mr. Lu.* But that was not his real name. Memories rushed in to fill the void the sedative had hollowed out in her mind; the imagery played like a film in fast-forward, starting with her arrival in Hong Kong all the way to the present. This was not a dream; she'd been taken. And Chung . . . Chung was most certainly dead.

She scanned the rest of the cabin and confirmed her gut feeling: they were alone.

"Tell me about Nick," her kidnapper said and took a loud, crunching bite of apple.

"Excuse me?"

"You've been mumbling on and on about Nick for the past hour. What is he to you?"

She folded her arms across her chest. "Nick is none of your business."

He smiled at her—that perfectly symmetrical, polished, bone-chilling smile he'd flashed her when they'd first met. He had shed the suit coat and tie, his expensive and highly starched collar now open. There was a hint of tattoo ink above the V-neck undershirt, and his wiry forearms, now visible as his shirtsleeves were impeccably rolled to just below his elbows, were also painted in rich designs and symbols of black ink. She saw the symbol for "discipline" just above his right wrist.

"The subconscious sings unbridled when the conscious mind is caged," he said. "Do you love him?"

"Where are you taking me?" she asked, shunning his probe.

He did not answer and instead took another bite of apple, staring at her while he chewed. He no longer looked like the businessman she had met, but instead a predator of sorts. *A predator and a murderer,* she corrected herself.

"Where are you taking me?" she asked again, emphasizing each syllable, her anger rising in tandem with her fear.

"You answer my questions, and I'll answer yours. That's how it works, Dr. Chen."

A chill ran down her neck. *Dr. Chen . . . oh God, he knows my real identity, but how?*

"I'll ask you again—tell me about Nick?"

"Nick is a friend," she stammered. "Now where are you taking me?"

"I'm taking you to see my organ-harvesting operation," he said flatly. "Does Nick work for the American CIA?"

"No. Where specifically are you taking me?"

"Hong Kong. Are you in love with Nick?"

"No," she snapped. "Where in Hong Kong?"

"That is a lie, so it appears our question-and-answer time is over," he said and took another bite of apple.

She tried to swallow, but her mouth was too dry. Staring at a bottle of water on his tray, she tried to moisten her lips with her tongue, but it was futile.

To her surprise, he handed the bottle to her.

She took it and inspected the cap to see if it had been opened. The tamper seal was intact.

"Don't worry, it is just water," he said, bemused.

She narrowed her eyes at him. The loathing she felt for him was beyond words, but it was not enough to trump her thirst. She unscrewed the cap and sucked down half the bottle, glaring at him as she did. To get out of this situation alive, she needed a cool head. Antagonizing him would not help her cause. What she needed to do was stall the inevitable. She had to give Nick and Zhang time to reconstruct the events at the museum and pursue her. Undoubtedly, they were playing catch-up, and it was unlikely they would leave Xi'an without first knowing her location. If her captor was telling the truth about Hong Kong, then help was a plane flight away, and that wasn't good enough. She suddenly remembered the wireless transmitter Zhang and Nick had insisted that she wear, and a wave of hope washed over her. She subtly felt for the lump on her sternum where she had taped it between her breasts, under her bra.

"Looking for this?" he said, reaching into the front right pocket of his expensive slacks and dangling the transmitter in front of her.

A wave of nausea washed over her. She wasn't sure which was worse: having lost her lifeline to Nick and Zhang or knowing that this monster had strip-searched her while she was unconscious. She shuddered at the thought of his hands crawling all over her.

"If you were counting on a valiant rescue, I'm afraid your friend Nick will not be able to help you. The only person on this planet who knows where you are right now is me."

"I still don't understand what this is all about. Why did you take me?"

He took a final bite of apple and set the core down on his plate. He brushed his hands together delicately, the mannerism strangely feminine. "My name is not Mr. Lu," he said, looking at her.

"I figured that out already."

"My real name is Xue Shi Feng. I am the Chief Operations Officer of Nèiyè Biologic," he said. "You don't look surprised, Dr. Chen. Why is that?"

"We've suspected Nèiyè Biologic was behind all this since the beginning."

"Since Tung Wan Beach?"

"Since Peter Yu's murder," she replied.

He nodded. "Yes, that was bad luck, him being a CIA spy. Now that I think back on everything, killing Yu was the beginning of the end. When I discovered he was CIA, I should have transferred his girlfriend to our Shanghai office and put everything on hold until he lost interest in our operation and shifted his attention elsewhere. But the problem was that I didn't have time. Our clients don't have the luxury of time, you see. Mother does not have the luxury of time."

"What are you talking about?"

"She's a truly remarkable woman, my mother. The sacrifices she made, the love and devotion she showed me growing up . . . I would do anything for her. I'm sure you can relate. I'm sure you feel the same unconditional love for your mother."

She nodded cautiously.

"Good, so long as you know this is not personal. Your blood type, physical characteristics, exemplary physical health—these matches are purely coincidental, I assure you. Despite the good fortune, it did create quite the conundrum for me. It would have been so much easier to have simply had you killed. Kidnapping is so much more complicated and dangerous."

The expression he wore was disturbing, and she felt a chill rise up her spine. Her stomach tightened, nearly giving back the half bottle of water she'd drunk.

"It was clever of you to use Gang Jin to contact me," he continued. "Very, very clever. I didn't see that coming. Then the money wired promptly from an offshore account in good standing. The false credentials your people prepared were flawless. Not a single red flag popped up during our vetting process until . . ." He smiled, licked his lips, and then wiped them dry with a napkin. "Do you want to know what was your undoing? Do you want to know your foil?"

She stared at him, desperate to know but not willing to give him the satisfaction he craved.

"It was your face. I could never forget a face like yours. You are a modern-day Helen of Troy. A true archetypal beauty that no amount of digital camouflage can hide."

He reached out to stroke her cheek, but she jerked her head back.

"I do my homework, Dr. Chen," he chuckled. "I know all about your little task force. I know about the mighty Commander Zhang and the sly Major Li . . . may he rest in peace."

"You murdered Li," she said, more an accusation than a question.

"Of course. He got too close. You were all getting too close."

"Zhang will find you, and when he does, you'll pay dearly for what you've done."

"Maybe, but I doubt it. Despite all his bluster, Commander Zhang doesn't have the mental faculties to compete in this game.

As a unit, your task force was formidable—Zhang was the brawn, you were the brains, and Li was the guile—but separate you from each other and what's left?" Feng chuckled. "Nothing but an acronym."

She felt her face flush, and she looked away from him. There was truth in his words, and suddenly she wondered if her fate was sealed. Could Zhang find and rescue her on his own? But as tears rimmed her eyes, hope whispered in her head.

Zhang isn't alone . . . he has Lankford and Nick. Feng probably doesn't know that Lankford is still alive, and Lankford is every bit the tactician that Li was. And Nick has escaped Feng's hit squads on three occasions. That's why he kept probing me about Nick. Maybe he's not afraid of Zhang and the Snow Leopards, but he's afraid of Nick, and he's definitely afraid of the CIA . . .

"Did you know I'm the one who chose the name of the company, not Dr. Yao?" he said, interrupting her thoughts. "Nèiyè was entirely my idea."

She nodded.

"Do you know the meaning of the word?"

She shook her head.

"The origin of the term comes from Daoist meditation," he said with entirely too much self-satisfaction. "It means 'inner training'—the cultivation of the mind, body, and spirit of the self by the self."

Epiphany washed over her like cold rain. "Nèiyè Biologic—self-cultivation through biology . . . self-cultivation through CRISPR."

"Very good, Dr. Chen," Feng laughed, clapping his hands. "No one ever makes the connection. People love to think in their little boxes. Not you. I knew I could count on you to appreciate my vision."

"What vision is that?" she asked, taking another drink of water.

"To fix the broken genetic machinery inside each and every one of us. To stop the suffering and the pain. Defects passed down from father to son, from mother to daughter, will soon be eradicated. Soon, very soon, I will be able to live in peace," he said and then in a whisper added, "Soon I will be able to slay the beast inside."

"Are you ill?" she asked, the physician in her looking him over as she would a patient.

"Ill? No, just hungry." He laughed. "Always and forever hungry—until I can cleave and replace that which ails me. Just a few more trials. A little more data, and I should be ready."

"You want to use CRISPR on yourself?" she asked, incredulous. "You intend to edit your own genome?"

"It is my life's ambition," he said, smiling at her. "And Yao's."

"CRISPR Cas9 is dangerous," she said, as if talking to a child playing with fire. "You know they tried this in Guangzhou. Junjiu Huang experimented on nonviable human embryos to remove the gene responsible for the blood disorder beta thalassemia, but the success rate was less than forty percent."

"Huang is an amateur," Feng sneered. "His team is years behind us."

"So you've solved the problem of off-target mutations?"

Feng shrugged.

"Then how do you prevent the CRISPR Cas9 complex from acting on other parts of the genome you don't want affected? How do you prevent unintended germ-line mutations?"

"If only we had more time. There is so much I could show you, so much I could *teach* you."

"I'm sure," she said finally, her voice barely a whisper.

"We'll continue this conversation later," he said, watching her like a salivating wolf eyeing its prey. With an odious smile, he settled back into his chair and crossed his legs. "You look like you are getting sleepy again," he said, unfolding a magazine from the selection in the large holder beside them on the bulkhead. *Immunobiochemistry*, she saw was the name of the journal.

And then she did feel sleepy. And dizzy.

"The water," she said, her voice slurring. "How did you . . ."

Her eyelids became heavy—iron curtains once again lowered between her and the disturbing man sitting across from her.

"So trusting, even now," he chuckled to himself as he thumbed to the next page of the journal.

Then he was gone behind her eyelids.

And she drifted off into a nightmare that a little voice sang would soon become her reality.

CHAPTER 27

Citation X executive jet
En route to Hong Kong International Airport
1715 hours local

Nick felt nothing except the crushing weight of time as he willed the biz jet to go faster in pursuit of the man they'd identified as Xue Shi Feng. After leaving Agent Ling and her MSS team stranded on the side of the highway, they'd worked with lightning efficiency. Based on museum security camera footage, a stop at Nèiyè Biologic headquarters, and a radio conversation with Xi'an air traffic control, they'd developed a complete tactical picture. Dash was with Feng in one of the Nèiyè corporate jets flying south to Hong Kong, and the bastard had a fifty-five-minute head start. The Citation X that Zhang had "acquired" from a friendly regional asset cruised one hundred and sixty knots faster than the older Citation II that Feng was flying. Simple math told Nick that they would whittle a full forty minutes off of Feng's lead by the time they landed. Depending on Feng's next move, there might still be time . . .

He looked at his watch for the thousandth time since takeoff.

This is all my fault. I'm the one who agreed to her plan, but then I stayed behind in the van. It was my job to protect her. Now it's my job to get her back.

Zhang settled into the seat across the aisle from him. "We've only been airborne for fifteen minutes, Nick."

"I know," he said, "but this is killing me. That maniac has Dash, and there's no telling what he intends to do with her."

Zhang nodded. "I feel the same pressure as you."

Nick made eye contact with the Snow Leopard Commander. "If he touches one fucking hair on her head . . ."

"Don't worry, Nick. I have a team mobilizing to the Hong Kong airport as we speak," Zhang said, his voice low and confident. "The instant Feng's plane touches down, we'll take him."

"Feng is clever. He knows we're onto him, which is why he took Dash as a hostage. This is his end game, and she's his insurance policy for getting out of China alive."

"I assigned my best Snow Leopard sniper to the team. If necessary, we'll make sure that doesn't happen."

Nick nodded.

The lavatory door opened, and Lankford emerged. He ambled over to join them and took the bucket seat in front of Zhang. "All right," Lankford said, swiveling the chair around to face them. "Can somebody please explain to me why the hell this bastard would kidnap Dash and fly to Hong Kong? And don't say he's using her as an insurance policy for getting out of China."

Nick looked at Zhang and then back to Lankford. "I think that's exactly what's going on."

Lankford shook his head. "No, it doesn't make sense. If Feng wanted to disappear, he would have made arrangements to fly directly to Vietnam—somewhere that Zhang doesn't have jurisdiction and can't easily marshal resources to intercept him on the ground. In that scenario, he's in the wind before we even get clearance to land. But in this scenario, he knows the odds are stacked against him."

"In that case, maybe Feng tipped off Ling and the MSS. Maybe Ling raiding our van was a critical component of his plan," Nick said, brainstorming out loud.

Lankford rubbed his chin. "Interesting theory. If you're right, our arrest and detainment would have certainly given him all the head start he needed. What do you think, Zhang?"

"The timing of Ling's raid does seem remarkably coincidental. I wonder if Feng knows we're not in MSS custody. I wonder if he knows we're in pursuit."

"I sure as hell hope not," Nick said. "If he thinks we're out of the picture, the airport team will blindside him. Easy day."

"So once again, why Hong Kong?" Lankford asked. "What is so important in that damn city that Feng needs to protect it at all costs? And why drag Dash there with him?"

Nick's heart skipped a beat as all the puzzle pieces clicked together in his mind: corpses washing up en masse on Tung Wan Beach with missing organs, the stolen shipping container lost at sea during a storm, Major Li murdered at the Port of Hong Kong while talking to a cargo superintendent, no rumors or reports of illegal organ harvesting at hospitals or medical facilities on land . . .

"We had it backward," he mumbled.

"What's that, Foley?" Lankford said.

"This whole time, we've been operating under the assumption that Feng's organ-harvesting operation was operating at a facility in Hong Kong and then shipping the corpses to sea for disposal," Nick said. "But we had it backward. The operation itself is at sea, and the bodies are offloaded for disposal, probably incineration. I wouldn't be surprised if the only reason we found any bodies at all is because the container washed overboard in the storm."

"Are you saying Feng is using a hospital ship for his operation?" Lankford said.

Nick nodded. "Or something like that. When I was with the Teams, we had an operation in Somalia go bad, and we had to CASEVAC a couple guys to the USS *Nimitz* for level-one trauma care. Since I was the Eighteen Delta, I rode along in the bird. I was amazed at the surgical suite onboard the carrier. Why couldn't Feng retrofit a similar facility on a merchant vessel? It would be the perfect way to disguise his operation and keep it forever away from prying eyes."

"That's one helluva theory," Lankford said. "But if you're right, then that means we have another problem."

"Feng did not take Dazhong to be his hostage," Zhang said, completing Lankford's thought as his complexion went pale. "He took her to be a donor."

"We have to locate that ship before Feng lands," Nick said. "We should start with satellite imagery."

"Don't look at me," Lankford said.

"You do work for the CIA," Nick said. "Spying on China is kinda your job."

Zhang frowned.

"Thanks for reminding him, Foley," Lankford grumbled. "But contrary to what you might think, I don't have a dozen dedicated satellites in geosynchronous orbits over China at my beck and call. If satellite data are what you're after, then talk to Zhang."

An hour passed with Zhang making calls on his sat phone, trying to requisition current and historical satellite imagery of a two-hundred-nautical-mile radius around Hong Kong. The stone wall of bureaucracy the Snow Leopard Commander seemed to be facing made Nick actually appreciate the US defense complex, which he had once assumed had no equal in the realm of unco-operative gatekeepers and walled gardens . . . Oh, how naïve he had been. Of course, Zhang's job was made more difficult because he could not utilize the normal chains of command and contact within the Chinese intelligence and counterterrorism structure. While there was no evidence of a specific breach, they all agreed it was inconceivable that Feng could have achieved what he had in Xi'an, Discovery Bay, and Hong Kong without some sort of inside information—something Lankford pointed out with great delight and to which Zhang was forced to reluctantly agree.

Zhang's phone rang, and he picked it up on the first ring. He listened for a beat and then unleashed an angry tirade in rapid-fire Chinese. Red-faced, he hung up the phone and turned to Nick. "That was my team leader on the ground at Hong Kong International. It appears Feng changed his flight plans. The bastard took a page from my playbook and diverted to Zhuhai. Meanwhile, my guys are stuck on Lantau. They're trying to secure an operational helo as we speak."

Nick was about to suggest they talk to their pilot about diverting to Zhuhai, when Zhang's phone rang again.

Zhang picked it up, and this time he spoke in English: "Zhang . . . Damn it! Have air traffic control track that bird. I want to know exactly where Feng goes. We'll be on the ground in thirty-five minutes. Have your team kitted up and ready to go. The mission has changed. We're going to be conducting a maritime assault . . . Yes, you heard me correctly, a maritime assault . . . Leave that to me."

Zhang slammed his sat phone down on the armrest. "Feng had a helo standing by at Zhuhai. ATC is reporting that he took off without clearance and that there was nobody at the airport to stop him."

"What the hell do we do now?" Nick said as a wave of dread washed over him. "Feng is taking Dash to the medical ship. If we don't get to her soon, she's as good as dead."

"The situation is bad," Zhang said, "but I know a guy who can help."

"Oh, Jesus, not this again," Nick said, shaking his head. "Who is it now . . . a deckhand on a buoy tender?"

Zhang grinned as he pulled up a number from his contact list. "No. This time I'm bringing out the big guns. I happen to know the captain of the *Hai Twen* CCG-1115—a Coast Guard cutter with helicopters and everything we need to support a maritime assault."

An electric charge of anticipation coursed through Nick's body, and his mind went to work visualizing the op.

"It's going to be risky. Depending on how that ship is staffed, a lot of innocent people could die," Lankford said.

"Yes, but if we don't act, the next time we see Dash will be with a pile of corpses inside a Conex box," Nick said.

Lankford nodded.

"One way or another, this ends today. Let me make the call, and then we'll brief the op. This is going to be a first for me," Zhang said as a smile crept across his face. "Fortunately, we have a Navy SEAL on the team to plan the assault."

CHAPTER 28

"Hospital Ship" **Huangdi**
104 miles south of Hong Kong in the South China Sea
0525 hours local

Dash gave up struggling against the leather straps binding her wrists and ankles. She had pulled and twisted until the skin beneath burned like fire. The wetness under her left hand told her she was bleeding. She was strapped to what could only be described as an operating room table with wheels. That, combined with the flimsy cotton hospital gown they had dressed her in, left no doubt in her mind what their intentions were.

A chill ran down her spine, and she pushed the terrifying thought away.

She'd woken up this way, which meant they had kept her drugged since her last recollection of consciousness on the jet en route to Hong Kong. She suspected she might be at sea—aboard a hospital ship—but the gentle rocking she felt might just be her own nauseating disorientation. The room she was in appeared to be a lab—she could see a hooded workstation behind her over her left shoulder and a row of workstations to her right. There was also what appeared to be an HPLC machine near an oval-shaped door, which meant a high-tech, remotely operated microscope was nearby. Someone had spent a lot of money on this room.

The oval door opened, and a woman entered, dressed in gray surgical scrubs, with a larger man pushing a cart. Dash was immediately reminded of the anesthesia cart—with its hep-locks and IV needles and bags of fluids and drawers of meds—from her residency and fellowship. Her skin began to crawl, and her throat tightened.

"Please," she choked out as they approached. "Please, there is a mistake. You have to help me."

Neither of the attendants responded or even looked at her. The female nurse began to assemble an IV setup on the cart. Their faces blurred as tears filled her eyes, and she tried again to twist her wrists free from the restraints.

"Please," she begged, focusing her gaze on the woman. This woman had to possess empathy. If she could just make eye contact—just establish an emotional connection. "Look at me, please."

"How are you feeling, Dr. Chen?" a voice said.

Dash blinked away the tears and saw that someone new had entered the room. His face was familiar, and so were his hungry, dark eyes. He smiled at her and clasped his bare, sinewy forearms behind his back.

"You must be so excited," Feng said. "I cannot imagine how it must feel to be in your position—to know that your life will be sacrificed to save such a great and noble woman."

"What are you going to do to me?" Dash asked and immediately regretted it. She knew already, and she hated that she sounded weak. But this was not how she wished to go out of this world. Not after everything she'd risked over the past three months.

Feng sat on a black rolling stool and rolled over to her. He leaned in—uncomfortably close—smiling widely. His eyes burned with anticipation and excitement. After studying her for a long moment, he picked up a remote control and pressed a button. The mirror on the wall behind him suddenly became transparent, and she saw an old woman lying propped up in a hospital bed, connected to a host of monitoring equipment.

"She's suffered so much," he said, gazing lovingly at the old woman. "To think how close I came to losing her. But then you came along, her guardian angel, to save her in her moment of greatest need."

Terror seized her. "Help!" Dash screamed, pulling against her restraints with renewed vigor. "Help me! Somebody—please!"

"She can't hear you. Nobody can hear you, Dr. Chen," Feng said, shaking his head. "Well, nobody that cares."

She felt her throat tighten.

This is going to happen.

Oh God, this is going to happen.

"Think of this as the first step in the quest for immortality, Dr. Chen. Your organs will be harvested, transplanted, and edited to match my mother's alleles with CRISPR. Within a month, your organs will be her organs, which means no more antirejection drugs, no more dialysis, no more diabetes, no more pain or weakness or deterioration. So you see," he said cheerfully, "even in death, a part of you will live on."

"You're insane," she said and began to sob.

The man shooed the comment away with his hand, as if it was a familiar argument he had fended off before. "Yes, yes," he said with mocking irritation. "Me and Louis Pasteur, Hippocrates, DeBakey, Galen, Rhazes, William Harvey, Christopher Wren, Joseph Lister, William Morton, John Gibbon—my God, we could go on forever with a list of the company I keep."

"You are nothing like them," she hissed. "They were great scientists who didn't go around murdering people."

"Oh, please," he said with a wave of his hand. "Do you really believe that all went well with Karl Landsteiner's early work, or that the family of Gibbon's first patient had reason for thanks? Don't be naïve. There is no progress without sacrifice."

"You're delusional if that is what you think this is."

He gave her arm a patronizing pat. "Don't fret, Dr. Chen, your sacrifice will not go uncelebrated. The work we do today is an important step toward achieving my ultimate vision."

"What the hell are you talking about?"

"Editing genes in transplant organs is only phase one of the path to immortality. Phase two is where the real transformation occurs."

Keep him talking, she told herself. *Anything to drag out the inevitable.*

"I don't understand. What is phase two?"

Before he could answer, the large male nurse grabbed her left arm at the wrist and elbow, gripping her painfully with all of his strength. Eyes downcast, the female nurse swabbed her forearm with a cool alcohol prep and then pulled the cap off of a large IV needle, the green hub pinched in her gloved fingers. Dash watched the woman insert the needle, and she felt a sharp pain in her forearm, followed seconds later by a cool ache as the nurse established a saline drip.

"Well, enough with the small talk," Feng said, still smiling as if they were having tea on a first date. "Time to move onto the matter of your deception and the administration of punishment."

She turned to him. "My deception?"

"You lied to me, Dr. Chen, about both your identity and your intentions. Because of you, my entire operation is now under the microscope. Because of you, my career, my reputation, and Nèiyè Biologic itself are in jeopardy. Your colleagues will be coming for me, and for that, you must be punished."

A new and horrible dread washed over her. What could possibly be worse than what he already had planned for her? What could possibly be worse than having her organs cut out against her will and gifted to another? She looked at the ceiling, refusing to give him the satisfaction of seeing her fear. She waited for her head to swim, for whatever preanesthesia meds they were pumping into her to take effect, but she felt bright-eyed and normal, except for the burning in her arm from the saline IV.

"You see, normally, after a crime such as yours, I would subject you to the Five Pains. But given the circumstances, I've been forced to be a little creative." He laughed, and it was the most obscene sound she'd ever heard.

He leaned in, his lips beside her ear, his breath warm on her face. "You will be the first to truly experience what we do here," he whispered. "To *fully* experience it. You see, I have instructed the nurses to administer only succinylcholine, a depolarizing

paralytic, during your procedure. You will be completely paralyzed, but you will not be given any other anesthesia. You will have
no sedation. You will have no pain medications. You, Dr. Chen,
will experience fully every moment of the procedure—as we draw
the blade across your lovely abdomen . . ." With his fingers, he
untied the knot keeping her gown closed and spread the flaps
open, exposing her naked body beneath. He dragged the tip of his
index finger down her abdomen to the top of her pubic hair, making her jump against the restraints. ". . . as we open you, remove
your kidneys, your pancreas, your liver—which I've instructed the
surgeon to save until late in the procedure so you don't drift away
too soon. Then, if all goes well, you will still be alive to feel the
snap of the shears as we split your sternum." Next, he ran his
finger gently down her chest, from the bottom of her neck, down
between her breasts, making her jump again. "You will fade away
after we excise your heart, ceasing the flow of blood to your brain,
a prison in which your mind will be screaming silently in anguish
until you die."

Leaving her naked and vulnerable, Feng moved toward the
oval door.

She stole a glance and took in all the details of this monster
and the sadistic grin lingering on his face. She searched for the
perfect thing to say to take away some of his pleasure. Unable to
think of anything, she began to cry instead.

At the threshold, he said, "See you shortly, my dear," his voice
almost cheerful, and then he was gone.

As the tears streamed down her cheeks, she wondered if Nick
and Zhang would find her body floating in the sea. With what
Feng had planned, for Nick's sake and for whatever it was he felt
for her, she hoped not.

CHAPTER 29

Lead H155 helicopter
Ninety-two nautical miles southeast of Lantau Island, Hong
  Kong
0615 hours local

If Dash's life were not on the line, Nick might have actually been enjoying himself—kitted up in the back of a helo, the blue China Sea screaming by two hundred meters below as they made their low-altitude stealth approach on the hospital ship. The assault force was divided between two helicopters: Zhang's team of six was in the lead bird; Nick and his team were trailing. The operators sitting beside him were all Chinese, and although their chatter was foreign to him, the mood and camaraderie was not. They were relaxed, confident, and ready to go. The weapons they held were different from the SOPMOD M4s his SEAL teammates had carried, but the intimate way they handled them was familiar. With a few tweaks of fate, this could easily be a SEAL Team. Nick had planned the details of the assault with Zhang's support, and the team was as ready as a foreign team could be. Maritime assault was *the* legacy mission of choice for the SEALs—that is, before perpetual combat in the deserts and mountains of the Middle East forever changed the force. Now Nick was preparing to execute the mission he'd always dreamed of, and the stakes could not be higher. The woman he loved was on that ship, and he suspected that mere seconds would determine whether she lived or died.

He had not, until this moment, permitted himself to acknowledge his true feelings for her, but there it was. He loved her. He loved Dash. The timing of this epiphany could not be worse. Instead of feeling excitement at the realization, he recognized it for what it was—an emotional liability. Personal stakes added stress and made for a dangerous distraction during what should otherwise be just one more operation in a log of hundreds of direct-action missions he'd completed. Hostage rescue, covert intel gathering, seek and destroy, capture or kill—they were all the same. But not this one.

Not today.

"Two minutes."

Zhang's voice snapped him back from the mental precipice he'd best stay clear of for the next thirty minutes or more. He held up two fingers to the Snow Leopard beside him, who passed the signal down to the next operator. Around him, men began the familiar kata of last-minute gear and weapons checks.

"You okay?"

Nick looked at Lankford, who sat beside him on the canvas bench seat.

"On time, on target," he answered, but he knew Lankford could see past the operator bravado.

Lankford put a hand on his shoulder. "She's going to be okay, Nick. We'll get her."

Nick nodded his appreciation to the CIA man.

"One minute."

Nick slid forward to the edge of the bench and keyed his mike.

"We're team two, clearing to starboard," Nick said, calling Zhang, who was in the lead helicopter. "Team one—that's you, Commander Zhang—will clear to port." Zhang repeated the order in his earpiece in Chinese. The men on Nick's team all spoke English, but Zhang was translating this critical detail so there could be absolutely no confusion.

Nick then held up one finger and gestured to himself. The operator across from him held up two fingers, the next operator three fingers, all the way around to Lankford, who was six—their numbers in their stick. Lankford was no SEAL, but he was blooded in combat and an asset in a gun battle. This was a short-fuse op, and they needed numbers.

The operator across from Nick opened the helo cargo door. Nick gazed out the opening and looked below, noting the frothy wake of the ship they were trailing. Only seconds remained.

"Two shooters on the fantail—on radios—they're engaging with rifles . . ." said Zhang's voice.

The report was followed by the loud belch of fifty-caliber machine-gun fire as the lead helicopter strafed the enemy security force.

"The fantail is secured. We have movement aft from amidships. At least a dozen men."

Nick felt his helicopter bank right, the pilot matching the arcing swath of green foam below. The hospital ship's captain had just made an evasive turn starboard—a pointless attempt to foil the assault by the profoundly more maneuverable helos.

"Team one is onboard," came the call from Zhang.

Nick felt the helicopter flare, slowing to match speed with the moving ship. Then the pilot yawed the nose left and banked to place the open door just a few feet above the fantail. Nick tapped the Snow Leopard across from him on the helmet, and the operator leapt onto the fantail deck, moving quickly to his right, the next man in line following a split second later. In seven seconds, all six of them were aboard and advancing along the starboard side of the fantail. The roar of rotor wash disappeared as the helicopter rose and banked hard away from the fantail. The bird would execute a two-hundred-seventy-degree circle and come along the starboard side of the ship to provide gun support.

Nick took a knee and surveyed the fantail over the sight of his rifle. The bodies of the aft deck security team lay in bloody heaps, having been cut to pieces by the fifty-caliber machine guns. The fantail of the hospital ship was set up as a helo pad, and Nick noted a commercial helicopter lashed down to deck eyes.

That has to be Feng's helo, Nick told himself. *Which means Dash is here.*

Automatic gunfire erupted to his left.

"Heavy contact forward, port," Zhang said in his headset.

"Contact forward, starboard," another voice said, the accent thick but the English understandable.

Nick's fire team took a knee. A high-velocity round whizzed past Nick's head, pulling a trail of sparks as it ricocheted off of the rail beside him. Nick sighted in on a moving figure—sixty yards ahead and moving aft along the deck rails. He squeezed the trigger. A three-round burst crumpled the target, painting red modern art all over the deck. Another round hit the nonskid deck by his left thigh. A burning sting lit his leg up as a piece of shrapnel tore through his pants and clawed his flesh just above his knee. He raised his weapon and searched along the railing of the bridge tower. When he saw a muzzle flash slightly to the left, he sighted in and squeezed the trigger twice. The shooter dropped his rifle and stumbled to a knee but then managed to scurry to safety through a hatchway in the white metal wall of the bridge tower.

"Check the bridge tower," he ordered. "Move forward—we need cover."

Nick's heart was shouting for him to find the nearest ladder and get belowdecks to rescue Dash, but the operator in him knew that would never happen if his team was cut to ribbons here. He signaled for team two to advance. As two pairs of Snow Leopards slid along the side rails, Nick and Lankford moved left, taking cover behind what he thought was a generator box. The deck-mounted structure measured approximately two meters wide by one meter tall and was positioned at the edge of the yellow paint circle marking the helo landing zone. Nick pulled in tight beside Lankford, who raised his rifle above the top edge of the rectangular metal box and fired. Nick peered over his rifle, scanning around the right side of the structure. Two of his Snow Leopards were hunched down behind a large yellow cart. Beyond them, he saw two of Feng's guards running aft, spraying bursts of fire from their JS 9s everywhere. Nick placed his red holographic targeting dot on the forehead of the first man, squeezed the trigger, and watched the head explode in a puff of red. The other shooter ducked and took cover behind an angular structure rising from the deck.

"You think this is a generator box?" Lankford yelled over the gunfire.

"I think so," Nick said, searching for more targets. A barrage of gunfire rained down on them from above, pinging off of the top of the metal box barely big enough to conceal them. Lankford popped up, fired a three-round burst, and then dropped back down.

"I hope you're right," the CIA man said.

"Why?" Nick asked without looking over. He saw another figure move across the deck passage that connected the forward area of the ship to theirs. He was about to fire when a muzzle flash made him pull back. A split second later, the metal box shrieked in protest as several enemy rounds carved out metal chunks where Nick's face had been.

"Because," Lankford said, returning fire, "given the position, it could be a fuel depot for the helicopters, in which case"—he paused and fired again before turning back to Nick—"you picked a really shitty spot for cover."

"Then let's shoot these bastards and get the hell out of here," Nick said as he leaned around the box and fired.

"Resistance at inboard hatches," Zhang announced.

Nick peered around the right corner again, found no targets, and then shifted left behind Lankford and peered around the left side. He spied two open doorways leading to the lower superstructure, and every few seconds, there was a burst of gunfire from each. Nick checked his watch. They'd been on the fantail now for nearly four minutes.

"Zhang," he said into his mike, "we don't have time for this shit. They're pinning us topside on purpose. We have to get down there and rescue Dash. Right fucking now."

A figure appeared in the doorway, and Nick lit up the opening with a barrage of gunfire. To his right, he heard the other two Snow Leopards engaging more targets forward on the starboard side. He had lost sight of the third pair behind him, but he heard occasional bursts of gunfire that told him they were still in the fight.

"We do not have control topside," Zhang said in his headset. "If we sortie below, they will pursue and cut us down from behind. I will not put my team in a crossfire."

Nick had drilled this scenario dozens of times, and Zhang was right. But this was his environment, and where there was a will, there was a way.

"Here's the new plan. Team one stays topside, along with five and six from team two," he said. "You secure the deck and then meet us amidships when possible. One, two, three, and four from team two will take the rear ladder wells and assault the medical spaces below."

There was a long pause, punctuated only by gunfire in both directions. Zhang had put him in charge, but the Snow Leopards needed their leader to concur before they deviated from the plan as briefed. Nick waited. After an eternity, Zhang's calm and even voice again filled his left ear, but this time rattling off instructions in Chinese before switching back to English at the end.

"Team two is now four man. Proceed belowdecks," Zhang said.

"Roger that."

"And Foley?"

"Yes."

"Good luck."

Nick looked at Lankford, who stared back at him and nodded. "I'm with you," the CIA man said. "Let's go get our girl."

"Cover fire on my mark," Nick called into his mike.

Lankford nodded.

"Three, two, one, mark."

A beat later, the Snow Leopards lit up the deck with cover fire. Together, he and Lankford sprinted from the cover of their rectangular box, bullets ripping up the nonskid around them as they ran. At the raised ladder well—shaped almost like a white metal port-a-john—they flanked the closed door, weapons up. Nick spun the wheel to undog the latch, then flung open the hatch. Lankford fired a volley down the hole, and then Nick led them into the ladder well.

The staccato ping of bullets hitting the outside of the ladder well reverberated as they descended the narrow ladder-style rungs. Nick cleared ahead as Lankford protected their flank. At the landing, Nick moved left and took a knee, scanning down the long, gray-white passageway stretching toward an oval hatch. For the moment, the passageway was deserted, but that meant nothing. Feng's security forces could be anywhere. Nick felt Lankford's hand on his shoulder as the CIA man moved past him. He waited a moment, clearing their six, and then fell in behind Lankford, who was now leading the charge to the next decision point. They continued down the passageway to the oval hatch painted with the number twenty-four. Inboard of the hatch, there was a descending ladder.

"Which way?" Lankford asked.

"I don't know," Nick said. "My gut tells me we go amidships, to the middle decks."

"Agreed."

"Forward or down?"

Nick shook his head.

"Just pick."

"Down," Nick said. He grabbed the oval hatch, shut it, and dogged the latch. Then he pulled a spent magazine from a pouch on his kit and jammed it tightly between the handle and the latch. It would not stop someone truly determined, but it might slow them down.

"One, this is Three," a voice said in Nick's ear. "We are clear on level one, port side to a ladder. Advance or descend?"

"Advance and report. We need to locate the medical suite," Nick said into his mike. "One is moving down to level two."

Nick descended the ladder to the second deck. He cleared at the bottom, and Lankford leapfrogged to take the lead, repeating the procedure from before. Moments later, they were crouched on either side of another hatch labeled thirty-eight, except this hatch was shut. As before, a ladder well occupied the space inboard of the hatch, except this one provided access up and down. Nick made a quick glance up and down and mouthed the word "clear" to Lankford.

Lankford pointed at the hatch and then the descending ladder.

Nick was about to gesture down when he noticed a placard on the wall beside the closed hatch with Chinese hanzi.

"What's that say?" he whispered, nodding at the placard.

Lankford glanced up. "It says 'surgery ward.'"

Nick keyed his mike. "Three, One. Ready to rescue the package, level two. Starboard side. Hatch number thirty-seven."

"Roger, One. What are your orders?"

"Descend to level two and support on the port side."

"Roger, backtracking to the ladder at hatch thirty-eight. Stand by."

"We going to wait for them?" Lankford asked.

Every fiber in his being wanted to say no, but the operator in Nick knew that it would be a mistake. He nodded and tightened his grip on his rifle. Gunfire from the firefight raging thirty feet above them echoed off of the ladder and metal hull in a surrealistic way.

"One, Three in position," came the call from the other half of team two.

"We breach on my mark," Nick said. "Clear the deck aft to front, beam to center. Kill anyone not Dr. Chen."

"Copy all," came the reply.

Nick looked over at Lankford, who gave an awkward thumbs-up. Nick grinned tightly and felt an unexpected surge of kinship for the CIA man.

Nick took a long, deep breath and then called into his mike: "Three, two, one—Go!"

CHAPTER 30

Dash wanted to scream, but the realization that she could not filled her with terror, amplifying the need to scream all the more. She could feel her arms and hands twitching, then her thighs. Her eyelids fluttered uncontrollably. She realized that she needed to take a long, deep breath, but no matter how loudly her brain ordered her chest to heave and her diaphragm to drop and suck in a long, cool breath of air, her body did not get the message and simply twitched uncontrollably instead. A moment later, the twitching stopped, and she felt her head grow dizzy as the unheeded call for oxygen became all-consuming.

"There it is," a man said.

"A seven and a half tube, please."

"On her chest."

"Sorry, I see it. What's her Pulse Ox?"

"Still ninety-four."

"Okay, here we go."

She felt a rubber-gloved hand on her forehead, tipping her head back. Then two gloved fingers probed her mouth, twisting and forcing her teeth apart. She ordered her jaw to clamp down, to bite off the invading fingers, but her jaw stayed slack. The fingers prodded, and next she felt cool metal on her tongue, followed by a sharp pain in her jaw as they readied her for intubation.

"I've got the cords."

"Here is the tube."

She should have been gagging, and although her *brain* gagged at the sensation of the metal rod down her throat, her body did nothing.

"Suction."

Another tube scraped painfully down the back of her throat, and then the sound of saliva being suctioned filled her ears.

"Tube."

Her throat burned with pain as the small tube was removed and the much larger endotracheal tube was pushed through her vocal cords and down into her trachea. Then the metal rod was gone, and the pain in her jaw eased. A moment later, a burst of cool air filled her lungs.

It took a few seconds, but then the horrible sensation of suffocating slowly dissipated, as did the dizziness and the feeling that she was fading away. As her wits returned, she suddenly found herself wishing she had actually blacked out. The horrible sensation of the tube forcing air into her lungs and then relaxing slowly—too slowly—as the air hissed out of her became overwhelmingly claustrophobic. She wanted to breathe faster. She needed to breathe faster, but the machine didn't care. Above her, a hazy white cloud hovered. She tried to blink—to clear away the tears that blurred her vision—but she found it impossible to pull her lids down across her eyes. Her pulse quickened, and she could actually hear the *swish swish* of the blood coursing through the arteries at her temple.

"She's a little tachycardic," a woman's voice said.

There was some shuffling around, and then she felt a squeezing band of pressure on her left bicep, which then slowly faded away.

"Her blood pressure is up too," a man's voice said casually. "Did you give her the Versed?"

"Yes—three milligrams. And the ketamine drip is running as well as some fentanyl."

"Okay. Maybe she's a little dry. Open up her saline."

"Are we almost ready?" asked a voice she recognized.

A tidal wave of panic washed over her. It was the madman, Feng. The man who planned to harvest her organs and dump her mutilated corpse in the ocean. The fear was all-consuming, and to fight it, she told herself that any moment, Nick would burst through the door. The next sound she heard would be the sound of Nick snapping the madman's neck. And then he would tell her she was safe, and he would hold her . . .

A blurry figure came into her line of sight, obstructing her teary view of the ceiling. With all her might, Dash willed her eyelids down, and after a moment, they obeyed, slowly drawing a dark line across her field of vision. Her tears, cooled by the air, rolled down onto her temples and then dripped into her hair. The machine gave a hiss, her lungs filled against her will, and it made her lose her concentration. Her lids slid back up to half-mast, and her vision was filled with the clear view of Feng wearing a surgical mask and taunting her with his eyes.

"You may wonder what is going on, so let me explain. I've replaced all the medication vials with saline. The surgery team has been instructed not to shield you from the sensations that are coming. Your wits will not be dulled. Your pain receptors will not be numbed. You will feel each stroke of the knife as I cut your organs free. Only the succinylcholine will remain, to keep you paralyzed and still."

Her stomach lurched, but nothing came up. Inside her head, she screamed—screamed for her life at the top of her lungs, but the only sound she heard was the chuckle of Xue Shi Feng and the hiss of the cruel and callous ventilator mechanically keeping her alive.

"The slush is ready. We can start anytime."

My God, they're going to do it. They're going to slice me open while I'm awake. Please, God, no . . .

With all her might, she willed her heart to stop pumping the oxygenated blood to her brain. If she could just stop her heart—just die now—she would be spared the agony of being carved and ripped apart piece by piece.

She felt hands, multiple hands, on her. The thin sheet they had covered her with was pulled away, and cool air licked her bare skin. Although she couldn't see it, she knew four pairs of eyes were ogling her sprawled and naked body. Something cold and wet spread across her belly, and she knew exactly what was happening.

"Prepping," someone said.

They whisked the freezing liquid across her skin; she felt it drip down her sides as they splashed it across her sternum and breasts. Then she felt a burn as they swabbed between her legs. Her nose filled with a familiar smell.

Betadine. They're prepping me with Betadine. Why bother if this ends with death?

But of course it wasn't for her. It was for her organs. They didn't want to contaminate their organ cultures. Rough hands now pressed surgical towels over her chest and abdomen, and again she felt violated by a hand between her legs. For a moment, she felt a tug of regret that Nick had never seen her naked, that they had never . . .

"What the hell was that?" someone said.

"Keep working. We must start immediately," Feng's manic voice said.

"That sounded like gunfire," said a woman's voice this time.

"My God, are we under attack?"

It's him! It's Nick. He's going to save me and kill this bastard.

"I have an army of men protecting us. Get started." Feng paused. "Where do you think you're going?"

She heard the *pop, pop* of gunfire, closer now.

"Give me the damn scalpel. I'll do it myself."

There was a moment of commotion, and then Feng was whispering in her ear. "It's time, Dr. Chen. Let us begin."

Panic gripped her. They were too late. There was no cavalry in the nick of time in real life.

"Guard the door and kill anyone that comes through it," Feng ordered.

Not Nick. Please don't let anything happen to Nick.

She felt a gloved hand on her chest, her skin pulled taut between strong fingers, and then the blade . . . gentle contact at first, but then a terrible, searing pain erupted just below her breastbone as the blade flayed her open.

She screamed in silent terror and with deafening agony, but no one could hear her.

No one could hear her scream . . .

CHAPTER 31

Nick watched Lankford undog the hatch and push it open. He advanced through the oval-shaped opening in a combat crouch, sighting over his rifle. The immediate passageway was deserted, but shadows were moving in his peripheral vision. This area of the ship had been completely retrofitted and had the look and feel of a hospital instead of a merchant vessel. An expansive frosted-glass window stretched along his left, and he ducked down below the midline. Lankford squatted and slid in beside him, their backs pressed against the metal half wall.

Nick mimed smashing the window and then engaging the targets inside.

Lankford nodded.

Simultaneously, they popped up and smashed the frosted glass with the butts of their rifles, averting their faces as the glass shattered and fell in exploding sheets to the floor. A beat later, they were sighting over the aluminum frame.

Nick registered a million data points in a split second: laboratory benches, an empty hospital bed in the center of his room, an IV stand, a vital sign monitor on rollers, and ducking in the corner, a man in a black uniform swinging his rifle to bear. Nick squeezed his trigger without hesitation—sending a 7.62 mm round tearing through the center of the man's face. Blood, brains, and bone exploded out the back of the man's head and splattered the pale-green wall behind. Before the body hit the ground, Nick swiveled right. With the window gone, he straddled the half wall and stepped into the room. He looked back at Lankford and signaled for the CIA man to remain in the outboard passageway, advancing in parallel with Nick. He then heard three pops from his Snow Leopard teammates, who were advancing on the port side of the ship but were separated by at least one, maybe two, divider walls.

He scanned left and right, moving forward through the room, but there was no other movement.

"Clear," he said.

At the next doorway, he paused.

Gunfire erupted from his right, and he saw the muzzle flash from Lankford's rifle.

"Clear," Lankford said.

Nick depressed the lever and swung the door open. He crossed the threshold and cleared the empty room, which was a virtual copy of the first. Except here, he found the gray pantsuit and shoes Dash had been wearing bunched in a pile beneath the bed. He picked up the clothes, just to be sure, and a black lace bra and thong fell to the ground. Heat and rage erupted inside.

"Coming to you," Lankford called over the radio.

The knob on the passageway door moved, and Nick trained his rifle on the door just in case, lowering it when Lankford's face materialized.

Lankford eyed the clothes in Nick's hand. "Are we too late?"

"There's still a chance," Nick said, his words a hiss through clenched teeth. "We need to find the operating room. We go together, okay?"

"Of course," Lankford said.

Nick dropped Dash's clothes and was out the door and into the passageway in a flash. He felt Lankford fall in behind him and hoped he was clearing their six. Nick had never felt less focused on a mission. Rage and terror were driving him now. Without pausing, he headed into a crossing hallway that joined the port and starboard passageways.

"Wait," Lankford said, jerking Nick by the shoulder.

A shower of high-velocity rounds exploded from the hallway and tore chunks from the wall, pinging off the iron framework. Nick collapsed backward into Lankford and crouched at the corner.

"Thanks, bro," Nick said over his shoulder. He had to calm down and focus or he would get them all killed, including Dash. He grabbed one of the flash bangs from the ammo pouches on his kit as he spoke into his mike.

"Three, One. We've got shooters in the crossing hallway. I'm tossing a flash bang."

"Go," the Snow Leopard said in his ear.

Nick rolled the concussion grenade around the corner. A beat later, lightning flashed, and thunder erupted in the passageway. Nick slid around the corner on his knee and felt the tap on his back as Lankford passed behind him. Four uniformed figures were standing in tactical crouches, but they were not engaging with their weapons. Disoriented from the flash bang, he could see them desperately trying to clear their heads and their vision. Nick and Lankford engaged simultaneously, and in less than two seconds, they had all four shooters sprawled on the floor in growing pools of red.

"Clear," Nick said. "Keep moving." He heard the desperation in his own voice and said a silent prayer they weren't too late.

In hunched crouches, they advanced ten meters down the passageway to an aluminum-framed set of double doors. The doors were set up in a manner Nick recognized, like the sliding entrance to an operating room. He crouched beside an access panel, his left hand just millimeters from the push button that would open the doors.

Lankford nodded at the placard on the wall. "This is it—the operating room." He spoke into his radio. "Three, One. We're at the OR. Ready to breach."

"One, Three. We have a problem," the Snow Leopard said, calling from a mirror-image position on the port side of the ship. "We have no access to the OR from the port side. Give us one minute to circle back and cross to your side."

Nick's chest tightened. By now, the voice keeping time inside his head was screaming at him.

"Copy that, but there's no time," he said and locked eyes with Lankford. "We're going in."

Nick held up his left hand. Three fingers up, which he quickly counted down to one and then slammed his fist into the button.

The double doors hissed open.

Still in a crouch, Nick slid through the door, his body low and his rifle up. He was aware of the tracer rounds that zipped over his head but was unable to pull his gaze from the horror in the center of the room.

"Nick!" Lankford screamed from his right. "Behind you!"

Nick blinked and twisted left. His left pectoral muscle burned like fire as sutures popped and the knife wound that Dash had sewn shut reopened. As Nick spun left, his mind registered the uniformed security guard pointing a pistol at his head, and in that millisecond, he realized he was too late. He hadn't cleared his corner, and now he would die for it. But instead of seeing a muzzle flash, Nick watched the man's head snap violently to the left as a round from Lankford's rifle tore off the bottom of the man's jaw. Another rifle burped—this time to his right—and Nick spun to the threat. But instead of targeting him, this guard was aiming at Lankford and squeezed off a second round a microsecond before Nick's bullet blasted through the guard's left eye socket.

In his peripheral vision, he registered a third person moving right to left. Nick led the target and sent two rounds flying that found real estate in the man's forehead. He scanned the room and took an inventory of the remaining personnel. Dash lay sprawled on the OR table, hidden by blue drapes except for the large oval of orange-stained skin in the center, where her chest and abdomen were exposed beneath harsh white light. A nurse, dressed in blue scrubs, cowered in the corner. Two other similarly clad figures stood by the table: a taller man with his hands raised over his head and a shorter man holding a scalpel in his gloved left hand—a hand coated in Dash's blood. Nick fixed his gaze on the long, vertical incision stretching down her abdomen.

"Don't shoot! Don't shoot!" the surgeon hollered in shrill, panicked English. "I'm a doctor. Please, don't shoot."

Nick tensed his finger against the trigger of his rifle.

A shadow swept along the far wall, and Nick ticked his gaze right just long enough to confirm it was Lankford flanking and not a new threat. The surgeon capitalized on the moment and flung the scalpel at Nick's face. Nick ducked reflexively, and the flying razor cleared the top of his head by a scant centimeter.

An enemy guard materialized in the doorway to their right and provided cover fire for the fleeing surgeon. One of the two operating lights above the table shattered in a hail of glass and sparks. Nick dropped to a knee, raised his rifle, and dropped the shooter just as the blue-gowned surgeon cleared the room. Nick squeezed off another round that shattered the glass door as it recoiled off the doorstop. Nick brought his rifle back to center and fixed his sight on the tall doctor, still standing frozen by the table.

"Get out," he barked at the gowned assisting surgeon and then turned to the nurse. "You too."

Whether they spoke English or not, he didn't know, but they scurried from the room just as his radio crackled in his ear.

"One, Three," came the call in his radio. "We're coming in behind you."

"Roger," he said. "We have the package."

Nick fixed his attention on the naked female figure laying on the operating table as the two Snow Leopards from the port side joined them in the OR.

"Oh shit," Lankford said to his right, and there was pain in his voice. "I'm hit."

Nick glanced at the CIA man. "How bad?"

Lankford winced. "I'll live."

Nick nodded, then tore down all the blue drapes around the operating table, slinging his rifle under his left arm as he did. He laid one of the blue curtains across Dash's lower body, covering her from the waist down. He checked her vitals on the machine and exhaled relief at the heart-shaped pulse icon on the LCD display. He shifted his gaze to her face. Her eyes were half open, staring up at the ceiling. But there was something in her eyes. Recognition? Awareness? Not the dull, vapid stare indicative of sedation.

There's something weird with the anesthesia.

He was no anesthesiologist. He stared at her, not sure what to do next.

After a brief hesitation, he closed the clip on the IV that went into Dash's arm, stopping any sedatives flowing with the IV fluids. It was also possible that anesthesia was being blown into her lungs from the ventilator. He looked back at the monitor, which showed her blood pressure in green numbers, stable but a little high. The pulse rate was flashing in red and showed one hundred forty beats per minute.

Is she in shock?

But her blood pressure was high, if anything.

What the hell is going on here?

He looked back at her. A long incision, starting at the base of her breastbone and extending down to her pubis, was filling with crimson blood. The blood reached the edges of the wound and then began to spill out onto her Betadine-painted skin, running in little streams over her sides and onto the table. Nick snatched a stack of gauze sponges and packed them into the entire length of the wound. As he worked, an alarm sounded, and he looked up to see that the pulse rate was now one hundred sixty. His own heart rate shot up with fear and worry as he pressed the gauze firmly to staunch the bleeding.

"Nick," Lankford called out, his voice still strained. "Nick!"

"What?" He turned.

Lankford was on the floor, one of the Snow Leopards kneeling beside him and pulling out a medical blowout kit from a cargo pocket.

"Is she okay?"

Nick blinked and swallowed hard—felt the tears spill onto his cheeks—and looked down at Dash's abdomen. The wound was long and gruesome, having parted the skin and subcutaneous fatty tissue, but it was only a first-pass cut. The surgeon's scalpel had not cut through her fascia into the abdominal cavity. With sutures, she would be fine.

"Yes," he said. "Are you okay?" There was a small puddle of blood forming around the CIA man where he sat half upright on the floor.

"Don't worry about me." Lankford grimaced and said, "That short doctor—the surgeon who threw the scalpel at your face—that was Feng."

"What?" Nick said.

"Feng was performing the operation," Lankford said. "I'm positive."

Nick turned to the Snow Leopard who was guarding their six.

"Come here," he ordered.

The operator joined him at the operating table, and Nick took the man's gloved left hand and pressed it on top of the stack of gauze piled on Dash's stomach.

"Hold this firmly," he ordered.

"How long?" the Snow Leopard asked.

"Until I get back or the bleeding stops," Nick said, shifting his gaze to Dash's face. He gently brushed a stray hair from her forehead. Her eyes ticked up. "You're okay. You're going to be fine," he said to her. Then, he kissed her cheek—tasted cool tears—and stepped away from the table.

"What are you doing?" Lankford asked.

"I'm going after Feng," Nick answered.

"He can't go anywhere," Lankford said. "Zhang will have control of the ship any minute now. We'll get him, Nick, don't worry."

Nick shook his head. He looked at Dash, her body violated by the madman's knife, the tears shining on her cheeks.

"Take care of these two," he said to the lead Snow Leopard, gesturing to the two people he cared most about in the world at this moment.

The operator nodded.

And without a backward glance, Nick sprinted out of the operating room to find the madman and mete out justice.

CHAPTER 32

Nick left the OR and advanced forward, clearing rooms and gliding along walls until he reached the transverse passageway. Directly across the passage was an oval hatch, indicating to him that the doorway he was standing in marked the end of the hospital ward. He stuck his head through the open doorway and glanced left. Clear. He took a knee, glanced right. Clear. He crossed the passage in two strides and pressed his back against the far wall. He exhaled, quickly stuck his head into the hatch, and pulled it back, pausing to register what he had seen. The room appeared to be a crew's mess—a long table in the middle with flanking bench seats. In the back wall, he'd spied a large serving window, closed now by a segmented metal roller door. On the port wall stood a beverage station, which was empty except for two large cylindrical coffee dispensers. He did not register any other details of significance.

Nick took a deep breath, counted to two inside his head, and then burst through the hatch, scanning forward and then turning left to clear his left rear corner, as he always did. Being alone, he could not simultaneously clear both corners.

Unfortunately, he chose wrong.

Pain exploded in his neck and the back of his head as something heavy struck him from behind. As he crumpled to his knees, clutching his rifle to keep from losing it, he wondered whether Feng had known he would—out of habit and training—turn left as he entered, or if the madman had just gotten lucky. He didn't intend to let the bastard live long enough to ask him.

Nick dropped his left knee and rolled left onto his hip, spinning his rifle up and back as he did. Halfway around the arc, his weapon struck something immobile, the entire rifle suddenly twisting in his grip. His right index finger, which was inside the trigger guard, torqued painfully at the joint. The instant before he lost control of the weapon, he squeezed the trigger. The weapon spit fire, but the bullet sailed wide of the target. A glint of light off steel caught his eye as Feng slashed down with a curved knife toward his throat. Still holding the forward grip of his weapon with his left hand, Nick jerked the barrel up to block the attack. The sling caught and pulled taut, and Feng's knife passed through the heavy canvas like it was butter. The maniac smiled, jerked the rifle from Nick's grip, and flung it to the other side of the room.

Nick pivoted on his right elbow, ignoring the throbbing pain in his index finger, and kicked his left leg blindly in a wide arc. His boot hit something soft, and Feng grunted. He continued his spin, rolled onto his hands and knees, and popped to his feet. He surveyed the man before him. Feng was a head shorter and looked to be at least sixty pounds lighter, but instead of finding eyes filled with fear at confronting a blooded Navy SEAL, Nick saw only rage—and something else, something he had seen in the eyes of jihadist zealots he had hunted in Iraq and Afghanistan. A hunger to die.

Next to Feng's left foot lay a fire extinguisher with a smear of Nick's blood across the base. This made Nick suddenly aware of the river of blood streaming down the back of his collar from the gash that had opened up from the impact. His gaze flicked to the blade in Feng's left hand.

So he's a southpaw.

Reflexively, Nick reached for his SOG bowie on the front of his kit but found it missing. His stomach sank when the little voice in his head reminded him that he wasn't a SEAL anymore, and he wasn't wearing his kit. Feng laughed at him but then did something Nick did not expect. He opened his left hand, let the knife fall to the floor, and kicked it. Then, with both hands, he grabbed at his scrub top where the neckline formed a *V* and tore the shirt off his torso with such ease that the fabric might as well have been tissue paper. He tossed the shredded garment to the floor and tipped his face up, emitting a chilling howl. When he lowered his face, his eyes seemed to be glowing with maniacal blood lust. Nick could not help but marvel at his opponent's torso. From neck to navel and from shoulder to elbow, the man was a muscular, sinewy canvas of overlapping tattoos—hanzi, symbols, and creatures. The middle of his chest displayed a wolf face, mouth open and snarling, the bottom jaw disappearing beneath the waistband of his surgeon's scrub pants. Feng shifted into a fighting stance; he was like a coiled viper, wound tight and ready to strike.

It's like Bruce Lee and Satan had a child, Nick thought.

"I am Feng, both student and master of the Five Pains," the man said in clipped, flawless English. "Let us begin with the first pain."

Feng's right hand struck with lightning speed, the first two fingers extended. Nick was too slow to block the jab but moved just enough that the fingers failed to gouge his eye out, the nails instead laying open a deep cut extending from beneath his left eye all the way into the hairline at his temple. In seconds, Feng's hands were back up defensively, guarding his smiling face, the sinewy cords of muscle in his forearm reminding Nick of a tangle of woody vines.

Nick swallowed hard while resisting the urge to wipe away the blood flowing down his left cheek. He had not actually seen the strike, just a blurry streak in the air, and he wondered how anyone could move that fast. He hunched into a combat crouch, shifting his weight onto the balls of his feet and raising his own hands. The next gouging blow came without warning, but he managed a partial deflection, Feng's fingernails this time tearing a chunk from his right ear.

The blended martial arts style he had learned in the SEAL Teams—borrowed heavily from the Israeli Defense Forces' Krav Maga—was designed to be universally lethal against all variants of hand-to-hand combat. But he had never encountered anything like this. He had never sparred with someone like the man standing before him. Feng was kung fu perfected, a weapon honed over what must have been decades of disciplined and dedicated training.

I'm screwed, he thought. *I'm going to lose.*

The next attack from Feng was a combination, but the punches proved to be a feint, because Nick didn't see the brutal kick directed at his left knee until it was too late. Instinctively, Nick shifted weight to his right leg, absorbing the blow by letting it drive his left leg backward—probably the only thing that prevented his knee from snapping. But the pain was immediate and severe. He felt his knee instantly begin to swell with blood rushing to fill the joint cavity. Hopefully, no tendons or ligaments ruptured. He could still bear weight, but only by ignoring the pain.

Feng dropped his hands to his side and bounced gently up and down on his toes. Then he began to circle.

"You are Nick, yes? An American military man?"

Nick said nothing but sidestepped to match Feng's rotation on his unstable left leg while trying to anticipate the next attack.

"How is it that your military is so feared, if this is how your warriors fight?"

Feng's voice hit a high-pitched crescendo, and the man was airborne, his right foot flying toward Nick's head. Nick juked right, avoiding the foot but not the elbow that smashed against the side of his face so violently it knocked him to the floor. He crawled on his stomach, searching the ground for anything he could use as a weapon. The fire extinguisher caught his eye, and he lunged for it, rolling right a split second before the madman's knee struck the ground where Nick's head had just been. The force of Feng's knee was so great that Nick thought, had it connected, it would have split his skull open like a sledgehammer, spilling his brains onto the floor. And then, to Nick's dismay, Feng sprang instantly back to his feet with no hint of pain from the impact.

He grabbed the fire extinguisher with both hands and rolled to face Feng.

A flash of blue raced toward his face. He raised the fire extinguisher just in time to deflect an arcing kick. Feng's shin crashed into the canister, knocking it from Nick's hands and sending it careening across the deck. Feng grunted in pain, and Nick seized the opportunity to crab toward Feng's discarded knife, which lay under a nearby table. He dove for the weapon, and his fingers found the hilt. Without needing to look, he knew a savage attack was coming, and he rolled onto his knees, slashing in a broad horizontal arc, opening a deep laceration along the killer's thigh. Energized by his successful strike, Nick sprung back to his feet. His left knee responded by howling with pain, and he immediately shifted his weight to his good leg.

Feng floated left, his body flowing like water in a way that defied physics. He laughed and taunted Nick with his defenseless posturing—arms loose at his sides, chin up, feet dancing. Not once did Feng's eyes tick down to the bloody gash across his thigh, which Nick noted was bleeding profusely. He waited patiently for Feng to close the gap. Eventually, Feng stepped in. Nick slashed at the man's neck, but Feng spun an arm around, easily deflecting the blow. The block felt like someone had smashed a piece of firewood into Nick's wrist. Feng laughed once more with an eerie, maniacal howl that sounded to Nick like the shriek of a bird of prey the instant before it tears apart its quarry with razor-sharp talons.

"You know I'm better than you, Nick. In a minute, I will reclaim my knife, and when I do, I'm going to give you the same gift I offered Dr. Chen. I'm going to slice you open and rip out your organs while you watch. A fitting reversal, don't you think? You will fulfill your lover's death sentence, while she is powerless to stop me."

Rage consumed Nick. He drew his right hand back, ready to slash at Feng's chest, when a voice from his past screamed inside his head.

He's baiting you, Foley, barked the voice of the Master Chief who had taught him hand-to-hand combat years ago. *Don't let him make your fight his fight. Fight your fight. If your opponent uses a short reach, stay long. If his reach is long . . .*

"Fight short," Nick mumbled to himself. He pulled the knife back and held it close to his body. He crouched and slid left just as Feng's foot whizzed past his temple. Despite his opponent's short stature, Feng fought with a long reach. On top of that, Feng was lightning fast. Even without his injured knee, Nick realized he was not built to trade blows and kicks with Feng. He needed to get *inside* of that reach—inside where he could grapple and, in doing so, leverage his bulk and sixty-pound weight advantage.

Getting inside to grapple was going to hurt, but Nick knew he needed to commit to the strategy before Feng took out his good knee. Nick advanced quickly and directly, stepping inside the range of Feng's reach. He tried for a takedown, but the mad-man only smiled and danced backward, landing a painful jab on Nick's sternum for the effort. Nick closed again, this time faking upward with the knife. But when Feng swung his ironwood arms to block, Nick spun in a full, tight circle, driving his left elbow, the true weapon for this attack, at the side of Feng's head with all his might.

The impact made a loud crunch, and Nick couldn't tell if the crunch was from Feng's temporal bone cracking or his own elbow shattering against the killer's skull. From the pain that shot up his arm, he figured the best-case scenario was both. Without missing a beat, Feng spun right, stepped through Nick's legs, and grabbed him by the kit. The smaller Chinese man used his angular momentum and positioning to throw Nick, but Nick anticipated the countermove. It's exactly what he would have done. As he fell, Nick clutched Feng and used his weight to accelerate their rotation, spinning Feng beneath him. He landed with his full weight on top of the madman, while driving his elbow into the center of Feng's chest. His two hundred ten pounds and their combined momentum multiplied the impact force. Nick heard a satisfying crunch and felt his opponent's sternum crack in half beneath him. Feng screamed like a wild beast as the ragged ends of his breastbone tore through soft tissue—undoubtedly damaging both heart and lungs. Nick switched the knife from his right hand to his left, arched his back, and slashed deep across the maniac's throat. An explosion of blood soaked Nick's face and neck as he sat up, swung his leg around, and straddled his opponent's chest. He drew back the knife for a second strike but saw that none was required.

It was over.

And then hands tightened around his throat like iron claws.

Suddenly, Feng's fingers were crushing his windpipe, cutting off the air and bringing a sharp, ripping pain, the likes of which he'd never felt before. He stabbed downward, sinking the blade all the way to the hilt somewhere in the tattooed villain's torso, but he couldn't see where. He blinked furiously, trying to clear the blood from his eyes. How was this man not dead? Nick's head begin to swim as the viselike fingers expertly cut off the flow of blood in his carotid arteries, starving his brain of oxygen. Somehow, he'd lost his grip on the knife. He groped for the handle, desperately wanting to stab again, but he couldn't feel it anywhere. As the world started to go black, his final thought was to slip both of his thumbs up and under the thumbs that were choking the life out of him.

The move bought him a moment of relief, and he felt the whoosh of blood moving up his neck once again. His vision returned, and he stared down.

To his wonderment, Feng's face was perfectly composed. He saw no fear, no pain, no panic—just cold, black eyes with a laser focus Nick had never witnessed before. Despite the blood pouring from his body, the maniac maintained perfect concentration. Just below Feng's Adam's apple, the white cartilage was splayed open and bloody bubbles formed and popped as air hissed from his trachea. On each side of the gash, geysers of bright-red blood shot several feet into the air in twin carotid fountains with each beat of Feng's heart, but the grip on Nick's throat did not waver. In fact, Nick felt the man's ironwood fingers squeezing tighter and tighter, driving Nick's thumb knuckles deep into his neck. How was Feng not unconscious? How was he not dead? Most of his blood volume was already on the floor, and yet he was still trying to crush Nick's windpipe.

But time was Nick's ally now.

As dark clouds once again crept into his visual field, the blood gushing from Feng's neck began to weaken. With each heartbeat, the arcs became shorter and shorter as the last of the madman's blood leaked from his throat. Eventually, it was little more than a pulsatile pool, dribbling onto the floor.

And yet the iron claws persisted, clenching his throat.

Feng's eyes clouded and then drifted slowly up and to the left as the life began to leave him. His shoulders sagged. His head lolled to the right, but somehow the man's fingers were still suffocating Nick. With all his might, Nick gripped the dying man's thumbs and twisted. He heard twin *pops*—as if he'd just wrenched a drumstick from a turkey—and the dislocated thumbs finally went limp. A beat later, his attacker's hands collapsed into the lake of blood pooling on the floor with a soft splash.

Nick rolled off of the dead man's chest and backpedaled away, feeling the warm blood soak through his cargo pants. He crabbed backward with both lingering fear and disgust, imagining that somehow Feng's corpse was about to reanimate and finish the job.

He sat with his back against the wall, massaging his throat and coughing violently. He closed his eyes and used four-count tactical breathing to regulate his rasping breath until another coughing fit seized control.

"Team two, this is lead. We have control of the ship. Report status," he heard Zhang's voice say, but far away. He reached up and found his earpiece dangling, and he shoved it back into his ear canal, then pulled the mike to his mouth. He tried to talk, but he couldn't stop coughing.

"Nick, this is Lankford, over . . . Nick, this is Lankford, do you copy?"

Unlike Zhang's call, Nick heard fear and worry in the CIA man's voice. A sudden pang of panic gripped him. Something was wrong. Was it possible she bled out?

He keyed his mike again and tried to talk but could only manage a single raspy word: "Daaashhh?"

Nick felt tears well in his eyes and looked at the dead man in the lake of blood. *Oh my God, while I was fighting this maniac, Dash died on the table.*

Then, as if reading his thoughts, Lankford said, "Dash is okay . . . She's awake, and she's asking for you, Nick."

Nick was on his feet, the pain in his knee and throat now just background noise. He scooped up his assault rifle and forced himself to methodically clear for threats as he moved toward the only door that mattered now.

A smile crept across his battered face as he keyed his mike. "Tell her I'm on my way."

CHAPTER 33

The first piece of her humanity that Dash reclaimed was the ability to blink. A minute later, she was able to move her eyes. Then, as her body metabolized the succinylcholine in her bloodstream, she was able to move her jaw, then her diaphragm, and then her fingers. The moment she'd started wiggling her fingers, she really got their attention. The three men in the room with her—two Snow Leopards and Lankford—were powerless to help her. None of them had any medical training to speak of. The next five minutes were absolute torture as she had to suffer the agony of being fully conscious and intubated with her gag reflex restored, all the while lacking the muscle tone and dexterity to disconnect the ventilator and rip the breathing tube out of her throat. When she was finally able to manipulate her arms, she extubated herself.

When that was done, she cried. And when that was done, she had one of the Snow Leopards help bandage her abdomen from sternum to pubis—fixing the gauze in place that Nick had packed into her incision.

Now she sat naked on the operating table, her legs dangling off the side, waiting for the strength to stand. But before that happened, she began to shudder uncontrollably.

I'm just cold. Malignant hyperthermia is an extremely rare complication of succinylcholine. The drug is nearly gone. The half-life is only five to eight minutes, so I will feel more myself any moment.

Seeing her shake, one of the Snow Leopards left the room. He returned thirty seconds later with a heavy cotton blanket and draped it over her back and shoulders. Then he helped her gather it closed in front.

She looked up at him. "Thank you," she wheezed, barely able to speak the words.

Lankford, who she just now realized had been shot, hobbled over until he was in front of her. He met her eyes and gave her his best smile.

"Are you okay?" he asked.

"Where is Nick?" she whispered.

"He went after Feng."

Dread washed over her, and she suddenly felt like she might vomit.

"Call him," she said.

Lankford keyed his radio and made the call.

Her heart skipped a beat when she heard Nick's raspy voice come back over the radio.

The next thing she knew, he was there, standing in the doorway. At first, the look of him startled her. Tears came unbidden. His left cheek and temple glistened with blood. Another small stream trickled down the right side of his neck from a gouge in the top of his ear. But none of this compared to his neck, which was so bruised, it had turned black along his trachea and on both sides.

"What happened to you?" she sobbed.

"Feng," he said simply, and then he came to her.

"Me too," she said, looking down at her stomach.

"Are you okay?" he asked as his eyes—those strong Navy SEAL eyes—filled with tears.

"Yes," she said and eased herself off the operating table and onto unsteady legs.

He unslung his rifle, set it on the table, and then opened his arms to her.

She collapsed against his chest as tears continued to stream down her cheeks. She closed her eyes and felt his strong arms envelope her. He pulled her closer, until she could hear the pounding of his heart in his chest. After a long embrace, she loosened her grip on him, and he did the same. She tilted her chin up, closed her eyes, and waited for his lips to find hers. And into this kiss, they both poured all their joy and their pain, all their hope and their fear, and shared a moment of profound and fragile communion that only two strong yet wounded souls can recognize. She felt the kiss through her whole body, and when their lips parted, she shuddered.

She exhaled and opened her eyes. A black-clad figure in the doorway caught her attention. She shifted her gaze and locked eyes with Commander Zhang. The look on his face was strange and one she hadn't seen before, but before she could blink, he turned his back on her and walked away.

"Not at all how I had imagined our first kiss," Nick said, staring down at her and smiling.

"But you had imagined it?" she said, meeting his stare.

"Many, many times."

She hugged him, but this time, she was acutely aware of the searing pain along her wound. She winced and bent at the waist.

"We need to get you dressed and then on a helo to a hospital," he said.

"Agreed, but the two of you," she said, looking from Nick to Lankford and back again, "are coming with me."

And for once, neither man argued with her.

PART III

CHAPTER 34

Xi'an, China
Two days later
0850 hours local

Nick noticed that Dash let go of his hand the instant Zhang pulled up to the hotel in a hired car. She hadn't really been "holding" his hand anyway—more like letting him hold hers. It was fine, Nick decided. Emotionally, this was a challenging time for all of them, but especially her. He opened the front passenger door for her and then climbed into the back. His abused muscles, bones, joints, lacerations, and throat all screamed out in pain as he contorted his body to get into the cramped rear seat. But the physical pain he was feeling paled in comparison to the growing apprehension he felt about the meeting he was headed to with Agent Ling. The female MSS agent had given them forty-eight hours to rescue Dash, complete their operation, and turn themselves in or face dire consequences. This was them following through on their half of the bargain, but to Nick, the impending drive to the Ministry of State Security field office felt like walking the green mile.

"I don't know where Lankford is," Nick mumbled as he buckled his seat belt. "He never came down this morning."

"Due to the severity of his injury," Zhang said, "yesterday, Lankford requested medical attention. A heated debate ensued among my interagency peers on the matter. Some individuals felt that the best care for someone like Mr. Lankford would be rendered at the prison in Guangzhou. Others suggested a military hospital, where he could be kept under armed guard. A third contingent argued that he be sent to the closest civilian hospital in Xi'an for immediate care."

"And what camp were you in?" he asked, meeting Zhang's stare.

"None of these," Zhang said, straight-faced. "I determined that the decision was one best made by the US Consulate, so under the cover of darkness last night, I arranged for his safe transport to Beijing and communicated the three options for his care. Apparently, your government thought of a fourth option, which involved placing Mr. Lankford on a red-eye flight to Germany. It seems they have excellent hospitals in Germany."

Nick couldn't help but grin to himself—*Lankford, you slimy bastard, you never even bothered to say good-bye.*

Zhang glanced at him in the rearview mirror.

"Thank you, Zhang," Nick said, meeting his compeer's gaze. "You didn't have to do that."

"Yes, I did," Zhang said. "I owed him at least that. And it was the same offer I tried to extend to you at dinner last night, but you interrupted me three times, so I gave up. You're a very stubborn man, Nick Foley."

"The only way I'm leaving China is if they drag me out kicking and screaming," Nick said, glancing sideways at Dash as Zhang pulled out of the parking lot.

"Depending on how this meeting goes with Agent Ling," Zhang replied. "It very well might come to that."

They rode in silence the rest of the drive. The macabre events on the "hospital" ship had deeply affected all of them, Dash most of all. Clearly she had been traumatized, but the depths of that trauma and the long-term psychological impact, only time would tell. He'd tried to talk to her about it last night, but she had said she was tired and had retired early to her room. When they had met again this morning, she had just smiled at him wordlessly.

As they walked from the rental car to the office park, Nick wondered if the Chinese symbols on the dark glass doors said Ministry of State Security or if they concealed their presence under the guise of "farm bureau" or some equally nebulous ruse, like some of the spookier US agencies with letters for names were prone to do.

"I recommend we show restraint and gratitude toward Agent Ling and her colleagues," Zhang said sternly, his hand on the door handle. "After all, we could be having this interview in a federal detention center."

Nick shrugged. He did not feel the same level of confidence about their situation as Zhang. He wondered if, after today, he would ever see Dash again. Perhaps they would escort him to a plane waiting to whisk him out of China forever. With Lankford gone, perhaps he would become both scapegoat and consolation prize, and Ling would order him straight to prison. Hell, this was the MSS . . . Perhaps the only way he'd leave this building was in an urn.

Zhang, still waiting for a response, kept his hand on the door handle and his eyes on Nick. The shrug, apparently, was not sufficient.

"I'll be nice," Nick grumbled.

"Thank you," Zhang said and pulled open the door. As Nick passed, he whispered, "If not for yourself, then for Dr. Chen."

They were made to wait on a sofa that looked pretty enough but did nothing good for his neck and back. No one spoke. Nick alternately shifted his gaze between the wall clock and Dash. Now and again, she would pull gently and absently on her silk blouse. He wondered if the incision on her abdomen was hurting her.

"Are you all right?" he whispered when he thought he saw her wince.

"I'm fine," she said with a wan smile, but her mind seemed to be somewhere else.

Her answer sounded very "American," the one language he knew how to read between the lines in. Physically, Dash was fine, but emotionally, how could she be? After the psychological and physical abuse she'd sustained strapped to that operating table, it was a wonder she wasn't a basket case doped up on Valium and Xanax. Her presence here was a testament to her strength of character. But in Nick's experience, even the toughest, most steely nerved, badass frogmen weren't immune to the effects of post-traumatic stress. Trauma of the magnitude she'd survived wasn't something that a mind could come to terms with overnight. The journey would be long and fraught with guilt, anger, and nightmares.

He knew this from personal experience.

"I'm sorry, Dash," he said softly.

She looked up, coming back from wherever her mind had gone, and smiled. "What are you sorry for? Saving my life? Exacting justice on the psychopath who tried to harvest my organs without anesthesia? Or for taking care of me these last forty-eight hours?"

"I'm sorry for dragging you into this."

"You didn't drag me into this. I left Beijing first, remember?"

"Yeah, but if I hadn't called you that morning in Hong Kong, Feng would have never targeted the task force."

"That's simply not true. Your call saved hundreds of lives, Nick—maybe thousands. You helped us fill in the pieces of the puzzle that led us to Nèiyè Biologic and Feng. We owe you. China owes you . . . again," she added and looked at Zhang.

The Snow Leopard Commander nodded. "She's right," Zhang said, but his expression was statuesque—a mask concealing whatever real emotions the elite counterterrorism operator was battling inside at the moment.

"So what do you think will happen to us?" Nick asked.

Before Zhang could answer, the receptionist behind the counter called to them in Chinese.

"They're ready for us," Zhang said and stood. "You have my support, Nick," the Snow Leopard added, clapping him on the shoulder.

"So you changed your mind," Nick said with a sideways glance, "and you're not arresting me?"

"Not if the MSS arrests you first," Zhang replied with a hint of a smile.

The woman led them through frosted-glass doors and then down a short hallway that ended at a door of black glass. Nick peered inside the room as the woman held them at the threshold while she talked with a stern-looking fellow dressed in a black suit. A large, oval-shaped wooden conference table occupied the center of the room; it was inlaid with regularly spaced black leather writing surfaces, each with a microphone and a black rectangular speaker box. The table was like something out of a spy movie, and nothing like the field-erected plywood workstations he had come to know in the TOCs of Iraq and Afghanistan.

The receptionist stepped aside and gestured them in.

At the end of the table sat Agent Ling Ju, flanked on each side by powerful-looking men in dark suits who sat stiffly with their hands folded on the table. Ling looked just as angry as the last time Nick had seen her. Zhang walked into the room with casual confidence and selected a seat at the opposite head of the table from Ling. Nick noticed that her scowl seemed to deepen.

Nick elected to cross behind Zhang and take the seat to his immediate right. He expected Dash to take the seat on Zhang's left, but instead she also passed behind Zhang and dropped into the empty seat beside Nick. To his surprise, she reached over and gave his leg a hopeful squeeze under the table before placing her hands in her lap.

Ling looked expectantly past Zhang into the hallway behind. After an uncomfortable pause, she said, "Where is Mr. Lankford?"

Zhang sniffed. "Who?"

"Chet Lankford," Ling repeated. "The self-professed American CIA agent guilty of conducting espionage against China, whom you removed at gunpoint from my custody forty-eight hours ago."

"Oh yes, that Chet Lankford," Zhang said with a straight face. "I'm afraid I don't know."

"What do you mean you don't know?" Ling hissed.

"He accompanied us to Xi'an yesterday and was booked in the same hotel as the rest of us. This morning, when it was time to leave for this meeting, he did not come down to the lobby. When we phoned his room, he did not answer. When I questioned reception, they said that Mr. Lankford had checked out of the hotel in the middle of the night. Where he went after that, I do not know. Hopefully, he will be along shortly. I assure you he was informed about this meeting."

Ling narrowed her eyes at Zhang. "Do you think this is a joke, Commander Zhang?"

"No, far from it."

"Then you must think me a fool," she said.

"No, Agent Ling, not a fool."

"Evasion is the hallmark of guilt, Commander Zhang. When we find Mr. Lankford, I can assure you that he will be treated accordingly."

Zhang nodded. "I understand, but since Mr. Lankford is not present, I cannot speak for the man."

"I think you already have," she seethed and then opened a black leather folder on the desk in front of her before continuing in clipped, angry Chinese—her eyes on whatever was in the folder.

After only a few sentences, Zhang held up his hand, interrupting her. "Excuse me, I would ask that for clarity and transparency—and out of respect for Mr. Foley, who does not speak Chinese fluently—that we please return to conducting the meeting in English."

Ling dropped her black pen on the papers in front of her. "If Mr. Foley was the valuable asset you claim him to be, would it not be imperative that he speak Chinese?"

"My apologies, ma'am," Nick said, his voice cracking. Zhang reached over and squeezed his forearm, hushing him before he could continue.

Ling pursed her lips and nodded. "Very well," she said, now staring at Nick. "Since the outcome of the meeting will determine his fate, as well as yours," she added, eyeing Dash, "we will continue in English." She picked up a piece of paper from her folder. "Now . . ."

"I'm sorry to interrupt again, Special Agent Ling—may I call you Ju?" Zhang said.

"You may not," she answered, her face now red with irritation, a vein on her forehead pulsing.

"Very well," Zhang continued, unfazed. "Agent Ling, I sincerely apologize for the incident in Xi'an. I know you had no way of knowing that you were inadvertently disrupting a joint task force counterterrorism operation. And while the task force forgives your ignorance and interference—"

"*You* forgive *me*?" Ling interrupted, rising from her chair. She leaned forward, placing her hands on the table and looking very much like an angry she-lion ready to pounce. "Are you insane?"

So much for restraint and gratitude, Nick thought. Perhaps Zhang really was nuts. Nick's fate was in this woman's hands, and here Zhang was, antagonizing her and trading jabs like this was some sort of lover's spat. *Should I intervene?* he wondered. *Throw myself on the mercy of the proverbial court?* He looked over at Dash, who looked back at him with equally confused eyes.

Suddenly, Ling seemed to regain control of herself and sat back in her chair. "Perhaps it is you who were in the dark, Commander Zhang," she said, forcing a maternal smile. "We were not out for a leisurely drive and happened upon your happy band of marauders. That is the correct word, is it not, Special Operator Second Class Foley—marauders?"

Nick met her gaze. "That's not the word *I* would choose, but I understand the point you're trying to make," he said. There was only so much shit biscuit he was willing to eat.

"What word would you choose, Petty Officer Foley?"

"It's Mr. Foley—I no longer serve in the Navy—and the word I would use is 'team.'"

"Team?"

"Yes, team. We were operating as a team. Not unlike the type of interagency Special Operations teams you participate with in the course of doing your job here at the Ministry of State Security."

"But you are not a Chinese citizen, Mr. Foley. You are not employed by the Snow Leopard Commandos, nor any agency of the Chinese government. In fact, your employer is the Central Intelligence Agency. The only 'team' you are aiding is one actively conducting espionage against the People's Republic of China, which makes you an enemy of state."

"That is where you are wrong, Agent Ling," Nick said, his voice hardening. "I work for Water 4 Humanity. I am not, and never have been, an agent for the CIA. I offered to help look for a missing American expat in Xi'an. Period, end of story. I was not working under contract, nor was I, at any time, engaged in espionage against China."

"If you don't serve the CIA, who do you serve?" Ling said, leaning forward.

He thought carefully and then simply said, "Justice."

"Justice?" Ling echoed with a contemptuous laugh.

"Who are you to mock him?" Dash said, raising her voice. "Must he remove his shirt so you can see the scars of his sacrifice?"

Ling glared at her but said nothing.

"Must I?" Dash shouted, her voice cracking as she stood to face the three MSS agents at the end of the table. With her jaw set in defiance, she raised her silk blouse to show the vertical incision—raw, pink, and angry—that stretched from her breastbone to her pubis. "And I was one of the lucky ones," she said. She released her blouse, reached into the unzipped mouth of her purse sitting on the floor beside her chair, and then flung a stack of A4-sized, full-page, glossy photographs across the table. The imagery was both gruesome and haunting—a collage of eyeless corpses missing noses, fingers, genitalia, and organs.

"If you aren't moved by Nick's sacrifice, then maybe you care about hers, or his, or hers, or his," Dash continued, flinging photograph after photograph across the table at Agent Ling. "This is the work of a madman. So when Nick says he served justice, maybe now you appreciate what he is talking about."

Gooseflesh stood up on Nick's arms and legs as he stared at Dash in wonderment. Despite the red rancor on her face, she was trembling uncontrollably. He had no words to express the emotions he felt for her in that moment. She was fearless . . . She was his champion.

He looked back at Agent Ling and saw in her face that she was beaten. She had lost. Even if she had the authority to prosecute Nick, she would have to do so with the knowledge that whatever punishment she meted, it was punishment meted without honor.

At this crescendo, at this turning of the tide, Zhang pulled a paper from his uniform pocket. He unfolded it and set it on the table in front of him. "I have a letter from the Central National Security Commission, signed by Deputy Chairman Hu Zedong, granting me full discretion and authority in this investigation. But before we discuss any more details of this case, I must ask your fellow agents to excuse themselves."

"Excuse themselves? And why is that?" Ling gestured to the agent on her right, who rose, retrieved the letter from Zhang, and then carried it back to her.

"I'm afraid that they do not hold adequate security clearances for the conversation we're about to have," Zhang said softly and smiled.

Special Agent Ling scanned the letter. After a beat, she scowled and dismissed her subordinates with a wave of her hand. The two MSS agents stood and exited the room via a door behind their boss.

Zhang spoke before she could say anything.

"As you can see from this letter, Mr. Nick Foley was granted a temporary clearance to work with the SLCU as a special consultant."

"This letter is from the Central National Security Commission?" Ling said, her voice resonating with surprise.

"Yes," Zhang said. If he was relishing the moment, he made no sign of it.

Nick made a concerted effort to conceal his own shock. Was this for real? If so, when had Zhang reached out to the deputy chairman? Before or after Major Li's death? If after, then he had taken an incredible risk for Nick.

"That letter confirms that Mr. Foley is, as he stated, a part of my *team*. Furthermore," Zhang added, cutting Ling off before she could get a word in edgewise, "this is not the first time Mr. Foley has risked his life for China. A few months ago, he was instrumental in unmasking and preventing a bioterrorism plot that, had it unfolded, would have resulted in the loss of thousands of innocent Chinese lives. I would tell you more, but the incident has been classified above your pay grade."

"You are referring to Beijing?" Ling asked, a flash of recognition in her eyes.

"I am not at liberty to discuss the details, but our government owes Mr. Foley a debt of gratitude," Zhang said. Then, with a subtle sideways glance at Nick, he said, "Consider that debt repaid."

Special Agent Ling looked down at the letter again as if trying to ascertain if it was a forgery.

"All this infighting and suspicion between us is distracting us from the real issue," Dash said. "Our task force's operation was compromised, and as much as you'd like to blame the Americans, they're not the ones responsible. Our colleague, Major Li, was murdered because he started asking the right questions about the wrong people. Feng might be dead, but this investigation is far from over. There's more going on here than meets the eye."

Ling exhaled long and slow through her nose before saying, "I'm inclined to agree with you, Dr. Chen." She picked up a remote control off the table and pointed it at a flat-screen television mounted on the far wall. The television flickered to life, and on the display was a video feed of a Chinese woman—attractive and in her midthirties—sitting alone at a small table in a small room. The woman was fidgeting in her seat and looked nervous. "This is Chow Mei, Mr. Feng's executive assistant at Nèiyè Biologic. She and I had several lengthy and insightful discussions yesterday. As it turns out, Ms. Chow is quite a wellspring of information concerning both the personnel and the day-to-day operations at Nèiyè. You see, after Commander Zhang liberated Mr. Foley and Mr. Lankford from my custody at gunpoint and left my vehicle disabled on the side of the road, I had no choice but to collect my thoughts. As I watched the traffic, it occurred to me that the only reason a man with a service record as impeccable and distinguished as Commander Zhang would possibly behave so out of character was either because he was under duress or because the stakes were so high that he had no other option. Clearly, the former was out of the question because he had been the one pointing guns at my team, which left me with only one conclusion. So while all of you were on the hospital ship, I took a team to Nèiyè Biologic headquarters."

Nick could see Zhang nodding with unrestrained satisfaction in his peripheral vision as Agent Ling spoke. The mood in the conference room had shifted now, from outright hostility to one of tentative collaboration. Nick listened, without interruption, as Ling shared her findings—the most notable of which was that the company's CEO, Yao Xing Jian, had left the country two hours before the events at the Terracotta Warrior Museum, and his current whereabouts were unknown. Ling went on to say that none of the employees questioned thus far admitted to having any knowledge of Feng's black-market operation or the secret hospital ship. She concluded by pointing at Dash's gruesome photographs, still untouched on the conference table, and saying, "Which brings us back to this—an illicit organ-harvesting ring being run by a respected company in Xi'an right under our noses. It's despicable."

"What I'm about to say might come as a shock to everyone," Dash said, "especially given what happened to me on that ship, but I believe that Feng's organ-harvesting operation is the red herring in this case."

Ling screwed up her face at the comment. "How can you say such a thing? You've just proven that Nèiyè Biologic had an entire supply chain established for the harvesting, sale, and transplant of organs on a grand scale."

"And not just regular organs," Zhang added. "We now know that they were selling genetically modified organs for a premium price. Would that not be worth a fortune?"

"Fortunes are relative," Dash said. "Nèiyè Biologic is a billion-dollar company. They made more revenue last year on biomedical technology sales than they could make in a decade selling designer organs on the black market. The risk-reward proposition is completely upside-down. Why risk billions to make millions? And besides, if the goal is really to sell designer organs, why not make it a legitimate business unit? Why lie, cheat, murder, and steal your way into the segment when you could create an entirely new industry? They have the infrastructure in place to do it."

"Because Feng was clinically insane," Zhang said.

"Insane, but not an idiot," Nick countered.

Dash nodded. "There has to be something more going on. Feng hinted as much when I was strapped to that operating table."

"You didn't mention that before," Zhang said, looking surprised. "What did he say to you?"

"I can practically hear him," she said, squeezing her eyes shut. "He said, 'Editing genes in transplant organs is only phase one . . . Phase two is where the real transformation occurs.'"

"Then what the hell is phase two?" Nick asked.

"I can't prove this yet, but I believe that everything Feng was doing—both legal and illegal—was wrapped up in a quest for immortality. When we were at the Terracotta Warrior Museum, before he kidnapped me, he spoke with great authority about the First Emperor and his obsession with the Elixir of Life. I think Feng was modeling his life and work after Chancellor Li Si, the architect of the Five Pains and steward of the First Emperor's quest for eternal life. The mutilated, tattooed bodies we've collected are evidence of Feng's pathological channeling of Li Si. The rest is evidence of his obsession with immortality."

"What are you saying—that his plan was to stop aging by replacing people's old, worn-out organs with healthy, young organs?" Nick asked.

"In phase one, yes," she said. "In fact, that was his plan for me. He intended to gift my organs to his dying mother. But as far as what phase two entails, I need more time with the documents and patient records we recovered from the hospital ship. Give me another twelve hours to continue digging, and I should have some answers."

Zhang leaned forward. "While Dr. Chen conducts her investigation, I think the three of us have our own digging to do. I'm not ready to let Yao Xing Jian off the hook. The timing of his disappearance is practically an admission of guilt. With Feng out of the picture, we need to learn everything there is to learn about Yao."

"And there is also the matter of Major Li's murder to be investigated. There are political implications that must be considered in both cases," Ling said.

"Agreed, but something else has been bothering me," Zhang said, fixing his gaze on Ling. "How was it that your team arrived at the museum at just the right moment to interrupt our covert operation and enable Feng to kidnap Dr. Chen and escape? This could not have been coincidence."

Ling pursed her lips and leaned back. "We were conducting a counterespionage sting."

"You were chasing Lankford?" Zhang asked.

"Yes, and Mr. Foley," she said with a quick glance at Nick before looking back at Zhang. "We had intelligence implicating them in the murder of a young female Nèiyè employee in Xi'an. Naturally, we linked Major Li's murder to them as well. I was tasked with finding them and bringing them in, and my group received a tip that morning as to their whereabouts."

"Are you responsible for the hit on our safe house in Hong Kong?" Nick asked, turning back to glare at Ling and making no effort to conceal his rising anger.

"No," she said. "My orders were to locate, apprehend, and interrogate—period."

"If not the MSS," Nick said, "then who has been trying to kill me?"

"Undoubtedly, the same people who killed Major Li," Ling said coolly. "Mercenaries, I suspect, hired by Feng."

"No way it's that clean. I went black," Nick said. "Hired guns don't have access to the type of pooled intelligence necessary to pull off the hits they did."

"Just what are you implying, Mr. Foley?" Ling said, her voice hardening.

"That one of your agents is compromised, Agent Ling," Zhang said, beating Nick to the punch. "And before we do anything else, we need to find out who and rectify the problem."

CHAPTER 35

Dash stepped back from the wall and looked at the product of her labor.

This was the first time she'd ever made a "case wall," similar to the variety depicted on television shows about detectives solving long, complex, conspiratorial murder cases. She was a doctor; she was a CDC emergency responder and epidemiological researcher. She was not a detective . . . and yet looking at her handiwork from the past day and a half, she might be able to convince people otherwise. Photographs, maps, autopsy reports, research notes, patient files, Nèiyè Biologic laboratory documents, and on and on—all connected by different-colored lines. And in the middle was a picture of Xue Shi Feng. She stared at his picture with contempt. To think that he had literally been within seconds of harvesting her organs, cutting her liver, kidneys, pancreas, lungs, and heart out of her while she was alive and conscious.

She shuddered, which made her incision sting.

She pinched her silk blouse and held it out away from her stomach. It was the lightest, softest blouse she owned, but even the slightest touch along the wound was an irritant. She looked down the V-neck at the bumpy, ugly suture work that ran down her stomach and disappeared below the waistband of her pants.

"I look so ugly now," she said and let go of her shirt.

It could be worse, she reminded herself, looking at the section of wall with photographs of the corpses. *I could be one of them.*

She looked back at the photograph of Feng. She knew much more about the man now than she had eighteen hours ago. By far, the most fascinating medical file she'd gained access to from the hospital ship data server was Feng's electronic health record. She was excited to brief the rest of the team on her findings and equally excited to hear the new intelligence they had unearthed. She'd heard from Nick that Ling had identified the MSS leak, but he'd only hinted about the rest.

The door to the conference room abruptly flew open, startling her, and in strode Zhang, Nick, and Ling. Zhang had "found" a recently vacated space in a two-story civilian office complex within a mile of the Xi'an MSS building. The previous tenant had not moved out their furniture and workstations. Personal mementos and office decorations still adorned a few of the offices, making Dash wonder if the tenant had actually moved or if Zhang had simply commandeered the facility for the week.

"Nèiyè Biologic is on fire," Nick said, walking straight up to her. "The entire facility is burning to the ground. It was burning when we got there with our team. We got nothing, absolutely nothing."

"Then it's arson," Dash said, looking from Nick to Zhang. "No other explanation."

"Agreed," Zhang said.

"Was anyone hurt?"

"Unclear. Initial reports indicate the fire started before the office opened, but it will take time before we know how many employees, if any, were inside."

"What now?" she asked.

"Now we brief," Zhang said, taking a seat at the table. "With our investigation hitting a brick wall, it's probably best that we all share our findings and then decide next steps as a group. Dr. Chen, would you like to go first?"

She nodded as the others took a seat. "Probably the most interesting thing that I've discovered," Dash said, walking over to her case wall, "is that Feng had Prader-Willi syndrome."

"What is Prader-Willi syndrome?" Agent Ling asked.

"Prader-Willi is a rare genetic mutation in which several important genes are missing on the fifteenth chromosome. A host of issues are associated with this syndrome, but the hallmark characteristic is incessant, insatiable hunger—a gnawing, visceral hunger that cannot be quelled no matter how much or how frequently the patient eats."

"That sounds horrible," Nick muttered, his stomach rumbling as if in agreement.

"Oh, yes," Dash said. "It would be a life of torture. I believe Prader-Willi was the source of Feng's psychopathy. Suddenly, his low-empathy, sadistic tendencies and his preoccupation with punishment begin to make sense. I cannot imagine the lens he must have perceived the world through. For someone with Prader-Willi, life would seem a great injustice, and ordinary people, spoiled and undisciplined."

"That makes total sense, but what does Feng having Prader-Willi have to do with organ harvesting?" Nick asked.

"Excellent question, Nick," she said. "And I'm not sure I have a complete answer yet, but the short one is this: Prader-Willi syndrome has nothing to do with organ harvesting but a great deal to do with CRISPR. I believe Feng's ultimate goal was to leverage the research Nèiyè Biologic has been conducting on CRISPR Cas9 so that he could someday use CRISPR on himself to repair his defective chromosomes by editing back in the genes he's been missing since birth."

"Then why hadn't he done it?" Zhang asked. "Why hadn't he used CRISPR to fix his genetic defect already?"

"Because CRISPR Cas9 editing is tricky. The mechanism was discovered in bacteria only a few years ago, and like every new technology, there are glitches that need to be worked out. The problem that all CRISPR practitioners face is preventing off-target mutations and unintended manipulations. Feng understood the implications of living with a faulty genetic code better than anyone. The last thing he'd want to do is use CRISPR to try to edit back in genes on chromosome fifteen but in the process inadvertently delete other critical genes elsewhere in his genome. Feng was a man of discipline. His entire existence was about discipline. Most people with Prader-Willi become morbidly obese from constant eating. Not Feng; his health record shows he's been practicing calorie control his entire adult life. I cannot imagine the self-control necessary to live that way."

"A fascinating finding," Ling said. "Thank you, Dr. Chen."

"Oh, I'm not finished," Dash said, shooting the agent a wry smile. "Feng was experimenting with CRISPR on the transplant organs. The organ recipients were already very sick people. They were the perfect test subjects because they had nothing to lose, and because they were receiving black-market organs, they were willing accomplices to the crime. He didn't have to worry about any of these clients suing him or going to the police if the CRISPR therapy went wrong. Equally important, the genetic modification he was trying to perform on the organs—relatively speaking—was an easy one. He was only trying to manipulate one thing: the alleles needed to ensure major histocompatibility complex matching between the transplant organ and recipient. Think of it as practice before the actual game."

"Okay, that makes sense," Zhang said, "but I'm still confused about the big picture. Why risk the company? Why not just practice CRISPR on rats until he was confident enough to use it on himself?"

Dash sighed. "I don't have an answer to that, Commander, only a theory—and my theory might sound a little crazy."

"Feng is dead, Nèiyè Biologic is burning to the ground, and Yao is missing," Nick said. "At this point, Dash, I think we're okay with crazy."

"Okay," she said with a little shrug. "Everything I've just described dovetails neatly into the Elixir of Life hypothesis I proposed before. I believe Yao and Feng had been working on this together from the beginning. In fact, did you know that Yao and Feng are the same age? They went to the same primary school together. I found a magazine interview from last year, in which Yao talks about founding the company. Feng was employee number two; he's been Yao's right-hand man for nearly two decades.

When I combine this information with bits and pieces of the conversation I had with Feng, a very clear picture emerges. Some time ago, Yao and Feng embarked on a grand quest together, a quest that dates back over two thousand years to the First Emperor of China and his chancellor."

"History repeating itself?" Ling asked, looking dubious.

"Yes, as it tends to do. The quest for the Elixir of Life has seduced many rich and powerful men over the millennia," Dash said, eyeing them each in turn. "The quest for immortality. I think this was what Feng meant when he talked to me about phase two of the project. The organ transplant and reprogramming was simply a baby step toward the ultimate goal of life extension via CRISPR. If they could figure out how to use CRISPR to fix Feng's Prader-Willi syndrome and program cellular histocompatibility in people after organ transplant, then why not shoot for the moon? Why not tackle all the genes responsible for chronic disease and aging? Even now, some of the greatest minds in medicine are postulating that aging is nothing more than a genetic disease, one that we pass down from generation to generation. It's not so different from Prader-Willi syndrome, just more complex. For Nèiyè Biologic, CRISPR is the chalice that holds the Elixir of Life. Once they solved the problem of off-target mutations, Yao and Feng would have the power to decide who lives and who dies in this world."

Nick and Zhang stared at her in silence as they processed the implications of her theory. Even the normally argumentative Agent Ling had no rebuttal or rebuke for her this time.

Finally, Nick spoke, and all he said was, "Whoa."

"I know," she said. "It even sounds crazy to me."

"Assuming you're right, what is the end goal here—a new generation of designer babies that grow up to be immortal?" Ling asked with the hostility in her voice absent for the first time since Dash had met the woman.

"Modifying the germ line is certainly a possibility, but this technology would not be constrained to zygote modification. Mature adults could be altered; certainly, this was their intention.

I believe that Feng and Yao were seeking the Elixir of Life not for their progeny but rather for themselves."

"And for anyone willing to pay enough to join them," Nick added. "Maybe it's time we start wondering about their client list."

"Yes, Nick," Zhang said with a cynical smile. "I think you have just had an epiphany that changes the nature of this case."

"Don't look at me," Nick said, staring with admiration at Dash. "This was all Dash—all I did was suggest the obvious."

An electric silence filled the room until Dash took a seat, smiled, and said, "Your turn."

"First and foremost, we found the leak," Zhang said. "And our initial suspicions were correct. A technician in Ling's office has been passing confidential data to a third party in exchange for bribes. That third party has been identified as a paramilitary black ops unit for hire known as OTK. We have communications linking OTK to Feng, and we believe this outfit is responsible for both the attempts on Nick's life and Major Li's murder. The compromised MSS technician has been taken into custody, and we're putting together a team to root out and take down OTK in China. But as satisfying as these developments are, Yao is still missing."

"What do we know about Yao?" Dash asked, looking at Ling.

"Yao is a charismatic self-made billionaire with a reputation for shrewdness. Interviews with Nèiyè Biologic staff reveal him to be inspiring when he's on the public stage and yet insular and unapproachable during the course of regular business. According to Feng's assistant, Yao left the management of day-to-day company operations entirely to Feng, rarely venturing from the executive floor. She also said that Yao was never in the office—he spent his time traveling abroad weekly to meet with investors and business partners. She paints a picture of Yao as nouveau Chinese royalty—the king of Nèiyè Biologic, intent on building a biotechnology empire. This depiction is very much in keeping with your analogy of Feng channeling Chancellor Li Si. Both men seem to have taken their roles literally. Attempts to extract personal information on Yao from his personal assistant have been frustrating, as she is tenaciously loyal to him, even under the threat of prosecution."

"The Nèiyè headquarters didn't burn down by accident," Nick said, looking at Zhang. "I think it's safe to assume he gave the order."

"Which means that despite uncovering Feng's organ-harvesting operation and finding the hospital ship, Yao has something else to hide. Something so valuable that he would rather destroy the company than let us discover it," Zhang said.

"I agree," Dash said. "And to find the answer, we have to find Yao. The only question is how."

Agent Ling smiled. "The same way we always find powerful people with secrets—we follow the money."

CHAPTER 36

Xi'an, China
2130 hours local

The next ten hours were a whirlwind of events the likes of which Nick had not seen outside of combat. The powerhouse combination of Zhang and Ling pulling strings and calling in favors from every corner of the Chinese intelligence complex was akin to watching two conductors direct the London Symphony Orchestra through two different musical scores simultaneously. As the evening waned, Zhang asked Nick to "take a walk" with him. He led Nick out the back door of the office to a garden courtyard nestled in between the U-shaped wings of the building. Zhang gestured to a sidewalk that snaked out of the courtyard and circled a small manmade lake in the middle of the well-manicured grounds shared by several other office buildings. After twenty meters of mutual silence, the conversation began with a question that knocked Nick off guard right from the start.

"Nick Foley," Zhang said, adopting the formal speech pattern he fell into whenever he was showboating, "if you were a fugitive of the state, on the run from the Chinese Snow Leopard Commandos and the Ministry of State Security, where would you go?"

"Is this a hypothetical question," Nick asked, eyeing Zhang uncomfortably, "or am I about to get a ten-minute head start in a game of let's 'play hide and seek' with the American traitor?"

Zhang tried to stifle a laugh and failed. "Please just answer the question. If you were on the run, trying to evade detection and capture from the likes of us, where would you go and what would you do?"

"All right, I'll play along," Nick said. "Do I have resources?"

"Yes," Zhang said. "You're a billionaire."

"Nice. Do I have international connections I can leverage?"

"Yes, of course, your company has numerous international contacts in the biotechnology space, especially in Europe."

"Then in that case," Nick said, "I would fly out of China on my passport, via a private jet, to a neutral, politically agnostic country that appreciates the value of money . . . a place like, say, Switzerland. I would land at a private airfield and enter the country on a false passport so that my trail died in the air. I would not disembark the plane until it was inside a secure hangar. I would pay cash bribes to eliminate any paper trail and to silence anyone and everyone who possibly could have seen my face. Then I would travel to another country in the EU by hired auto under an alias to a private residence—owned and kept by a trusted partner, located in an obscure, unpopulated region—where I would regroup and plan my next move."

"Sounds to me like you might have some experience as a hunted man on the run."

"Not until recently," Nick said, "and I'd like to keep it that way, thank you very much."

The corner of Zhang's mouth curled into something resembling a smile. "Nick, your intuition on this matter is impressive. Here's what we know. Yao left Xi'an on the day of Dash's kidnapping at zero five hundred on his private jet heading west. His flight plan listed his destination as Astana, Kazakhstan. But this was just a refueling stop. The plane landed, refueled, and took off again. Astana air traffic control reported that Yao's jet was headed for Munich, but German airport officials report no record of Yao's plane landing in Munich, let alone entering German airspace. Maybe he landed in Switzerland, maybe Austria, or maybe

Poland. Regardless, we believe that Yao is somewhere in central Europe, but that is where the trail stops."

"So what's your plan? Wait for him to make a mistake or hope he shows up on CCTV in some major European city? That could be one helluva long wait."

"I have no intention of waiting, which is why you and I are having this conversation alone . . . I need a favor."

Nick stopped walking and turned to face the lake. "What kind of favor?"

Zhang stopped and stood next to him. "I was hoping you'd agree to contact Lankford and see if the CIA would be willing to assist us in locating Yao. Your government has a much closer working relationship with the intelligence agencies in central Europe than mine. To be perfectly honest, neither Agent Ling nor I have any relationships outside China that we can leverage."

"What makes you think Lankford would be willing to help us? If I were Lankford, I'd be pretty irritated with China at the moment."

"Because if it wasn't for me, he'd be sitting in a Chinese prison right now."

"Good point," Nick said. "What made you do it, by the way? Why'd you get him out?"

"There's supposed to be a code of honor in our business, even between adversaries. I have history with Lankford. Ling doesn't. I couldn't trust her to do the right thing."

Nick thought back to his time in Afghanistan and all the different tribal leaders and warlords he'd interacted with. With some, he'd felt the code. With others, not so much. He blew air through his teeth. "I can make the call, and Lankford might want to help us out of a sense of obligation, but a capture/kill operation in central Europe is going to require approval at a level above Lankford's pay grade. We have to give him something to work with. What does the US have to gain from all this?"

Zhang reached into his pocket, pulled out a folded piece of paper, and handed it to Nick. Nick opened it and looked at the hanzi characters arranged in what looked like a printout of a spreadsheet. Mixed in with the Chinese was a smattering of names spelled out in their appropriate English characters. One of the names, James Jericho, sounded familiar.

Nick looked at Zhang. "You do realize I can't read Chinese. This means nothing to me."

"I know," Zhang said. "But we're on the clock, so I only translated the English names of relevance."

"Okay, well, what is this?"

"That is a list of Yao's clients for Project Penglai."

"What is Project Penglai?"

"According to Dr. Chen, Penglai Mountain is the mythological home of the eight immortals, and it is the location where the First Emperor of China believed he would find the Elixir of Life. She believes Project Penglai is phase two of Yao and Feng's plan. Everyone on this list is a billionaire, a titan of industry, or a politico. Without exception, the men and women on this list occupy coveted positions of power and influence. You should recognize many of the names."

"James Jericho the US senator?" Nick asked.

"Yes."

As Nick scanned down the list, now with the proper context, more and more of the names sounded familiar. He saw a global media mogul, a Silicon Valley legend responsible for funding many of the world's most famous social media companies, several international heads of state, a prominent investment bank CEO, and so on, and so on.

"Where did you get this?" he asked, not looking up from the paper.

"I sent a team to Yao's private residence this morning. He covered his tracks quite well, but not well enough. With the help of the cybersleuths at Unit 61398, we were able to defeat the encryption on a number of files stored on a USB memory stick locked in a hidden safe."

"These are the people who run the world," Nick said.

"Yes, Nick, and by buying a slot in Project Penglai, they intend to continue running the world for a very, very long time. Until this moment in human history, death was the great equalizer. Rich or poor, strong or weak, famous or obscure—none of these things matter to death. Mortality has always been nature's governor. Fortunes must be passed down, leadership must change hands, opportunities must be given to the young as the old fade away. But now, it appears Yao intends to change all that. By offering immortality to the rich and powerful, for the first time in history, they can cement the world order."

"Holy shit, Zhang. This is unbelievable. We're talking the mother of all conspiracies."

Zhang nodded. "There are many Chinese names on the list I recognize. Now we know why Peter Yu and Major Li were murdered and why we are still not safe. All of these individuals have a great incentive to keep this information hidden. They are playing the ultimate long game. Managing today's scandal is nothing for someone who plans to live forever."

"This list is the ultimate international cabal," Nick said. "With their resources and connections, we don't stand a chance to stop them."

"Which is why we must act immediately," Zhang said, looking out at the water. "I assure you that forces are at work against us even now. The men and women on this list wield enough influence that it is only a matter of time before Agent Ling and I lose our authority or worse. Time, it seems, is against us."

"It always is, brother," Nick said.

"So will you help me? Will you call Lankford?"

"Yes," Nick said, turning to face Zhang. "Just to be clear, what is it exactly that we're asking for?"

"American assistance locating and capturing Yao."

"Are you thinking a 'joint' spec ops task force—US and China?"

Zhang nodded. "It would be the first."

Nick rubbed his chin. "And what about the international cabal? Most of these folks fall into what I'd call the 'untouchables' category."

"Yes, Nick, I know this term, and I agree," Zhang said. "My hope is that if we take Yao and his biotechnology, then the cabal will dissolve organically. Without Yao and the Nèiyè CRISPR Elixir of Life, there is no cabal."

"For a glorified door-kicker, you're surprisingly cerebral, Zhang," Nick said with a smirk.

"For a former frogman, you're surprisingly funny," Zhang fired back.

After a mutual chuckle, each at the other's expense, Nick said, "All right, I'll make the call, but I'd prefer to make it in private."

"Of course," Zhang said and extended his hand. "The list, please."

Nick grinned and handed the paper back to Zhang so he could take his leave. When the Snow Leopard Commander was well out of earshot, Nick retrieved the ultracompact satellite phone that Lankford had given him and dialed the number that Lankford had told him to call only in emergencies. The phone took several long moments to connect, but when it finally did, Lankford picked up on the second ring.

"Well, that didn't take long," the familiar voice said on the line. "I haven't been gone eighteen hours, and you already need my help."

"Nice to talk to you too," Nick said, pacing on the sidewalk. "You make it out okay?"

"Yeah, thanks to Zhang . . . Everything all right, Foley?"

"Yes and no. I'm fine and so is Dash—well, given the circumstances—but the case has taken a turn for the worse."

"That's not good. Is there something I can do?"

"I sure as hell hope so, which is why I'm calling. Are you sitting down?"

"No, Foley, my ass is fucking killing me. Thanks to you, I don't know if sitting will ever be comfortable again."

Nick couldn't help but laugh. "Sorry, man, bad choice of words. Just lean against a wall or something, because what I'm about to tell you is going to knock you off your feet."

CHAPTER 37

Sofitel Hotel
Xi'an, China
0318 hours local

Sleep was the monster under the bed . . . the nightmare in the closet that crept out only once she turned off the lights.

Despite the incapacitating weariness she felt, she didn't have the strength to face her tormentor again. She looked at the clock on the nightstand. It read 03:18. She wondered if she'd gotten any actual sleep since turning in at midnight. Probably less than a half hour, because the minute she closed her eyes, she was back on that operating table—naked, paralyzed, and with a breathing tube snaked down her throat. The reenactment was always the same. Feng's masked face would appear over her, taunting her with those smiling, sadistic eyes. He would run his gloved fingers across her skin, caressing her before picking up the scalpel. Then he would cut her—opening her from sternum to pubis—except in the nightmare, her insides spilled out, and she screamed . . . silent in her dream but aloud in real life.

How long will this torture go on? Will I never be able to sleep again?

Her eyes rimmed with tears, and for an instant, she thought she was going to sob, but she was too exhausted for yet another emotional release. So she just lay there staring at the blurry red numbers on the digital alarm clock.

At 04:12, she switched on the bedside lamp, picked up her phone, and called Nick. He answered on the second ring. "I need you," she said, with no hesitation and without apology.

"On my way," he said, and a beat later, he was knocking on her hotel room door.

She opened the door and stood there in her nightshirt, looking at him.

"Are you okay?" he asked.

"No," she said, her voice catching in her throat.

He stepped across the threshold and gently wrapped his arms around her torso, letting the door swing shut behind him. He held her for a long time . . . held her until she was ready to let go.

"Nightmares?" he asked.

There was no judgment or pity in his voice, just the solemn empathy of someone who was experienced in battling the demons of the night.

She nodded. "Will you stay with me?"

"Of course."

She walked to her bed and climbed in. He slipped in beside her but refrained from touching her. She rolled onto her side, putting her back to him. They stayed that way for several minutes before she spoke.

"As soon as I fall asleep, I'm back on the ship, strapped to the table, and he's there."

Nick said nothing, but she could feel his eyes on her.

"I'm paralyzed and cold," she continued. "Then . . . he cuts me."

He began caressing her head, gently tracing his fingertips front to back, from her forehead, across her temple and ending behind her ear. It immediately soothed her, reminding her of how her mother stroked her hair when she was a young girl.

After a comfortable silence, he said, "In my dreams, I'm in Afghanistan. When I was stationed in the Hindu Kush, we conducted a raid on a Taliban compound. The spooks assured us there weren't any civilians present, but they were wrong. We got overrun by enemy fire, and the LCPO called in a hellfire strike. The missile hit the compound. Innocents died that night . . . women and children . . . I don't know how many times I've relived the event."

"Does it ever stop?" she asked, tears rimming her eyes.

"No, but you get stronger. On the good days, the nightmares don't come . . . and for the bad days, there's Ambien."

At this, she couldn't help but smile, and the humor seemed to take the edge off her dread. She let him continue caressing her hair, and she began to get drowsy until a terrible thought snapped her awake again. In a few hours, Nick was leaving with Zhang on a secret operation to capture Yao.

"Do you have to go?" she asked, craning her neck to look at him.

"I don't have to go," he said. "But without me, the mission is less likely to succeed."

"Did you plan the rescue mission to get me off the ship?"

"Yes."

She nodded. "Will you be involved in the planning of the mission to get Yao?"

"Yes."

"And will you participate in the assault?"

"Yes."

She turned away from him.

"If you want me to stay, I will," he said. "Just say the words."

"If you stay and Yao evades capture, then I would have to live with the knowledge that everything that happened to me— everything I survived—was for naught. Yao will resume his work. He will find another Feng, and more innocent people will suffer and die. I couldn't live with that."

"That's why I have to go," he said.

"But if something happens to you, I couldn't live with that either."

"Nothing's going to happen to me," he said.

"You promise?"

"I promise."

"Hold me," she said.

He spooned his body against her and wrapped his right arm lightly around her torso, careful not to press her still healing wound. She cradled his forearm and closed her eyes. Her respiration fell into synch with his, and the heat of his body warmed and relaxed her like afternoon sun on an autumn day. Despite her best efforts to stave off drowsiness, sleep found her—but this time, instead of being strapped to a madman's operating table, she dreamt of her eighth birthday, and her father, and a beautifully painted puzzle box with a secret inside.

CHAPTER 38

Former Navy Expeditionary Medical Spaces, Building Four
Landstuhl Regional Medical Center
Five kilometers south of Ramstein Air Force Base
Rheiland-Pfalz, Germany
0945 hours local

Nick stifled a completely inappropriate yawn and raised his eyebrows in surprise. He didn't feel tired, despite only getting four hours of sleep last night. Truth be told, he was bored, stuck waiting in the dark conference room at the end of the empty office space for the Navy EMU. The EMU had been abandoned since 2014, when the drawdown from Iraq and Afghanistan had obviated the need for a special space for the coordination of care for Navy SEALs and other special missions' personnel. The reason Lankford had chosen this space was obvious, but Nick would have greatly preferred a homecoming not in Landstuhl. The first time he had visited this place was when he'd accompanied two teammates wounded in Afghanistan—one of whom had died. The second, he was recovering from his own wounds. No happy memories existed for him in this place.

"Good morning, Mr. Jones," a familiar and sarcastic voice boomed causing Nick to look up. Lankford stood at the doorway, his arms crossed over his chest so that the cane dangling from his left hand swayed back and forth in front of his khaki 5.11 Tactical cargo pants—the uniform of nonuniformed personnel in the wartime theater.

"Good morning," Nick said, hesitating because he was unsure what name to call Lankford. He couldn't remember if the longtime spy was using a new alias. Damn, he was tired.

"Let us have the room," Lankford said to the younger man standing beside him.

"Yes, sir, Mr. Lankford," the man said, answering Nick's silent question.

"You got a lot of fucking balls, Foley," Lankford said, offering his hand and a tight grin. "I'll give you that."

Nick shook the CIA man's hand and then noticed the profound limp as Lankford hobbled to the table. Nick dropped into a chair, but Lankford stayed on his feet.

"Feels better to stand," Lankford grimaced, pointing at his ass. "Thanks again for giving me a matched set."

"If it wasn't for you, I wouldn't have a functioning cerebral cortex. Thanks for taking a bullet for me."

"You'd do the same," Lankford said. "How's the knee?"

Nick shrugged. "Strained ligaments and internal bruising."

"Will the injury affect your work?"

"I might not look like it," Nick said, gesturing to his badly bruised neck and face, "but I'm operational," Nick said. "What about you?"

Lankford waved his hand. "Nah," he said. "It's all spin, right? The after action makes me look so good for staying black, tracking you guys down, coordinating the assault, and helping take down the psycho who killed Peter Yu. Hell, it almost appears like I know what I'm doing. Shit, they may even give me a medal." Lankford leaned his hands on the table beside Nick and sighed. "Unless you get me sent to prison for helping the Chinese—again. You know they were the *objective* of my last assignment, right?"

Nick nodded. "I know I put you in a tough position," he said. "But this is big. You got the file I sent on the high side?"

"I did," Lankford said, then shrugged and pulled a large rolling chair out from the table, maneuvering to balance himself on the less injured ass cheek.

"And you saw the list of names—including one particular US senator who is a total pain in the ass. No pun intended," Nick said, trying not to laugh.

"I did, and I sent it up the chain with my recommendations that we participate, if only to control the fallout."

"And what did the brass say?"

Lankford shrugged. "I'm here, ain't I? Helping you and your Chinese girlfriend yet again. Oh, and let's not forget the always lovely and accommodating Commander Zhang."

"Dash stayed home this time," Nick said, smiling. "I think she earned it."

"And then some."

"So this is officially approved?" Nick asked.

Lankford laughed. "This is unofficially approved, Foley. Which means if it goes well, my bosses will all put themselves in for a commendation, and if it goes to shit, they'll deny they knew anything about it."

"And what happens to you?"

Lankford shrugged. "If we succeed, I keep my job. If we fail, maybe you and I can open a dive shop somewhere. I've always wanted to open a dive shop."

"It won't come to that," Nick said with a smile. "So what do you have for me?"

"The location is a mountain retreat in Austria. High altitude and possibly fortified. The cybersleuths have confirmed that this is where Yao went, and they are ninety-five percent sure that he has not left since his arrival."

Nick started to open his mouth.

"Don't ask me how. They just know."

"Does he have a security detail?"

"Satellite imagery indicates a sizable force."

"How big?"

The CIA man pursed his lips and shook his head. "Maybe two dozen guys at the most. I'll be supplying you six shit-hot shooters from Ground Branch—all ex-SOF guys like you. Shit, you may even know some of them. And you said that Zhang was bringing some guys?"

"Yeah, eight Snow Leopards."

Lankford nodded. "Anything for me?"

"Ling is here," Nick said.

Lankford pushed away from the table. "Why would you bring that bitch?"

Nick screwed up his face. "Like I had a vote in the matter."

"Where is she?"

"With the plane at Ramstein right now."

Lankford sighed and shifted his weight from one leg to the other. The wince on his face told Nick the man was far from recovered and would not be participating in the assault. "Well, it is what it is. I'll try to play nice."

"Thank you," Nick said. "What about air?"

"We have air assets for your HALO INFIL and EXFIL. The Germans offered airborne fire support as well, but that will depend on the weather at altitude. I'll run the op from an airborne TOC with my Ground Branch counterpart. The team is standing by at Ramstein, probably within pissing distance of the Chinese. I suppose the next order of business is to meet up and have a nice, cozy multinational preop brief, which you're going to give, by the way."

"Yeah right," Nick said, rolling his eyes.

Lankford exhaled and put a hand on Nick's shoulder. "Before we bug out, I need to talk with you privately."

Nick shifted uncomfortably. "Isn't that what we're doing right now?"

Lankford arched his back and rolled his neck. "Look, Nick. I don't want you to take this the wrong way, but I need to know if you're all in on this."

"What the hell is that supposed to mean, exactly?" Nick asked and folded his arms across his chest. "You know me. I'm here, aren't I?"

"I know that, Nick," Lankford said. "But there's nothing simple about this operation. We have reason to believe that a number of the people on that list are up there on that mountain, meeting with Yao as we speak, including a US senator and a number of other high-profile Western allies. However this goes down, you have to be thinking about more than meting out justice. I need you to think containment as well."

"I get it, dude," Nick sighed. "All you need to remember is that I'm loyal to America above all else, and I will do what serves her interest first, foremost, and forever."

"I was hoping you'd say that."

"Nonetheless, there is one caveat—Feng was a sick, evil motherfucker. Feng worked for Yao, and it's starting to look like Yao might work for the folks on this list. If we go in there and find people strapped to operating tables, getting their organs harvested, oh brother, God help everyone in that compound."

"In that case, when facing a choice between capture and kill, err on the side of kill," Lankford said.

"Anything else?" Nick asked.

"Yes, this mission is all about containment and data recovery," Lankford said, holding his gaze. "If any Americans or Europeans are taken into custody, you own them. Captives are segregated—we get ours; the Chinese get theirs. And we need absolute control of the data—especially those pertaining to American nationals and connections. Don't give the Chinese anything. Is that going to be a problem for you?"

"No," Nick said. "But keep in mind that Zhang and Ling are probably having this exact same conversation right now in reverse. Don't forget that Yao is a Chinese national and that this is his biotechnology. I wouldn't be surprised if they want to take him alive and Zhang has orders to confiscate any and all laboratory materials and intellectual property. We're going to have to be fluid and see how the op unfolds. This is a joint operation. We have to trust Zhang to do the right thing and not get into a pissing match while we're prosecuting the target. If things get wonky at the scene, we can always try to work something out that benefits everyone post-op."

Lankford clenched his jaw. "I like Commander Zhang; he got me out of China when Ling would have arrested me as a spy," he said. "But I can't afford to trust him. Not when it comes to this. Which is why my orders are to confiscate any data linking Americans to this plot and hand it over to the DNI at all costs. Understood?"

"Understood," Nick said.

"And you're with me?" Lankford asked.

"Hooyah," Nick said.

Lankford laughed. "Let's go brief this shit," he said. He handed him a small case the size and shape of a ring box.

"Aw man, you shouldn't have," Nick said. "I'll need to sleep on it before I say yes," he added with a laugh.

"Don't be a smartass," Lankford said. "That's a micro Bluetooth transmitter receiver. Uses bone conduction or some such shit. Put it in the opposite ear from your primary earpiece. No one will see it, and it will allow me to communicate with you on a separate encrypted channel during the op. You cool with that?"

Nick nodded. "Sure," he said, slipping the box into his cargo pocket. "But we won't need it. Everybody wants the same thing here."

Lankford wrapped an arm around his shoulders. "You are one bleeding heart, kum ba ya, sonuvabitch, Foley," he said. "But for this op, I hope you're right."

CHAPTER 39

USAF C-130
24,000 feet above the Hohe Tauern National Park
Austria
0240 hours local

Nick bounced the heel of his boot up and down against the steel deck of the C-130. He wasn't anxious. He wasn't afraid. This was simply what he did before an op. His engine was up and running, and if he didn't dissipate some of that energy, he just might burn up.

To his left sat the six American CIA special operators, kitted up over black snow pants and Mountain Hardwear coats without insignia. To the right, the Chinese Snow Leopards were dressed all in white—the only splash of color being a snarling snow leopard set against a background of royal blue on the patches that adorned their left shoulders. Even their weapons were white. How in the hell were these two teams—who were sometime enemies—supposed to take this compound together? It didn't help that both Zhang and Lankford insisted that the Chinese and American operators be segregated into divided teams for the assault. He knew Lankford's reasoning, and he suspected Zhang and Ling had similar nationalistic motives. No one wanted a foreign government to control information on any embarrassing connections between Yao's clientele and their own high-ranking government officials or private-sector

A-listers. Those connections were best kept secret and dealt with internally. What the respective governments did with the information he recovered, he preferred not to think about. He was a door-kicker—an instrument of foreign policy, not its creator.

Usually there was chatter between teammates at these moments, but tonight the black-and-white operators were either staring at their feet or sizing up the men across the aisle. This was not the type of crew that needed pep talks, but tonight Nick felt like he needed to say something before the drop to try to bring them together. In the SEALs, that job had fallen to the LCPO. He sure as hell wasn't an LCPO, but who else on this airplane would take the initiative if he didn't? He blew air through his teeth and decided that if the right moment presented itself, he'd give it a shot.

He looked down the line, studying faces in the low red light of the droning aircraft.

He didn't recognize any of the Americans, but he knew several of the Snow Leopards from the assault on the hospital ship. One of the Snow Leopards, the operator he knew only by the call sign "Three," met his gaze and nodded. Nick held up three fingers and then bumped his fist against his chest—acknowledging the horror they'd faced and triumphed over on that sadistic ship just days ago. The Snow Leopard smiled and mirrored the gesture. Nick let his gaze drift down the line. All the men were hunched forward on the benches due to the bulky parachutes on their backs. They had their weapons slung tightly to the side to avoid fouling their chutes, and their kits were loaded with miscellaneous gear, extra magazines, and blowout kits. They wore helmets with tipped-up NVGs and their oxygen masks slung like fighter pilots to the side. Only Nick had a hard black case fixed to his chest, containing the tablet device necessary for navigation during the descent to the target.

Besides the men on the plane, two other operators—one former Marine sniper and one Snow Leopard sniper—were already in position on the ridge line overlooking the target. Both snipers had checked in earlier to provide their scouting report of the target. The reports had matched: three guards on the compound roof and four roving patrols on the portico. Another two operators had been tasked with disabling the private gondola that ran between the mountain retreat and the valley below as well as a pair of helicopters, which satellite imagery had shown shuttling personnel to and from the compound.

Nick looked forward toward the front of the aircraft, where Lankford sat uncomfortably, cocked to one side on his less-injured ass cheek. The CIA man had a laptop propped on the seat beside him and was scanning a bank of monitors at his station. This aircraft, in addition to providing INFIL transportation, would also serve as an airborne Tactical Operations Center. It had pissed Ling off to no end when Lankford had made it clear that she could not be aboard the Command and Control Aircraft for the operation. Lankford reminded her that had their roles been reversed, she would never let him aboard a sophisticated Chinese aircraft crammed full of classified equipment. She'd responded by reminding Lankford that he had just last week been operating as a spy on Chinese soil and that this was simply quid pro quo. To which Lankford had told her she could either respect his opsec or go fuck herself. Then, before the CIA man could tell her which option *he* preferred, Zhang had intervened. After a heated discussion in Chinese, a compromise was reached, with Ling being placed in charge of the operation to secure the gondola and helicopters. She would run command and control at the base camp, with her primary objective being to secure the perimeter and prevent any personnel from entering or exiting the scene. Lankford had insisted that American operators be on each of those actions as well but relented when Nick had quietly pointed out that they were better suited having more Americans at the target.

What a piss fest.

Lankford turned his head and met Nick's gaze. "Five minutes," he said. Nick watched his lips move, but the voice spoke on the open channel in his left ear with a millisecond's delay.

Nick nodded and then looked across the aisle at Zhang. The Snow Leopard Commander looked up but did not make eye contact. Things had been different with Zhang since the hospital ship. Sometimes he acted like the Zhang that Nick had come to know and trust, but other times, he sensed a coldness—not quite overt hostility, but close. Strange.

Nick gestured across his lower face with his left hand, the signal to secure oxygen masks, and all the men across the aisle complied.

"Buddy checks," he said when his mask was in place, and the men began checking each other's chutes and packs and then their own weapons.

"Thumbs up if you are up on the secure," Lankford said in his right ear now.

Nick looked up and held the CIA agent's eyes and then gave a thumbs-up.

"Good man," Lankford said on the secure channel. "Remember what we talked about. America first. Tug on your glove if you understand."

Nick gritted his teeth—he hated this spooky-ass shit—and then adjusted the strap on his right glove.

"Good." Then Lankford's voice shifted to his other ear and said, "Three minutes."

It's now or never, said the voice in Nick's head.

He unsnapped his harness from the bench seat and stood. A dozen sets of eyes looked at him.

"Everyone here is a seasoned operator; we all understand what it means to be a team. If we don't operate like a team, some of us are going to die. That's not going to happen tonight, do you understand? Not on my watch. Tonight we are not Americans. We are not Chinese. Tonight, we're a band of brothers—brothers on a mission to help keep the world a safe and decent place. I say we do our job and let the politicians and bureaucrats worry about the rest."

"Hooyah," came a call from one of the CIA Ground Branch operators.

"Hooyah," the rest of the American team said in unison.

Zhang finally met his eyes, and the corner of the Snow Leopard's mouth curled up into a crooked grin. He hollered something in Chinese, and his men barked the same battle cry in echo.

Nick nodded. "Let's do this."

"Two minutes," Lankford said over the radio.

Nick raised two fingers and gestured for everyone to get up. Nick moved to the front of the line and led the black-and-white operator parade to the rear of the aircraft, stopping at the bright yellow-and-black line beside what looked like a traffic light. He steadied himself under the awkward weight of his gear as the C-130 made a gentle turn to the left and then leveled off again. The pilots—experienced Air Force Special Operations aviators— were experts at challenging insertions. At the moment, they were making last-minute corrections based on winds and temperature to ensure that the team would have a clear path to land on the target. There was a sudden pressure change, then a loud *clunk*, and the rear ramp began to lower. Frigid air flooded the cargo hold, and his ears popped immediately. The deck lowered to an angle a hair below level, and then the traffic light switched from red to yellow.

After a beat, it flashed green.

Nick walked to the rear of the platform, spread his arms out, elbows bent, and fell into the night.

At twenty-four thousand feet, the icy-cold air clawed at his skin, penetrating his wind-resistant clothing like it was cheesecloth and chilling him to the bone. The wind raged against the loose fabric of his jacket sleeves and pants, flapping and snapping it against his skin as he strained to keep his arms open and out and his legs spread and bent at the knees. The night was black as pitch, with no moon to light the tops of the clouds. Tonight's free fall would be shorter than most jumps since the target was located at an elevation of twelve thousand feet. Nick had jumped from much higher altitudes, but the C-130 was limited by a modest ceiling. His plan was to open chutes at fifteen thousand feet—low enough to minimize vulnerability, but still high enough to navigate to the target. He felt dampness on his neck as he penetrated the cloud deck. City lights appeared, Zell am See below and Salzberg in the distance. Seconds later, the lights of Salzberg winked out as the northern mountains came between them.

Nick pulled his left arm in and watched his altimeter spin down. The others would be watching the glow from the light on the back of his helmet and waiting for his call. At fifteen thousand feet, he crossed his arm over to his chest, pulled his legs in slightly for bracing, and called, "Three . . . two . . . one . . ."

He clamped his jaw hard and pulled the silver ring on his left chest harness.

The chute deployed, and he felt the powerful tug of deceleration—jerking him hard in the crotch and tightening around his chest. He breathed a sigh of relief that his chute wasn't fouled and reached instinctively for the risers. Without looking, he grasped the handles and took control. He tugged, slowing his descent, creating the sensation his body was rising. He pulled harder on the left riser, banking away from the lights of Zell am See and toward Grossglockner.

With his right hand, he snapped open the top of the hard plastic case on his chest and flipped up the screen on the navigation computer inside. The target was preloaded, and he immediately saw a green box and then his red glide slope information—left and below—the white lines that would lead him directly to the portico of the target building. He said a silent prayer that the data had been loaded correctly and he wouldn't slam face first into the side of the mountain in the dark.

God, I hate this shit.

Nick tugged on both risers, but with more pressure on the right handle, and watched as the glide slope line slowly merged with the computer-generated lines. As long as he maintained this alignment, he would glide in and land in the center of the drop zone. He tilted his head up, looking over the nav screen into the dark, hoping to see lights from the target. Nothing yet. He looked back at the screen and the changing numbers on the left bottom. The top number gave his altitude—13,700 feet—and the lower number his ETA to the target, 2:12.

"Two minutes. Bravo team set?"

"Set," the American sniper replied in his headset. "Three on the roof and another five on the portico. Call the first shot."

"Stand by," he answered.

Nick clicked his night-vision goggles into place, and the world came to life in eerie green and gray. The mountain looked closer than three thousand feet away. Through the NVGs, he could now clearly see the two-story compound—a miracle retreat built into the side of the mountain face. Satisfied with his approach, he no longer needed the glide slope. He clicked it off and collapsed the screen into the hard case on his chest.

"Target visual. One minute."

"Got it," someone said in his left ear—one of the Americans.

"In sight, Nick. I am number two behind you." Zhang's voice. The idea that it would be him on his six somehow was more comforting than one of the Ground Branch guys. Yes, they had trained just like him—were likely former SEALs or Army SOF in fact. But he had battle history with Zhang.

"Bravo—on my call. Light your targets now."

"Check."

"I has mines target," came a thick Chinese accent. "Left center."

"Check, Bravo two."

The portico was rushing toward him now. He hated this part. The security patrols—five in all—were roving about just as Bravo had said. He could see the glow of their cigarettes as he closed in. He unsnapped the thigh band that held his SOPMOD M4 in place.

"Engage targets, Bravo," he said.

He saw the flashes on the ridgeline, two thousand feet above the target house, and then came the chaos as the snipers engaged. Two figures collapsed on the roof in gray-green cinema. A third raised his rifle but then arched his back and fell from the roof onto the portico, nearly crushing a man beneath him.

"Security is engaging at the base of the gondola," Lankford's calm voice called in his left ear.

The remaining compound guards were scrambling for cover at the edge of the building, their rifles raised and scanning up the mountain face. Two were struggling to pull out NVGs from thigh cases dangling from their belts.

Nick pulled the risers hard, stalling his descent with near perfection, as he pedaled his feet and crossed over the concrete wall at the edge of the portico. He shifted his weight back, kicked his left foot forward as he landed, then dropped onto his right knee and pushed up on the fittings at his shoulders to open the quick release for his chute. He felt a tug, and then the chute was free. He raised his rifle in a quick, smooth arc as the chute blew away over his head. Two men were crouched beside a door, and one more was running on his left. Nick put his green dot from his infrared sight on the running man's head just as his chute caught the man's attention.

Nick squeezed the trigger twice, and the man's head erupted in a geyser of black and gray—the universal color of blood and guts in the monochrome world of NVGs. The target pitched backward and crumpled to the ground. Without a pause, Nick was up, moving left and engaging another target. He fired on the run, the first round wide right and the second catching the target in the throat. He glanced over his shoulder and saw Zhang firing on the move beside him. As the Snow Leopard Commander drifted right, Nick continued left, leading their teams in a mirror image sweep of the portico. A muzzle flash ahead caught his attention, and he spied an enemy shooter kneeling, partially obstructed by a billowing parachute. Nick feinted right, then flanked hard left, and fired on the go, two rounds hitting the man center mass as a round from the right—possibly from Zhang's rifle—blew the top of the guard's head off.

In seconds, it was over. He was crouched beside four American operators and could see Zhang's Snow Leopards lined up on the right side.

"Rooftop movement," came the American sniper's calm voice. There was a flash, but Nick couldn't hear the distant crack of the sniper rifle through his helmet and the earpieces he wore in both ears. "Tango down," the sniper reported. "You're clear on the roof."

Nick chopped his hand toward a pair of large metal double doors that led inside. The rest of the facing wall was outfitted with floor-to-ceiling plate-glass windows—affording the occupants a spectacular view of the mountains or the occasional assault team storming the portico. Nothing he could do about that . . . or was there? Why funnel through the doors when they could blow out the glass and waltz in? Nick strafed the wall of glass with a prolonged burst from his M4, but the glass did not shatter.

"That's ballistic glass," Nick barked on the open channel, and Zhang repeated the comment in Chinese.

A beat later, the double doors flung open. Two guards sprinted out, rifles at the ready, but the joint team cut them down midstride before either man could squeeze off a round. A third guard poked his head out, but upon seeing his teammates' fate, he pulled back just as a round from Zhang's rifle blew a chunk out of the doorframe. The door hinges were apparently spring loaded, because Nick watched the doors draw closed under their own power.

Nick's left earpiece crackled with Lankford's voice. "On thermal we see multiple bodies retreating deeper into the structure, but others are fanning out to make a stand in a central room. Looks like four—no, five figures taking up defensive positions." The CIA man dispatched tactical information with the same proficiency as a sportscaster calling the play-by-play of a football game on TV.

"Stay low," Nick said, warning his teammates as he advanced on the entry doors. There was no way to know the ballistic rating and longevity of the glass, which made it an unreliable barrier. Like an exclamation point to this thought, machine gun fire erupted somewhere inside, spraying the ballistic windows and the inside of the heavy doors with bullets. The glass panel to Nick's left fractured in a spider-web pattern but did not blow out. As he stepped over the fallen guards, he mentally noted that none of the hired security personnel they'd engaged so far appeared to be Chinese.

Upon reaching the double doors, Nick took a knee.

Only one way to do this properly.

"Grenade," Nick said, looking at Zhang as he pulled a grenade from his kit. Zhang nodded and repeated the word in Chinese on the open channel. They both got low. Zhang pulled on the right door handle and eased it open; Nick rolled the grenade through the gap. A beat later, the grenade exploded and did its work. Nick pulled a second grenade, this time a flash bang—a nonlethal grenade meant to stun and disorient—and repeated the operation with Zhang. He waited for the flash and the loud crack, and then he was up and moving through the doors. He advanced in a tactical crouch, scanning over the barrel of his weapon. Gunshots echoed. He turned toward the muzzle flash, knelt, sighted on the prone target, and ended him with a double tap to the head. Instantly he was up and moving again, clearing the left corner behind him. Zhang moved in a mirror image and cleared the right corner.

Corners cleared, Nick surveyed the space. Two identical white leather sofas faced each other in the center of the room. Mid-century lounge chairs flanked the sofas, and silver floor lamps arced over the seating area. The expensive furniture was shredded by Nick's grenade. The rear of the room was occupied by a long bar—bottles, glasses, mirrors all shattered. Nick checked the security guard he shot.

Deader than dead.

"Clear," Nick said. "Looks like everyone else has pulled back to the rear of the building."

"The only thermals I hold now are your men," Lankford said. "I'm getting interference from the structure. It must extend into the mountain."

Nick looked at Zhang. "We have them trapped now. Nowhere left to go."

"My count is eight security dead. If Lankford's intelligence is good, there should be only two or three guards left. Anyone else is a high-value target."

"We take the HVTs alive," Nick said over the open channel. "That's an order."

The American operators acknowledged, and then Zhang parroted the order in Chinese.

The last thing Nick wanted to do was shoot some American politician or German ambassador. They had no way of knowing who on Zhang's list might be in attendance with Yao tonight, but the intelligence clearly suggested a gathering—a conclusion that was reinforced by the large security presence.

"In your experience, how accurate is CIA intelligence?" Zhang asked, cupping his hand over his boom mike to muffle the question.

Nick smirked. "About fifty percent."

"It is the same with our operations," Zhang said. "My point is simply that we have no idea what or who we will find inside. We need to show . . . what is the word . . ."

"Restraint?"

"Yes, Nick. That's it. We need to show restraint. Do you understand what I mean?"

"Yeah." He nodded. "But we also need to breach while we still have initiative."

"Agreed, let's go," Zhang said, and he motioned one of his men forward. He spoke to him in Chinese, and the man slung his rifle and approached a heavy metal door at the back of the room. The Snow Leopard pulled a breacher charge from the bag on his left thigh.

"My priority is Yao," Zhang said to Nick, holding his eyes. "We need to interrogate him. And there may be other Chinese nationals involved who need to be held accountable."

"Are you trying to say, 'You take yours; we take ours'?"

Zhang responded with a single nod. Nick wondered what Lankford thought of the exchange, but he supposed he knew. They had prepped for this.

"I can live with that," Nick said. It was the only way.

The Snow Leopard at the door came back and spoke in English this time.

"Charge is set," he said. He held up a small device in his hand like an Apple TV remote.

Zhang nodded. "We set a heavy charge for this door," he said. "Let's pull back onto the portico."

They all moved outside and pulled back a safe distance.

"Go," Nick said.

He flipped up his NVGs and turned his head away.

The explosion was so violent, for an instant he wondered if the portico was about to tear loose from the mountain and send them plummeting to their deaths. But the foundation held, undamaged, and Nick donned his NVGs and led the assault team back inside. He moved swiftly through the first room, past the bar and through the door they'd just breached. The room on the other side appeared to be a formal dining room, with place settings for many set along the mahogany dining table.

"Clear," Nick said, moving swiftly through the dining room. At the back of the room, there were two cased openings: one left, one right.

He glanced at Zhang. "You go right."

Three CIA operators followed Nick through the cased opening into a long hallway with doors along the left side. "Clear these rooms," Nick barked. He took a knee and held his sights down the hallway, advancing as his men cleared.

"Bedroom," came the first report. "Clear."

They repeated the operation, room by room. Nick expected gunfire but heard none.

"Zhang, what have you got?" Nick asked on the open mike.

"A large kitchen, food storage, laundry facility, mechanical room—all clear," the Snow Leopard reported. "What about you?"

"Half a dozen bedrooms—more like luxury suites," Nick said. "The beds have been slept in, but there's nothing left behind except some dirty towels and rubbish in the trashcans."

"My guys will sweep for DNA," Lankford said in his ear. "Forget that shit. Find Yao."

"Nick, I found something," Zhang said. "Looks like an elevator."

Nick motioned for the operators to follow him, and he looped back around. "Coming to you," Nick said. When he reached Zhang, he found the Snow Leopard Commander standing in front of a metal door. Nick surveyed the frame. "Where's the call button?"

"I don't know," Zhang said, dragging his gloved hand down the seam.

"Breach it, and then we can check the shaft. We can rope down if we need to."

"Rather difficult approach," Zhang said, his face a frown.

Nick shrugged. "Blow it and we'll decide."

Breacher charges were set and detonated. When the dust cleared, smoke billowed from the gaping hole where the door had been. Nick took point once again and led the team back. As he peered inside the shaft, a bullet whizzed past him, embedding in the wall beside his head. Nick dropped to a knee, sighting over his rifle and trying to see through the smoke. He didn't need to call the contact, as the other five men on both sides of him were already pouring gunfire into the smoke. He unleashed a volley with the others and then barked, "Hold fire."

All gunfire ceased instantly.

When the smoke finally cleared, what he saw inside was *not* an elevator shaft but rather another hallway. He chopped his left hand forward, and together the team moved down the hallway. They stepped over three dead shooters on the floor. A fourth was sitting up against the wall—blood painting the wall behind him and pink bubbles coming from his blue lips. Again, none of the shooters were Chinese, he noted wryly. All four looked Eastern European.

"Last stand?" Nick said, glancing at Zhang.

The Snow Leopard Commander nodded as he stepped over the fourth guard to stand shoulder to shoulder with Nick. "It would appear."

At the end of the short hallway stood two doors—one right, one left.

"Only two rooms remain," Zhang said.

"Fitting, don't you think?" Nick replied.

"Yao must be sheltering in one of them."

Nick nodded. He'd been going left all night, no point in changing now. "I'll take the room on the left with my guys covering; you take the one on the right with yours."

Zhang smirked at this suggestion and then simply said, "Agreed."

"Whatever or whoever you find in that room belongs to us, got that Foley?" Lankford barked on the secure channel in his right ear. Nick could hear the unbridled frustration in the CIA man's voice. So far, the op had been a total bust. The next ten seconds would prove whether they'd scored a clandestine treasure trove or wasted millions on a snipe hunt.

Rifles up, Nick converged on the left door as Zhang moved right.

They paused, traded glances, then kicked open their doors simultaneously, the American operators behind Nick and the Chinese behind Zhang. Nick entered the room and scanned quickly for threats. There were none.

A distinguished and familiar-looking Chinese executive was seated at the head of a table. Yao was the only person in the room. His legs were crossed at the knee and his hands folded in his lap. Light glinted off the silver cufflinks at the wrists of his tailored shirt. And despite the small hole in the center of his forehead, he was smiling. A single rivulet of blood dribbled from the hole. It flowed inside the curve of his right eye socket, along the side of his nose, and down his cheek and dripped from his chin. Clutched in his lifeless hands were two white envelopes.

"Clear," Nick hollered over his shoulder. "Securing the scene."

"As am I," came Zhang's neutral voice in his ear. "Clear here as well."

"I hope you picked the right fucking door, Nick," Lankford said on the secure line.

Nick ignored him and looked around the room over his rifle. The room appeared to be a lab of some sort. There were three stainless-steel refrigerators in the back and then workbenches with Plexiglas hoods over them. To the left was a large desk with a twenty-inch flat-screen TV monitor and computer. There were several other computers at workstations along the wall, but unlike the one with the large flat screen, these computers were all smashed, the tops on the floor and the motherboards removed. To the rear of the room was a reinforced steel hatch—like the kind on a ship. Nick peered inside and stared down a tunnel carved into the mountain. The tunnel descended steeply and seemed to stretch into infinity. Whoever had been with Yao had escaped through here.

"Are there computers, Nick?" Lankford demanded in his right ear.

Nick saw no way he could possibly answer, so he coughed twice, the equivalent of a double click on a mike.

"Just plug in the USB drive that I gave you. It has an auto-run program that will grab everything. It's wicked fast. You need only a few seconds."

"I found Yao," Nick said on the open channel for everyone, including Lankford, to hear. "He's dead. Bullet to the head." He snatched the envelopes from the dead man's hand and shoved them into his cargo pocket. He walked over to the desktop computer, inserted Lankford's flash drive into a USB port, and kept talking. "I've also got a tunnel in here. Looks like it goes—"

He paused midsentence.

Something was beeping . . . and the frequency was accelerating.

"Bomb!" Nick shouted and ran.

He was diving for cover when the 'explosion' happened.

Instead of a burning blast, all Nick heard were a series of anti-climactic *whump*s followed by a puff of gray smoke. Not a bomb, but self-destruct charges rigged inside the laboratory comput-ers, undoubtedly triggered when he inserted the USB drive. He doubted he would have been injured had he not made it out. As it was, his strained left knee was screaming at him from his dive out of the room. Nick shook his head.

Shit. Lankford is going to be pissed.

313

An outstretched hand appeared in front of Nick's face. He looked up and saw Zhang. They clasped hands, and the Snow Leopard Commander pulled him to his feet.

"What happened?" Zhang asked, peering into the room.

"Computers were booby-trapped," Nick said.

"You need to check the other room, Nick," Lankford barked in his ear on the secure channel. "You need to see what Zhang found."

"So they killed him," Zhang said, staring at the dead CEO alone at the table.

"Yep," Nick said. "You surprised?"

"No," Zhang said, shaking his head. "Just disappointed. I desperately wanted to talk to Yao. It would have been . . ." Zhang paused for a moment, his gaze distant, and then mumbled, "It would have been better for everyone if we could have ended this tonight."

"Stop jabbering with Zhang and get your ass in the other room," Lankford barked in his ear on the secure channel. "You need to see what Zhang found."

"Got a tunnel to clear," Nick said, gesturing to the hatch. "Why don't you and your guys get started while I check out the other room?"

"This is a joint operation, Nick. I think you should come too," Zhang suggested.

"Helicopters on the portico in less than ten mikes," Lankford said, and then, in his other ear: "He's playing games, Nick. Don't take that shit from him."

"Sure," Nick said, "but first, let me clear that other room." He marched toward the other doorway, but the Snow Leopard Commander stopped him with a hand on the shoulder. Then Nick watched Zhang pull a grenade from his kit.

"What are you doing?" Nick asked.

"There is a computer stack in this room as well," Zhang answered. He tossed his grenade inside. "It is undoubtedly booby-trapped too."

"What the hell is happening, Foley?" Lankford screamed in his ear.

The Snow Leopard Commander stayed upright, barely flinching as the grenade exploded in the other room. Then he turned to Nick. "Regrettably, there was nothing I could recover from the room," he said. "How about you?"

"Same. Nothing at all," Nick said. He resisted the urge to finger the envelopes in his cargo pocket.

"Then it is time to go," Zhang said, clapping him on the back.

As they walked away, Nick glanced over his shoulder at the American and Chinese operators who were rushing between the rooms, trying to find anything of value and trying just as hard to prevent the other team from finding and securing anything they'd missed. He shook his head.

What a cluster . . .

Nick thought about Dash and about the madman Feng, who had nearly killed her. He thought about Yao, who had secretly pulled the strings all along. He knew there were others in bed with Yao—powerful actors who could snuff out a life with a text message and a wire transfer. He knew both the American and Chinese governments wanted the immortality technology that Yao and Feng had developed and that both governments had hoped that tonight they would get it. He also knew that Lankford was right—a powerful cabal was behind all of this. Yao's murder proved he was not, and never was, the ringleader of this shadow organization. Whoever led the cabal had deemed the CEO enough of a liability that even his brilliant mind and vision weren't enough to save him. Project Penglai would live on, just not at Nèiyè Biologic.

"Yao is dead. The high-value targets eluded us, and the computers were destroyed. Was this mission a success, Nick?" Zhang asked as they stepped outside.

A blast of crisp, clean mountain air swept across the portico.

Nick inhaled deeply and discreetly switched off his transmitters.

Then, staring into the black, he clasped a hand on his friend's shoulder and said, "I think for you and me, it was the best we could have hoped for."

CHAPTER 40

Landau and Associates Architectural Firm
Central Germany Division Headquarters
Eiselbener Strasse 46
Berlin, Germany
1430 hours local

Nick didn't want to be here.

His body was battered and bruised from head to toe. He ached in places he didn't even know a man could ache. The last time he'd felt this torn up was at the end of hell week in BUD/S. He groaned his displeasure at the world. He had done his part—done more than either government could reasonably ask of him. Now he didn't want to talk to Lankford about why he had not secured the site. He didn't want to argue about Zhang, the Chinese, nationalistic interests, secret cabals, or how Agent Ling was going to become a problem for everyone. He didn't want the CIA man to hard press him for a job. And he didn't want to have to turn him down again. But most of all, he didn't want to waste another second in any place that wasn't Beijing.

The only thing that mattered to him right now was going home to Dash.

"Are you okay, sir?"

He looked up at the pretty young girl—blonde hair, blue eyes, Eastern European features—who was eying him with more than a little concern and feeling maybe some irritation of her own.

"I'm fine," he said, then remembering the bruised train wreck that was his face, he added, "Just uncomfortable. I was in an accident recently."

She nodded and smiled at him.

"Would you like some water? Or perhaps tea or coffee?"

"Black coffee would be awesome," he said.

"I'm sure Mr. Kent will be with you any minute," she said in her clipped German accent. Her desk phone beeped. She smiled and held up one finger, taking the call.

After a brief conversation in German, she returned the receiver to its cradle. "Mr. Kent will see you now. I can bring your coffee in if you like."

"That would be great," he said, rising slowly, silently cursing his aching knee as he did. "Danke Shon," he added, thereby depleting the entirety of his German language skills.

She opened the mahogany door and ushered him into an office larger than most apartments he'd lived in. Lankford stepped out from behind an imposing claw-foot desk and extended a hand. Nick shook it firmly.

"Thank you so much, Katrina," he said.

"Of course, Mr. Kent," she said. "I'm getting Herr Foley some coffee. May I get you another cup?"

"Yes, please," the CIA man said, and the door closed behind Nick. Lankford gestured to the two oversized leather seats beside a matching couch that formed a sitting area beside the expansive window.

"Mr. Kent?"

"Clark Kent," Lankford replied.

"No," Nick said, shaking his head.

"Yes."

"Your NOC is Clark Kent?"

Lankford tried to keep a straight face but failed and busted up laughing. "I'm just fucking with you, Foley. It's David Kent."

Nick chuckled and eased himself gingerly into the chair. "Nice digs compared to your last gig," he added.

Lankford—now Kent—laughed out loud.

"I earned it," he said, taking his own seat. He straightened the cuffs on his tailored shirt. Nick decided Lankford did, indeed, deserve it. Especially when he noticed the CIA agent leaning hard left because of his recent gunshot wound.

"I couldn't agree more," Nick said. Then, the fatigue suddenly hit him like a bus. "Look, I know we need to debrief this thing, but I'm going to be honest with you. All I care about is getting home. I hope you're not planning on keeping me around for a couple days so everyone and their uncle can talk to me."

"It's not going to be like that," Lankford said. "First things first, thank you for everything. Had you not agreed to help me find Peter Yu, we never would've had closure, and we certainly never would have stopped Feng and Yao. I owe you."

"Even after getting shot in the other ass cheek?" Nick jabbed.

Lankford smiled. "Yeah, even with that. As you pointed out, I sucked you into this mess, so no foul there."

The door opened, and Katrina delivered them their coffees—in porcelain china cups, he noted—and then left quickly, closing the door behind her.

"You have questions about the compound?"

Lankford nodded. "Don't you?"

Nick sighed. He did have questions, he supposed. He just wasn't sure he gave enough of a shit to wait around for the answers. He'd had enough of spy games and murderous psychopaths for two lifetimes. Yes, he longed for the truth, but he knew that Lankford, and others like him, would continue to ask questions and prosecute targets until the truth was birthed. He was just too damn tired to live at the pointy tip of that spear. All he wanted now was to get back to his real job and to Dash. But if he shut his eyes and plugged his ears, two weeks from now, when his batteries were recharged, future Nick would regret not knowing. He fingered the envelope in his left cargo pocket, debating the best time to hand it over.

"Not really," he said at last.

Lankford listed in his chair and then crossed his legs, pain on his face. "Did you get a look in the other room?" he asked.

"You mean the one Zhang dropped a grenade in?"

"Yes."

Nick shook his head. "There was nothing left to see, as far as I could tell."

"Did Zhang take anything from the room? Anything before he tossed that goddamn grenade?"

Nick shrugged. "I don't think so. He claimed he didn't find anything."

"And you trust him?" Lankford asked.

"With my life," Nick said simply.

Lankford nodded.

"This isn't over, Nick, I'm afraid. We've uncovered something enormous—something that has been rumored in the intelligence community for decades but over the years has morphed into an urban legend worthy of scorn and mockery. But this cabal is real, Nick. They have their tentacles so deep into so many corporations and governments that they may represent the greatest threat to security on earth right now. The existence of Project Penglai and the membership list you obtained is the first credible evidence that the legend is true. I have to pursue this. I could really use your help."

"Count me out," Nick said. "This thing—this cabal or whatever—is unnerving. But that's why we have guys like you that can track the beast down and drive a stake through its heart. I'm done monster hunting, sorry."

Lankford smiled and handed him a business card with two sets of numbers written on the back. "The top number is my new personal cell. The other number is my secure line. Stay in touch, Nick, and the next time you're in Germany, you owe me a dinner."

"Me owe you?" Nick said and laughed. "I seem to remember you stiffing me with the tab last time. I think *you* owe *me*."

Lankford shifted in his seat and winced. "My association with you has resulted in my inability to sit comfortably for the rest of my life. But fine, if you won't buy me dinner, I'll settle for a drink." He held Nick's eyes. "Time will pass. You'll heal. Dash will heal. That little voice will come back. You might change your mind. If you do, call me. We would love to have you back on the team, Nick."

Nick sat pensively and watched Lankford take a sip of coffee. Then he reached into his cargo pocket. "I do have one thing that might help inform your decision about how to handle our new shadowy friends," he said and handed the envelope to Lankford.

"What's this?" Lankford asked, smiling. "A formal letter of apology?"

Nick shook his head, and Lankford's face changed, sensing the dark gravity of Nick's final gesture.

"That envelope was clutched in Yao's dead hands when I found him."

Lankford's eyes widened.

"Addressed to me? Personally? How the hell is that possible?"

Nick shrugged. "It would seem your suspicions about the cabal's tentacles being everywhere are true."

Lankford opened the envelope and read quickly. Then he looked up, all the color and humor gone from his face. "Did you read this, Nick?"

Nick nodded. "I didn't think you would mind, under the circumstances. I needed to know if I was secure after leaving the scene."

"You're not," Lankford practically whispered. He looked up at Nick again, his voice heavy with dread. "None of us are."

Nick stood. "Well, that's another good reason to check out of the game. I'm just gonna have to hope that these bastards don't have time to worry about an NGO worker bringing clean water to poor people in China. That being said, if you do happen to take down these motherfuckers, please send me a note. Until then, I'll be looking over my shoulder."

He extended his hand to the spook, but Lankford ignored it.

"Where do you think you're going?" the CIA man said, waving the letter at Nick. "We're not done talking. I need to know everything you know about this."

"I don't know anything else," Nick assured him. "That letter is the only gold nugget I mined in those mountains, and I just turned it over to you. As far as I'm concerned, the less I know, the better."

"There must have been something else," Lankford pressed, his anxiety almost palpable. "Something on Yao's body or in the room? Something that Zhang said, or that he didn't say, that was a red flag? C'mon, Foley, think."

Nick shook his head. "I already told you, that's all I got."

Lankford stood. "Has anyone else on our side seen this letter?"

"No."

"What about Zhang?"

"No."

"Did you tell Dash about it when you phoned her?"

"Don't be ridiculous."

Lankford nodded. "Good, keep it that way."

Nick turned and walked toward the office door. "You said you'd have a plane waiting for me at Templehof with instructions for the pilot to take me wherever I wanted to go. Is that really true?"

Lankford nodded. "Where will you go?"

"Beijing," Nick said with a tired smile. "It's time to go home."

EPILOGUE

Nick knocked on the door to Dash's apartment. She'd invited him for a home-cooked dinner, recompense for the dinner of ruined risotto and never-cooked lamb chops she'd missed when bodies had washed up on Tung Wan Beach. Even though only two weeks had passed since that night, for Nick it felt like a lifetime ago. They were not the same people now that they were then.

They were something else, but what that something else was, he could not articulate.

"Coming," she called from inside, her voice harried yet upbeat.

She opened the door and greeted him with an ear-to-ear smile. She wore a blue apron, cinched tightly around her narrow waist, and she had a smudge of flour on her cheek. The aroma of cooking bacon hit him a second later, and his stomach growled loudly.

"My stomach says hello," he said.

"Hello, Nick's stomach," she laughed, bending at the waist and addressing his midsection. "Would you and Nick's body like to come in?"

Grinning broadly, he stepped into the apartment. They stared at each other, both hesitant. Instead of embracing her, he affectionately wiped the white streak of flour from her cheek with the pad of his thumb and said, "Looks like you're still at it."

"Yes," she sighed. "I ruined the first batch and had to start again."

"Sounds familiar," he said. "We must have attended the same cooking school."

She laughed at this and closed the door behind him.

"What's in the bag?" she said, looking at the ornate paper bag he was holding in his left hand.

"It's a surprise."

She narrowed her eyes at him. "I hope it's not a present, because I don't have one for you."

He shrugged. "Maybe, maybe not. You'll just have to wait and see."

She smiled and led him inside. He tried to follow her into the kitchen, but she stopped him at the threshold. "No, no, no," she scolded playfully. "Go take a seat at the table. Dinner's almost ready."

He followed orders and took the seat facing the kitchen. Instead of wine or beer, the glass at the top of his place mat was filled with orange juice. A knowing grin spread across his face. "If I didn't know better, I would have thought I'd stepped into Grandma's Kitchen," he said. "Smells like pancakes and bacon."

"You're quite the culinary detective, Nick," she called from the kitchen. "Does Zhang know about this secret skill of yours?"

"I sure hope not," he said. "We wouldn't want your government to think I'm actually an undercover food safety inspector."

"You could definitely be deported for that."

A beat later, she appeared with a plate in each hand and set one at her place and one in front of him. His plate was filled with an enormous Belgian waffle, a side of bacon, and a mound of scrambled eggs. She scurried back to the kitchen and returned with a dish of softened butter and a bottle of real maple syrup.

"What do you think?" she said expectantly.

He made a show of inhaling the symphony of aromas wafting off his plate and then said, "I think I've died and gone to heaven." Then he popped a piece of crispy bacon into his mouth. "Perfect," he said, chewing.

He saw her blush with pride as she took her seat across the table. Unlike him, instead of going straight for the bacon, she smeared a layer of butter across her waffle and then grabbed the maple syrup bottle and methodically began to pour tiny dollops into each of its square divots—something he used to do as a kid with his Eggo toaster waffles. He stared at her, smiling and chewing.

"What?" she asked, feeling his eyes on her.

"Nothing," he said, but what he really meant was *you're so adorable.*

They ate their "breakfast for dinner," making small talk and grinning at each other like nervous high school kids on a first date. When they hit a lull, he asked her about returning to work, and she told him that Director Wong had offered her two weeks' vacation. She said she had refused, insisting that working kept her mind occupied and held thoughts of the hospital ship at bay. She then told him about the rumors that she was next in line to become the department head of the Office of Disease Control and Emergency Response and that accepting the position would mean saying good-bye to lab work, probably for the rest of her career. He asked her if Wong had offered to replace her on the task force, and she shook her head. Then he asked her if *she* wanted to stay on the task force, and she said, "If I were to quit, I'd feel like I was letting Zhang down . . . What would you do?"

"I'm an unreliable counselor," he said.

"What do you mean by that?"

"I mean that I rarely follow my own advice—the operation in Austria is proof of that."

She smiled wanly, stood, and began clearing the dishes, a signal he took to mean she was ready to put the topic to bed for the evening. Despite her protests, he helped her with the dishes, and then they relocated to the sofa in the living room.

"Oh, I almost forgot," he said, jumping up and retrieving the paper bag from the dining table where he'd left it. He settled back onto the cushion beside her, this time close enough that their thighs were touching. He looked at her, and she met his gaze, her deep-espresso eyes both hesitant and expectant. "I have something for you," he said.

"Okay," she said, her lips curling up in the corners.

He reached into the bag and retrieved the puzzle box—her puzzle box, now meticulously reconstructed and restored. He had done all the physical reparations himself, but for the painting, he had hired a local artist. He presented it to her and watched her expression.

"Oh, Nick," she gasped as she accepted it into her hands. "You fixed it for me. I don't know what to say . . . It's beautiful." She worked the puzzle box with expert, practiced efficiency, sliding and shifting the concealed wooden panels. "It works perfectly."

"There's more," he said. "Look inside."

With the box now open, she peered into the inner chamber. Delicately, using her index finger and thumb, she retrieved a silver chain and animal totem pendant. She looked up at him, tears rimming her eyes. "How?" was all she could manage to say.

"I went to see Gang Jin. I thought he deserved to know what happened. When I told him about your kidnapping and what happened on the hospital ship, his face turned so red I thought he was going to have an aneurysm. Cursing himself, he unclasped your pendant from his neck and insisted I return it to you. 'A lucky charm,' he said, 'should never be separated from its true owner, even if given as a gift with good intentions. Tell Dazhong that I'm sorry, and tell her never to take it off again.'"

She closed her eyes, pressed the little silver rat totem to her lips, and kissed it. Then she handed the chain and pendant to him, swiveled in her seat, and lifted up her hair in the back. "Will you put it on me, please?"

"Of course." With thick, calloused fingers, he fumbled with the miniscule clasp but eventually got it secured around her delicate neck. "There you go," he said.

She turned around to face him and immediately threw herself into him, wrapping her arms around him. "Thank you, Nick. Thank you, thank you, thank you," she mumbled, her mouth pressed against his chest.

He returned the embrace and stroked her back with his right hand. "You're welcome."

She suddenly let go of him, and she looked at him with hungry eyes.

He leaned in and kissed her, long and slow and passionately.

When they parted for air, she said, "I want you."

"I want you too." He leaned in and began kissing her neck, breathing in the smell of her.

"Not tonight," she whispered, her mouth next to his ear. "I'm not ready. Will you wait for me?"

He pulled back and met her gaze. "Yes . . . for you, I'd wait until the end of time if that's what you asked of me."

"I won't make you wait that long," she chuckled. Then, she lowered her eyes. "I'm still healing," she murmured, the double entendre not lost on him. "I want our first time to be without regret . . . *and* without restraint."

"Me too," he said with a crooked grin.

She leaned in and kissed him, this time even more passionately than before. His hands roamed, exploring her waist, hips, and thighs, until he reached the threshold of his self-control. Abruptly, he pulled away from her. "There's something else."

"Yes?" she asked, panting in synch with his own heavy breathing.

"A letter . . . for Commander Zhang."

"What letter?"

"In Austria, when we hit the compound, Yao was already dead when we breached."

"Yes, I know. Zhang debriefed me."

"I was the first one to find the body. Yao had two envelopes clenched in his fist. One addressed to Lankford and one, I'm pretty sure, addressed to Zhang." He reached into the bag, pulled out the sealed envelope with Chinese hanzi hand-scribed in red ink on the front, and handed it to her.

She straightened her blouse, smoothed her skirt, and resettled herself on the sofa cushion before accepting it. "Yes, this is addressed to Commander Zhang," she said, inspecting the envelope. "You did not open it?"

"No," he said. "I didn't have to, because I read Lankford's letter."

"What did it say?"

"It was elegant, simple, and poignant. I can't remember the exact wording, but the message was essentially threefold: One, they are a secular, enlightened order that has existed for centuries, intervening as necessary to keep the world from descending into apocalyptic chaos. Two, they know intimate personal and professional details about Lankford and me. And three, that Yao paid the same price we will pay if our actions further jeopardize their veiled existence."

The color in her cheeks blanched until her complexion went pale. "And you kept this information from Zhang? Why?"

"Because I wanted to talk to you first. I know Lankford. I know how he operates. With Lankford, it's not about ego or professional accolades. Before taking any future action against the cabal, he would consult me, even if his boss said otherwise."

"Because you were named in the letter?"

"Yes."

"And you think Zhang wouldn't?"

"I think Zhang might view the letter as both a boast and a challenge, while downplaying the threat. After the operation, everyone was amped up on adrenaline. We were all emotional, and that's normal. I thought it best to let things simmer down a bit. I was worried Zhang might act impulsively without first giving him some time to decompress. If he gets upset about that decision when he gets the letter, then I know I made the right call."

"Do you think I'm named in Zhang's letter?" she said, her voice betraying her nerves.

He took a deep breath. "Given Major Li's fate and your role on the task force, it would not surprise me."

She nodded, took the letter from him, and stood.

"You're not going to open it?"

"No," she said, walking over to where her purse hung on a hook by the apartment door. She placed the letter inside. "I will give it to Commander Zhang and see what he does. As you said, his reaction will tell us as much as, if not more than, the contents of the letter itself."

Instead of coming back to the sofa, she began to pace the living room.

He'd felt the same anxiety after first reading Lankford's letter. He watched her for a long moment before saying, "Forget about the letter. Come, sit with me."

"I don't like it," she said, fingering the charm around her neck.

"I know," he said. "Me neither."

"They're probably watching us right now."

"I doubt it," he said, with far more conviction than he felt.

"These are powerful men, Nick. They murdered Major Li without consequence. Who is to say they won't decide to do the same to us? I don't want to spend the rest of my days looking over my shoulder and wondering when they're coming for me."

"I feel the same way."

"Then how can you sit there so calmly?"

"Because I know that if they wanted us dead, we'd be dead already. I view the letter as a truce of sorts. As long as the operation in Austria stays our last and final action against the cabal, then the war is over. I accomplished my mission: Peter Yu's body was found, Feng is dead, Yao is dead, Nèiyè Biologic is finished, and you're safe. That's all that matters to me. I have no intention of pursuing them. The only thing that matters to me right now is you."

She stopped pacing and looked at him. "Do you really mean that?"

"I do." He stood, walked to her, and wrapped his arms around her waist. "I think it's time we go back to what we were doing before I pulled out the letter."

She took a deep breath, grinned, and then tipped up on her toes until her lips were a centimeter from his. "What letter?"

"I love you," he breathed.

"I love you too," she whispered and pressed her lips to his.

GLOSSARY

AFSOC—Air Force Special Operations Command
BC—Buoyancy Compensator
BUD/S—Basic Underwater Demolition School
CASEVAC—Casualty Evacuation
CDC—Centers for Disease Control and Prevention
CIA—Central Intelligence Agency
CONEX—Intermodal, standardized shipping container
CRISPR—Clustered regularly interspaced short palindromic repeats (DNA editing tool pronounced *"crisper"*)
DB—Discovery Bay
DCER—Office of Disease Control and Emergency Response
DPV—Diver Propulsion Vehicle
Eighteen Delta—Special Forces medical technician and first responder
EMCON—Emissions Control (Radio Silence)
EOD—Explosive Ordinance Disposal
EXFIL—Exfiltrate
HALO—High Altitude-Low Opening (parachute)
HPLC—High-Performance Liquid Chromatography (analytical chemistry machine used to separate, identify, and quantify components in a sample mixture)
HUMINT—Human Intelligence
INFIL—Infiltrate
KPI—Key Performance Indicators
LCPO—Lead Chief Petty Officer
MARSOC—Marine Corps Special Operations Command
MEDEVAC—Medical Evacuation

MSS—Ministry of State Security, a.k.a. the Guoanbu, China's intelligence and security agency (CIA analog)

NGO—Non-Governmental Organization

NOC—Non-Official Cover

NSA—National Security Administration

NVGs—Night Vision Goggles

OGA—Other Government Agency

OPSEC—Operational Security

OTK—Chinese paramilitary security contractor for hire

PDA—Personal Data Accessory

PLA—People's Liberation Army

QRF—Quick Reaction Force

SAD—Special Activities Division

SCLU—Snow Leopard Commando Unit

SEAL—Sea, Air, and Land Teams, Naval Special Warfare

SERE—Survival, Evasion, Resistance, and Escape

SIGINT—Signals Intelligence

SITREP—Situation Report

SOCOM—Special Operations Command

SOG—Special Operations Group

SOPMOD—Special Operations Modification

TOC—Tactical Operations Center

Unit 61398—China's Cyber Warfare division of the PLA

W4H—Water for Humanity (The NGO Nick works for)